John's Pond

Donna Lynch

Copyright © 2023 **DML Publications**

All rights reserved. No part of this publication may be reproduced, distributed, or transmitted in any form or by any means, including photocopying, recording, or other electronic or mechanical methods, without the prior written permission of the publisher, except in the case of brief quotations embodied in critical reviews and certain other noncommercial uses permitted by copyright law. For permission requests, write to the publisher, addressed "Attention: Book Rights and Permission," at the address below.

Published in the United States of America

ISBN 978-1-960159-61-8 (SC)
ISBN 978-1-960159-01-4 (HC)
ISBN 978-1-960159-02-1 (Ebook)

DML Publications
222 West 6th Street
Suite 400, San Pedro, CA, 90731
www.stellarliterary.com

Ordering Information and Rights Permission:

Quantity sales. Special discounts might be available on quantity purchases by corporations, associations, and others. For details, contact the publisher at the address above.

For Book Rights Adaptation and other Rights Permission. Call us at toll-free 1-888-945-8513 or send us an email at admin@stellarliterary.com.

Peace and happiness are available in every moment.
Peace is every step. We shall walk hand in hand.
There are no political solutions to spiritual problems.
Remember: If the Creator put it there, it is in the right place.
The soul would have no rainbows if the eyes had no tears.
Tell your people that, since we were promised
We should never be moved,
We have been moved five times.

An Indian Chief, 1876

Acknowledgements

This has been a long journey, but a blissful one too, so I hope I remember all those who have helped with advice and suggestions along the way.

First I would like to thank Ann Speyer for taking time after her day time job as a librarian to help with editing one of my several drafts. I'm grateful she agreed to work with me, when I, a stranger, randomly asked her after hearing her do a laudable talk at the library.

I would also like to thank Carole Johnson, a retired policewoman and friend, who guided me with her expertise regarding guns and police protocol.

Mary Jo Everson, I want to thank you, too, for sharing your knowledge of guns. I'm still waiting to hit the shooting range with you.

Jaime Tracy, you are an incredible writer and I thank you deeply for reading the manuscript and giving me your thoughts and blessings.

And lastly, but not forgotten, I'd like to thank my dear friends, Bob and Doug, for holding their faith in me during the last rewrites. Their encouragement kept me focused and determined no matter what hindrances had stepped into my path.

Table of Contents

Acknowledgements iv
Chapter 1 1
Chapter 2 4
Chapter 3 7
Chapter 4 13
Chapter 5 16
Chapter 6 20
Chapter 7 22
Chapter 8 26
Chapter 9 29
Chapter 10 33
Chapter 11 39
Chapter 12 41
Chapter 13 46
Chapter 14 51
Chapter 15 55
Chapter 16 59
Chapter 17 62
Chapter 18 68
Chapter 19 70
Chapter 20 76

Chapter 21 81
Chapter 22 90
Chapter 23 94
Chapter 24 101
Chapter 25 108
Chapter 26 116
Chapter 27 123
Chapter 28 126
Chapter 29 132
Chapter 30 138
Chapter 31 144
Chapter 32 153
Chapter 33 159
Chapter 34 164
Chapter 35 170
Chapter 36 179
Chapter 37 186
Chapter 38 191
Chapter 39 196
Chapter 40 208
Chapter 41 214
Chapter 42 218
Chapter 43 227
Chapter 44 230
Chapter 45 234
Chapter 46 239
Chapter 47 243
Chapter 48 251

Chapter 49 257
Chapter 50 263
Chapter 51 267
Chapter 52 274
Chapter 53 280
Chapter 54 285
Chapter 55 292
Chapter 56 298
Chapter 57 300
Chapter 58 308
Chapter 59 314
Chapter 60 323

Chapter 1

Even before the thunderheads rolled across the Mashpee sky, shrouding it in darkness, Tobin knew the storm was coming. Just as he knew the outcome of the trial before the verdict came. Just as he knew his fate. He felt the chill in his bones, its icy fingers trailing down his spine. Was this the same way his father, the Wampanoag's medicine man, knew things, too?

Leaves flipped in the trees, flashing their silvery underbellies like a darting school of fish. A heavy raindrop torpedoed Tobin's brow. A barrage followed, pelting his bare mahogany arms below the sleeves of his T-shirt. He whistled for Brownie.

"Here, boy!" he called. The chocolate lab plodded over to the two-toned, red and white '59 Ford F-100. Tobin helped the old dog into the cab and let him settle onto the bench. Even though it was only a short trip to the market, he could not deny Brownie this simple pleasure. His hips weren't so good these days. Other than sleeping, riding was his favorite pastime. At the market, Tobin planned to pick up some maple syrup, dried corn, sunflowers seeds and raspberries for the *nasaump*, porridge, he was going to make for his mother, who was not feeling well. There was a time when he could gather all the berries and herbs from around his property, but the vines were barren now.

As the rain blasted the windshield, the wipers struggled to keep up. Tobin slowed the truck to a crawl. Through the deluge, he missed the black-and-white that pulled behind him until he saw the flashing lights in his rearview. *What now?* He thought as he pulled over. He'd done nothing wrong, yet it seemed they had made it their special mission to harass him.

He rolled down his window as the officer approached.

"That dog vicious?" the officer asked, keeping back and looking warily at Brownie.

"Nah, he wouldn't hurt a fly. Would ya, ole pal?" Tobin said, scrubbing Brownie behind the ears. The dog licked his hand. "Good boy."

"License and registration."

Tobin recognized the officer immediately from their previous run-in at John's Pond: the nervous rookie.

"Like you don't know who I am," Tobin muttered, as he rummaged in his pockets for his wallet. *Crap*, he thought, realizing he'd left it at home. "I don't have it on me. I only have the registration," he said apologetically, opening the glove compartment and handing the white card to the officer.

"Step out of the car."

"Huh? It's pouring—there's no need. . . ."

"I said, *out*."

Shaking his head, Tobin complied.

"I need to see your hands," the officer stated.

Tobin raised his hands. "What's your problem?" he asked, taking a step forward. "I didn't—"

"Stay right where you are!" the officer commanded, his hand hovering at his holster. "You kidnapped the Matthew's girl—it's all over town."

"Kidnapped? I didn't kidnap anybody."

"Don't try to get out of this."

"Out of what? I don't know what you're talking about! Laurie is home and has been for quite some time!"

"Nope. Haven't heard that."

"Check for yourself," Tobin insisted. "You have no reason to hold me."

Tobin blinked rapidly as the rain drenched him and ran into his eyes, blurring his vision. *He must really have an axe to grind to want to stand out here like this* Tobin thought.

At least the rain ran off the brim of the cop's hat. Tobin reached into his jacket pocket.

"Hold it right there!" Suddenly, the cop's .38 special was aimed at him.

"Whoa! I don't have a weapon! Only a bandana—to wipe my face. See?" Tobin said, pulling it out.

Simultaneously, a deafening crack of thunder shook the ground and a flash of lightning struck nearby—close enough that Tobin could feel the heat, the electricity, and taste the ozone in the air. Like sucking on pennies—or was that blood? The cop was staring at him wide-eyed, his mouth agape. Then he appeared to be talking, but Tobin couldn't make out the words. For a moment everything seemed bright around him, then he went out of focus and teetered, clutching his chest. It burned. He pulled his hand away and it was covered in blood, mingling with the rainwater in streams down his arm.

"You. Shot. Me," he gasped, sinking to his knees. He heard Brownie howl, then he lost consciousness.

Chapter 2

Six Months Earlier

The question was whether or not the Mashpee were a tribe. If not, what in the hell were they?

A low net of threatening gray clouds stretched across the Boston skies. Tobin Horvarth wondered what effect this gloom would have. A water department crew repairing a broken pipe had rerouted him and somehow he missed a detour sign. A driver honked at him when he stopped to ask for directions. "Okay, okay," he said, waving them on.

Life as a recluse was better than this madhouse, he thought.

He parked his red and white '59 pickup in the huge garage, a block from the courthouse. Locking his truck, he stood there for a moment. Then, dressed only in a blue windbreaker, jeans and sandals, he joined the crush of shoppers dodging puddles and white-collar workers in dark trench coats shielding themselves from the slapping wind and rain with their newspapers.

His people just wanted to preserve the land for future generations. But the whites thought it was too far away to worry about the kind of life their grandkids would face when water was full of detergent and fertilizers and there was no wood to keep them warm in the winter.

A maddening vision invaded his mind—Mashpee, his small Cape Cod village surrounded by woods of pine and oak, mushrooming into a city. He hastened down High and Pearl Streets, trying to concentrate on where he was headed. It was scary to think of not having trees, crystal lakes and clean air.

Looking around Boston, he now had a better understanding of his tribe's greatest fear.

When he entered the empty lobby of the historic granite skyscraper at Post Office Square, he headed down the corridor to the courtroom. It was filling quickly. The media were packed inside, snapping photos from every angle and scrawling busily on yellow pads. Tobin scanned the room before taking a seat next to his father and Uncle Basil. Near the podium just behind the lawyers, a sketch artist was already drawing away. *Probably making a spectacle out of us. Newspaper headlines are not what we're about.*

Tobin's jaw stiffened and his mouth dried up. He folded his twitching fingers in his lap and warily scrutinized the stone-faced crowd: white townies he'd once considered friendly. They were whispering, their eyes shifting from the lawyers to the Wampanoag.

In spite of not allowing enough time for the weather and traffic, Tobin felt he really hadn't missed a whole lot. Except being able to speak with his family before the judge appeared. He'd been away at Keene State in New Hampshire for nearly two months. He wanted to be sure that everyone was okay, especially his sister, Hannah. She'd written him once a week in the beginning, filling him in on what was happening at home and school. But her letters had stopped, causing him to wonder if there was something going on he should know about.

Attorney Morin, one of the best trial lawyers in Boston, hired by a private benefactor, addressed the jury with his opening remarks. "As we understand it, the issue being carved out by the judge and being presented to you good people for determination is the following: is the plaintiff a tribe today?"

Today? Did something change when I woke this morning? Before Tobin's people could even try to get their land back, they had to prove who they'd always been? Ridiculous. But when it came to the white man's law, what did he know?

Morin began to take the jury on a tour of three hundred years of Mashpee history.

"Basically, we'll be offering evidence to prove four facts. I may repeat them one more time before I am through. First, the plaintiff is and always has been a group of Indian people, that is, people of ancestry who are conscious themselves of being Indian and are recognized as Indians by the outside world. "Second, that this group of people has lived on the lands of Mashpee for hundreds of years.

"Third, that the Indians on this land have made up a cohesive, permanent community with a common heritage and many shared ways of living, some of which carry the imprint of the past to this day, as you will hear during this trial.

"And fourth, that Indian communities in Mashpee have always had their form of organization and leadership."

One by one, historians, anthropologists and sociologists were called to the witness stand by both sides. It was going to be a long day. Neither Tobin nor his friends could see much chance of winning back the sacred acres swindled so long ago. But their parents and grandparents were chasing after their last hope. And Tobin couldn't blame them.

Every five minutes or so, lawyers bumped heads with each other and the judge. Bench conferences, they called them. And all this fancy talk. But could they deliver?

Chapter 3

Tobin's mother, Myra, and his sixteen-year-old sister, Hannah, were waiting for him and his father with Myra's famous clam pie with its thick cream sauce and buttery flaky crust, still hot from the oven. Kissing them both, Tobin hung up his jacket on the wooden coat rack he'd made for his mother's birthday when he was twelve.

After digging in, Tobin said, "I should go away more often."

"No," both his mother and Hannah said in unison.

"Missed you guys, too," he said with a smile.

"How're you doing in school, son?"

"Great, Ma."

"It's always great with you," Hannah piped in.

Tobin shrugged. "What can I say? 3.5 GPA."

Hannah's face twisted.

"Keep those grades up, honey."

"I intend to, Ma," he said, looking around the table. They were good people—decent people who tried hard to do the best they could with what little they had. And now the one thing closest to their souls, their spirits, their beings, could be snatched from them. Forever. His heart burned from the pain of that possibility.

His father nodded. "Stay focused."

"Any progress, James?" Myra asked her husband, with hope in her voice as she handed him his plate.

"No, Myra. Better off staying home."

"I want to go next time. I think it would be fun," Hannah said.

Both Tobin and his father looked at her in disbelief.

"Interesting, anyway," she said, reaching for another helping of mashed potatoes.

Tobin pushed the dish closer. "Trust me," he said, "don't give it another thought. It'd be the most boring day of your life." Tobin knew his sister's real fascination had more to do with just going to Boston than the trial itself.

"Can you tell how things are going?" Myra persisted.

"It's too soon. We've got a long way yet."

Tobin nodded.

After dinner James went out onto the porch to sit in the rickety old rocker and smoke his pipe. Hannah cleared the table, and Tobin picked up a dishtowel.

Hannah gave Tobin a surprised look. "This is a first."

"Any hassles at school?" Tobin asked.

The elementary school had been cool because it was their own haven. But at Falmouth High, where his sister was now a sophomore, kids from more than one town were mixed up. Tobin surmised that it had to be a big adjustment.

"Some. But I can take care of myself."

"I know you can."

Tobin was only four when Hannah was born. She was so small— so precious. He swore her little restless hands and feet were telling a story. Or maybe she was just hungry. He would feed her a bottle or shake her rattle and she would smile. He would look in when she was sleeping, and cover her with the pink blanket covered with yellow butterflies his mother had hand-sewn when she was carrying Hannah. Tobin vowed he would watch over his baby sister always.

"Have you met anyone?"

"Hmm. Met a lot of people."

"You know what I mean." She gave him a swat on the arm with the dishtowel.

"I have to keep my grades up and baseball takes the rest of my time. I don't have room for girls."

"Sure you don't. A handsome guy like you?"

"There's a ton of good-looking guys in college, Hannah."

"But not like you," she said, winking.

"That's for sure," he said, winking back.

"Cut it out," she said, giving him another smack.

"Holy mackerel! You're getting strong, baby sister! I better be careful."

"I've learned everything I know from you."

Tobin had taught Hannah a few basic self-defense moves he had learned from his Uncle Basil as soon as he saw she was getting breasts and boys were noticing her more. He also taught her about body language and how important it was to look alert and confident whenever she was walking alone. He hoped, however, she would never need to use those defense moves on anyone.

The house fell dark and quiet. Tobin's father was going to bed at 8:00 instead of his usual 10:00; but he would be up again if anyone were sick or dying. Tobin didn't require much sleep after pulling college all-nighters, so he decided to read. He had been lucky to get a leave of absence. Tomorrow he would tackle the science project on evolution Professor Collingsworth had assigned. Tonight, though, it was *Baseball Memoirs of a Lifetime.* First he wanted to say goodnight to his sister. When they were horsing around earlier, he had a feeling she was holding back something. In fact, he was sure of it.

Tobin and Hannah had always shared the same bedroom. As they grew older, their mother had sewn together a navy canvas with a massive white star to hang down the middle of the room for some privacy. She told them it was the North Star in the night sky. "To watch over you," she had said. Then, when Tobin was thirteen, he found some plywood and added a partition. It made the small room look even smaller, but they were just happy to have their own space.

Hannah's light was still on, so he walked to her side of the room. Tobin called it the "Rainbow Port." She had painted a huge purple, lime, and cherry arch above her miniature dolls from Japan, Holland and Ireland. His walls were more subdued in earthy browns and greens, plastered with posters of Red Sox greats—Yaz and Ted Williams. Hannah was at her small table, stringing together glass beads in ocean shades of indigo and jade. He stood there and watched for a moment. She seemed absorbed in making the necklace; he wasn't sure if she knew he was there.

"For anyone special?" he finally asked with a smile.

"Gayle. Her birthday's tomorrow. I'm just about finished. I'll shut off the light."

"Don't hurry. It's still early for me." He sat on the end of her bed. "Who're you hanging out with lately?"

"Theresa and Gayle. And a few others. Why?" she asked, now looking up at her brother. Hannah had been friends with Gayle and Theresa since first grade; they were from the same tribe. They had similar interests such as their doll collections to finding unique shells on the beach and making their own necklaces and bracelets.

"I don't know. I'm just curious, I guess."

"You're wondering if I made any new friends?"

He nodded. "Have you?"

"I've tried." Her eyes filled with tears. "It's not easy, you know."

"I know."

"It just hurts sometimes. Those white kids can be so cruel. Why?"

"We've been in a cocoon too long. There's a lot of crap out there. We just never knew it before. We rarely left our grounds. Granddaddy used to say, 'If we weaken, the vile will kill us. No evil can channel where it cannot be received.'"

"What does that mean?" she asked, wiping her tears.

"It means if you stay tough, they won't be able to slaughter you."

"Ha, ha," she said, rolling her eyes.

"Trust me. Don't show them you're afraid."

"I'm not," Hannah said defensively.

"Good, because fear will only swallow you up. Remember fear's only a state of mind and it's useless," he said, rising from her bed.

"That's all? Just not be afraid?" she asked.

"Pretty much. Once that's gone, what's left?"

She looked at him gratefully. "Thanks."

"What's a brother for? Sleep tight."

Lying back in bed, Tobin started thinking about the court case again. Was it possible to get back what was taken from them so long ago—being who they were? Was the battle over before it began? How much grief will his people have to endure before they realize that the ones who have the most resources, clout and revenue will prevail? He would have to keep his dark thoughts to himself, though. He didn't want to hurt his family. They had lost so much over this claim. Two tribe members had been fired from the Selectman's office and the fire chief was asked for his resignation. Still, Tobin was damned proud of their standing up for what they believed in.

Finally, he slept. The banging of hammers and the clamor of saws and heavy equipment made him rise. He quickly got dressed and hurried out the door. In the mist, trees were tumbling like a tornado was sweeping through. He rushed around pleading for the workmen to stop, but they ignored him. Some even laughed. He felt he was standing still as the things he loved most in his small town were being annihilated right before his eyes. He couldn't take on an army and he knew it. He had never felt more helpless in his life.

"Stop! Stop! You're destroying the land!" he ran about yelling. But no one seemed to be listening. It was like they never saw him. Raccoons, rabbits and deer scrambled for a safe place in their fright. They were his friends, coming to know him as he had come to know them. What would happen to them? Where would they go?

"Don't you see what you're doing? The animals! They need a place to live!" he cried.

"Go away, Indian! You have no say," said a monstrous woodsman in blue jeans and red suspenders. Tobin saw the huge axe coming at him. He tried to run and stumbled.

Without warning, a pine trunk nearly clobbered him. He dodged away like lighting. Then another and another fell around him as he barely escaped being crushed. Just when there seemed to be no way out, he woke. Beads of sweat lined his face. Shaken, he got out of bed and wandered into the kitchen in his shorts and socks. He was surprised to see his father sitting at the kitchen table in his bathrobe drinking tea.

"Can't sleep either?" James asked.

"Nah, not really. Is the water still hot?"

His father nodded.

Tobin fetched a tea bag from the tin canister on the counter, grabbed a mug and poured water from the kettle, then sank into a chair. He spooned three heaps of sugar into his cup.

"All that sugar," James said, shaking his head, "not good for you."

"It sweetens me."

"You're already a good boy, Tobin. Stay that way."

Tobin wanted to say, "I'm a man now, Father," but didn't. He knew his father was telling him to stay cool and level-headed, no matter what happened between their family and the white folks. They sat immersed in their own thoughts. Then Tobin looked over at his father. "Dad, they can't take away who we are."

James rose from the table.

"Nope," he said, clutching his cup, "but they can damn well strip us of everything else."

Chapter 4

Laurie Matthews opened the front door to retrieve the *Standard Times*. She walked through the living room into the sunny kitchen where her parents were having breakfast. She tossed the paper on the spotless counter and yanked open the refrigerator. While pouring grape juice, she glanced at the front page. Intrigued with the headlines, she missed her glass.

"Watch what you're doing!" her mother scolded, not even glancing up from the material in her briefcase. She worked in the Selectman's office and for Frank Morgan, a big land developer. Her father saw what happened but kept quiet.

Laurie wiped up the spill with a paper towel and threw it in the wastebasket under the sink. She sat down and began reading. Eleanor Matthews tapped her coffee cup with a spoon, then looked pointedly from her daughter to her husband.

"Sorry, Dad," Laurie said, handing him the sports section, the only part of the paper he read before heading off to work.

"No problem, sweetheart. Something interesting?" he asked.

She didn't hear him. She was too immersed. "Wow, it's all over the papers! This has really gotten big."

"It certainly has," Eleanor replied disapprovingly, steadily refilling her cup.

"I heard Senators Brooke and Kennedy, even the President, are getting involved," Laurie announced.

"Those Wampanoag are getting an awful lot of attention," Eleanor murmured.

"Isn't it wild? I think the natives should sue for their land."

"I think it's absurd," Eleanor remarked.

"Who started this?" Laurie asked her mother.

Eleanor cocked her head regally, arching one brow. "We're doing them a favor," she said, with her perfect red fingernails poised on the cup, about to take a sip.

"Is that what you think?" Laurie asked.

Eleanor's blonde hair seemed even lighter against the black suit she wore. Laurie wished her mother was as sweet as she looked. Since the Indians had filed their claim, her mother's sweetness had gone sour and her prettiness had turned ugly. She wasn't the same.

"Dad?" Laurie implored, looking for some back-up.

Donald peered over the newspaper, his plastic frames halfway down his nose. Looking into her father's dark eyes, she knew they held secrets. One thing was certain, he was a good man who would not hurt or judge anyone.

"I'm staying out of this one," he said in a soft voice.

Laurie knew her father loved them both and hated to take sides, even when his views were opposite her mother's. And Laurie believed this time his feelings *were* contrary.

"We're taking their most precious possession. You think we're doing them a favor?" Laurie asked.

"You and I don't seem to be communicating," Eleanor said.

Laurie had been following the trial since it began. She and her mother didn't have the same opinions on the matter. Laurie thought the natives had every right to fight for what was once theirs, but her mother thought otherwise, generating tension between them.

"What else is new?" Laurie mumbled, taking her dishes to the sink. She hurried out of the room. Seconds later, she raced out the front door. "Bye, Dad," she yelled.

"Have a good day, sweetheart."

"You, too."

Her father was also on his way out. He was an accountant for Savory and Burns, a big retail firm in Quincy. Laurie wondered how he traveled that distance every day. She knew the traffic would get heavier in time as more people moved to the Cape or vacationed there in the summer. For now he didn't seem to mind the commute.

Laurie saw her mother standing in the doorway, arms crossed, watching her as she drove off. A few colorful leaves drifted onto the newly paved blacktop. Their flawless lawn was now shrouded with them.

Charlotte Dunbar, the Matthews' fifty-year-old widowed nosey neighbor, nicknamed "Snoopy" by Laurie, was pruning the last of her blue and purple hydrangeas. *Mary, Mary, quite contrary*. Charlotte stopped and watched as she drove by. They exchanged small waves.

"Get a life, Snoopy!" Laurie said out loud. With the windows up, Charlotte couldn't hear her, but Laurie bet the witch could read lips.

Chapter 5

A morning sky of apricot and gold softened the nippy air. Little crystals of frost shimmered on the ground— a sure sign of a cold winter to come. Tobin and his father were on the road again, headed to Boston. They had gotten an early start. Uncle Basil and other members of the tribe followed behind Tobin's pickup in an old Chevy wagon. After twenty minutes of driving, Tobin saw his father gazing at a farm off to their right. His father had once told him about the time he visited an old friend in Vermont fifteen years earlier. His friend had a beautiful working farm and ever since then his father had a desire to own one.

"Look," James said, pointing at a doe and her fawn standing in the sun, nibbling the grass.

Tobin glanced into his rearview mirror and saw the others pointing, too—thinking of their next meal, no doubt. Still, his people respected and prayed for the animals, even when they planned to kill them for food.

There were only a few cars on Route 93 and the journey along the south shore was peaceful. Tobin looked over at this father. James Horvarth had always been stalwart. But could he handle losing the trial?

"They'll spoil what's pure and natural," James said, staring out. "Maybe it's too late."

"Don't forget, Father, we've got the best on our side." James didn't reply; he remained glued to the window.

They drove on in silence. Tobin thought his father was praying. He wanted to turn on the radio, but his father wasn't a rock fan. His mind drifted to baseball. The season was months away, but he couldn't wait to be on the field again, turning a double-play and hearing the crowd roar.

Breaking the silence, a white car zoomed by, chased by a cruiser.

"Serves them right. Speeding like that," James said.

If I had a sports car, I'd be booking it, too, Tobin thought. "Was that a Camaro or a Firebird?" he asked.

"I'm not sure. Not good with newer cars. A Camaro, I think."

In the stretch of highway ahead the cruiser turned on its siren and lights, but the driver kept going. After a few minutes they could no longer see either car. Tobin noticed his father shaking his head.

As they traveled farther, they saw the police had finally caught up. Tobin slowed down. A young officer was standing by the driver's window, his ticket book in hand. He was smiling at locks of blonde hair.

"I doubt she'll get a ticket. Maybe a hot date instead," Tobin said.

"How do you know it was a girl?"

Tobin looked at his father. He was grinning. They laughed.

The judge appeared and they stood. Another predictable day. A handful of spectators was sitting in on the trial. Tobin was becoming more and more frustrated. He wondered how long this absurdity would last. When the plaintiff finally rested after the better part of the day, the defense presented its case.

Jeanne Stockman, a sociologist from Boston College, defined the meaning of "tribe" for the defense from the two books she'd been studying by American anthropologists George Murdock and Julian Stewart.

"Would you tell us in substance first Dr. Murdock's definition of the tribe and then Dr. Stewart's?" Defense Attorney St. Pearce asked.

"The basis for a definition of 'tribe' that George Murdock uses emphasizes the sovereignty of a particular group that a tribe is known by, and I quote here, 'original and definitive jurisdiction over some sphere of social life in which the organization (tribe) has the legitimate right to make decisions having a significant effect on its members.'"

"Is Dr. Murdock's definition recognized by anthropologists as being an authoritative definition?"

"Yes, it is."

"Now will you outline for us Dr. Stewart's definition?"

"Dr. Stewart's definition deals more with cultural aspects of tribal organization. He relies on three characteristics. The first one is basically the sovereignty one, that is, that a tribal group is fairly simply organized and independent and self-contained and with that is the understanding that it's usually a fairly isolated group. The second aspect has to do with cultural uniformity."

Cultural what? Tobin's head pounded. Are they imbeciles? "This is crazy," he wanted to yell. Get to the damned point and move on. It was all he could do to hold his tongue.

He shifted in his seat and saw an attractive young woman sitting to his right, a few benches back. He took a second look. She was wearing a pink sweater and a black mini-skirt, her long slender legs crossed. In her lap were a notebook and pencil. *Why is this beautiful white girl taking notes?* Why was she so interested? He couldn't imagine any male in the room concentrating on anything else after seeing her, especially the young hotshots running the show.

"He was referring to the idea that most people in the community conform in terms of their values and behavior to a certain general standard. It's acceptable by everyone. The third characteristic is that the culture of the tribe is unique relative to other cultural traditions. Those are the three aspects."

Using these criteria, Stockman concluded the Mashpees were not a tribe.

Where'd this woman come from? She knows nothing about us. Just takes a survey, reads a couple of books, then decides we're not a tribe? No sovereignty? We were here hundreds of years ago, taking care of our own land, our own people. We've always had a medicine man, still follow the old ways. We'd still be in charge of Mashpee if the whites hadn't taken over.

The cross-examination of Stockman was extensive, detailed, and at times bitter. Questioned on her knowledge of the Mashpees, her methodology, and her definition of "tribe," she finally had to acknowledge that neither of the writers on whom she relied for her definition actually used the term *sovereignty* in his definition. Morin returned repeatedly to the witness's definition. Finally, at the request of the court, Stockman read the portion of Stewart's work she used to formulate her definition. Though admitting that the quotation did not contain the troublesome word, she maintained that it was implied.

Tobin was still thinking about the girl, though he knew she had not noticed him. A few more hours, he kept telling himself, and she'll be history.

Tobin pretended to pick up something off the floor and turned around for a third time to look at her. Her powder blue eyes, almost translucent, locked into his. He imagined she was rising from her seat, in slow motion, walking toward him, her platinum hair flowing over her shoulders. She stopped and her index finger signaled him to get up. A sap for beauty, he did. The twin hills of her sweater loomed above a petite waist. She took his hands in hers as she moved closer to him. With her breath upon him, he waited for her kiss.

Something shook him back to reality. The last time Tobin had been aroused was by someone in *Playboy*. But this was no centerfold: she was real. He was glad the judge wasn't entering or leaving the courtroom—the trial was beginning to seize his attention.

Chapter 6

After a late supper Tobin strolled along the swamp to John's Pond. This was his second home. Even in evening's darkness Tobin glided through the trees like a hawk in flight. The murmur of the wind and the cry of a coyote from the cranberry bog packed his ears. After all the city noise and congestion, the woods seemed more divine than usual. When he reached a clearing near the pond, he removed his shoes, walked to the edge of the bank and sank his feet into the cold water.

He couldn't get the beautiful white girl from the courtroom out of his head. She had sat on the wrong side of the room; he didn't know who she was or where she came from. The cool water relaxed him. That night he went to sleep not thinking or dreaming of her.

The next day on the way to Boston, however, he was eager to see her again. When there was no sign of her in the courtroom, he was bummed—and relieved. His focus should never have been on her anyway. The trial was going downhill, in spite of their expert witnesses and lawyers. He felt useless just sitting there, but there was nothing he could do to make things come out right. Tobin searched for her face again.

"Who are you looking for?" his father asked.

"No one, really," Tobin shrugged. He didn't realize he had made himself so obvious. His dad was always tuned into things. Tobin swore his father had some kind of special radar. *Must have something to do with being a medicine man*, he thought.

"I don't believe she's here today, son."

"Huh?"

"Come on, Tobin. I'm a man, too. Beauty comes in all sizes and colors. Some young and some not so young. And something that pretty can't be disregarded," James said with a smile.

He and his father had never discussed women, sex or even relationships, but Tobin saw the respect his father showed his mother. They loved each other very much, and this was the kind of love he wished for himself.

Tobin stole a final glance, hoping he had missed her. He noticed how impeccably dressed the other side was. Claiborne dresses and Lauren suits and silk ties, right of out of *People* magazine. The Wampanoag women wore simple cotton dresses and the men had on chinos or Wranglers and a casual or flannel shirt. At the beginning of the trial, many had come to court heavily feathered, proudly wearing buckskin leggings, long fringed vests and dresses with beaded moccasins—until the judge put an end to it. They looked too Indian and that might sway the jury. Now they just looked defeated, and the jury would see them that way.

Listening to the big shots on the podium made Tobin sleepy. When he shut his eyes for a moment, the heavy stench of perfume and deodorant permeated the room, making his stomach churn. The restlessness—a man's nagging cough and the clearing of irritated throats—were like being in church. The only things missing were the small voices of children. And serenity. A woman across the aisle sneezed. Tobin opened his eyes and said, "God bless you." She looked at him and then turned away.

Tobin said quietly, "You're welcome."

Chapter 7

Laurie wove her way through the crowded corridors at Falmouth High and ran into her two best friends, Sharon and Pam.

"Hi, guys! What's up for tonight?" Laurie asked.

"My parents are going out. Wanna stay over?" Sharon asked. Sharon Rodney was tall, close to six feet, and slender with long, dark brown hair and deep green eyes. She worshiped attention. The more she got, the more she would bat those fake eyelashes. And Sharon never left the house before dotting a mole above the left side of her lips. Modeling school was Sharon's first thought. Actually, her only thought. Laurie thought she was perfect for theater production, especially with her known dramatics.

"Sure. What time?" Laurie asked.

"They're leaving at eight, but you can come anytime."

"The guys will be there, too," Pam said excitedly, her face cocking to one side. With short, ash-brown hair, turquoise eyes and an adorable dimple on her left cheek, Pam Courtney was similar to Sharon in build except a tad shorter. Pam, a people pleaser, was branded Sharon's patsy by her boyfriend.

The girls wore trendy clothes, usually short denim skirts, blouses and pullover sweaters with clogs on their feet. The three cheerleaders were attractive and popular. They were the ones all the other girls tried to emulate.

"Great," Laurie said, with little enthusiasm. She thought it was a perfect time to cut ties with Brian Shannon. She wanted him to understand that all there could ever be between them was friendship.

The other four were more intimate, but she wasn't interested in him that way.

"Hey, Laurie, neat report," Pam said.

"Indians turn you on, huh?" Sharon added, grinning.

Her two friends snickered. The teacher had assigned a special current events report. Laurie had written about the Indians' lawsuit, and it was one of the few chosen to read to the class.

"Got an 'A'" Laurie retorted, grinning back.

As they parted to go to their next period Sharon swiveled around and hollered to Laurie. "Don't forget the chips." Without turning, Laurie signaled with her hand that she'd heard.

Sharon and Pam had been friends since fifth grade. When Laurie came to their school in her sophomore year, they liked the way she looked and dressed and particularly the way the boys paid them added attention whenever she was around. They quickly invited her into their little group. Seeing it could be beneficial to her new environment, Laurie gladly accepted. The three of them soon became inseparable.

The students had a half hour to eat their lunch. The six of them always sat at the same table in the cafeteria, nearest the lunch line. The very cool, black-haired, blue-eyed Rob Kilroy was Sharon's boyfriend, and smiley, brown-eyed Mike Holloway was Pam's. Brian was the school's star quarterback, Rob his best receiver and Mike a linebacker on defense who was always good for a sack or two.

Rob enlightened the group with a joke like he did every day at lunch. This time Laurie was sensitive to the subject. He was making fun of the Indians. This irritated her. She disapproved of anyone ridiculing another for their race or culture.

"So the kid says to his mom, 'No way am I going to eat a native turkey for Thanksgiving,'" Rob recited. Everyone laughed. At that moment, a heavyset Indian boy wearing moccasins and a headband edged by them. Sharon grimaced.

"Why are you so against them?" Laurie asked her.

"If they knew how ridiculous they look in those dumb costumes."

"It's part of who they are," Laurie returned.

"Rob's part Scot, but he's not wearing a skirt or carrying bagpipes," Sharon shot back.

Maybe if he were in Scotland. Laurie decided to end it.

Rob was sitting at the end of the long table. He turned his chair slightly, extending his long legs toward the aisle where students were passing. He nudged Mike. "Watch this."

He stuck out his foot and tripped an Indian boy carrying a full tray. Food flew everywhere.

The group all roared with laughter, except for Laurie.

"Are you all right?" she asked, bending down.

The boy nodded. As Laurie helped clean up the mess, she sensed eyes on her.

She looked up at her friends. "He could've gotten hurt."

"Oh, lighten up, we're just having a little fun," Rob responded.

"Yeah, that's right," Mike Holloway echoed.

"Laurie's always feeling sorry for people," Pam declared.

"Yeah, especially them," Sharon added.

"I just don't think anybody should be treated that way," Laurie scowled.

"She's got a rare quality," Brian said, defending her.

"Yeah, she sure does. She's an Indian lover," Rob said.

"You son-of-a-b—"Brian yelled and rocketed out of his seat. He raced toward Rob and punched him low. Rob bent over gasping, holding his stomach. Laurie wondered if it was the impact of the blow that made his color fade or if he was about to throw up. Brian was unrelenting. He had Rob in a headlock, pounding him over and over.

"Stop! Stop! You're going to kill him!" Laurie screamed.

"Help him, Mike," Pam shouted. Mike just stood there.

A throng of students gathered around the table. Some were cheering, egging them on, while others stood stunned to see Falmouth High's best in a fight.

"Take back what you said! Now!" Brian hollered.

"Okay. Okay. I'm sorry," Rob said, his voice dropping.

"Let him go. He said he was sorry," Laurie pleaded. Laurie had never seen Brian like this. Two male teachers intervened before he finally calmed down.

"Thanks," she said to Brian, half grateful, half scared by his rage.

"People shouldn't make accusations. That's how rumors get started," he said as they emptied their lunch trays into the trash and stacked them on a metal cart.

"God forbid," she said under her breath as the bell rang.

"What? Did you say something?"

"No. See you later," Laurie said. She walked in the opposite direction.

Chapter 8

When Tobin arrived at his Uncle Basil's, he found him sitting on the porch step, whittling a wolf. His brown Lab, Brownie, was lying on the ground near him. Fallen leaves nestled around them like flames. Tobin patted Brownie, then sat on the step below his uncle. "You do nice work."

Basil stopped and pulled out a chunk of wood from a burlap bag. "Here," he said, extending his callused hands, "finish yours."

"You still have it?" Tobin asked, amazed.

Uncle Basil nodded.

Tobin had started the wolf before he left for school. His uncle handed him a knife and Tobin began carving. For years Tobin watched his uncle create fine-looking animals from blocks of wood and soon whittling became a pastime for him, too.

Uncle Basil was special. He never had children, and Tobin was like a son to him. When Tobin's father was busy performing rites at weddings or funerals, overseeing tribal ceremonies and counseling young and old, he and Uncle Basil would fish and hunt together. They would take long walks through the woods and Basil would tell him war stories.

"What're our chances, Uncle Basil?"

"We have to believe in ourselves and hope for the best."

"It's like we're beating our heads against the wall. It would take a miracle."

"Miracles happen all the time."

Tobin wondered if his uncle believed that, because they needed one. An all-white jury sure wasn't going to increase the odds.

Uncle Basil changed the subject. "You putting your money away?"

"Yup. And counting the weeks."

In May, Tobin and his uncle were heading for the Big Medicine Wheel on a peak in the northern part of Wyoming. His uncle said it was a sacred place, like none other in the world. Tobin had worked summers and saved a grand. Uncle Basil had money from his wife's insurance policy. Not much, but enough.

"I feel the Wheel calling," Uncle Basil said, his eyes glowing as if he could see it right in front of him. Tobin wanted to make this happen.

Uncle Basil shook himself from his reverie and took a long look at Tobin's carving. "Nice work, yourself."

Tobin examined his small creation and nodded. "Who taught me?"

Uncle Basil smiled.

Tobin wanted to tell his uncle about the girl in the courtroom, but he didn't. What was the point? What was there to tell? He would never see her again, and even if he did, what difference would it make? After carving for a while, Tobin stood up, brushed the shavings from his pants and placed his work in the burlap bag.

"It's getting late. Ready to go?" Tobin asked.

Every weekend, Friday nights usually, weather permitting, his people met at John's Pond where they had a few beers, burgers and hot dogs and much laughter. It was something they had done for as long as Tobin could remember.

"Nope. I'm going in and getting settled for the night," Basil said as he rose from the step.

"You're not coming?"

"No. I'm going to pass this time."

Tobin found it strange that his uncle turned him down. It was the one day of the week he looked forward to, especially since Aunt Dot died, and he always enjoyed himself.

He did look a little tired, but he was getting up there in years. Even his faithful companion, Brownie, who played non-stop when he was younger, could barely retrieve a stick a few yards these days.

"I'll see you tomorrow."

Uncle Basil nodded as he shuffled slowly toward the front door.

Chapter 9

Tobin drove down a long dirt road, dense vegetation on either side, to a large open field where a dozen or more cars and trucks were parked, mostly 60's models: a Country Squire Wagon, a Dodge Dart, a beat-up '60 Chevy pickup, a Suburban and an El Camino. He recognized his cousin's '66 green Mustang, one he wished he had. It was a sharp car and fast. Tobin grabbed the six-pack of Budweiser on the seat next to him, got out of his truck and followed a grassy pathway to the picnic grounds. In the distance, his cousin Charlie Cowen was strumming the guitar and others were singing. Here, they could forget about things they could do nothing about.

As he walked toward the bonfire, a squirrel scurried past him to a nearby pine tree, closely followed by another. A dog was barking not far away, as if joining in the fun. Tobin greeted his relatives and friends. Steamed clams were passed around. Burgers and hot dogs were being charcoaled over the fire. It was great seeing everyone let loose and being themselves.

"Hey, Cuz, how's it going?" Charlie Cowen asked during a break after playing a set.

Tobin nodded. "Great," he said, perched on a nearby log with a bucket of steamers between his legs. As he was digging into them, Clyde Jason Phillips, known as CJ, approached him. CJ was almost twenty-one, unmarried with a kid. With a small paycheck working in a liquor store he could barely support himself, never mind anyone else. *Not for me*, Tobin thought. He wanted a future. *Something more. Better…*

Tobin tried to ignore CJ but he was a leech—rough and big-mouthed. This time was no different. He had been that way since his boyhood, evoking hurtful name-calling. *Jolly Green Giant.*

"How come you haven't gotten yourself a girl?" CJ asked, sitting down beside him.

"What—and end up like you?"

"I was dumb," CJ admitted.

"You said it," Tobin returned as he rose from the log to empty his bucket, then refilled again.

Tobin hoped to find someone he cared about, but he refused to settle for just anyone. He wanted to be in love and get married before he started his family.

"Hey, by the way, where's Uncle Basil?" CJ asked.

"He said he's had enough of you," Tobin offered with a smirk, inhaling a large clam dripping with butter.

"Are you sure he didn't mean you?"

Swallowing, Tobin raised an eyebrow, "Never know."

"This is a first for him," CJ remarked, as he walked away.

"It happens."

It was true. Uncle Basil had never missed one of these gatherings. Many inquired about him. They expected to assemble around him again and listen to his stories about World War II and Vietnam. Some were funny, others sad. Either way, Uncle Basil knew how to amuse and engage people.

Tobin joined Charlie and a few others in a game of archery. Tobin had been shooting bow and arrow since he was seven. Rarely missing a target even then, he was better at it now.

Suddenly, a bank of black and whites barreled through and surrounded the area.

"What the hell. . . ." Tobin heard CJ say.

The officers leaped out of their vehicles, guns pointed, scaring the crap out of everyone. Silence fell over the forest. The only sound was the crackling of the fire.

Tobin approached confidently. "Something wrong, officer?"

"Stay right where you are. Don't move another inch," a young officer hollered, directing his .38 special, a little unsteady, at Tobin's chest. Tobin wondered how tough these uniformed guys would be without a gun or no badge to flash.

"What's this all about?" Tobin asked, standing still and keeping his voice even.

"You're disturbing the peace."

"What?"

"You heard me."

"You must be kidding. We've been coming here for years," Tobin said, his calmness waning, his arms folded in front of him. He could hear his father's voice, *You're already a good boy, Tobin. Stay that way.*

"There's been complaints," the officer claimed.

"From who? There's nobody around here for miles."

"Shut up, kid," said an older officer. "You old enough to drink?"

Tobin ignored him. "You're on our land. You're trespassing."

His people nodded in agreement.

"Did you hear that, boys? We're trespassing," the young policeman relayed to the rest. They chuckled. "We have every right. And if you don't shut up, you're going to jail."

"What gives you that right?" Tobin asked.

"That's it. I've had enough of your flip mouth. Get in the cruiser," the older cop said, abruptly, pointing his gun from Tobin to the vehicle.

The Mashpees rushed forward, shouting and waving their arms angrily. Another cop fired a warning shot into the air. They halted, frightened.

"Anyone else wants to be arrested?" barked the tall, bald-headed officer. His glare alone was intimidating.

Some just shook their heads, while others kept shouting in spite of the officer's threat.

"You can't do this," Tobin blurted angrily.

"That's what you think," the cop said, with an assured grin. "Take him, boys."

Two burly officers walked up to him, one holding handcuffs. Tobin's first instinct was to fight them; instead he gave in. These cops were looking for a confrontation. He wouldn't give them the satisfaction. *You've seen too many TV Westerns. We're not the bad guys.*

Chapter 10

Laurie drove around the block a few times before finally pulling up to the Rodney's house a few minutes before nine. *I have to do this.* When she walked in, Pam was shutting off lamps and Sharon was lighting candles. The record player was on, the volume low.

"Ah, the final touch," Sharon said, blowing out a match.

"How romantic," Laurie said sarcastically, taking a bowl from the buffet and spilling a bag of chips into it.

Sharon and Pam hurried to the bathroom to check their makeup and hair. They fussed far too much over those particulars, even more so when they were meeting the boys. Laurie picked up a stack of albums from the stereo cabinet and, slipping off her shoes and curling up on the sofa, sifted through them. Half the LPs belonged to Sharon's parents. They had joined a record club and they let Sharon choose something she liked every other month. Setting aside Tony Bennett and Frank Sinatra, Laurie placed some of her favorites, *Chicago and The Eagles*, on top of the pile.

Laurie waited until the girls came back into the room and sat down. "Listen, I've got to tell you something."

They peered at her.

"What? You're pregnant?" Pam asked after sucking a long drag from her Marlboro.

Laurie grimaced. "Fat chance."

"What is it then?" Sharon demanded.

"I have to let Brian know there's no chance for him and me."

"What!"

"Are you nuts? I'd die for him." Sharon held her heart, nearly falling to the floor.

"Why?" Pam cried.

"He's a nice guy and all, but the feelings really aren't there."

Sharon and Pam looked at each other. "The feelings really aren't there," they echoed in unison.

"He's class president, captain of the football team. And his daddy owns the bank. What more do you want, girl?" Sharon probed.

"That's not everything," Laurie said.

"Apparently not," Pam said, coughing as she choked either on her cigarette or on Laurie's last remark.

"And it's not about what I want—it's about what I feel. Or what I don't feel in this case."

"There's so many girls out there wanting him," Sharon emphasized.

"Yes. Exactly. That's why I have to let him know that I'm not interested, so he can move on. It's not fair to him. To either of us."

Something inside of Laurie was changing. This little clique of theirs was growing old, stagnant. She was searching for something different. But what? Maybe someone different. Before anything else could be said, the doorbell chimed. When Pam went to let the boys in, Sharon glared at Laurie.

"Maybe you better rethink this," Sharon said.

Laurie just looked at her. There was nothing to rethink. She had made up her mind. Brian had great looks and a nice personality and she knew he was crazy over her, but there had never even been a spark between them. At least as far as she was concerned. Everybody thought they should be together and to make them happy, she agreed to date him. It was wrong of her to do that. What about her happiness—didn't that count?

The boys came in, each carrying a six-pack of Heineken. Brian's father was a fan of the Dutch brew and he liked to entertain. Mr. Shannon had cases stacked up in his garage. Brian would help himself when the occasion called.

"Want a beer?" Brian asked Laurie.

"Sure. Why not?"

He opened the bottle and handed it to her.

Sharon wasted no time ushering Rob Kilroy, who should have been named "Killjoy," to the kitchen and began making out with him.

Laurie wondered what Sharon saw in him. He was a known heartbreaker. As soon as a girl fell for him, he would ditch her. She was certain Sharon would be next. Laurie tried to warn her friend, but she refused to listen. Rob was such a charmer. He even tried to come on to Laurie once. "You're so pretty, maybe we could go to the movies some night?" She told him straight out, "I got your number, bud. Bug off!" Even if she were attracted to him, she would never consider going out with him knowing her best friend was crazy over him. If she had told Sharon about his advances, it would have only started an argument and Sharon wouldn't have believed her anyway. Laurie was glad Rob got the message.

Pam stayed in the dining room with Mike most of the evening, drinking and slow-dancing. Mike was an all right sort of guy—nice looking, of course. Pam likely would have opted for someone else, otherwise. Mike could easily be identified as a follower. He rarely expressed ideas of his own. Maybe because his parents did everything for him. He could be such a wimp at times.

"What happened when you saw Principal Donovan?" Laurie asked Brian when they sat on the couch.

"A few detentions."

"That's it?" Laurie asked, shifting to face him. "No suspension or anything?"

"Nope."

"Rob, too?"

"Yep."

She wondered if the Indian boy would have gotten off as lightly. She doubted it.

Laurie and Brian drank and munched on chips and pretzels while the other four were preoccupied in other rooms. Brian and she had smooched many times. His kisses were okay, but not sensational. She knew he wanted more, but how could she? Even if her hormones were raging.

She wasn't ready to give all of herself to anyone. Her mother had warned her early on, "Boys have one thing on their minds. You could get pregnant. You don't want a bad reputation." Laurie had no intention of having sex, at least not at the time, but when Sharon and Pam went to Planned Parenthood one day she tagged along too, and got on the pill just to be safe. But nothing ever happened between her and Brian and never would. That was why she knew it had to come to an end.

Softly singing the lyrics to Neil Diamond's "Sweet Caroline," from time to time Laurie would look at Brian. He was handsome. Definitely. His body was lean; he had nice blonde hair, big hazel eyes and a smile other girls would kill for. Was she crazy?

He seemed as nervous as she. Before he had too much to drink she had better let him know how she felt. It made her feel phony to pretend there was anything other than friendship between them.

"Brian, let's talk," she said, letting her stocking feet touch the floor and feeling around for her shoes.

"I know what you're going to say," he said, rising from the sofa, walking to the stereo, and brushing his blonde hair with his hand.

"You do?" she asked, surprised.

"I'm not stupid," he said, his back toward her, crouching to change the records. Then he slowly rose, turned and faced her. "Is there someone else?"

"No. There really isn't," she said, shaking her head.

In front of the fireplace, Brian picked up an ornate framed photo of the Rodneys and stared at it for a moment. Then his gaze returned to Laurie. "Did I do something wrong? Is this about the fight?"

"No. Absolutely not," she said.

"What is it then?"

She swigged down some beer. Before lowering the bottle to the coffee table, she looked up at him. "I like you a lot, I really do. It's just that. . . ."

Returning the framed picture to the mantel, he crossed his arms in front of him and inhaled deeply. "I don't turn you on."

She felt like saying, "Yes, this is true," but she couldn't hurt him. "No," Laurie said, shaking her head. "It's me. I'm just not sure what I want. It's got nothing to do with you," she lied.

"Can we remain friends?" he asked.

"Of course we can. Always."

He lowered his gaze. "Nice." He walked back to the stereo. "What do you want to hear?"

"You pick," she said with a smile.

Brian didn't seem too let down. Maybe he felt the same way she did all along, but was afraid to let anyone know, even her.

The room soon blared with Crosby, Stills, Nash and Young.

The girls shooed the boys out at midnight so they could clean up before Sharon's parents arrived home. They blew out the candles, disposed of empty beer bottles, washed bowls and cleaned ashtrays. Then they opened up the front door to air everything out. Fifteen minutes later, the house was back in shape. The girls washed up and donned their pajamas.

"It's Laurie's turn to share the bed. Sorry, Pam, you get the floor," Sharon said as she strolled out of the room to the hall closet.

"Lucky you," Pam said to Laurie with a grin.

Sharon was a restless sleeper who liked to spread out like an octopus. Even in Sharon's queen size bed, Laurie would awaken with the dead weight of an arm or leg across her.

"If she starts tonight, I'll push her off the bed," Laurie vowed as Sharon hauled in a sleeping bag.

"What was that?" Sharon asked.

"Oh, nothing," Laurie said.

Pam and Sharon settled against the maple headboard, Laurie lay on the folded comforter.

"So, Laurie, what did you say to Brian?" Pam inquired.

"I told him how I felt."

"How'd he take it?" Sharon probed.

"Better than I thought. I told him I just wanted to be friends."

"He accepted that?" Pam asked.

"He seemed to. I mean, what choice did he have?"

"I can't believe this," Sharon said, rolling her eyes with her head rattling as she stretched her legs.

Laurie furrowed. "Your smelly feet are in my face."

"Nobody asked you to lie that way."

Suddenly, the sound of a motor could be heard. Laurie leaped from the bed and peeked out the window from behind the shade. "Your parents are here."

"Shut off the light," Sharon ordered as Pam scrambled toward the sleeping bag.

Laurie slipped under the covers with Sharon. Just as Laurie started to doze, a knee shoved the middle of her back. Was it deliberate? *It's my life, Sharon.*

Chapter 11

On Monday morning, Tobin stood in front of the judge with disheveled hair and clothes, his hands cuffed. The judge was quietly talking to the clerk of court. Wired from no sleep, Tobin spoke before the judge addressed him.

"Your Honor, we didn't do anything wrong. The police just. . . ."

The judge and the clerk turned and glared at him. Then the judge covered the mike. "Excuse me. Am I talking to you?"

"No, sir."

"Then be quiet. Wait till I'm through, or you'll go back where you came from. Do you understand me?"

"Yes, sir. I do."

Behind bars since his arrest on Friday night, Tobin had had enough. Now he sealed his lips and only spoke when spoken to, saying only what His Honor wanted to hear. He apologized for wrongs he hadn't committed. He wanted to kick himself, but remaining in jail would only upset his family.

Tobin's parents were in the house waiting for him. Uncle Basil was there, too. Tobin was glad Hannah was at school. He wandered onto the porch and opened the door that led into the kitchen.

"Are you okay?" Myra asked, greeting him with sad eyes and gently touching his arm.

"I'm fine, Mother."

"What happened? Why did they arrest you? What'd you do?"

"Nothing, Ma," he said abruptly. He didn't mean to sound snappy with her. He was just exhausted; he hadn't gotten much sleep in that cold cell. He had been too stirred up to rest anyway.

"Myra, the boy has done nothing wrong," James said, backing up his son while he stirred his coffee. Uncle Basil was sitting at the table next to him. They had been drinking coffee and discussing what had happened since early morning. Even though neither one was at the gathering Friday night, their friends had filled them in.

"I don't understand. How can they do this? If he didn't do anything wrong, how can they arrest him like that?" his mother demanded.

"The law can do what they want. They'll try to provoke us any way they can," Uncle Basil said, handing Tobin a cup of steaming herbal tea.

"Well, what the hell are we going to do about it?" Tobin asked.

"What *can* we do?" James had been through it all before.

"They've got us by the balls—let's face it."

"Tobin!"

"Sorry, Ma, but it's true."

The men nodded.

Tobin sipped the tea. "What's this? No coffee?"

"It will help take the edge off," Uncle Basil said.

Tobin dumped the tea in the sink. "It's time we did something."

Chapter 12

Laurie plopped her overnight bag in the foyer, flung her sweater onto the sofa and darted to the kitchen. She opened the refrigerator, took out the carton of milk, then scurried over to the cookie jar on the counter and helped herself to a handful of peanut butter cookies she and her father had baked a couple of nights before. As she sat at the counter dipping a cookie into her glass, Eleanor, looking lovely in her brown slacks and a pale yellow V-neck sweater, struggled in from the garage with more Filene's bags than she could manage.

Laurie ran over to help, grabbing a few from her hands.

"What's in here?" she asked, peeking into one.

"Christmas presents."

"For me?" Laurie asked, stuffing another cookie in her mouth.

"There are other people I buy for, besides you."

Laurie grinned. She knew what a soft touch her mother was about gifts.

"Maybe I better wrap them. I don't need you snooping before Christmas," Eleanor said, heading out of the kitchen. Then she paused in the doorway. "You'll spoil your dinner."

A few seconds later, her mother's voice resounded from the living room.

"Laurie, please pick up your things."

"I will."

"Now would be nice."

"O-kay."

Still gulping her milk, Laurie seized her sweater and backpack and headed upstairs. Halfway up she turned around. She had caught a subtle scent of her father's favorite musk, Royal Copenhagen. "Is Dad home?"

"He's in the den. At least he was when I left."

Continuing upstairs to her room, she rushed to her bureau and yanked open the top drawer, extracting the civics report folded under her pajamas. Then she sprinted back down to the den. She knew her mother would be busy for a while, giving her some alone time with her father.

Among the built-in bookcases were mullioned windows that captured the afternoon sunlight. In front of them were a brown leather sofa and two ginger-clad chairs. Her father was engrossed in his work when she peered in. Clients' files were piled on his mahogany desk, along with a calculator, a pewter stein chock-full of pencils and pens, and a letter opener. An old manual typewriter occupied the top of a file cabinet to his left.

Laurie tapped on the doorjamb. He looked up. "Do you have a minute?" she asked.

"Yeah, sure. Come in, sweetheart."

"I wanted to show you this," she said, handing him her paper and settling into one of the chairs.

Laurie had decided not to say anything to her mother. It was bad enough she had skipped school, telling her friends she had an awful headache. She thought actually being in the courtroom would help her write a better report, which it had. When she read it out loud in class, however, ridicule orchestrated by Pam and Sharon orbited the room. With all the racket, her friends heard little or nothing about what she wrote, especially how it ended.

Her father adjusted his glasses and began reading.

I guess I was ignorant, to say the least. The only thing I really knew about the Indians was what I had read in books and seen on television. They were never the heroes. In fact, just the opposite. But living here and getting to know them, I've found that they're really nice people. No different from you or me. So what if they wear paint on their faces or beads around their neck. We shouldn't judge them on the way they dress or choose to live their lives. They respect our culture; we should respect theirs.

The Wampanoag were here long before we were. Our people forget they're the ones who taught us how to farm. They've been a tribe forever. Saying they haven't is just another way to force them to abandon their claim. But they're too strong to give up.

For years, the Indians did a good job taking care of their small village. They minded their own business and kept things running smoothly. Then we barged in and turned their lives upside down. What right do we have, trying to keep something that never belonged to us in the first place? We stole their land and we should give it back.

Donald finished reading. "I'm very proud of you, Laurie. And for so much more than the 'A' at the bottom of the last page here," he said, smiling as his eyes filled with tears.

She leaped out of her chair and ran over to hug him. "Thank you, Daddy," she said.

Later that evening, as Laurie was pouring gravy over her meat and potatoes, she thought how peaceful it was at the dinner table for a change when her mother started in again.

"Do the Wampanoag really think they're going to win?"

"Why not? They have a chance."

"You're young, Laurie. You have a lot to learn."

"Maybe I'm young, but I know what's right."

"Everything will be taken care of properly through the court system," Eleanor continued, buttering her bread.

Laurie grew tired of listening. She hated arguing with her mother, and lately it seemed that was all they did.

"Where are you going?" her mother asked when Laurie rose from the table, picking up her plate.

"I've got homework."

"I have your favorite tonight—strawberry shortcake."

"No thanks," she said, scraping her half-finished plate into the wastebasket then stacking it in the dishwasher.

"The teachers should give you kids a break. After all, you'll be graduating soon."

"Guess not," she said, leaving the room.

Eleanor cleared the table and brought out dessert for her and her husband. "Let me tell you what they're planning now. . ."

Donald slapped his cloth napkin on the table and stood up.

"And where are you headed, Donald?"

"I've had enough, Eleanor."

Her mouth closed. She looked stunned.

"What do you mean?" Eleanor finally asked.

"Lay off them awhile. Will you please?"

"Aren't you interested?"

"Interested is one thing. Obsessed is another. You're taking this too far."

"Well, I'll be," she mumbled.

Laurie had unloaded her schoolbooks and notebook paper on the desk when the phone by her bed rang. It was Sharon.

"Pam and I are going Christmas shopping. Wanna come?"

"Sure. I'll pick you guys up."

Laurie had slipped on her jacket and slung her pocketbook strap over her shoulder when she saw her mother standing there.

"Where are you going?"

"To the mall."

"What about your homework?"

"I'll do it later."

"Get home early. It's starting to rain. Supposed to get very windy. Be careful."

Laurie nodded, shutting the door behind her. Mom, I know you care about me. You used to care about all people. What changed you?

Chapter 13

Inside the mall, the girls stopped in front of Sheldons, an expensive clothing store. Admiring Gunne Sax dresses on the mannequins, they decided to venture in. They marched in and out of dressing rooms, goofing around. Pam sported a sleeveless, black velvet maxi and Laurie decked herself out in a white disco gown with rhinestones. When Sharon wiggled into a snug-fitting mini dress, black background splattered with shimmering specks in hot pink, turquoise, gold, and purple, she stole the show.

"You look totally hip," Pam said to Sharon. "Doesn't she, Laurie?"

"Yeah," she said, giggling. "I think we all do."

Adding Christian Dior sunglasses and silk Gucci scarves, the girls resembled Vogue models as they paraded up and down the aisles. The store manager didn't seem to mind; he grinned the whole time. The girls' performance increased sales. After returning the dresses and accessories to their proper racks, the girls left the store with their arms around each other's shoulders.

"Was that fun or what!" Pam exclaimed.

"Where to next?" Laurie asked.

"We have to get the guys something," Pam sighed.

"It's getting late. Maybe we better," Sharon said.

In Filene's, after tossing woolen hats on their heads, the girls slipped gold and silver bangles on their wrists and large hoops in their ears. They lingered at the makeup counter and stopped to squirt Chanel on themselves, but quickly moved on through the mall knowing they still had to find gifts for their boyfriends. Or at least Sharon and Pam did.

"So, what are you getting Brian for Christmas?" Sharon asked.

"We are just friends, remember? If I get him something, he'll get the wrong impression," Laurie said.

Sharon glowered at her. "So you're getting him nothing?"

Laurie nodded. "That's right."

Pam piped in. "You can't do that. What if he gets you something?"

"I don't think he will."

"But what if he does—how are you going to feel then?" Sharon quizzed.

I am going to feel like a heel. "I can't worry about it."

"This is stupid. We're *all* friends," Pam emphasized.

"It won't work," Sharon added.

Laurie stopped and stared at her. "What do you mean? What won't work?"

"You can't just be a friend to him."

"Why not? Brian and I already talked about this."

Sharon shook her head. "You could've waited till after Christmas." Laurie just shrugged.

Her friends looked at her as if she were a terrible person. Christmas or not, they weren't going to make her feel guilty. Laurie hadn't thought about it before, but they were right in a way. It could be an awkward situation. The six of them had celebrated Christmas together the year before and exchanged gifts. She and Brian had just met. They hadn't started dating or anything, but he did give her a cookbook, obviously one his mother had picked out for him. It was nice of him anyway. She had given him a new Cross pen, one of the many her father received from clients. It was like a "Hello, glad to meet you" present. But that was then. They had no reason to impress each other with gifts now. But now what? Since the rest were going steady, would she and Brian be comfortable being around them? And if one of them found someone, there would be an oddball in the bunch. Unless they both got lucky. That would work. Or would it?

Suddenly, Laurie noticed three Indian girls headed toward them. She had to find a way to distract her friends. She spotted an instant photo booth and nudged Pam.

"Let's go," Pam grinned, grabbing Sharon.

The three of them rushed inside, crunched into the small seat and closed the dark curtain. They dropped in the quarters and snuggled close, making faces for the quick flashes. Minutes later, the strip of glossy images appeared. Laurie quickly gathered the photos, admiring them.

"Let me see," the other two whined in unison.

Laughing at the silly faces they made, the three argued about who was getting what but finally managed to decide. Remembering she had a small pair of scissors in her makeup case, Laurie cut the glossy strips. She gave Pam and Sharon the ones they wanted, and she kept the rest. As the girls pushed the curtain aside, Laurie hoped by now the Indian girls would be out of sight. They all nearly smacked into one another.

"Oh, look. Here come three little Indians," Sharon remarked, scanning the Wampanoag girls up and down.

"Aren't they cute?" Pam said scornfully, raising her brows. Then she looked at Laurie, expecting a response. Laurie wished she could disappear.

"I hope the camera doesn't break," Sharon said sarcastically, watching the other girls head toward the photo booth.

Two of them just walked past, but one paused just long enough to say, "Hi, Laurie."

"Hi," she said, wondering how this girl knew her name but, then again, her trio was well known. Still, she was flattered just the same.

"Hey, Laurie, who's your friend?" Pam asked, looking back at them.

"I don't know who she is."

"Yeah, right," Sharon said with a nasty smile.

Believe what you want, Laurie thought.

As they were getting ready to leave the mall, Laurie saw Tobin Horvarth coming out of Eli Baker's, a clothing store for tall men. She was certain he was six feet tall, maybe taller. She learned who he was when she read about his arrest in the newspaper. He looked even more handsome than when she saw him in the courtroom. Despite the fact that it was only a glimpse, her heart started beating faster and her palms became sweaty. She had never met him.

Hannah's two friends, Gayle and Theresa, hurled incredulous looks when they walked past the white girls.

"Laurie's nothing like them. She's really nice," Hannah said.

"Sure. If you say so," Gayle said.

"Laurie was the one who helped Kerry in the cafeteria that day."

Hannah's friends' blank looks told they had no clue what she was talking about. "Remember when Rob tripped him, and his lunch went everywhere? She helped Kerry pick up his tray."

"Oh, yeah. Right after that, those two white boys got into a fight," Gayle said.

"That's right," Theresa buzzed in. "I heard one of them call Laurie an Indian lover. And that's when the fight started."

"It was Rob Kilroy who said it. And Laurie's boyfriend, Brian, got mad," Hannah relayed.

Tobin was strolling their way when they came out of the photo booth. He was their ride.

"Come in with us. C'mon," the three implored, grabbing his hand, pulling him back toward the booth.

"At least take a picture with your sister," Gayle insisted.

Outnumbered, he gave in.

"Tobin, you look too serious. Smile," Hannah said.

"I'd bet he'd smile if Bo Derek was next to him," Theresa teased.

The first flash captured Tobin's laugh.

Hannah and her friends rushed over to a bench to look at the pictures.

As Tobin stood there waiting for them, something caught his eye on the mall floor. He bent down and scooped it up.

"Hey, you forgot. . . ."

"What?" Hannah asked, raising her head.

"Nothing," he said, staring at the photo cupped in his hand.

Chapter 14

A light breeze whistled across the window sill in Tobin's bedroom. The cool morning air stirred him. He glanced at his wind-up clock. 7:20 A.M. How good his own bed felt, after that flimsy cot in the jail cell. It made him appreciate what he had, even though they didn't have much. After tossing and turning a couple of times, he finally got up and slipped on a pair of jeans and a T-shirt.

After a trip to the john, he went into the kitchen and put on the kettle. Waiting for the water to heat up, he rifled through the junk drawer for the tube of adhesive. The crack in his wall needed a temporary fix. Finding the glue, he laid it on the kitchen counter and picked up the whistling pot. As he added milk and sugar to his coffee, there was a knock on the door. Through the windowpanes, he could see it was CJ Phillips. Tobin wondered what he wanted. He hoped his few words with CJ on Friday night hadn't been too encouraging.

"What are you doing here?" Tobin asked when he opened the door. CJ was dressed in torn farmer's overalls and a Red Sox jersey. His brawny arms bore heart tattoos with the names of old scores.

"What kind of greeting is that?" CJ asked.

Tobin rubbed his neck and looked at him.

"I need to talk to you."

"What is it?" Tobin asked coolly.

The law knew CJ. Too well. Although Tobin had to admit he himself was becoming no stranger to the police. CJ, though, was on probation more than he was off. His ex-girlfriend, Ellen, had taken out several restraining orders against him, but he ignored the injunction each time. He ended up in jail once or twice. Tobin had lost track.

CJ looked around nervously and when he saw Tobin's mother walk from one room to another, he clammed up. Tobin wondered what sort of jam CJ had gotten himself into this time. CJ had begged for his help when he gambled away his child support money. Feeling sorry for his poor kid, Tobin lent CJ fifty bucks that day, but made it clear to him it would be the last time.

"Let's go outside," CJ said.

Tobin let CJ lead the way, closing the door behind him. They walked into the backyard toward the old chicken coop with its slanting roof. They hadn't had chickens in years. The family once sold eggs to the locals, but that was a long time ago.

"What's going on?" Tobin asked.

"One of the jurors got a phone call—a threatening one."

Tobin tilted his head, squinting. CJ had his attention now. "Who told you this?"

"Don't matter."

That's true, Tobin thought. He didn't care. Still, he wanted to find out who had threatened whom and why. "What'd he say? I mean, I assume it was a guy."

"Yup. Sure was."

"And I suppose it was a woman he threatened?"

"You got that right."

"Is this a guessing game or what?" Tobin asked CJ.

"Okay, man, let me tell you what he said: 'You know which way you better go.'"

"Hmm," Tobin murmured, crossing his arms over his chest. "You know which way you better go," Tobin slowly repeated. "Is that right?" he mused quietly, peering into the distance. "I don't suppose this person identified himself?" Tobin asked as he slowly turned and looked at him.

"Nah. That woman juror—the one that got threatened. . . ." he stuttered.

"Yeah?"

"She's been blabbing on the bus. Ain't she supposed to keep her mouth shut?"

"She shouldn't be discussing the trial—with anyone. Who is this woman? What's her name?" Tobin grilled.

"Don't know. I'm sure I can find out if you want me to."

"Just give me a minute," Tobin said, gesturing at CJ to stop talking.

Walking across the brown lawn, Tobin bent down and picked up an old weathered baseball, left behind from his practicing days, and threw it high into the sky far past the end of the property into the woods. CJ watched in awe.

Brushing the soil off his hands, Tobin turned toward CJ. "How can I be sure this is all true?"

"I got good sources. They've always been right before." CJ was looking superior. Bad boys somehow had ways of finding out stuff, and CJ was like a sleazy encyclopedia. He stared at Tobin. "What're ya going to do?"

"What am *I* going to do? You're the one who's got the contacts. First thing, get the facts straight. We need names—proof. We can't go to Morin and Huffington with something made up or second hand. Things get twisted. You know what I'm saying?"

"Yeah," CJ said. "I gotta be careful. I can end up behind bars."

Though Tobin was actually a few months younger, CJ looked up to him as if he were a big brother. "You started something; you're going to have to follow through now. You'll be doing our tribe a favor. A fine one."

"Do you think that dude called the other jurors, too?"

"It's possible," Tobin said, frowning. "Keep your ear to the ground and see if you can find out who that woman is. At least it'll be a start."

"You got it," CJ said as he headed toward an old '59, camouflaged Jeep in the driveway. Tobin waited until he got in and started it up.

To his amazement the ugly jalopy purred. He watched until it was out of sight, then he went into the house and straight to his room.

He sat down on his bed, trying to figure out what to do next. He knew the last thing he was going to do—tell his folks. What was the sense of giving them false hope? If some of the jurors were replaced with non-whites, maybe then the Wampanoags would have a better chance. With an all-white jury, his people were doomed. *Damn, he's got to come through for me.* Tobin never thought he would be asking CJ for anything. But even a slime ball can come in handy.

Chapter 15

Everybody needs a refuge, Tobin thought as he sat under an awning of pine trees on the pebbly beach, watching jumping fish make halos on the calm water after cleansing rains. The tallest boy in fifth grade, his height had made him feel awkward and clumsy. When one called him the "Jolly Green Giant" and others started teasing him too, he wanted to run away and hide forever.

It was here at John's Pond he had retreated that day. He sat in the sand near the water's edge with his arms around his knees, fighting back tears. Horizontal lines of blushing pink hovered above the water. Brilliant red, orange and yellow leaves flickered in the low sun. The only things moving were the ducks coming toward him. He stretched out his arms to release the bread crumbs from his fingers. It wasn't long before he had started to feel better.

Now, he was sitting in the same spot, ten years, later, his people and the whites again at war. In spite of the conflict, like the big old trees circling the pond, his tribe's roots were long and deep. Who he was, where he came from would always be sealed in his soul.

His tribe had been pretty much in control of their little village for many years, but now the rich were moving in. Taking over. Developers were buying up all the vacant lots, closing Mashpee land to hunting and fishing, destroying the ancient ways. They were building flashy homes, supermarkets, and malls. The whites, blind to the beauty of the natural world and used to getting their way, had grown vicious. The earth was the center of his tribe's existence. Surely all the venom couldn't touch this place.

Tobin stood up. Lavender clouds drifted over the pond. He watched the ripples, nudged by the breeze, playfully kiss its shore.

Tobin dialed the operator to get Morin and Huffington's number. James Horvarth had it somewhere, but Tobin would never scour through his father's affairs. He had to tell the lawyers what he had learned. Whether they believed it or not would be another story. CJ didn't know the name of the woman being threatened. The caller feeding CJ this information was anonymous. The whole thing could have been made up. Tobin needed to find out. He had jumped in his car and driven a couple of miles down the street to a small market where there was a pay phone. He went in, grabbed the first thing he saw, a bag of chips, and took the change to make his call.

There were two booths outdoors. The first one, he discovered after he deposited all his coins, was out of order. This time when he went inside the store, he simply handed the cashier a dollar bill and asked her for change.

"We can't do that," she replied.

Tobin looked at her dumbfounded.

"You—you have to buy something."

"I just bought something. Potato chips—remember?" he said to the skinny girl with braces, who didn't look much more than fourteen.

She gave him a vacant look.

"Fine, give me a pack of gum."

"What kind?"

"I don't care. Anything."

Tobin pocketed the change and Juicy Fruit and went back outside to make his call. This time the only working phone was in use. The guy on the phone, back turned and huddled in the corner of the small booth, looked like he wanted to keep everything he was saying private. After ten minutes, Tobin whistled some, finally getting his attention. The man snapped his index finger in the air, swiveled and continued talking. Tired of waiting, Tobin rapped on the door.

"Hold on a minute," the occupant said to whoever was on the phone. He glared at Tobin.

"How much longer you going to be?" Tobin asked.

"Okay. Okay. I'm getting off." The fellow, thirtyish, wearing a blazer and jeans, rolled his eyes. "I have to go," he said loudly to the person on the other end of the line. "Don't worry I know what to do. Don't forget what I said. I mean it."

He hung up abruptly and jerked open the booth's door. Stepping out, he exhaled an annoyed breath, gave Tobin another nasty look, straightened his jacket and strode off.

Tobin hurried in to make his call. The attorney's secretary answered, keeping him on hold for what seemed like forever. He didn't know it would be such a hassle getting through. Minutes passed and the change dwindled quickly. "Please deposit another twenty-five cents more." As Tobin deposited the money, he was suddenly mesmerized.

The beautiful blonde from the courthouse was driving into the store parking lot. She was with a friend. *Damn.* She pulled into a spot where his view was blocked by three other vehicles. He had more important things to deal with now anyway. "Get over it," he said out loud while trying to get a glimpse, still wishing he could see her Camaro.

"What was that?" the secretary asked.

"Oh, nothing."

"Mr. Huffington is in court. And Mr. Morin is with a client. May I take a message?"

"No, thank you. Is there a good time to reach them?"

"Well, it's hard to say. They're very busy. If you leave your name."

"I'll call back. Thank you," Tobin said and hung up. After all that. He had thought about leaving his home number, but then his parents would want to know all the particulars when he received a call back. It would stir up too much commotion, and he couldn't afford that before CJ could get the names he needed. Without those, it was only hearsay. Tobin hoped there were no warrants out for CJ. Tobin didn't want him locked up—not before he came up with the entire package this time. Tobin had heard of mistrials and hung juries, but he couldn't remember exactly what it took, or if it was even possible in this type of lawsuit.

Before leaving the booth, Tobin checked again to see if he could see the blonde girl. The cars that had been in the way were gone, but so was the one she was in. *Another time—maybe*, he thought.

Chapter 16

Laurie had been invited over to Sharon's house for lunch. She liked eating there anytime. Mrs. Rodney made the best homemade chicken soup ever. Her baked macaroni and cheese smothered with sweet tomatoes deserved an award, too. When she arrived and entered the foyer, a flustered Mrs. Rodney greeted her. She was out of the bread she needed for the casserole she was preparing for their lunch.

"I can run to the store, Mrs. Rodney. That's no problem."

"Oh, that's sweet of you, Laurie. Sharon, why don't you go with her? You can run in. You know what I get. It will save time."

"I planned to anyway."

"Wonderful. Thank you, girls. I'll have everything just about ready by the time you get back."

Laurie stayed in the car while Sharon ran into the store. Humming to Kenny Nolan's, "I like Dreamin" on the radio had her thinking about Tobin. She didn't know why; she didn't even know him. She found him good-looking, but he was no more attractive than Brian or any other cute guy. And it seemed like he could stir trouble easily. Or was it the other way around? Trouble found him? Before she could figure it out, Sharon was back in the car.

Leaving the parking lot, Laurie spotted Tobin in a phone booth. A horn's blare blasted her out of her trance. The black Lincoln swerved to avoid hitting them. Laurie slammed on her brake.

"What the hell are you doing?" Sharon yelled, flying forward in the seat. The angry driver pulled past, showing his fist. "Are you crazy? Didn't you see him?"

I saw him all right. But not the 'him' you're talking about.

"No," Laurie said, shaking her head. "No, I didn't. One minute he wasn't there—the next he was." She had only inched onto the main road when it happened, so even if they had collided it would've been a minimal dent, since the other guy was moving at a snail's pace. *Count on Sharon to blow it out of proportion.*

"Are you blind? For Chrissake!"

"We didn't hit him. Sorry. Jeez, it's not like I did it deliberately."

At least Sharon had missed seeing Tobin. She likely had been looking in the mirror again at her hair or makeup—which was a blessing since she was in no mood to listen to Sharon's derogatory mouth. Laurie was afraid she would defend Tobin. But why? Were they meant to meet for real? Or was it only her fantasy?

When they got back to the house, Mrs. Rodney had white linen and sterling candlestick holders on the table. Everything looked White House elegant, as usual. Cold cuts, pickles, olives, cheeses and fruit, and a homemade lemon meringue filled china plates. All this food before the spinach and lamb casserole even came out of the oven. Laurie wondered how they all stayed so thin.

"She almost got us killed," Sharon blurted to her mother. "I thought I was going to go through the windshield." Biting into her colossal roast beef sandwich, Laurie nearly bit her tongue.

"Did something distract you, Laurie?" Mrs. Rodney asked.

"No," she fibbed, wiping the mayonnaise from her lips with a linen napkin. Sharon had a tendency to go overboard at times, and Laurie knew Mrs. Rodney was aware of those times. "The man seemed to come out of nowhere."

"You have to be careful. Your eyes have to be on the road always. I wouldn't want anything to happen to you girls," Mrs. Rodney said.

"Yeah, and you don't want to crack up that new car of yours," Sharon added.

Laurie turned toward Sharon's mother. "I really am a very conscientious driver."

"Oh, honey, I know you are. That's why I don't worry when Sharon leaves with you. Well, there's no sense dwelling on something that didn't happen."

Did you hear your mom, Sharon?

When the subject changed to the girls' plans for the following year, Laurie was relieved. Sharon perpetually argued with her mother about going to modeling school.

"Modeling years are short. I think twenty-six—that's when they retire you. Then what would you do? What about working for the airlines? You'll get to travel all over. I think you'd make a great flight attendant," Mrs. Rodney said with a smile. "Don't you think so, Laurie?"

Laurie didn't hear her. Her mind had floated back to Tobin. Seeing him close up, he was better looking than she remembered.

"Laurie!" Sharon said loudly.

"Huh?"

"My mother is speaking to you."

"I'm sorry, Mrs. Rodney."

"It's okay. You probably have a lot on your mind."

"The way she's been spacing out lately, you'd think she was in love or something. Probably feeling bad she broke Brian's heart," Sharon said.

Hardly. But let that last theory rule, Laurie thought.

Chapter 17

"Thanks, Tobin, for bringing me here." Hannah smiled, staring up at Boston's skyscrapers surrounded in puffy gray clouds. Before they parked the car, Tobin had driven past the John Hancock Tower, Old State House and the Old North Church, a few of his sister's favorites.

"My pleasure."

Although she had been hinting for him to bring her here, Hannah had no idea he would actually do it. It was sort of his gift to her. At least Boston was pretty at Christmas. It felt good to get away from it all, but that wasn't going to solve anything—as much as he would like it to.

Suddenly, it dawned on him that he could accomplish more here than make his sister happy. He pulled out his wallet and found the address. "I have an errand to run. Why don't you get some shopping done?" He glanced at his watch. It was twelve o'clock. "I'll meet you back here in an hour. In front of Jordan Marsh. Don't go anywhere else."

"I won't." She bounced away happily, blending into the sea of holiday shoppers.

She never asked him where he was going, and he could tell she was too enthralled to care; she was happy to do her own thing. Hating to leave Hannah any longer than he had to, Tobin walked swiftly down Washington Street, crossing Tremont through the Public Garden.

After the elevator door opened on the 10th floor at 360 Beacon, he went right to a woman at the front desk. She directed him three quarters of the way down the hall to a glass door with polished brass letters. *Morin and Huffington, Attorneys at Law.* Very impressive, he thought as he stood in front of it for a moment. *Hmm. Maybe someday I'll have an office with fancy letters* on my door. But was that really appealing to him? He was an outdoorsman, an environmentalist, a baseball player—even a park ranger. *No. If I had to be cooped up in an office all day, I'd go out of my mind.*

"Excuse me," Tobin said to the secretary sitting behind the desk. "I need to speak to Mr. Huffington or Mr. Morin."

"What is your name, sir?"

"Tobin Horvarth."

She looked blankly at him.

"Oh, I'm sorry—I'm from Mashpee. They're representing us. Our tribe, that is. We—"

"Mr. Horvarth, I don't see you down here," said the strawberry-haired woman, looking in a big black book.

"Oh, I didn't make an appointment. I was in the city, and I just thought I'd stop by, hoping to catch one of them."

"You really need to call in advance if you want to see either one of them."

"I called yesterday, but they were in court."

"I'm sorry," the secretary said.

"I have to speak to one of them—today. It's very important."

"I don't see how that's possible, Mr. Horvarth."

"Can't you make it possible?"

"Wish I could help you out, but Attorney Morin is with a client and Attorney Huffington is in court again. You can leave them a note if you'd like," the middle-aged woman suggested with a sympathetic smile, handing him a small pad and pen.

How the hell am I going to explain on paper that a juror was threatened? What choice did he have? He left the note and returned to Hannah.

Tobin and Hannah wandered happily along the city sidewalks. Red, green, orange and blue lights flickered on the bare trees. Santa Clauses rang their bells on every corner, and a handful of carolers were singing,

"Oh, Holy Night." The department store windows glittered with garland. After devouring Jordan Marsh's famous blueberry muffins and a cup of hot chocolate, they watched ice skaters with woolen scarves and gloves glide carefree across Frog Pond.

"Oh, Tobin, I wanna live here. I love this place—the noise, the excitement, the tall buildings," she said smiling with open arms, as if she were trying to embrace it all.

Surprisingly, his sister was becoming her own person with her own tastes. She was growing up fast. Tobin thought about how everyone he knew, including himself, was growing or changing in some way: older, wiser, stronger.

Tobin noticed people of all colors sauntering in and out of the stores—without any hassle. No stares. Nobody razzing. *A classic Heinz 57 variety*, he thought, smiling to himself as he scanned over everyone in his path. They were only about one hundred miles from home, yet it was like they were a world away. Was this Hannah's real attraction? He wished life could be so easy in his own town. Maybe someday, he thought.

Peering into a Filene's window, they saw Mickey and Minnie dancing in their Christmas attire. All around them, children stared, awed. Like the white kids at the Pow Wow who would point and smile when he was a kid, and he would hold their hands and dance with them. Then he gave each one a feather or a bead to remember him by. Tobin never thought those same kids would be so hateful when they became older.

Suddenly, the sky opened up and sprinkled fresh whiteness, soft and hushed. Tobin put his hand on Hannah's shoulder. "Come on, Sis, it's time to go."

"Do we have to?" she asked, eyes imploring.

He was enjoying himself as much as she was, and the snow shower gave them a real feel for the holidays. He also knew the slick streets would make the driving difficult with everyone rushing to get out of the city at the same time before it got worse. Only a couple of inches had been predicted. But in New England, weather was unpredictable.

"We should, it's late. I'll bring you back again."

"You will?"

"Of course," he said, remembering The Common on the way to the lawyer's office. Maybe we'll even take a swan boat ride."

"Okay," she said, satisfied. "Let's go."

He had meant what he said. Hannah could be stubborn at times, but she was good company and she now seemed so much older than she had when he had left for college. Once they got through the city, the ride home was easier. The snow turned to rain and the traffic back to Cape Cod was light.

They had just pulled into the driveway when he saw car lights in his rearview mirror. Tobin quickly spun his Ford pickup around, his headlights now shining on the camouflaged Jeep.

"What's he doing here?" Hannah asked, recognizing their visitor.

"I'll take care of it. You go into the house," Tobin told her.

Hannah hesitated. "Do I have to?"

"Yes. Go!" he demanded, shooing her with his hand.

Reluctantly, she got out of the car and shut the door. Walking slowly toward the house, she turned around every few steps. Even she knew CJ was bad news. In spite of her good sense, Tobin felt the less he told her the better. At least for the time being, anyway.

He watched his sister for a moment, making sure she had gone inside. Then he got out of the truck and went to talk to CJ, who was still sitting in the Jeep. *And you can stay right there,* Tobin thought. *You're not getting an invitation to dinner.* Any more meetings between them would have to be set up somewhere else.

Sticking a Winston in his mouth, CJ used a lighter with a large flame.

"What'd you do, stay up all night?" Tobin asked him, noticing the dark circles under his eyes.

"Not quite," he said, blowing out smoke. "Actually, it was easier than I thought."

"Never mind how you got it. Just tell me what you have," Tobin insisted.

"That woman juror, the one that got threatened. . . ."

"Yeah, what about her?"

"Amelia Smart is her name. Her name don't fit her. If she was smart, she wouldn't say nothing."

Tobin looked at him, waiting for more.

"She's a housewife."

"A housewife? Is that it?"

"Yeah. No."

"Well, which is it?"

"That's all I know about her. But there's something else."

"Shoot," Tobin said impatiently, his fingers tapping the Jeep's door.

"The caller—he got to the others, too."

"What are you saying? He threatened them?"

CJ nodded. "Yup. Sure did."

"How?"

"Don't know. He said he'd break limbs or worse—if they don't go the right way."

"Who the hell is this guy?"

CJ shrugged.

"You've got to find out who he is."

"He's slick. He knows what he's doing. Must be a pro."

"You'll just have to be slicker. We've got to get him, or we won't have a fighting chance—we'll lose the trial for sure."

"I'll do what I can."

Tobin stared at him. "Not good enough."

"*Okay*. I'll find out who the bastard is," CJ said.

"Now you're talking."

CJ shifted the Jeep in reverse, backed into an open field, then switched gears and pushed the gas pedal to the floorboards, spraying mud. Tobin jumped back just in time. Then he stood there until the Jeep's taillights became little red dots and a large snowflake made him blink. *What are you really up to?*

Chapter 18

Laurie was stretched out on the big blue velour sofa in the living room, reading Seventeen, when Eleanor came in and began rearranging the crocheted pillows in the overstuffed chairs. Before Eleanor cleared her throat, Laurie knew she had something on her mind by the way she was acting.

"I haven't seen Brian around lately. Did you two have a fight?"

"No," Laurie said flatly, lowering the magazine. She figured Brian's parents must have said something, since her parents and his were friends and they had been with the Shannons the night before. Her mother obviously knew something. She was just waiting for Laurie to come out with it. Laurie had avoided filling her in because she knew her mother would knead her for the particulars. Then she would go on about how wonderful Brian was—give her all the reasons why Laurie had made a mistake.

And she was right.

"He's not sick, is he?"

"No. I can't be stringing him along. I let him know I just want to be friends."

"Oh, that's too bad. I thought it was more serious than that."

Laurie sighed deeply. "Well, it's not."

"What a shame. He's such a nice boy. You two looked so good together, too."

Laurie shrugged. "I guess."

"You guess? You don't think so?"

"No, he's okay—he's just not for me."

"Do you want to talk about this?"

That's exactly what I don't want to do. She had already heard more than enough from Sharon and Pam. And she knew she hadn't heard the end of it yet.

"Not really. There's nothing to talk about. I just don't feel anything for him—you know what I mean?"

Maybe her mother didn't know. Or maybe she did and she always just accepted her lot instead of looking further. Although, Laurie believed her father was a premium catch.

"Honey, maybe the two of you need some time apart. I'm sure you can resolve this, you know, work it out. I wouldn't wait too long, though. He's handsome—and smart. There're a lot of young women who would be glad to have him."

They're welcome to him.

"I think eight months is time enough," Laurie said, although her mother's hearing seemed blocked.

Laurie felt she was missing nothing. In spite of his prized looks and popularity, Brian had little else to offer. Nothing about him excited her. And those feelings couldn't be pulled out of a hat.

"The Shannons are well-respected in this community, Laurie."

Give it up. "Mother. He's not for me."

Eleanor let out a long sigh, shook her head and strode from the room.

At least this gave them something else to argue about besides the trial, Laurie thought.

Chapter 19

When Tobin finally reached the narrow shaded path to the old cottage where CJ lived with his alcoholic father, he noticed CJ's Jeep was gone. Tobin hoped he was busy finding out who was threatening Amelia Smart and the others, though if he had, getting in touch with the lawyers would be like trying to contact a celebrity. *First things first, he thought.*

Tobin looked around. To the right of the house was a dump of empty liquor bottles. An old push mower sat in tall, brown grass. A Model T Ford rusted into the ground, long out of commission, and an old steel plow, probably from the 50's, was left discarded in the field.

Before he reached the wooden door, much in need of painting, he heard a TV blasting. He knocked but nobody responded. He knocked harder. Then he heard what sounded like grunting.

"Hello? Anybody around?"

"Come in, come in," he heard a raspy voice repeat. Tobin opened the door and stepped into the entryway. The living room was on the right.

CJ's father was lounging in a worn recliner. Dressed in a fisherman's hat, a brown short-sleeved shirt, and stained tan trousers, he was hugging a half-full bottle of whisky and watching Name That Tune on a snowy screen. The rabbit ear antenna on the TV was useless.

"Who's that?" the gruff voice asked as Tobin walked into the room, hazy from an ashtray full of crushed Pall Mall butts.

"Tobin Horvarth, Mr. Phillips."

"James's son?"

"Yes, sir."

"What're ya doing here?" he asked, his words slurring, his eyes red and glassy.

"I'm here to see CJ."

Mr. Phillips shook his head. "That boy. I can't keep track of him. He's somewhere."

"I'll wait if you don't mind."

"Don't matter to me. Have a seat, boy," he said almost cheerfully, motioning to the couch.

Tobin assumed his visitors were far and few. "I'm fine," Tobin said after he took one look at the dirty sofa. There had been rumors that Mr. Phillips had beaten CJ when he was younger, although now the old man looked unable to swat a fly. It was easy to figure out how CJ ended up to be what he was.

"Like a drink?" Mr. Phillips asked, his hand waving the bottle.

Tobin shook his head. "Too early in the day for me."

"Ah, best time."

Always "best time," so it seems. Tobin wondered what had happened to CJ's mother. Did she die? Maybe her husband's drinking drove her away. Tobin couldn't remember CJ's mother ever coming to any school events; he wondered how long she had been gone.

Suddenly, the phone on the metal card table rang. Mr. Phillips made no effort to move. "Would you like me to get that?" Tobin offered.

"Nah," CJ's father said. "No one important. Machine will get it."

After four or five rings, there was a click. CJ's voice came on. "Leave a message. If you're lucky I'll get back to you. If you're not so lucky, I won't. You figure that out." *Typical.* Somebody listened for a minute. Thinking CJ's informant might be calling Tobin glanced over at the unmoving Mr. Phillips, then quickly dove for the phone.

"Yup. It's your dime," Tobin said, trying to sound like CJ. He thought he heard someone breathing but with the TV up loud, he couldn't be sure. "Anyone there?" Tobin repeated, but it was too late.

As he was returning the receiver, Tobin saw a neatly written phone number on a small pad of paper. Maybe it was the informant's. The exchange was the same, and the first two digits, 2-0, were his age, the remaining two, 4-0, were his age doubled. *That's easy*, he thought.

Preoccupied, he was startled when CJ rushed in. He stopped dead, wide-eyed, when he saw Tobin.

"What are you doing here?"

"I came to see if you heard anything."

"Oh, uh, not yet," CJ stammered, directing Tobin toward the front door away from his father.

"Nothing at all?" Tobin asked.

"There is one thing," CJ said quietly, pausing. "He's making his threats from a phone booth so he won't get caught."

"A phone booth?" Tobin remembered the man in the phone booth the day he tried calling the lawyers. He thought the man was having a tiff with his girlfriend, but it might not have been that at all. Maybe he had been hired by one of the big land developers—someone like Frank Morgan. Tobin didn't trust that man.

"Yeah, and he called juror number seven, too."

"When?"

"Yesterday."

"What'd he say?"

"Asked her if she knew where her daughter was. He told her she better keep a close eye on her. The little girl means everything to her and her old man. I hear it's their only child. They already had one die at birth. And they can't have no more."

Tobin understood why the juror would never tell under these circumstances.

"Her name?"

"Mary-Ellen Duquet. This guy targets the weak ones. Clever, ain't he?"

"Maybe not," Tobin said.

"What do you mean?"

"I think I may have seen him."

"Seen him where?" CJ asked, rifling through his pockets for a light for his cigarette.

Tobin thought he smelled of booze. Unless it was the stench from the house. "I'm not positive about this but. . . ." Tobin started to tell him and stopped. He wasn't sure he could trust CJ, who seemed more fidgety than usual.

"You said no secrets between us."

"Right, no secrets. But I don't want to put my foot in my mouth. You understand?"

"Yeah—yeah, I guess I do," CJ sighed.

"Well, there isn't much time. The jurors will be weighing it all before we know it."

"I'll have something tomorrow for sure," CJ said.

"Once you find out, give me a call. We'll meet somewhere." But not at CJ's house. Tobin had never known CJ to be ashamed of anything, but even he had to have a little pride.

"I figure mid-day. How's the General Store?"

"Sounds good. I'll be waiting." CJ could not care less about the trial. So why was he sticking his neck out? "See you tomorrow then. Goodbye, Mr. Phillips," Tobin said loudly from the doorway. There was no response.

"He's probably sleeping," CJ said.

Tobin nodded. *A nice way of saying he's passed out.*

Later that evening, Hannah pulled the checkerboard from the coffee table drawer and played a few games with Tobin. Hannah was good but Tobin was better as he sped to the opposite end of the board.

"King me!" he said with a grin.

Hannah reluctantly slapped on the black plastic piece, crowning him.

James challenged his brother to a game of chess. Anything to keep their minds occupied with something other than the trial.

"Come on, Basil. It's been years. I'm going to win, you know," James claimed.

"Ah, we'll see. How about it, Brownie—will he beat us?" His lab barked. Basil patted his head. "Oh, is that so? I have to agree with you."

"What did he say?" James asked.

Uncle Basil grinned. "Wishful thinking."

Listening to his father and uncle, Tobin smiled to himself. During ups and downs, Tobin knew it was their tight family bond that kept their morale high.

"King me," Tobin chorused for what seemed to his sister the hundredth time.

"King me," Hannah mimicked him. "It's no fun playing with you."

"We're not a poor sport, are we?"

"On the contrary, brother dear, I'm just letting it happen. You're going back to school soon. I don't want you to go back a loser. It would be dreadful for your image," Hannah taunted.

He hated to leave, but missed his friends there. He planned to double up on his subjects to keep his full scholarship that he was fortunate enough to receive. Studying hard and playing ball had paid off. He didn't want to blow it.

"So, what are you doing hanging around with CJ?"

"*Shh,*" Tobin said. "Keep your voice down!" Fortunately, their mother was engrossed with TV and the older men were too immersed in their own game to hear.

"You into something bad with him?" she asked in a whisper this time.

Tobin leaned forward. "No!"

"I don't believe you!" she said, leaning in. "He wouldn't be coming over here if something wasn't going on. That guy's trouble."

"I need you to keep quiet. We don't want to get Mom and Dad upset. When I can tell you, I will."

"You better," she said.

Chapter 20

"Mary Folks was chosen to replace the Smart woman." Eleanor paused. "My daughter just walked in, I'll call you later."

"Mrs. Folks is going to be a juror?" Laurie asked, tossing her backpack on the kitchen counter. She put her hands on her hips.

Her mother stared at her, nodding.

"I can't believe it. She is such a bigot."

"Laurie!"

"Well, she is. Everybody knows it. I can't believe they're allowing her to do this. This thing must be fixed."

"Don't be silly. The judge makes the decisions."

"He could be prejudiced, too," Laurie persisted.

"I don't know where you get these ideas in your head."

"Just because he's a judge, it doesn't mean he's perfect—or that he's right all the time."

"Judge Coleman got to this place, honey, because he knows what he's doing."

"Mother, I'm sorry, but you only see what you want to see," Laurie muttered, walking out of the room.

"How was lunch at the Rodney's?" Eleanor hollered to her daughter's retreating back.

That's it, mother, change the subject. That will take care of everything. "Great," Laurie yelled back as she continued running upstairs. That lunch had been two days ago. She wondered why her mother was mentioning it now. Laurie prayed she hadn't heard about her near-accident. Her car couldn't be taken away. Stuck in the house with her mother—that would be a drag.

In her bedroom, she turned on her record player. Flinging off her shoes, she sprawled on her bed listening to James Taylor. Seeing Tobin again had her thinking about him. She was wondering why he was using a phone booth. Didn't he have a phone at home? Couldn't they afford one? Maybe he was calling his girlfriend and wanted some privacy. No, not a girlfriend, she hoped. Just a friend.

Then she began wondering what Tobin would have done if she had run into that car while leaving the store parking lot. Daydreaming, she imagined him coming to see if they were all right—coming to her rescue. She closed her eyes and saw Tobin holding her in his arms as she pretended to be unconscious, hoping he knew CPR so that she could feel what his lips felt like on hers. Although with Sharon in the car, she wouldn't want Tobin to even approach. She would be too afraid. Everything would be ruined.

Walking through the kitchen, Tobin snatched the ringing wall phone.

"Hello."

"Is this Tobin Horvarth?" a man's voice said.

"Yes, this is Tobin."

"This is Mr. Morin. I got your note. I know you said not to call, but it looks like things are going to wrap up soon. The judge was informed and has already replaced Amelia Smart."

"Wow! That was quick."

"Unfortunately, he saw the rumor as unfounded. There were no more dismissals."

Tobin's mother wandered down the hallway with a handful of ironed clothes. He waited until she was out of sight. "I just heard that Juror Number Seven was threatened, too. This guy, whoever he is, called her and asked her where her daughter was. I'm sure the woman panicked. It's her only child."

"Sounds like he's picking the more vulnerable ones. I'll try to get word to the judge. I can't make any promises. If this woman's basing her decision on fear alone, though. . . ."

"That's my point. This man's frightened them so much—they don't know what else to do."

Had CJ enlightened him earlier, maybe something could have been done.

"The new juror is he—she, um…white?"

"It's a she and yes—she's white."

"That's not going to help us. Not that one non-white would make that much of a difference. The judge should at least have tried to even it out a little."

"I hear you. I know where you're coming from. I'll do what I can—but don't expect much," Morin paused. "If there is anything else, don't hesitate to call."

"Thank you. I appreciate it."

Tobin made sure his mother was still busy in another room before making a call. He dialed the 2040 he'd seen at CJ's. Tobin was about to hang up after the phone rang numerous times when someone said, "Hello."

"Who's this?" Tobin asked, not thinking.

"You must have the wrong number," a man said back.

"I don't think so. I'm a friend of CJ's."

"Who's CJ? Listen, I was just passing by, minding my own business. But that phone kept ringing."

"Whose phone?" Tobin insisted.

"It's nobody's—it's public.

"A telephone booth?" Tobin asked.

"Yeah, here at the Sunoco station."

"Where?"

"The Sunoco," he repeated. "The only one on Route 151."

"Thanks."

"You're not welcome," said a disgusted voice.

Checking his watch, Tobin realized in another hour CJ would be working at Martin's Liquor. Tobin planned to be there.

CJ was ringing up a customer's order. A distinguished old gentleman in a brown suit and pale yellow shirt looked as though he were stocking up for the year—or maybe just the week. Tobin counted six bottles of red and white wine, three of each, four bottles of Seagram's Seven and two cases of Bud.

"I'm going to give him a hand," CJ motioned to Tobin. "Keep an eye on the store, I'll be right back."

Tobin thought CJ looked quite professional, for him anyway. Tidy with clean jeans and a green and black plaid, flannel shirt. Even his Converses gleamed. Tobin paced in front of the register, head lowered. It seemed like hours instead of minutes before CJ came back into the store.

"So, what's happening?" CJ asked.

Looking out the glass door to be sure there were no more customers in the parking lot, Tobin backed him into a corner, knocking over a cardboard wine display. "What the hell's going on?" he asked, pointing a finger into CJ's chest.

"Nothing. Nothing at all. I don't know what you're talking about, man." CJ's eyes blinked rapidly.

Maybe he's afraid of me. "Don't play games with me. You're in contact with him, aren't you?"

"He told me I better keep my mouth shut."

"That isn't what I asked."

"Yeah—the dude called. But I don't know who he is—I'm not lying to you."

Tobin stared at him. "He said if I said anything to you, that he'd kill me—and you."

"Kill me?"

"That's what he said—and I believe him. This guy's dangerous. I heard he shot somebody. I don't want him to hurt you, man."

More like you're worried about your own skin. "What's the matter—you scared of him?"

"Nope," CJ said unconvincingly.

"Yeah, you are." Tobin looked at him. "A big tough guy like you."

CJ shrugged. Silence fell for a long while.

"What do we do now?" CJ asked finally.

"You still don't know who this guy is? And your informant won't tell you. Right?"

"He don't know nothing. Only what the big guy tells him." "And nobody knows who that is?"

CJ shook his head. "Nope."

"This is crazy. We'll never find out who's behind this in time, if at all. If only you'd been up front with me from the start. Are you supposed to call him back at some point?"

"Yeah. Tomorrow at noon."

"Good. I'll be there."

CJ stared at him. "Be where?"

"At the phone booth where he'll be calling you from." At that moment a customer wandered in. "I'll be in touch," Tobin said as he headed toward the door.

"Wait," he heard CJ say, but Tobin ignored him.

Chapter 21

Tobin waited in his car at the Sunoco station, keeping his eyes on the phone booth. A few minutes before noon, he saw a short, stout man, casually dressed, maybe late thirties or early forties, go in to use it. But it wasn't the same man he remembered that day at the market. Could there be more than one person involved? Or was this man just a regular person making an ordinary call? Playing detective was a new role for him. Bugging the booth had been a consideration, but he knew nothing about where to get one, let alone how to use it.

Binoculars dangled from his neck. Drawing attention was the last thing he wanted to do but when he thought no one was watching, he raised them to his eyes. He had never seen this man before, but that didn't mean anything. It only meant he had no reason to notice him. Tobin observed the man's facial expressions, but wasn't a lip-reader. And he certainly could hear nothing from where he was. What the hell, he thought. He leaped out of his car, hurried up to the booth and stood there. What if he had the wrong guy? His adrenaline told him otherwise. His first thought was to interrogate this suspect like a detective would, but he had no idea where to begin. Besides, it would take too much time, and that he, they, didn't have. He would get what he wanted the old-fashioned way.

Tobin busted into the booth and grabbed the phone. "Hello, who is this?" The line went silent.

"Somebody call the police!" Tobin heard a patron yell.

"Who was on the other end?" Tobin demanded from the man now staring at him.

"That's none of your damn business."

"Who hired you?"

"I don't know what the hell you're talking about. You've got the wrong guy."

"No buddy—I don't think so," Tobin said. "What's he paying you?"

"Who? Nobody's paying me anything."

"Did you go to drama school?"

"No, why?" the man asked, seeming bewildered.

"Because you're a damn good actor."

From the fear in the man's eyes Tobin could see he had intimidated him. Tobin would never lay a hand on him, but the guy wouldn't know that. Suddenly, three cruisers pulled up. *Always more than one. Don't they have anything better to do? It doesn't take half the force to restrain someone.*

"Okay, Tobin, what's the story? What are you up to now?" a heavyset cop asked, swinging his Billy club, as if he were getting ready to use it. A younger cop had his hand on his gun, playing badass.

"I'm glad you guys showed up when you did. I didn't know what this Indian was going to do to me," the man said excitedly.

"Yeah, I'm glad you're here, too," Tobin broke in. "This man's been threatening the jurors. Someone hired him. And he's been making his threats from this phone booth."

"He's got it all wrong. I'm a business man."

A shady one. Tobin looked at the bigger cop. "Ask him who he just called. Go ahead, ask him."

"Who was on the phone, sir?"

"My boss. I'm in insurance—Prudential. Here's my card," he said, handing it to the officer.

The officer took one glance and returned it to the patron. "Thank you, Mr. Waters. Sorry to have bothered you."

Tobin shook his head. "You're just going to let this guy go?"

"There's no reason to hold him."

"Can't you check with the phone company? They should be able to tell you who he was talking to."

"Why don't you let us take care of things?"

"That's the problem—you're not doing your job," Tobin said, raising his voice.

"I think you're getting out of control, Tobin," said the younger cop.

"Yes, that boy scares me," said Waters.

"Do you want us to lock him up? You pressing charges?" the older cop asked, surveying the insurance agent and looking disappointed that he seemed unharmed.

The man looked at Tobin as if he was afraid to say yes. "No. I guess not."

"Are you sure?" the cop asked, his club still in hand, obviously hoping to put Tobin behind bars.

"Yeah," he said nodding, brushing the wrinkles out of his clothes.

"Be on your way," the younger officer said, glaring at Tobin.

Tobin raised his hands and walked to his car. "I'm out of here."

Get a grip, Tobin told himself. Maybe he *had* made a mistake. But he wanted so badly to catch the guy who was going after the jurors. Nobody else was doing anything. The whole lawsuit was like running a marathon backwards.

The word was the jury had gone into deliberation, and the deputy clerk would notify James Horvarth when they were out. The tribe would soon know their destiny. The family sat tensely each day— waiting. Tobin and his sister kept the phone line open. They had told their friends not to call, and they made no calls out. None of his people could sleep during this time.

Thursday afternoon, Hannah wandered into Tobin's side of the room and perched in a chair. He was on the floor, poring over some baseball cards.

"Maybe this is good news. Isn't that what they say? The longer the jury stays out, the better our chances?"

Tobin couldn't tell Hannah what he knew or at least what he believed. "Usually," he said quietly. Winning the case would mean a hopeful future for Tobin and Hannah's generation, but even more so they wanted it for their mother and father and the other elders.

"Maybe there's a Great Spirit after all."

"Do you have doubts?" he asked. Tobin always had faith, believing in the Supreme Being. *He'll make things come out right.*

"I haven't really. Sometimes I wonder though. . . ."

"Don't ever let Father hear you say that."

"Never," she said, shaking her head.

Tobin had heard of juries taking as long as a week for ruling. No one wanted to leave the house for any reason until the word came. Myra was weaving a basket and Hannah was working on a quilt she had started for a Christmas fair but never finished. She stuck herself twice with a needle then threw down her work in frustration. Tobin picked up a novel but kept reading the same lines over and over again. James stayed at the kitchen table, paying the bills.

The old black phone on the wobbly end table hardly got a chance to complete its first full ring. James had been practically roosting on top of it for the past forty-eight hours. Tobin, Hannah and their mother stood only inches away with their arms folded.

James nodded a few times and barely said much of anything. Then he said, "Yes. Yes, we'll be there. Thank you. Good-bye." Sighing, James hung up the phone and smiled. "It's time to leave."

"Can we go? Please?" Hannah implored.

Tobin spoke up quickly, "I don't think it's a good idea, Father."

"Why not?" Hannah asked.

"Yeah. Why not?" Myra echoed.

"Mom, it may not turn out the way we want it to."

"I don't want to think like that, Tobin. And whatever happens, we should all be together."

"We'll go crazy, sitting home waiting and wondering," Hannah chimed in.

"There's no harm, son," his father finished up.

Ready or not, it had been a long four months. They just wanted to move on with their lives. Tobin hoped he was wrong in what he believed. As much as he wanted to be prepared, he wasn't. Either way, the control was out of his hands.

They picked up Uncle Basil on the way. The air was so thick with tension, Tobin's throat tightened. No one said a word, making the drive to Boston seem longer than usual.

In the courtroom, Tobin saw Attorney Morin talking to one of the tribal elders, a friend of his father's. The elder pointed in Tobin's direction and the lawyer strode over to him, leaned over the bench and said quietly, "Can I have a word with you?" Before he could answer, Morin said, "Meet me out in the lobby." Tobin stood up.

"Where are you headed? What's going on?" his mother asked.

"I'll be right back," he said, patting her hand and walking out.

The lobby was still bursting with lawyers, spectators, and others conversing. Morin was waiting behind the door and gestured to Tobin with a nod.

"Did you tell the judge about the woman whose child was being threatened?" Tobin left out that his life had been threatened, too. What was the point? If he was a juror, maybe it would matter. Although, it was only a threat—threats didn't scare him.

"He was informed."

"I see it did a lot of good."

"Well, it's hard to say. The case wrapped up sooner than we expected."

"Can't something be done?" Tobin asked.

"What's the juror's name?"

"Mary-Ellen Duquet."

"Duquet," Morin repeated.

Tobin nodded.

"The judge will probably request a lobby conference."

At times like this, Tobin wished he knew more about the system, or at least knew some of its terms.

"That's when the judge invites the lawyers from both sides—and Ms. Duquet—to discuss the matter."

"Then what?"

"She may be dismissed. Or he may tell her she'd be safer staying in the courtroom."

"So, what do you think will happen?"

"My guess would be she'll stay in the courtroom."

"You're basically saying you believe nothing's going to be done?" *It's all been a waste of my time.* The lawyer said nothing and shrugged.

Walking back, Tobin sat down next to his mother and sister. It wasn't so much the outcome he was worried about, but how his family would handle it. Maybe some of the holiday spirit would lighten the jurors' hearts enough to make the right decision. He prayed it would be so.

They filed in and took their seats in the jury box. Watching them, Tobin was beginning to perspire, and he felt like he was standing on a platform of needles. Practically holding his breath, he gripped his mother's and sister's hands. Their palms were clammy, their fingers restless. Many of his people were clutching one another. Some had their eyes closed, murmuring in their native tongue, while others had their eyes pinned open—waiting, as their hearts pounded.

Judge Coleman turned to the foreman. "Have the jurors reached a verdict?"

"We have, Your Honor."

"Please hand it to the bailiff."

The bailiff carried the folded sheet of paper to the judge. Judge Coleman opened it. There was dead silence in the courtroom. The bailiff returned the paper to the jury foreman.

"Would you read the verdict, please?" the judge asked.

In a slow monotone he read, "In the case of the Mashpee Tribe versus New Seabury, et al, we the jury, in the above entitled action, find to the question of whether the Mashpees constituted a tribe in 1790: No. We found them a tribe in 1834 and 1842, but not a tribe in 1869 and 1870. Also, the Mashpees were not a tribe in 1976. Therefore, they have not been a tribe continuously since at least 1790." Moans and cries from one side, sighs of relief and hoots of triumph from the other echoed in the courtroom. The judge slammed down his gavel.

"Let's have some order here."

When everyone quieted down, the judge said, "That's better." He paused. "The verdict will be recorded and entered into the minutes." He went on. "I want to thank the jury for their time and service in this case. You're dismissed."

Just like that, it's over.

The plaintiffs' attorneys immediately filed objections to the jury's findings. This was not the Christmas offering his tribe had fought and prayed for.

Tobin let out a deep sigh and slowly turned to his family, his mother first. Her eyes were full of tears. His father had already left to speak with other members about the outcome. Tobin was so frenzied himself, he couldn't think straight. Seeing the impact it had on his parents—all of his people—was painful. He put his arm around his mother's trembling shoulders.

"I'm so sorry, Mother."

"Me, too. Me, too," she repeated soberly.

In the midst of all the confusion, in the back of the room, closest to the exit, a crying woman in dark glasses, shabbily dressed, caught his attention. She was alone. Why was she sad? Why would she even care? When he looked again, she was gone. Tobin thought her to be elderly at first, but not after she dashed out of sight. Could it have been her? Was she afraid to be seen?

He needed answers. Hurrying into the lobby after her, he saw the elevator headed down and pushed the buttons to try and stop it. Too late. He sprinted to the back stairway and flew down them. He had missed the opening by seconds. Leaving the building in great haste, he nearly knocked over an old man in his way. The guy raised his cane high and hollered. "Where the hell you going!"

Tobin paid little attention to him, mumbling, "Sorry," and kept looking for the woman. He had no idea what he was going to say.

Suddenly, he saw her, rushing through the crowded sidewalk. "Hey!" he yelled. She turned slightly, locks of her blonde hair fell loose from the shawl she was wearing. Her oversized glasses fell to the bridge of her nose. He knew those eyes; he would never forget them.

"Wait!" he cried.

She stumbled and lost a shoe in a puddle. Before she could retrieve it, Tobin handed it to her. "It's you," he said.

"Me?" she asked, slipping her shoe back on.

"Yeah. I saw you in the courtroom. Taking notes. Are you a reporter or something?" he asked.

"No," Laurie said, shaking her head.

"Then why?"

"Why what?"

"Why were you there?"

"Oh. Current events report for my civics class."

"I see."

"I have to go," she said, rushing away.

Wait I saw you crying. Why?

He watched her disappear into the crowd. Then he went back into the courthouse. The townspeople hovered in the lobby, enjoying their victory. His people had gathered quietly in one corner of the foyer. They looked so dejected and lost and out of place standing there, it made his heart sink. He stood by them. There wasn't anything to say. It had been said in court. From the beginning it was like his people didn't exist. The lawyers and the system were only going through the motions—to make it constitutional. Now the show was over, the curtain was drawn.

"This greed will destroy our beautiful village," James said.

"We'll fight it further, Father. We'll win. You'll see." Tobin wanted to be optimistic, but. . . .

Pompous Frank Morgan strolled insolently up to Tobin. "Sorry things turned out this way, kid, but progress is what it's all about."

Tobin said nothing, curled his hand into a fist and socked Morgan square in the jaw. Blood dripped from Morgan's lip. A woman screamed. Court officers scurried to the scene, grabbing Tobin. Reporters wasted no time lapping it up. A photographer had gotten a lucky shot.

Regaining his composure, Morgan warily raised his hand. "No harm done. Let him be. Just a misunderstanding."

The two court officers released Tobin, watching him closely. James put his arm around Tobin's shoulders. "Let's go home, son."

Chapter 22

Laurie beat her mother home that afternoon as planned. *Mom's probably celebrating with the rest*. She needed this time alone.

Racing to her bedroom, Laurie glanced into a full-length mirror. *Pretty slick. My own mother didn't recognize me. But he did.* After slipping off the long flowered skirt, moss green shawl and brown scarf, she threw them in a paper bag with some other stuff she wanted to donate and hid them in the back of her closet.

What would happen to Tobin and the others now? The townspeople might as well have taken the Indians' clothes off their backs. That's how stripped her people had left them.

Hearing her father come in, she waited till he got settled in front of the five o'clock news before heading downstairs. Plopping down on the sofa beside him, she held off until a commercial.

"Our judicial system screwed up, Daddy."

Donald rose and turned off the TV. "I know," he said looking at her. "It's too bad. It really is."

"How can this happen? It's just not fair."

"Many things in life aren't, honey."

"But it's Christmas," she said, rising. Then she went over to the silver artificial tree and stooped to straighten a purple bulb.

"It sure doesn't make it any better, does it?"

"It must have been hard for you, Dad."

Her father had understood. He hadn't had it easy. Both his parents died when he was young. His mother died during childbirth, having his brother, who died shortly afterward. And at thirty-nine his father had had a major heart attack, leaving him weak the rest of his short life. Her mother had never suffered any real hardship. Both her parents were still living. And they were not only healthy but wealthy, too. Her mother had had it easy, as far as Laurie knew. If Eleanor had any sad stories, she kept them hidden.

"It isn't always easy, sweetheart, but you get through it somehow."

She sat back down on the sofa. "I'm going to UMass in Boston, Dad," Laurie said, looking at him. Her parents were paying for her college, and they also let her pick the one of her choice.

"What about Mount Ida? Change of heart?" he asked with a puzzled look.

"Yeah," she said. "I can study anthropology at UMass. Then maybe become a lawyer someday. All I know is that I want to make a difference—for them."

"You have a very big heart and because of that, you will."

"Why can't Mom be like you? What did the Indians ever do to her? Why is she so against them?"

"I don't know, honey," he paused, staring. "Maybe she has her reasons."

Laurie laid her head on his shoulder. "I love you, Daddy."

"And I love you."

At that moment, Eleanor bounced into the house. "Anyone home?" she asked, almost singing, her smile as wide as the open sky.

"Brace yourself," he said.

Eleanor gloated as expected. When neither of them showed an interest, she resorted to the phone to spread the news, calling her parents first, then her sister. By dinner she had mellowed, no longer as wound up with the excitement of coming out ahead. *Winning. Was that what it was all about?*

When Elaine and Frank Morgan invited Laurie's parents over for cocktails and hors d'oeuvre that same evening, her father utterly refused to go. "I see no reason to celebrate. What's done is done," he said to his wife.

"That's fine. I won't be out late. I'll fix the two of you something."

Laurie could tell her father wasn't happy about her mother going, but he knew trying to stop her would be a waste of time. She was a stubborn woman, and he hated arguments.

Eleanor threw together a tuna casserole for the two of them. It had been a long time since Laurie had eaten a meal with just her father. Besides, Eleanor should have known that going to the Morgans' house to party because the Wampanoag lost their land was her family's poor idea of a good time.

Maybe now her mother would get back to normal and all this hostility could end. There was nothing more to fight about. The townspeople had gotten what they wanted—control over land they could use recklessly to build more homes and shopping centers. The disappointment on so many faces in the courtroom had made Laurie so angry she wanted to get up and punch someone herself. And Tobin holding his sister and mother when the finding was read was something she would never forget. She had never known anyone quite like him. Each time she had seen him in action or read about him in the paper, the more intrigued she became.

"Daddy, would you like a hot roll?"

"Thanks," he said, taking one from the basket.

"I have to tell you what I did today," she said, in a low voice, leaning across the table.

He bent in to meet her halfway. When Eleanor walked through the room, they straightened up until she was out of sight.

"I dressed like a homeless person and went to court."

"You did what?"

"I went in disguise," she whispered.

"Where did you get the clothes?"

"Goodwill."

"Goodwill," he repeated, shaking his head. "Did anyone recognize you?"

"Are you kidding? I had on a long skirt. So ugly. A shawl knitted maybe a hundred years ago. With a ratty kerchief and those big sunglasses you get from the eye doctor's. You know, the ones patients leave in the basket to be recycled."

"You must have been quite a sight."

"I don't think anybody noticed. Well, maybe one person. . . ."

But her father missed that. She could tell he was too busy imagining the whole scene. He began to laugh. "You never cease to amaze me, Laurie," he said, when he caught his breath.

"I hope that's a compliment, Daddy?"

He nodded. "I'm a lucky man."

"Me, too. Lucky girl, I mean."

She thought about Tobin and his family and wondered how they were doing. At least they had each other. She could tell when she saw them in the courtroom they were a close family. And she knew that made all the difference.

Laurie had never gone without. Looking at all the gifts under the tree, she wanted to say to her mother, "This isn't what we want. We need you to listen. To understand," but she was afraid of hurting her feelings. They tried hard, almost too hard, especially her mother, to please her every year. The true meaning of Christmas was nearly lost. Forgotten. Even by her own family.

She wished she could have talked to Tobin outside of the courthouse, but the timing was off. She had to get out of there not only because she was afraid someone would find her out, but her emotions were bubbling over with sadness for him and his people. She was dying to meet Tobin, officially, that is. But she knew he would be going back to college soon and would probably stick close to home in the little time he had left. Sure, he would be back for the summer, although that seemed too far away.

Chapter 23

The aroma of freshly baked pastries permeated the cheerful coffeehouse in Keene, New Hampshire. French and Danish tarts, apple turnovers, chocolate éclairs, rosette, trifle, strudel, baklava and cream puff pies displayed nicely on spotless glass shelves spawned long lines of yearnings. Thick deli sandwiches served daily were also popular.

A jukebox was stationed in one corner of the room. Half a dozen small metal tables decked out in blue and white checkered tablecloths rested on blue-tiled floors. White-framed Norman Rockwell prints hung on pale blue walls, while a Bird of Paradise and a Bamboo palm sat by the entrance. Tobin enjoyed busing at this little place. It reminded him of a café back home where many of his people met regularly, keeping strong social ties. Every Saturday, he had tagged along with his dad and his Uncle Basil since he was knee high.

Clearing off some tables, Tobin glanced at a short male customer, around fiftyish, balding, sitting alone for quite some time. Suddenly, the man sprang from his seat and strutted over to the jukebox. He dug into his trousers for change and then deposited it into the slot and made his selections. When he returned to his table, he looked around. Then he glared at Tobin.

"You pocketed it, didn't you?"

"Excuse me?"

"I had a five-dollar bill. Right here!" he said, tapping his forefinger on the checked cloth. "You took it."

"No, sir. I wouldn't do that."

"Don't lie. You damned Indians steal everything!"

"You're wrong."

Mr. Henry, the owner, heard the commotion and came out from the back room to see what was going on. Heather, the main counter girl, filled him in. He hurried around the counter to the center of the room. "What's the trouble here?"

"He stole my money," said the irate customer.

Mr. Henry turned and looked at Tobin.

"It's not true, Mr. Henry."

"I go over to play some music. I come back—my money's gone."

"Tobin says he didn't take it and I believe him."

"They lie. Every one of them. Check his pockets," the customer insisted.

Tobin knew he didn't have to prove his innocence to his employer. But he had been the only other person in the room. What choice did he have? He didn't want to cause any problems for Mr. Henry. He was too nice a guy. So Tobin kept his cool and before any more was said, he jammed his hands in his pockets, pulling out the linings. A couple of pieces of crumbled paper, a few pennies and some chewing gum dropped to the floor.

"Are you satisfied? Or do you prefer a body search?" Tobin asked, his voice dripping with sarcasm. The man shook his head.

Tobin bent down and picked up the things that had fallen from his pockets. "Well, well, will you look here?"

Both men looked down at the same time. The five-dollar bill was stuck to the bottom of the customer's shoe. He quickly bent down, snatched the money and made no apology to Tobin as he headed out.

"Maybe it's best you don't come back here too soon," Mr. Henry called after him.

"Thank you," Tobin said to his boss.

Mr. Henry patted him on the back before returning to the back room. He was in his sixties and was fairly easygoing, unless one took advantage of his goodness. The two of them had a chance to chat one afternoon when it was quiet and Mr. Henry had told Tobin he had been in the restaurant business nearly all his life. He wasn't quite ready to retire yet, so when he saw this small place up for sale a couple of years ago, he thought, Why not? He had no one at home but his cat, Bailey, which he named his coffee shop after. His Vietnamese wife had divorced him years ago, and his two adult children were halfway across the country. He said he saw them once or twice a year, if he was lucky.

He caught Heather looking his way. A real sweet girl and easy to work with, she was born with one leg shorter than the other so she couldn't maneuver very fast. If it got too busy, Tobin helped her with the counter work, serving customers, and at times, he tallied up checks.

"What?" he asked.

"You were so cool. I don't know what I would have done."

"It was nothing."

"Yeah, right. Anybody else would have flipped. Punched his lights out."

"The thought went through my mind, believe me." Tobin was sweeping the floor when he saw her putting on her jacket. "You leaving?"

"Yeah. My cousin's getting married. I'm a bridesmaid. We have to be at rehearsal at seven." She grabbed her purse and headed toward the door, then turned and looked at Tobin. "Say hi to Richard for me."

Heather obviously had a crush on his college buddy, Richard. Richard and his brother Thomas were fraternal twins, though they weren't much alike. Thomas, the more serious of the two, was tall and gaunt with thick, wavy brown hair and a big bushy mustache. Richard, the carefree one, was short, on the heavy side, with absolutely no facial hair and a crew cut. Tobin managed to get along with both of them, in spite of their differences. He never really had much of a problem getting along with anyone, at least before the trial.

Heather, already energetic, perked up whenever Richard came in the coffeehouse. She liked listening to his jokes. Tobin had no idea where Richard came up with some of them. Some were original, others weren't, but just the way he presented them had Heather in stitches every time. And lately, it seemed Richard was noticing her more.

Tobin smiled. "I will. You'll probably see him before I do."

"Maybe."

"Catch you later."

"You bet."

Tobin was wiping off tables when Ralph Henry hollered to him from the backroom.

"Tobin, would you mind tallying up for the night?"

Tobin paused for a second. "Sure."

Tobin hated the job of balancing the register. Part of him feared if it didn't come out right he would be the first one blamed. He knew he had no reason to feel that way. Mr. Henry had always trusted him, been good to him, too. Mr. Henry had already given Tobin two twenty-five cent raises in just over a year. It was all the terrible things happening in Mashpee that made him edgy. Friends back home who had never taken a thing in their lives were now being accused, without any proof. Even though he was far away, inside his head he still lived with the battle that raged there and what happened tonight didn't help. However, he tried not to let it get the best of him. There was enough going on at school to divert him from stuff clouding his life.

Tobin added up the checks and the cash, deducting them from the money they started with that morning. He counted and recounted to be sure. It was perfect. Even if it wasn't, he told himself, he had nothing to worry about. He was an honest guy, had never and would never take a dime he hadn't earned.

Mr. Henry approached, "How'd we do? Okay?"

"Yes, sir. To the penny," Tobin said with a slight smile.

"Great."

When Tobin opened the door to the dorm room, he found his roommate, Austin Hanes, deep into an assignment. He thought Austin's name fit him. When he wore those heavy plastic eye frames for reading theories about everything, Tobin would refer to him as the reincarnated Mr. Einstein.

"Hey, Tobin, what do you have in the bag tonight?" Bakery leftovers were offered to the employees so Tobin always took something home.

Austin was sitting at a small sturdy desk, which had one of those desk lamps made for tedious drudgery, working this time on a major literature task. "I've been craving those clumps of fat and sugar creatively transformed into savory and decorative smithereens of delicious edibles."

Chuckling, Tobin dug into the small white bag, pulled out a colossal coffee ring loaded with icing and handed it to him.

"Damn. This will relieve my coiled muscles, for sure," Austin said, taking a huge bite.

"I brought something to swish it down with," Tobin said, reaching into another bag, extracting two Styrofoam cups filled with steaming cappuccino.

Austin sported a wide grin as he closed his books and turned his chair around to face Tobin, who was now sitting on the edge of his bed indulging, too. "Thank you," he said, as he took the cup, removed the cover and sipped. "Hmm, this is good. Hits the spot. Tob, I was blessed when I got you for a roommate."

"Got that right," Tobin smirked.

Living with Austin, Tobin got to share his last thoughts of the day with him. He didn't always appreciate his words to the wise but more often than not Austin tended to be right. It was as though Tobin had his own private counselor, and best of all—free of charge. Although tonight he didn't bother briefing him on the little incident that had taken place at the café. He'd only get himself all worked up again.

Gazing up at the enormous colorful print of Charlie's Angels pinned to the wall beside his bed, Austin asked Tobin, "Wouldn't it be grand to just hold one of those beauties?"

"Never."

"Never?" Austin asked, his brows creasing.

"Never for too long, that is. It could be torturous."

"Torturous?"

"Knowing we'd have to give them up," Tobin clarified.

"Oh. Who said we'd have to?"

Tobin's mind drifted from the Angels to her—the beautiful white girl, the one he saw—even met briefly outside the courthouse. He still didn't know her name. "I can't even imagine getting that lucky to begin with," Tobin said, quickly letting that thought go. "Besides, I'm saving myself."

"For whom?"

He still didn't know her name. "For whomever will have me," Tobin said with a small chuckle, thinking of her again: her hair— long and silky; her light blue eyes—translucent yet penetrating.

"You need to change your thinking pattern."

"Why? Do you seriously think it will help?"

"Of course. You've been depriving yourself, Tob."

"Right now, I don't feel deprived at all," Tobin said with a smirk, his mouth bulging.

He had never mentioned the girl in the courtroom to his friends or family, not even to his Uncle Basil. However, his father did witness him eyeing her in the courtroom. Still, he was afraid of ridicule. They would think he was crazy for even thinking of her, never mind wanting to be with her. Sometimes he wondered if he had ever seen her at all—but, of course, he had.

"She must have a million and one boyfriends," Tobin sputtered.

"Who?" Austin asked.

Tobin blinked, realizing he'd spoken. "Farrah, who else?" he said, looking at *Charlie's Angels*.

"I'm sure they all do."

"You have to prepare for this stuff."

"Prepare? What are you babbling about?"

"You know. Learn a little bit about women and their feelings."

"We got all the information we need right here," Austin reminded him, slapping the mattress filled with copies of *Playboy* and *Penthouse*.

"It's different when you're really with a woman. It doesn't always work the way you think it will."

"Then how do you know if you're doing the right thing?"

"You'll figure it out."

"I can't even get a girl to notice me."

Tobin thought maybe it was the bowtie and the laced wingtips that turned the girls off. He was a fairly good-looking dude. His dark brown eyes and curly brown hair accentuated his angular features. "Ah, you're looking too desperate."

"Think so?" Austin asked, his glasses on his nose, staring at Tobin.

"Relax. Let her come to you."

"I'll be dead by then."

"What women can do to us," Tobin said softly.

Chapter 24

The sun was bright, a few cirrus clouds in the sky. Students were having lunch outside under big elms rebounding with new green leaves. Tobin tried to get out as often as he could. He loved the outdoors; the cold never bothered him. Except for a day at the lodge skiing and a few movies with his friends, Tobin had kept his nose in the books this long winter, working hard to stay on the honor roll. He filled any extra time working for Mr. Henry at the café.

Tobin and Austin were sitting under a tree eating their sandwiches when they saw Bill Hogan, a popular senior around campus, coming their way.

"How's it going, Tobin?" he asked, with a pleasant smile as he walked past.

"No complaints. How about you?" Tobin replied, stunned. This was the first time Bill had spoken to him, even uttered a syllable. And he was usually the kind of guy who seemed to haul around a lot of prejudice.

"Fantastic. Couldn't be better," he said, hurrying off. "Great scrimmage the other night."

Every Saturday morning, Tobin and the Owls scrimmaged against local high school teams to prepare for game days. Tobin went three for four with three RBI's in another great defensive all-star performance, which seemed to be the norm in his everyday, on-field play.

"Thanks," Tobin hollered back, hiding a smile.

Three attractive girls who had walked past now turned around and gave a petite wave. Austin gave them a flutter back. They giggled and kept walking.

"Small attempt, but better than nothing, I suppose," Tobin pointed out.

"Are you kidding? I'll take it—any day."

"What do you know? Mr. Hogan put himself out. And it didn't even seem like it was killing him," Tobin remarked, looking over at his friend, who was still in awe as he watched the girls disappear into the distance.

"Darn. Maybe I should become an athlete," Austin said.

Not likely, Tobin thought. Austin was theatrically clumsy. "You'd be better as a political leader. Like the President or something. You'll get plenty of attention then."

"Exactly what this country needs. A Jewish president."

"How about an Indian president?" Tobin asked, raising his hand, laughing.

"Not a bad suggestion."

"Yeah, right, not in a hundred years."

Finishing up their lunch, they rolled the plastic wrap from their sandwiches into balls and shot for the basket nearby.

"Here he comes again," Austin said, nudging him.

"I wonder what he wants now."

Bill strutted their way and stopped in front of Tobin.

"Hey, Tobin. There's a frat party tonight. Why don't you come? You won't be disappointed—I can guarantee it. Lots of frills and perfume," he said, winking.

Without hesitating, Tobin answered, "Yeah. Sure."

"Great. See you at nine."

"Where?"

"36 Alpine," Bill said, rushing off to catch up with a pretty brunette.

Tobin was reasonably content most of the time, but every now and then he looked for something more. After the cops put a tight clamp on the good times he and his people had together at John's Pond, he wondered if they'd ever have fun again. He was flattered this popular white boy had asked him to the party, but it made him a bit suspicious, too. Bill had never given him the time of day before.

"Girls, girls and more girls," Austin dramatized, as they walked side by side along the cement walkway. "Lucky man. Who'd pass up the opportunity?"

"I could. I mean—why all of a sudden? Why me?"

"Why not? You're the big baseball star. Fame comes and goes. Grab it while you still can."

"I don't know. . . ."

"Do you need your head examined?"

"Come with me then."

"Who invites nerds?"

"I'm Indian. What's the difference?"

"You're better looking. I don't know. Clue me in."

"Nerds are supposed to be smart," Tobin teased, leaving Austin to go to his German session.

"I'll get you for that, roomie," Austin growled behind him.

Tobin raised his brows. "We'll see."

Parties never happened, at least not for him—until now. In spite of Tobin's suspicions, he wasn't going to pass up this special invite from Bill. Although Tobin never admitted it, he wanted to be popular. Who wouldn't? And if getting friendly with this group of kids was going to benefit him, then he was all for it.

When Tobin showed up at the party, kids were spread over the frat house like peanut butter on bread. And there were definitely girls—loads of them. And every one of them was fine, real fine. Short skirts, skimpy tops and heels were in. The heavy scent of perfume and burning incense wafted about the room. In one corner roosted a keg of beer with kids waiting in line for a refill. Smokers dragged away on cigarettes, fogging the house.

Walking in, he felt out of place until Bill Hogan saw him, signaling for Tobin to join him. Bill had a chick draped on each side of him, both dressed identically in tight black leather pants and bright red blouses. At first, Tobin thought they were twins but found out later the brunette and blonde were just best friends. Both beautiful though, of course. *Wow, Bill knows how to pick them.*

After Bill introduced him to two of his closest friends, he stood on a chair and made the big announcement. "Look who's here, everyone."

Everything ceased at once, froze, it seemed. Complete silence. Even the music had dropped. The bunch stared up at Bill. *King Bill.* Then there was a sudden shift in focus. All eyes were on Tobin.

"Yes, it's Tobin Horvarth. I think you all know him, our short stop. Our baseball star."

The gang whistled and cheered loudly. He heard a girl yell out, "Tobin's our man." For a split second, Tobin thought *fame*, and it felt rather nice.

"He's our main guest here tonight. Treat him right—give him whatever he wants."

"And what's that?" another sweet voice asked.

"You'll have to ask him that one." Everyone roared.

Bill waved his hands downward. "Enough. Enough." The group quieted and Bill seemed to delight in holding the reins. Finally, he said, "Ah, carry on."

The music blared again. Everybody resumed what they were doing before His Highness had launched his big broadcast.

"Can we get you a drink?" Bill asked Tobin.

"Sounds good to me."

"Super. Steven," he said, snapping his fingers, "get Tobin a beer. It is beer, right?"

Tobin nodded. "Yeah."

Bill's servants are sure doing their job.

"Better yet," Bill yelled to Steven, "get two. The line's getting pretty long."

"One's fine," Tobin blurted.

"Loosen up. Everything's cool. When's the last time you partied—hung loose?"

Tobin raised his brows. He wasn't going to admit this was the first one he'd been to since high school, other than the gatherings his people had, but his expression ratted him out.

"See, it's been awhile."

The first beer slid down easily and relaxed him; he decided there would be no harm in having another. After the second, he was able to open some. The more he talked, the more freely he accepted the oncoming drinks. Soon the girls were looking even prettier than when he first arrived. Becoming friendlier too, especially the two that were checking him out the moment he walked through the door. They were intrigued with who he was. Not just as the star of the baseball team.

"So, what's it like being an Indian boy?" asked Sam, short for Samantha, as she twirled his long black hair around her long thin fingers.

"No different than you. Why?"

"I guess I'm just curious," she said, her curves swaying all around him. In tight designer jeans and a skimpy tank top, she kept flipping her ash brown hair over her shoulders with every move. "I remember reading about Pocahontas once. Never known any real Indians though—till now."

The whites, Tobin thought, knew so little about his people and where they came from. They were almost as ignorant today as they were two centuries ago. But for once that didn't seem to bother him. "So what do you think?"

"Not bad. You're nice—and you're a hunk, too."

Tobin was thinking the same of her. Good-looking, that is. The place was steamy from all the bodies, and he was heating up, too. In his blurred vision, Sam's partially exposed breasts whenever she bent over him appeared enormous. He was conscious enough to know what was going on. She kept stroking him. His hair. His face. The brass medallion around his neck. And when she touched the upper part of his leg, he knew he had to leave right away.

"Got to go," he said, rising from his chair abruptly. "It's getting late."

"Stay for one more beer?" Sam pleaded.

"No. Thanks, anyway."

"Come on. Don't be a party pooper."

"Sorry. I really have to go. Good-night," he said, wondering if he was crazy not to stay.

"Oh, that's too bad," Sam said, sullenly. "The fun was just beginning."

Escaping outside into the cooler air, he had to admit Samantha's moves were working there for a while, but he knew it wasn't right. Even with all the brew he consumed, he wasn't ready. Besides, he had no real feelings for her. He didn't want to use her. And he surely didn't want the reverse.

On his way back to his dorm, he wondered why he was receiving all this attention. Did they really want to be his friend? They seemed sincere enough. Still, he was curious about the sudden interest. Did they know somehow he was still a virgin? It wasn't obvious, was it? He'd never told anyone, but he felt cheated. Everyone seemed to be having sex but him. Even Austin had done it once. It wasn't that Tobin hadn't had plenty of opportunities, because he had. It was just that he wanted to be in love first. Maybe he was a little old fashioned, but that's the way he felt.

It was close to 1:30 A.M. when Tobin entered his dorm room, quietly closing the door. Austin was snorting in his sleep. Tobin sprawled onto the bed and quickly dropped off. In the early morning, he dreamed of the courtroom girl. Holding her in his arms and making love to her. He woke up needing a cold shower. He eyed the clock on the desk: 8:20 A.M. Looking to his right he saw that Austin's bed was empty. Tobin never heard him leave. The two of them were supposed to meet Thomas and Richard for breakfast at 8:30 A.M. He knew his friends would be waiting to get the rundown on last night.

While Tobin was getting dressed, the courtroom girl entered his head again. He had seen so many pretty women the night before. Why did he have this strong attraction for this particular one? He had to confess he wanted to be a part of the white world, but he had rejected Sam. Would he have turned down the courtroom girl, too?

Chapter 25

On his way to the Pancake House, Tobin internally documented how good he felt. He felt terrific, in fact. No hangover. Maybe this was a positive sign—he could party more with his new friends and still be able to study and work and play ball proficiently.

At the restaurant, he spotted the guys right away at a table for four. Walking over to them, he could see they were just about finished with breakfast. Tobin looked at Austin before he grabbed a chair and sat down.

"Why didn't you wake me?"

"I tried. I tried my damnedest. You were zonked, man."

A slender middle-aged waitress hurried over to the table. "Coffee?" she asked.

"Please." As she turned away, Tobin added, "A raspberry Danish, too, please."

She nodded. "Got it."

"So, how's the man about town?" Thomas asked, after he scarfed down his last blueberry pancake.

"Yeah, tell us about your night," Richard urged.

"It was all right," Tobin said quietly. It seemed unfair to crow over the awesome time he had, especially when they weren't invited. Tobin and these guys had always done everything together.

"Just all right? What a boring description," Richard remarked.

"Tolerable? The smoke. It was so intense. And the wall to wall people—I nearly suffocated there. And if you're claustrophobic, forget it."

"I see you survived it," Austin said, finishing up the last bite of sausage on his plate.

The waitress arrived with Tobin's order. "Can I get you something else?"

"I guess not," Tobin said, glancing at his friends' empty plates. Sipping the steaming coffee, he felt their eyes upon him. "Okay, you win. The place was rocking. It was unreal. I never saw so many foxy ladies all at once," Tobin said, illustrating hourglass figures with his hands.

"Stop. You're making me miserable," Austin whined.

Richard brushed his forehead. "Yeah, well, you don't have to make us faint."

"What's the big man himself really like?" Thomas asked crunching his nose, his thick mustache battering his nostrils.

"He's just as you see him."

"Yeah, thinks his shit doesn't stink. Everybody kisses his ass," Thomas added.

"True. That about sums him up. But he made sure I got royal treatment and that's all I gave a damn."

Thomas stared at him. "Headed back for more?"

"Maybe he wasn't asked." Richard sounded hopeful.

"Actually, he did invite me to come again. In fact, he said anytime I wanted."

"Going?" Richard asked.

"If you all come with me."

They rose simultaneously. "Maybe in another life," Thomas murmured.

His friends were right. But that wasn't going to stop him from having a good time. He decided however that from now on, he would keep things to himself.

"What's happened to you, man?" Austin asked Tobin when he could barely get himself out of bed one morning.

"What do you mean? We won the game last night. My head hurts," Tobin moaned, slapping his palm to his forehead. "You got any aspirin?"

"Yeah. I'm not talking about the game. Or your head. Although that's enlarged a great deal."

Tobin didn't respond to his comment.

"Where is it?"

"In the top drawer of the desk. On the right side."

Unscrewing the cap, Tobin shook out two Bayers. Then he looked over at Austin. "What? What are you looking at?"

"You've changed."

"Changed? How?"

As far as Tobin was concerned, he was still the person he'd always been. Maybe Austin was jealous. Unless he just missed their late evening discussions. Tobin was still bringing home any leftovers from the café for him—not always the same day, though. And when Tobin *did* get home nights, after partying with his new friends, Austin was already asleep.

"Have you looked at yourself lately?"

Tobin glanced into a small ceramic mirror on the wall beside his bed, the one Hannah had made especially for him when he left for college, nearly two years ago now. "Whoa," he said, as he winced, stepping back.

"If you were white, it'd be even worse."

Tobin dared to take a second look. His eyes were bloodshot and there were dark circles beneath them. "Scary."

"Yeah. And another thing, I've been watching you play. You missed the ball twice last night and you struck out."

"It happens. No one's perfect."

"You're going to the dogs. Thomas and Richard have observed the alteration in you, too."

"All I did was take your advice. I'm just having a little fun. Is that so wrong?"

"No. But you've pushed beyond limitations. You have to set boundaries. This popularity BS has gone to your head."

"There aren't opportunities like this in Mashpee. We're still in college. It's supposed to be the best days of our lives."

What did Austin know? Yeah, his grades had fallen slightly, but he just hadn't had as much leeway to study. And yeah, he'd been drinking some, maybe a lot at times, but it hadn't changed him. At least he didn't think so. It never really got in the way of working or playing ball before, so he hadn't worried about it. Tobin still liked his old pals, hung out with them when he could. But he enjoyed chumming with Bill Hogan and the rest, too.

Tobin was already half wasted Saturday evening when Sam suggested that the two of them go to her dorm "for a quiet drink," whatever that meant.

"You lead the way," he said, easily this time. *I'm a decent guy*, he reminded himself. Though being alone with an attractive woman could be dangerous. Or just wonderful.

He surveyed the room. Towels and clothes, even bras and panties, were strewn everywhere. He tried not to look too closely.

"I'm really sorry about the mess. We don't have much company."

"Ah, it's okay," he said, shrugging.

Her bed was covered with school papers, candy wrappers and empty soda cans. She gathered a heap and dumped it on her roommate's bed. Then she shook out the psychedelic coverlet.

Sam motioned for Tobin to sit down while she went and lit candles and incense. "Help yourself to a beer." He looked around. "Over there." She pointed to a small compact refrigerator, masked with Wonder Woman and Superman Comics. He got up, wandered over and and bent down to open it. There was a carton of OJ and some beer—nothing else. He already had a buzz on but, he thought, *what the hell*.

"Can I get you one?" he asked.

"Yeah. Please."

He grabbed a couple of cans and strolled back over to the bed and sat back down. She shut off the light and sat down next to him. Now it was just the smell of vanilla, flickering candles and the two of them. Before he could utter a sound, though, she snatched his beer from him, pushed him down, climbed on top of him and kissed him hard on the lips. "Wow," was all he could say, seeing the wildness in her eyes and the urgency to get what she wanted—something, evidently, she'd been waiting for all night.

While Sam quickly undressed him, Tobin's head began to spin. He always thought first times were supposed to be perfect. Special. He wanted to slow the pace, enjoy every second, but at the same time he favored the way she took control of things. "Gosh, you are so damn sexy," she mouthed. He had never thought of himself in that way.

She lifted her tiny knit top over her head. He wanted to yell, "What are you doing?" Nothing came out. *So much for foreplay*, he thought. Or is this it? He'd only had a few drinks, so why couldn't he think clearly?

"You know, Sam, you're good-hearted. I really like you," he sputtered excitedly, not knowing what else to say, but meaning what he said.

"And I like you, Tobin. That's why I can't do this," she said, suddenly putting her top back on.

"What's wrong?" he asked. All of a sudden, she was turned off like a running faucet swiftly clamped after flowing full force.

"No one's ever said anything like that to me before. You're really sweet, Tobin. But don't be foolish. I could never be close to anyone. Love them the way they deserve."

"Why not? You're not the right girl for me?" he asked.

"I'm not the right girl for anybody. I just can't be happy with one guy. Never could."

"You're such a nice person. I don't understand."

"It's kind of you to say that, but I'm not as nice as you think. If I was, I wouldn't be this way."

"What do you mean? What way?"

"Sometimes I think you're naïve, Tobin." Tobin looked at her.

"See, my stepfather molested me when I was a kid. More than once actually. A lot. I figure—that's why I'm so horny. I don't know."

"Oh, that's awful. I'm really sorry, Sam. Have you seen anyone?"

"You mean have I seen a shrink?" She shook her head. "Nope. I didn't see the sense. They're divorced now. I don't see him anymore. It helps."

"Does your mother know?"

"Nah. She was too much in love with him—I couldn't tell her."

"That's crazy. He had no right. That sick son-of-a-bitch," he said, anger building rapidly in him.

"It's over now. There's no sense dwelling on it."

"I don't even know him and I want to kill him."

"He's not worth it. I used to feel that way."

The thought of what that man had done to her gnawed at him, but there was nothing he could say to make her feel better. It was too late for that. He couldn't imagine something that dreadful. He didn't want to think about what he'd do to someone who abused his sister like that.

"I shouldn't be telling you this, but you're a sweet guy and I really like you. . . ."

"What? What is it? What shouldn't you be telling me?"

"This was set up, sort of," she said, wincing.

"Set up? What do you mean?"

"Bill Hogan—he slipped me a few bucks."

"For what? Oh, no. You're not telling me. . . ."

She nodded. "I had nothing to do with this. It wasn't my idea."

"He paid you? He actually paid you to—?"

She nodded again.

Tobin shook his head in disbelief. "How much? Never mind. I don't want to know." *That no good swine,* he thought. All this time there was a motive to Hogan's geniality. *How stupid am I?* Then he looked at her. "Why? Why'd he do this?"

"I don't know. He thinks you're queer or something."

"Queer?" he questioned, stifling a small laugh. "Is that what you think?"

"No, of course not. I never thought that."

"But you did this for money?"

"No."

He stared at her.

"Okay. Yeah, maybe I did. Going through some tough times."

He shook his head again, not believing what a damn fool he was. "I just want you to know I'm not going to say anything—to anyone," she said.

"Do what you have to."

She sat beside him on the bed. "Listen, I feel bad about this. Maybe I shouldn't have told you. You going to be all right?"

"Don't worry about me."

"We did have some good times together," she said with a half-smile.

"Did we?"

"I know I did and I think you did, too. I look at it this way, he was paying me for something I wanted to do anyway." She looked at him. "We're a lot alike, you know."

"How so?" he asked, staring deeper in those mysterious gray-green eyes wondering what he'd seen in them. Now they looked not only faraway but also loveless.

"We're both looking for something we'll never get."

He wasn't sure what she meant by that. And he didn't bother to ask.

Sunday morning Tobin stayed in his dorm studying. He knew Sam had gone back to the party. Whether she told them what they wanted to hear he didn't know. And he didn't care. He wanted to believe she wouldn't, but then again he didn't know what to believe. It was like nothing ever happened between her, his new friends— nothing meaningful anyway. Oh well. Everything one did, good or bad, taught a lesson, he thought. Still, he was furious with himself for not seeing it coming. *What an ass!* But he had to move on.

Tobin showed up on the field early that afternoon to get in some practice. Joe Finn, his coach, was already in the dugout. Joe had been lecturing him but he'd only been half listening. It was time to turn things around.

"Hey, Tobin."

"Coach," Tobin said, sitting down on the bench, "I know I haven't been doing that great lately."

"You know, son, you're only here for a short time—get the most from it."

"I plan to, believe me. I've been doing a lot of thinking; I'm going to settle down."

"Glad to hear." Finn moved closer to him. "You're one of my better players. You got what it takes. Don't throw it away." The coach started to get up, then sat back down. "Another thing," he said, coming closer to Tobin so no one could eavesdrop. "These kids— the big shots—they'll end up nameless on the map after they leave here. You—you have a future. Don't screw it up," he said, rising and heading toward a couple of players who had arrived and were getting ready to warm up.

"Coach Finn?"

"Yeah?" he said, turning around.

"Thanks."

Chapter 26

May, 1977

Suitcases and duffel bags were packed and ready to go. When the day finally arrived for the Keene State students to leave for the summer, it was like a grand rally with the beeping of horns and squealing of tires.

Tobin said good-bye to his friends—his true friends. It was hard leaving, but he knew he'd be seeing them again after the summer. Besides, it was a break he really needed. New Hampshire's mountains were beautiful, especially in their fall foliage and when they were covered with snow. Still, nothing compared to the forests and ponds in Mashpee.

Tobin followed highway I-495 south, then took Route 25 to the Bourne Bridge. Driving the speed limit, he was able to relax and enjoy the ride, listening to his favorite rock station, WRKO. The sun was blinding, so he reached into the glove compartment for his sunglasses, then rolled down the window to let in the warm air. Spring always brought a mantle of lush, deep green to Mashpee, along with new "wash-a-shores." Each time Tobin came home, there were more buildings and less land. He heard conversations about another mall being built. He knew he would never be able to block progress.

Hannah ran out as soon as he pulled up, giving him a big hug, then helping him unload the truck. She's getting tall, he thought. And she seemed older—that babyish look was vanishing.

"What do you have in here? These bags are heavy," she complained.

"Couple of bats. Some balls. You know, the usual."

"They weigh a ton."

Tobin unzipped one of the bags. "Here," he said, handing her a new baseball. "This one's for you."

"Gee, thanks," she said, rotating it. "Maybe someday you can autograph it. Then it might be worth something."

"You don't think it's worth something now?" he asked grinning. The attention he received on the school field had given him a hint of what it would be like being a famous ballplayer. He had hoped a scout would have noticed him by now, but his late-night partying had hurt his chances. Playing on the Cape League this summer, his dream, seemed unlikely now, though his coach had said it was still possible.

"A few bucks maybe."

"I work hard for those few bucks." His mother held the screen door open. Dark eyes sparkling, she had a full smile like always when he came home.

"Hi, Ma."

"Tobin you're getting bigger."

"Nope. You're shrinking, that's all," he said with a smile, bending over to kiss her.

He went into his room to unload his things. Myra and Hannah followed. They sat on his bed talking with him while he filled his bureau drawers.

"Where's the famous medicine man?" Tobin asked his mother.

"Your father's at the Meeting House—with the preacher." She hesitated.

Tobin saw it in her eyes. Something was wrong. "What, Ma? What is it? Tell me," he implored, staring down at her.

She gave him a long, thoughtful look. "It's your Uncle Basil. He's not doing so well these days. They don't give him much time," she said, lowering her gaze.

"What do you mean?"

"It was the war....," she trailed, raising her head, searching his eyes. "And now they say he's got cancer."

"Cancer?" Tobin said with incredulity.

His mother nodded. "I'm afraid so."

"I wish someone had told me. I would have come home sooner," he said, looking at his mother, then over to Hannah.

"Your Uncle Basil didn't want you to miss any school. Besides, there's nothing anyone can do."

"He was doing okay when I was home last." Then Tobin recalled how his uncle had skipped the Friday night gathering and how tired he had looked.

"He hid a lot. You know the way he is. We visit as often as we can."

"I know you do, Ma. You have a lot to take care of here. I have to see him."

"Now?"

"Yeah," he said softly.

"You just got home. All that driving. You must be worn out."

"Doesn't matter. He's sick. I'll rest tonight."

"Tobin. . . ." Hannah said, looking disappointed.

"We've got plenty of time, Sis," he said, leaving the room and heading for the front door.

But his uncle didn't.

Tobin decided to go on foot to his uncle's house. He had been sitting too long in the car and his legs needed stretching. His double strides through the woods turned to a lope, and he was there in minutes.

Like many of the houses on that side of town, shingles were falling off the weather-beaten ranch and there were holes in some of the screens. Tobin tapped lightly and then let himself in. Nobody ever locked doors there.

"Uncle Basil, it's me, Tobin."

"In here," a weak voice answered.

Tobin walked through the small living room, through the tiny hallway and into the bedroom where he found his uncle in bed with a thin, tattered blanket over him. His eyes were droopy and his long hair, now mostly gray, reached his shoulders. Deep crow's feet magnified his tired eyes and pain lines crossed his forehead like spring streams.

"Good to see you," his uncle said feebly, trying to lift himself, his body trembling.

"Let me help you." Tobin got him up resting against the pine headboard with two flimsy, feathered pillows behind him. "Can I get you some hot soup?"

The older man shook his head. "It's my time, boy. It's time to return to the earth. I've completed my circle."

"You were doing pretty good the last time I saw you. What happened?" He knew his uncle had been lonely after Aunt Dorothy died, struck by lightning while clasping the padlock on the outdoor shed. Tobin wished he could have been around more to make his uncle feel less alone. Maybe he wouldn't have given up so easily, could have hung on longer. The outcome of the trial hadn't helped either.

"I'm wintry, boy. Things wear out. Bodies wear out. Even Wampanoag grow old, you know."

"More like you threw in the towel. You're not that old."

Uncle Basil looked away. "She always said you were the best. She was right."

Aunt Dorothy had thought the world of Tobin. He was the kind of kid who didn't mind running errands, fetching mail or picking berries. It was something he wanted to do; it made him feel good, and he wasn't looking for anything in return.

"Aunt Dorothy was a great woman, Uncle Basil."

"Royal, boy. Royal," his uncle said with a faint smile. "That wampum bracelet. You remember the one? Fetch that for me."

Aunt Dorothy had donated it to the museum. What made his uncle think of it now? "I'll see to it, don't you worry," Tobin promised.

"You keep it. Give it to your girl," he said, barely above a whisper.

"Uncle Basil, I can't. I don't have. . . ."

His uncle's lips tightened. "Shh. You will."

Brownie was lying at the foot of his bed, whimpering, feeling his master, his best friend in the world, slipping away from him. Brownie was like Uncle Basil's child, since he had none.

"My Brownie. . . ."

"Don't you worry—I'll take good care of him," Tobin said, his eyes welling with tears.

At that moment, Tobin heard the screen door slam and footsteps coming toward them. His father came into the room and stood beside them.

"Just in time, James," Basil said.

"Time for what?" Tobin asked.

He saw his father stare at his brother and nod his head.

"So soon?" Tobin cried. "No! No, you can't go! What about the Big Medicine Wheel? You and I are going there in a few weeks. Did you forget? This has been your dream. You can't give up." He turned to his father. "Dad, do something. Heal him."

"You go," his uncle said in a weak voice. "You go to the mountain."

Tobin walked closer to his bed. "No. Not without you."

"I'm tired."

"I'll carry you," Tobin insisted.

His uncle smiled wanly. "Hawu'nshech." Goodbye.

James bent over his brother, said a few loving words and kissed his forehead. "So long, dear brother."

Tobin sat on the edge of the bed and laid his head on his uncle's chest. "Please stay. I love you," he cried.

"Love you," the dying man said in a whisper.

Tobin lifted his head finally, looked at his uncle, then kissed him. Standing over him, Tobin and his father said three prayers, and Uncle Basil closed his eyes. The preacher arrived during the last prayer and said, "Ho, amen." Uncle Basil was gone.

Tobin couldn't move. Even though he knew his uncle's spirit would return to the earth, his heart grieved a grief he never experienced before, and one he never wanted to know again. Tobin wished he could breathe life back into his second father. He would miss the man who taught him so much. When he was ten he got his first pellet gun. Tobin was so thrilled he couldn't wait to use it. He ran over to his Uncle Basil's where he practiced shooting, using tin cans and glass bottles as targets.

On their first hunting trip, he shot a squirrel. Excited, he ran over to it. Seeing it lying there twitching and then motionless made his stomach flutter. He didn't know why he cried. He wanted the squirrel to get up again, chase its mate through the trees. But he knew that wasn't going to happen. He felt terrible. Afraid of what his uncle would think, he wiped his tears away quickly.

Uncle Basil knelt down beside him. "Life's too short for sorrow, boy. My dad, your grandfather, got your father and me each a gun the summer I turned nine. Oh, I couldn't wait to go hunting with the men. First shot—killed that bird. He didn't have a chance. My dad, my uncles, they'd been betting, even drinking beer. I laughed with them. Then, when nobody was looking, I went behind a bush and upchucked my breakfast." Hearing his uncle's story had made Tobin feel better.

Tobin stayed by his father's side for as long as he thought he was needed. "Dad, you going to be okay?"

James nodded.

"I need some fresh air." Tobin hated leaving, but he needed to be by himself. He wondered if his father was used to this kind of thing, since it was part of what he had to deal with, being a medicine man. Not everyone could be cured. But when it came to family, it had to be a lot harder.

"You go ahead," James said quietly, putting his hand on his son's shoulder.

Tobin gave his uncle's forehead one last kiss. Suddenly, he heard Brownie's whimpers. The dog knew his master, his best friend, had left. "Come boy." Together, they wandered aimlessly down the street and into the woods. Along the way Tobin picked up twigs and stones, chucking them as far into the air as he could. He climbed an elm tree, peering into the sky. The soft wind blowing his hair, he watched the hawks. He only wished he could grab hold of one of their wings and fly with them, through the valleys, over the lakes—up to the Bighorn Mountains. He would have to find another way to fulfill his uncle's dream.

Chapter 27

The next day, Tobin went to the museum across from Mill Pond, once run by his people. He was determined to find the wampum bracelet. His Aunt Dorothy had often helped out there, and for three years his people had worked hard to get this old place in shape. They were proud of their accomplishment. Now, town officials had destroyed everything by allowing the whites to take control; few visited, and less often.

He walked into the renovated house, a shingled half-Cape, at one time owned by a medicine woman named Mabel Avant. Two white women were tending the place. They both looked up when the old metal bell inside the front door rattled. He was their only visitor, and they didn't look too happy to see him. The ladies were both neatly dressed. One was middle-aged, maybe mid-forties, blonde and light-skinned. The other woman, he guessed, was in her late sixties. She had thin lips, her gray hair pinned back.

"Good afternoon, ladies."

"Hello," they muttered, then went back to what they were doing. He wanted to swipe the priceless items that meant so much to his people—arrowheads, pottery, beads and fossils—and return them to their rightful owners. He believed the more valuable ones had been lifted. Tobin remembered how excited his people were when the museum opened. It made him sad knowing others had now taken the place over, with little appreciation of what went into creating it. Not only sweat and tears but also laughter and love—love for a place that had safely kept their ancestors' precious possessions.

The ladies eyed him suspiciously. Aware of this, he stared back. His dark eyes were relentless and the women looked away.

Strolling through the rooms, he noticed paintings hung sloppily. He stopped and adjusted each one. Afterward, he picked up an old pipe and an axe from a wooden shelf and carefully examined them, wondering whom they had belonged to. Moving on, he gazed at the arrowheads displayed in locked glass cases. Even though he felt the museum was no longer sanctified, the native history there fascinated him.

The two women huffed, accenting huge sighs. He could see they wanted to close up, even though it was only one o'clock. *It is only a job to them*, he thought. But he wasn't ready to leave. Uncle Basil had counted on him.

Finally, to his amazement, he spotted the precious piece, but not where he expected. "Where did you get that?" he asked the blonde-haired woman, staring at the purple and white stones around her wrist, which he had obviously missed when he walked in.

"What?" she asked, her eyes widening innocently as she looked down at it.

"You are wearing my aunt's bracelet. I'd like it, please," he said, holding his hand out.

"Well," she said, her right hand fingering it, "I don't know. We'll need some information. What's her name?"

"Her name was Dorothy Horvarth. She worked here for years. Everyone knew her. Look it up."

Eleanor blushed and her eyes blinked rapidly. The older lady was already looking through the files.

"It doesn't belong to you," he said.

The two women glanced at each other. The older one, her brows raised, silently saying the boy was telling the truth. Then Eleanor unclasped the chain from her wrist and swung around toward him, dangling the bracelet in mid-air.

"Here. Take it. I have no use for it," she said, practically flinging it at him.

Thanks to his baseball reflexes he caught the chain of stones. Sure you don't, he thought, glaring at her.

Tobin headed straight to the cemetery next to the Old Meeting House, built in 1684 and converted into a church when the tribe adopted Christianity. It was the first Indian chapel in the United States. A historic copper plaque was hidden in nearby shrubbery, inscribed with the words, 'a record of a rugged race to be governed by the word of the Lord—indestructible.'

He remembered how he and his friends played hide-and-seek there when he was young. They read the headstones of local people, names that had meant little back then. Now there would be two here whose names meant a great deal to him. It seemed odd, unreal, in a way, but he knew it was just the beginning of losing those he cared for down the road. A part of life he would have to get used to.

Uncle Basil had found the perfect headstone for Aunt Dorothy. It was made of granite and sparkled with quartz. The word, "Twosome" was carved on the stone's face above their names. Tobin had asked his uncle one day when they visited her grave what "Twosome" meant. He said, "We'll be together always. Whether here or there."

"Whites are hard to understand, I swear. I have your bracelet, and I'm returning it to you," Tobin now said, patting the ground his aunt lay under. He dropped the hoop of gems into a small wooden box he had brought along with him, and then he scratched at the earth until there was a hole deep enough to put it in. When he finished, he brushed the soil from his hands.

"Better here than there," Tobin said out loud. "They had no right to it." Then he picked up a handful of leaves and a sprig from a nearby pine tree and placed it where his Uncle Basil's stone would be. "I'll miss you. Now you'll be with Aunt Dot. Your loving wife. Rest in peace, Uncle Basil," he said, wiping a tear.

He wondered if his people could ever rest. Tobin looked around at the stones. The sacred burial ground used to be for his people. Now non-Indians were being buried there, too. Was anything theirs anymore?

Chapter 28

Eleanor had cooked a pork roast for dinner with roasted potatoes and a medley of green and orange vegetables. She always served promptly at six every night in the kitchen, unless it was a holiday. Then they ate in the dining room, usually mid-day. After Laurie set the table, she and her family sat down to eat.

"I ran into that rude Indian boy. You know who I mean, Donald," Eleanor said, looking at him. "The one who's in the paper all the time." Laurie's father gave her mother a vacant look and shrugged.

"Tobin Horvarth?" Laurie asked excitedly. *He's back. He's back.* Her head whirled with thoughts of maybe seeing him again.

"Yeah, that's him. What an arrogant son-of-a-gun he is. He comes in—right when we're ready to close up for the day."

"What'd he come in for?" Donald asked.

"Looking for trouble, no doubt. I'm glad Hilda Snow was with me."

"Mother, please," Laurie said. "He wouldn't hurt you."

"How do you know that?"

"Because he wouldn't."

"He hit Mr. Morgan, didn't he?"

Donald shifted in his chair. "Mr. Morgan asked for it. I think I would have hit him, too. He doesn't know how to keep his mouth shut."

"I thought you liked the man."

"I like nothing about him. And I don't like you working for him either."

Bravo, Dad.

"You never told me," Eleanor said quietly.

"No, I haven't. . . ."

Laurie wondered if Tobin had any particular reason for stopping by, or if it was just a routine visit. After all, his people's possessions packed that museum. Why wouldn't he make an effort to see if everything was okay? It was probably his first visit to the museum since he had returned from college. *Of all times—when my mother was working.*

After cleaning up the dishes, Laurie headed to her bedroom. She had had months to figure out how she was going to see him again. Formally, that is. She still wasn't sure, but she'd be damned if she would let the summer slip by and miss her chance.

Lying on her bed, thinking about what she would say when she saw him, Laurie fell asleep. She was in the backseat of a car. A man was driving and woman wearing a bonnet sat on the passenger's side. It was a cool but pleasant day; the sun was out and the car windows were rolled down enough to let some fresh air in. The radio was on and she hummed to Louie Armstrong's "Wonderful World." She never felt happier. In the distance, she heard what sounded like rumbling followed by hissing and screeching of brakes. Then a loud whistling sound that seemed endless woke her. It was the phone ringing beside her bed. Half asleep, she reached over and knocked off the receiver, leaving it dangling.

"Anyone there?" Sharon yelled.

She sat up and pulled up the phone cord to her ear. "I'm here, Sharon. What's going on?"

"We thought we'd go get an ice cream. Then hang out at the beach. You up for it?"

"I guess so."

"You sound funny."

"I fell asleep. I had this weird dream," Laurie said, yawning.

"You don't have to come. Go back to sleep."

"No, it's okay. I want to."

"Well, in that case—could you drive? Your car is nicer than mine. People notice us in yours."

Suck up. Laurie was the only one among her friends who had a new car. At first, she had to admit, she liked driving. But after the Camaro had gotten christened umpteen times, she got tired of being their taxi. "Oh, all right."

"Can you hurry? Because we'd like to see the sunset."

"Yeah, yeah." *I'll get there when I get there.*

After stopping at the ice cream shop that had re-opened in April the girls drove to the beach. When Laurie pulled into a parking spot, she saw a father teaching his young son how to fly a kite. There was enough wind, and the yellow and red plastic drifted high in the sky. Then her eyes fixed on three toddlers playing in puddles left after high tide. Finally, she watched a young couple stroll barefoot along the water's edge, holding hands. At one point, they stopped, embraced and then kissed. She couldn't imagine Brian, or any other guy she had dated, ever doing something romantic like that.

"He still cares about you, Laurie," Pam said.

Laurie snapped out of her trance and turned toward her. "Who?" she asked, frowning.

"Brian, who else?"

"Oh, stop."

"I see the way he looks at you. He still has it bad."

"It doesn't matter. It's over," Laurie said, handing Pam a napkin after watching ice cream drip out of the bottom of her cone. Then she turned back and stared out the windshield.

"You can't tell me you like being alone," Pam remarked.

"Yeah. It's kind of nice, actually."

Laurie caught Sharon's eye in the rear-view mirror.

"You're crazy. You won't find anyone better."

"She might change her mind," Pam said, sounding hopeful.

"Nope. Definitely not," Laurie said, shaking her head, staring at the beautiful sunset, smiling to herself.

Sharon and Pam had been trying to get her back with Brian ever since they broke up. Not that she would have considered it. Maybe her friends were being thoughtful. She wondered, though, if they were only afraid that her separation from Brian might mess up their own relationships. Laurie had stayed friends with him even when he dated a girl named Suzie. That had only lasted a short time. And lately, he had been too nice and this was making her very uncomfortable.

Her friends' heads turned like robots every time a car slid into the beach parking lot. They never even saw the sunset. The real draw suddenly skidded in beside them.

"Look who's here," Sharon yelped, as tires squealed and Rob's blue Chevelle nearly sideswiped the Camaro.

"Should have known," Laurie muttered, staring at Rob and his faithful followers. "How convenient."

"We didn't know they were coming here," Pam said, innocently. "Did we, Sharon?"

Sharon shook her head. "Nope. It's a coincidence."

"Yeah, right," Laurie said. This was what Laurie despised about these two. One always backed the other.

Brian was sitting in the back seat, smiling. He winked at Laurie and she looked away. No matter what her friends were scheming, nothing was going to work. She was done with Brian. Done. Done. Done. She wished they would get it through their heads.

"Want a beer?" Rob asked, hanging the bottle out the window.

"Yeah," Sharon said, reaching for it.

"If you want to drink—go sit with him. I'm not getting in trouble for you," Laurie said.

Sharon's eyes rolled. "You can be such a prude."

Laurie thought it was sad—pathetic actually, that her girlfriends had to keep constant tabs on their boyfriends. So afraid of losing them—even for a day.

"You guys got any room?" Sharon called over to the other car.

"For you? Sure, babe," Rob said, sounding smashed.

"Pam, you coming?"

Pam looked at Laurie.

"It's okay, Pam. Go."

"You won't be mad, will you?"

"No. I'm tired anyway. I'm going home."

Just as the girls were getting out of Laurie's car, the cops pulled in—patrolling the area like they did every night. An officer stuck his head out his window to speak to the boys. The girls headed slowly toward the beach, looking back every few seconds to see what was happening.

Before taking off, Laurie decided to wait. If the boys got arrested, Sharon and Pam would need a ride home. She turned off the music, resting her head on the door.

"What are you guys up to? You wouldn't be drinking now, would you?" asked officer Marty Hensley, a friend of Rob's parents.

"Marty, you should know us better than that," Rob said.

Laurie couldn't believe Rob was calling the officer by his first name. She imagined Rob holding the beer between his legs while trying to shove the unopened bottles under the seat. He probably didn't have to bother—Rob's father was also friendly with the chief.

"I hope not. I wouldn't want your father down my back."

The police had to know the boys were drunk or halfway there, and yet they only told them to keep it down because the neighbors might complain. There were no threats, no arrests and no scaring them to death by pointing guns in their faces. A simple talking to and then they drove off. Laurie shuddered to think what would have happened if it had been Tobin instead of Rob in the car. But then she doubted Tobin would have done something that irresponsible to begin with.

Chapter 29

Tobin liked to keep in shape. Every evening, around dusk, regardless of the weather, he would go for a lengthy swim. One night, he heard light splashing and figured it was ducks or swans. *There'd better not be any other intruders.*

Minutes later, a girl in a bikini rose from the pond. Her body was like a magnificent sculpture and her skin was milky against the night sky, as clear as the water she emerged from. She was whistling a melody. He tried to recall it. From the light of the moon, he could tell it was the courtroom girl. He shook his head and blinked his eyes. Was he dreaming?

Afraid of frightening her, he hid behind a huge oak, where he had a full view. She was the most beautiful thing he had ever seen. Blended with the woods, he could look at her for as long as he wanted. Never taking his eyes off her, he watched as she ambled slowly to shore and wrapped a towel neatly around herself. He had to figure out how he was going to get her attention without startling her. He skimmed a pebble. She jumped at first, then she watched it skip across the water. He saw her looking through the trees.

She called out. "Someone there? Tobin Horvarth, is that you? Come on out."

He appeared from behind the tree. "You know me?"

"Well, we did meet briefly."

How could he forget? The day of the verdict, he ran out of the courtroom after her. "But you know my name."

"I've seen your name in the paper."

"Oh, is that so," he said defensively.

"Yeah. I like the way you stand up for yourself—and for your people."

He assumed she was referring to the time when he was arrested for disturbing the peace, or the time he punched Morgan. Whichever, it was something he preferred not to talk about; it wasn't anything he was proud of.

"I think you're very brave," she said.

"Thanks. I guess." He paused for a moment, ingesting what she said. He never thought of it as being brave.

"You guess?"

"I did what I had to do," he said, averting his eyes. "What is your name?"

"I'm sorry. I'm Laurie. Laurie Matthews. Nice to meet you—officially," she said, walking closer to him, holding out her hand.

He held it. Through her cool fingers, he felt warmth. Actually, he felt more. He wasn't sure what it was, but it was nice. "What brings you here?" Tobin asked, letting go, trying not to stare. Keeping focused on her words was hard.

"It's beautiful here—so peaceful," she said with a smile.

"Indeed it is." *Indeed it is? What kind of talk is that? What a jerk I am.* He felt like he was ten years old and noticing eleven-year-old Evelyn Klein for the first time. Seeing her shaking—trembling—he wanted to wrap his arms around her, settle her, let her know she had nothing to be afraid of. "You're shivering," was all that came out.

"I'll be fine."

"I won't hurt you," he said quietly, stammering.

"Oh, I know that."

There was silence.

"You think I'm scared of you?" she finally asked.

"I don't know. Maybe."

"I'm just chilly, that's all."

"Oh," he said, relieved. Still he was short on words.

"I need to get back into the water. Are you going in?" she asked, looking down at his trunks.

He nodded. Slipping off his sandals and shirt, he dove in. She let her towel fall and ran in behind him.

"*Tauh Coi!*" he yelled.

"Huh?"

"It's very cold," he translated.

"Only at first. Once you're in, it's like bath water." She was telling him what he already knew;—he had been swimming at John's Pond all of his life. Still, everything she was saying seemed new, fresh. He wondered how she stumbled across this area.

It was like he had his very own mermaid beside him. Her backstroke, her sidestroke—all her movements were incredible. "You're good. Where'd you learn how to swim like that?" Tobin asked her.

"We had a pool at our house—where we used to live in Newton."

"You had lessons?"

"My mom wanted me to, so I did. I was a lifeguard for a while. That made her happy," she said, rolling her eyes. "But I taught myself basically, before then. How about you? You're not bad either. Where'd you learn?"

"Here. Like you—it was second nature."

They swam around like two fish in a bowl, gracefully chasing each other in and above the water. Then Tobin vanished completely for a long time. He could hear Laurie shouting his name, repeatedly, her voice in a panic state. Then she dove in looking for him. When she surfaced, he appeared beside her, tossing back his long black hair, and blinking water from his eyes.

"How can anyone hold his breath that long?" Laurie asked with a deep sigh. "I'm good at holding mine, but not that good." Then she blasted him. "Don't ever do that again. You scared me half to death."

"I didn't mean to."

"I could see these big bold headlines, 'Man Drowns in Local Pond.'"

"Indian man."

"Huh?"

"'*Indian* Man Drowns.'"

"'White Girl's Fault,'" she said.

"No big loss."

"You really think that little of yourself?"

"Do you?" he asked.

"Do I what—think that little of you? If I did, I wouldn't be here."

"Wouldn't you?"

"Go to hell."

How could he be mad at her? She had been truly worried, and that touched him. It made him want to kiss that perfect face of hers, full of apprehension and anger. Instead, he laughed.

"You think this is funny?"

"No. No," he said, shaking his head. "Not at all. If only you could've seen your face."

She rushed to shore and grabbed her towel. "I have to go. Nice meeting you."

"Yeah, nice meeting you, too," he said watching her disappear into the woods. He stood confused. He had blown it. She was here and then an hour later she was gone, like none of it really happened. Everything had been perfectly fine. They were swimming and having fun and the next thing he knew, she was running away.

What had he done?

Laurie wondered if she should have gone there in the first place. Maybe it was a mistake—but how could she think like that? She wanted the chance to spend some alone time with him. And now that she had, she was more attracted to him than before. Even though they were with each other only a short spell, everything she learned about him she liked. He was brave, and caring. They both liked to swim. She mused over what else they might have in common.

She realized that the only way she was going to find that out was to go back there—to the pond. She was stubborn, too, but why did he have to make fun of her? Taking off abruptly might have ruined the best thing that ever happened to her.

When Laurie went to sleep, she had a dream like one she had a few nights before. The sun was shining so brightly she had to squint, but she saw it was the same two people. From the edge of the water, the lovely woman was reaching her hand out to her, and beside this fair complexion, smiling, was the dark-skinned man. They wanted her to go with them—she wanted to go. The man helped her into the boat. But when she stepped in and sat down, she realized she was alone. The couple had vanished, and there she was by herself— drifting. She awoke then. *Who were they? Why had they left her?* They seemed like real people. People she might have known once.

She dozed off again and this time she dreamed of Tobin and her, swimming at the pond. Afterward, they had lunch on shore. She had brought a picnic basket filled with sandwiches, a couple of apples, brownies and a bottle of Chardonnay she had stolen from her parents' wine chest. The wine made her silly, and she kissed him. He kissed her back. It must have been a nice kiss because she awoke with a smile on her face. She was ready to make up with Tobin Horvarth.

Half asleep, still in her baby doll PJs, she went downstairs to the kitchen, opened a cabinet and took out a box of Frosted Flakes. When she went to get the milk, she saw a note on the refrigerator. *Heading to your Aunt Cathy's. We'll be back tonight. Have a great day. Love Dad.* Her mother's sister lived in Wellesley, about an hour and a half away. They saw her as often as they could. Aunt Cathy was a few years older than Eleanor and her children were grown and gone. Laurie was very fond of her aunt, but she grew bored fast whenever she visited with her parents.

Looking out the bow window over the kitchen sink, Laurie could see clouds rolling in from the east. A single bluebird perched on the bird feeder. Charlotte from next door was watering her flowers. She looked up and beamed at Laurie with a witchy smile. *I'm keeping a watchful eye on you, my pretty.* Laurie quickly moved away from the window and shuddered.

While she was sitting down at the table with her cereal, the phone rang.

"What're you doing?" Pam asked.

"Having breakfast. Why, what's up?"

"Mike's getting his father's dune buggy!"

"Gosh, that's so cool. How'd that happen?"

"I guess it wasn't easy. We want to get out there before it rains.

Can you be here in half an hour?"

"At your house?"

"Yeah. Mike's picking us up here."

Sharon was muttering something in the background.

"What's Sharon saying?"

"She said don't forget your suntan lotion. No. She said hurry it up."

"I'll be over as soon as I get changed. Bye."

It was seldom that Mike's father would allow his son to take his pride and joy out for a ride. In fact, Mike had gotten the buggy only one other time and Laurie thought his father regretted it afterward. He had come along and waited on the dunes for them, watching closely. Then he checked the vehicle over thoroughly for dents and scratches. She remembered, though, how much fun it was. The sun, the sand, the bouncy ride in the metallic blue buggy. What a blast!

Chapter 30

During the summer Tobin worked for a large sanitary service. It was a rancid job, but the pay was decent—money he could stash away for Wyoming. He planned to keep his promise to his Uncle Basil. He was more eager than ever to see the Big Medicine Wheel. He stood on the back of the garbage truck as they drove through the southern part of town, the rich section. Daffodils were popping up everywhere. He jumped off the truck, retrieved the barrels, dumped them and hopped back on. Every so often a customer gave a wave or a nod. As they were leaving one driveway, a short, white-haired lady came running out her front door, hailing them.

"Wait! Wait!" she cried.

Pete, the driver, stopped the truck. Tobin jumped off and met her halfway. The little lady was out of breath, holding her hand to her chest. Tobin wondered what was so important that she had to wear herself out.

"Could you come to the back of the house? There's a dead raccoon!" she cried.

"That's not our job, Ma'am. You should call the Animal Rescue League," Tobin suggested.

"I'd appreciate it if you'd take it away for me. She flinched. "It's horrible."

Pete, who had popped his head out the window, had been with the company much longer than he had, and Tobin always thought of him as the boss man.

"She's got a dead raccoon!" Tobin shouted.

Middle-aged with a large gut and a long, gray beard, Pete was rugged-looking and could be intimidating, but he was really a softy. He lifted his hands in the air. "Whatever."

"I'll pay you," the lady told Tobin.

"No, that's okay. But just this one time. We're on a tight schedule."

"Thank you. Thank you very much."

Tobin walked into the backyard with her.

"Do you need a shovel?" she asked.

"No," Tobin said, shaking his head. He picked up the carcass with his gloved hands. The lady shuddered as she watched warily, her teeth clenched. Then she followed him, keeping a safe distance, as he carried it to the truck and heaved it in. The woman thanked him again and skittishly offered him fifty cents. Tobin hopped into the truck and held up the quarters.

"She's all heart," said Pete, with a toothless grin.

"Here," Tobin said, handing him the change. "Stick it in your kids' piggy banks." With two young kids at home, Tobin figured every penny counted.

Laurie quickly donned her bathing suit, jeans and a halter-top. Then she bent over, brushing her hair forward. Standing back up and lobbing her head back in position, she secured her long strands with an elastic band keeping the ponytail in place. There was no time for fussing. She wished not to miss out on even a moment. If she were late they might leave without her. They never had before, but this ride meant a lot to them.

She raised the garage door and had started backing her car down the driveway when she looked in her side mirror and saw the garbage truck in front of her house. Her father usually took care of bringing the barrels outside, but he must have forgotten. She hopped out of the car and ran back into the garage. As Laurie was dragging out the trash barrels, these big-gloved hands grabbed hold of them. In a rush, without looking, she apologized for not having them out sooner. "I'm really sorry," she said. "I totally forgot you were coming today."

"It's okay," a familiar voice said. She looked up and found herself gazing into Tobin's eyes.

"What are you doing here?" she asked, shocked to see him.

"This is my job. We don't usually do this route. But Manny—he's the guy who usually does—is sick today."

"Oh, you do this?" she asked, not knowing what else to say.

"It's a stinky job, I know," he said with a quick smile, "but the money's good. I'm saving for a trip to Wyoming."

"I didn't mean anything by it. . . ." she stammered.

"Hey, forget it," he said.

"About last night—I don't know why I acted the way I did."

"Listen, it's a new day," he said softly. They stood looking at each other until Pete beeped the horn, erasing their trance.

"I have to dump these."

"Yeah, sure," she said, standing dumbfounded, watching him take the barrels to the truck and bring them back.

"Have to go," he said, hustling down the driveway. The truck was moving as he jumped on.

"How about a ride later?" he called to her. "I get off at three."

She nodded fiercely, smiling.

"I'll pick you up at four."

"That'll be great," she yelled back.

Driving to Pam's, Laurie was in a world of her own. Seeing Tobin again ignited something inside her and she wanted to be with him— more than ever. She was still excited about the buggy ride, but the idea of a date with Tobin was more thrilling. She spent a lot of time with her friends—they did everything together. She never realized how much she was with them. Until now.

When she arrived at the Courtneys' house, Pam and Mike, Sharon and Rob were already in the blue metallic fiberglass buggy. *It's so sharp-looking*, she thought.

"Sorry, Laurie. There's only room for four." *Now they tell me.* "Brian said he'll drive you," Pam said. "We'll let you guys have the first turn on the beach."

"Okay."

She saw Brian waiting in his car. Laurie had forgotten the buggy could only hold four comfortably, or more important, legally.

"It's up to you," Brian said, out his window.

What the heck, she thought. "Sure."

Like a wild ride at a fair, there were screams and much laughter as they bounced over rolling dunes, holding on for dear life. In spite of all the fun, Laurie could hardly wait for four o'clock. Because of the predicted weather, an afternoon shower, Mike had promised to have the buggy back by three. *Perfect*, Laurie thought. She glanced at her watch. It was one-thirty. There was still plenty of time. At least she could bug out of there without having to make up a story.

While the two other couples had their turn, she was left waiting on the beach with Brian. She wondered if it was intentional. Everyone was hoping they would work out, but it would never happen.

"Why do you keep looking at your watch?" Brian asked her.

"I do? I guess I'm just hoping it doesn't rain before we have to leave. I want to get another ride."

"Doesn't look like it," Brian said, tilting his head, staring up into the sunny sky.

"I know. But it was supposed to."

"Well, since the weatherman was wrong, maybe Mike's dad will let him keep it longer."

Laurie prayed not. If she were late, Tobin would think she had changed her mind. She was lucky he had given her another chance. There was no reason for her to fret; Mike's dad had made it clear to his son he had to have the buggy back in the yard at three, no matter what.

"I'm glad we could stay friends," Brian said, looking at her.

"Yeah. Me, too."

"So what have you been up to lately?"

"I keep busy." Laurie aimed on keeping her responses short and vague.

"You dating anyone?"

"No, not really," she mumbled, wishing she could have replied with a "yes."

"Hmm. 'Not really.' Does that mean there might be someone?"

"I'm not going steady with anyone—that's all I'm saying." She was feeling very uncomfortable being left alone with him. She wanted to be nice—friendly—but she also didn't want to initiate any false encouragement, making him think there was hope for the two of them. She was thankful when the buggy was coming their way.

"Can't you keep it just a half hour longer?" Sharon pleaded.

"No. I really can't," Mike said.

"If his father can't trust him this time," Laurie said, "he'll never let him take it again. You want another ride, don't you?"

Brian convinced Rob to drive his car back to Pam's so that Laurie and he got *their* chance to ride paved roads in the buggy.

"Thanks, Mike. I had a great time," Laurie said, leaping out of the buggy at Pam's house and heading toward her car. Her girlfriends lingered, chatting with the boys.

"I'll see you guys later," Laurie said loudly, unlocking the Camaro.

They stopped talking and focused on her. "It's still early. Do you want to do something?" Pam asked.

"I promised my parents I'd clean the house," she lied.

Pam and Sharon stared at her. They knew how much she hated cleaning.

"Excuse me, you're doing what?" Sharon asked.

"They went to my Aunt Cathy's for the day. It was a way of getting out of going with them," she muttered, slipping behind the wheel of her car. Laurie drove off without looking back. Seeing the astonishment on their faces had made her smile.

Chapter 31

Tobin was waiting for Laurie, his red and white truck idling at the end of her driveway. She gestured, parked her Camaro in the garage and ran down to him. They were only a few hundred feet down the road when she made him stop.

"Could you please pull over?" she asked, combing her fingers through her hair.

Without questioning her, he did what she asked. She hopped out, bending over to shake her head. Then she took off her sneakers and began dancing on the pavement. "God, it's hot!"

Tobin tried not to laugh. He was afraid she would run off again. He wondered why she didn't just hang her beautiful legs out the door and dump her shoes that were full of beach sand.

"Where we going?" Laurie asked when she got back in.

He smiled. "It's a surprise."

"I love surprises."

Tobin removed his bandana and handed it to her. "Here, use this as a blindfold." He saw her looking at it. "Go ahead, wear it."

"Okay, I will, if you promise to drop hints along the way," Laurie said, folding it over her eyes and tying it behind her head. "Are you looking at me?"

He chuckled. "If anyone sees you, they'll think you're my hostage."

"Is this part of your plan?"

"It wasn't, but it's a thought."

"Maybe I'm reckless in picking new friends."

Tobin didn't respond.

"It ended up being a perfect day," she said finally.

"Yep. Not a cloud in the sky," he said, looking through his windshield.

"It seems like we've been driving forever."

"Always does when you're waiting."

"Not being able to see doesn't help," Laurie said.

"No, I suppose it doesn't."

"It must be horrible to be blind."

"Sight is a precious thing," Tobin responded, looking at the trees, the flowers—at her, then reminding himself to keep his eyes on the road. He couldn't believe she was sitting beside him. If she was blind, deaf or wheelchair-bound, he would still want to take care of her. He didn't know why he felt this way, he hardly knew her. But already he wanted to protect her.

"Are we almost there?" she asked.

"Soon."

Tobin drove another mile and veered to the left. A quarter of a mile down that stretch, he turned off to the right.

"We're going up a hill," Laurie said.

"Yup, I guess you're feeling the incline."

A few seconds later, the car was on level ground again. Tobin shifted and turned off the motor. "You can take off the blindfold."

Untying the bandana, Laurie wiped sweat from her brows and blinked. She looked up at the stone tower. "Where are we? What is this place?"

"C'mon, let's go in," Tobin said. They hopped out of the truck, shutting the doors.

He saw her reading the plaque above the opening of the tower, "Established in 1890, by Francis Bassett Tobey. Did he build this?"

"Not sure. The first tower was blown down in a storm in 1876. A second one was finished about ten years later, in 1886. This guy, Tobey, bought it in 1890 for his summer guests."

"He must've had a lot of money."

"Yeah. I would think."

Inside the stone structure, lovers had carved hearts with their initials or names inside. Tobin watched Laurie scan them. "Anyone you know?"

She shook her head. "No."

Climbing the tower's spiral staircase, they stopped on each level to look out a long window. Reaching the top, they witnessed miles of endless green patches of trees and fields, some with houses and small ponds, like the fish-shaped one below. And beyond Scargo Lake was the bay.

"Wow!" Laurie said. "It's beautiful."

"There's definitely history here," Tobin said, looking around.

"You knew about this tower?" Laurie asked him.

Tobin nodded.

"I didn't. There're probably a lot of places I've never been to."

"You haven't been here long."

"Two years," she pointed out.

"That's not very long, especially with all there is to see on the Cape. I think the people living here—they take it for granted. They know they can visit whenever they want. But they never do."

"So you mean if I was a tourist, nobody would suggest I come to this tower?"

He shook his head. "No, just the opposite, they probably would. It's a great attraction and they know it. They just wouldn't get around to seeing it themselves."

As Tobin pointed to the Sagamore Bridge to their left, the Provincetown Monument straight ahead, Laurie leaned lightly against him. In the gentle breeze, strands of her hair stroked the nape of his neck.

To distract himself, he said, "There are two legends about how this lake got here."

"Tell me both."

"Well, the first is about a giant named Maushop. He looked after the welfare of the Native Americans. They believed he played a great part in forming the Cape and the Islands. He taught the tribes— helped to unite them. The natives had much respect and admiration for him. Before he moved on, they wanted him to leave some sort of sign that he would continue to care about them."

Laurie stared at him.

"So, he dug this pond—Scargo Lake—as a gift to them, letting them know they wouldn't be forgotten."

Laurie suddenly looked awestruck. "I can't believe he made this pond all by himself."

"Don't forget, he was a giant."

"So that's how the lake got its name?"

"Some think so."

"Tell me the other story."

"Others believe the lake was dug for a beautiful Indian Princess— named Scargo. She was loved by this handsome young brave. He was going on a hunting trip, and he said when he got back he'd ask her father, the chieftain, permission to marry her. But before he left he gave her a gift."

"A gift?" Laurie asked, intrigued.

"A pumpkin. A pumpkin shell, actually. Filled with little fish. They got sick quickly, though. Some even died. It was too crowded for them in that small space. The princess got very upset. She ran to her father crying. She begged him to find a way to make the fish better."

"What'd he do?"

"He got the squaws to dig this lake out with sea clams—to give the fish a place to live."

"Sea clams? Didn't it take forever?" she asked, surveying the lake below.

"I don't think so. I bet though they worked from dawn to dusk."

"But I wonder why he felt he had to make something so big. Though, it's great that he did. It's a beautiful lake."

"Couldn't tell you. Maybe he thought about all the families the fish would have."

"That makes sense. Did they ever get married?"

"Yep. And they lived right here on the banks somewhere," he said, staring at the lake and the many trees encircling it, trying to visualize where they might have settled.

"That's incredible. I like happy endings."

"Me, too," he said, looking at her, still amazed he was with the girl of his dreams.

At that moment, two people drove up in a sedan.

"We're not alone anymore," Tobin said.

"It's okay." She sounded disappointed and that pleased him.

Peering over the ledge, they watched the middle-aged couple get out of their car. The man looked up and waved; the small woman gestured with her camera, slung around her neck, that she would take a picture of them.

"Of her and me?" Tobin asked, pointing to Laurie first, then himself.

"Yes! Yes! Picture of beautiful people," the woman said in an accent they didn't recognize. "Eye-catcher. Eye-catcher."

Laurie looked at Tobin and then back down at the woman.

"Eye-catcher," Tobin repeated, putting his arm around Laurie, drawing her closer. They smiled for the photographer.

Laurie skipped up the driveway, replaying everything that happened in her head. It had been one of the best days ever, a great time with her friends and an even more wonderful time with Tobin. He was beyond what she expected him to be. She only hoped he felt the same way about her. The door swung open just as she was about to turn the knob.

"Where have you been?" her mother asked, not giving Laurie a chance to answer. "You were with that Indian boy, weren't you?"

Laurie stood in the hall and just looked at her.

Her mother crossed her arms. "And don't lie to me. You've been seen with him."

Laurie knew right away who the informant was. Charlotte must have seen her in Tobin's truck. Snoopy rarely missed a trick. And she really liked stirring people up. "I'm not going to lie to you. Yes, I was with him."

Flustered, Eleanor walked briskly into the living room and began pacing. "I—I can't have this."

"Have what?" Laurie asked, as she flopped in the chair, laughing.

"I don't find anything amusing here."

"You're making a big deal out of this—I only went for a ride with him. I'm not marrying the guy or anything." *Except in my dreams.*

Eleanor stopped pacing, sat down on the sofa and fumbled through her purse. She took out an already open pack of Virginia Slims and one of those throwaway lighters, pulled out a cigarette and nervously lit it. Laurie wondered when she had started the nasty habit. A butt hanging out of her mother's mouth certainly soiled her sweet image.

"The signs were all there. But for the life of me, I never thought you'd get involved!"

Involved? What a weird term. I spend a few hours with him, and now I'm involved? Hmm. I don't think so—not yet anyway.

"Wait til your father hears about this."

"He's not filled with hate—like you."

"I never hated anyone. That's a very strong word. I've disliked people."

"Mother, you're a hypocrite."

"How dare you speak to me like that?"

"I'm sorry. It's just how I see it."

"I don't want you seeing him again."

Laurie wished Tobin and her were as close as her mother thought they were. But this new friendship was only in infancy. Although, if she felt this wonderful after being with him for only a few hours— who knew what could happen down the road?

"Mom, I'm almost eighteen. I think I can make my own decisions."

"As long as you're living under this roof, you'll do as I say."

Laurie stomped upstairs, slamming her bedroom door. Her mother would have to deal with it. Laurie had made up her mind; she was going to continue to see Tobin as long as he wanted to see her. Was she trying to defy her mother? No. Tobin fascinated Laurie, and he had for a long time. It was too bad her mother would never approve of him. Anyway, the secret was out. Her mother certainly wouldn't advertise that her daughter had been with Tobin. But now that Charlotte had seen them together, the whole town would eventually find out. Laurie had to tell Pam and Sharon before they heard the news through someone else. If only they could see Tobin through her eyes, they would welcome him. *Dream on.* Truth was, all they saw was the color of his skin.

Laurie stayed in her room and turned on the stereo, volume up high. The white walls and shades were stenciled with small daisies. Every shelf and surface was bursting with a large collection of stuffed and porcelain rabbits. When she was little, she had her father read Beatrix Potter books to her every night.

She kicked off her shoes and scrambled onto the bed, pushing aside the sheer pink and white canopy. She reached over and picked up the phone on the nightstand to call Sharon and Pam, then decided against it. Her mother's disapproval was enough for one day.

Lying there, Laurie thought about Tobin and their time together. Every moment was special—the way he smiled at her, his laugh and the way he told stories. She couldn't think of one thing she didn't like about him. He seemed too good to be real. Before Laurie knew it, it was close to six o'clock. No way was she going downstairs to have dinner with her parents. She could still hear her mother's tainted words. Laurie felt sorry for her father, knowing he'd have to suffer through a meal while his wife went on endlessly about his daughter being involved with an Indian boy, disgracing the family. Then her mother would pressure him to do something about it.

There was a knock on her door.

"Who is it?" she asked.

"It's Dad. May I come in?"

Hopping off the bed, she shuffled to the door and opened it. He brought her supper. She was hungry from the long day, just not enough to face an earful from her mother. "You didn't have to do this. Thanks," she said, taking the plate, filled with ham, mashed potatoes and mixed vegetables.

Donald sat at the edge of her bed, while Laurie perched at the vanity, toying with the food.

"I told your mother I'd talk to you."

Laurie shook her head, on the defensive right away. "Daddy," she said, her eyes filling up. Then she stood up and went and sat beside him. Laying her head on his chest, she started to cry. "Mom's making a big deal out of this. I took a ride with him. That's all."

He wrapped his arms around her trembling shoulders. "I know," he said softly.

When Laurie sat up, her father folded her hands in his and looked at her. "I'm not going to tell you to stop seeing him, honey. I have no right to tell you who you should or shouldn't hang around with. You're old enough to make your own choices."

"I wish you could tell Mom that."

"Your mother—well, you know the way she is. She just doesn't want you to grow up," he said, shaking his head. "As long as he doesn't hurt you."

"He wouldn't—I know he wouldn't."

"I trust your judgment, Laurie. But to keep peace here at home, for the time being anyway, you're going to have to keep things to yourself."

"I will, Daddy. I promise," she said, blinking away tears. Her father gently patted her knee.

"He's a good person," Laurie said quietly.

Her father nodded. "Eat your supper," he said, rising from the bed and walking to the door.

He was the only one, so far, on her side. Still, it was a start. *And people can change*, Laurie thought, with a fragile smile, as she finally took a bite of the food.

Chapter 32

Laurie pushed the snooze button twice before getting up. Knots twisted her stomach. She hated quarreling with her mother, but she had no intention of letting Tobin go. *Maybe if she got to know him she'd like him. But let's face it, she'd never give him a chance.*

She dressed quickly, hoping to beat it out the door, but just as she got to the bottom of the staircase her mother was standing there.

"Hi honey, can I fix you something to eat?"

Laurie wondered what had changed her. Where was all this cheeriness coming from? She was acting like nothing happened. Maybe it was her way of making up?

"Thank you, but I don't have time."

"Why don't you skip school today—and come to work with me?"

Laurie stared at her. *Something's up. Why would I go to work with you?*

"There are some people I'd like you to meet."

"People?" Laurie asked.

"There's a young man—a little older than you—who just started working for us. He's very handsome. And smart," Eleanor said with a smile.

And non-Indian, Mother?

"Thanks, but I have a final today."

"I thought you were done with them?"

"I did, too."

Laurie saw more frustration than disappointment on her mother's face, and decided to get out of there before anything got started. "Sorry, I've really got to go. Maybe another time," she said, hurrying out the door.

Laurie was having a hard time paying attention in school. Part of it was her mother. Things between them had gotten so ugly. But mostly she could hardly wait til the end of the day to be with Tobin again. They had made plans to meet at John's Pond. Laurie was experiencing some powerful feelings when she was around him. Sharon and Pam were usually the ones she talked to about this stuff, but they had no idea she was even seeing Tobin. And there were some things she just couldn't talk about with her father.

Laurie and her friends stopped to chat in the corridor before their English class.

"You're coming over tonight, right?" Pam asked.

"Tonight, uh, no. I can't." Laurie hoped she wasn't stuttering.

"What do you mean, you can't? What's going on?"

"Nothing. I promised my dad I'd go shopping with him." Sharon and Pam were looking at her strangely. "It's my mother's birthday," Laurie blurted.

"I thought your mother's birthday was in March? Your father had a huge bash—she hit the big one, a year ago. We got drunk. Remember? Everyone was plastered—they didn't even know we were, too," Sharon reminded her.

Oh, damn, they remembered my mother's fortieth.

"Oh, did I say birthday?" Laurie asked, trying to sound casual.

"Yeah, you did," Sharon said.

"Sorry. I meant anniversary."

Laurie had to be more careful. Her friends weren't stupid. And they knew her well. Maybe better than she thought.

"If you say so," Sharon said, her eyes narrowing, before she hurried into the classroom as the first bell rang.

The students were seated at their desks by second bell, busily writing in their notebooks. Shifting in her chair, Laurie noticed Sharon's dubious glances. Or was it her imagination? Pam was twirling her hair around her finger. She only did that when something was bothering her, of if she was trying to figure out something. Laurie was starting to feel paranoid.

When the teacher shut the classroom door against noise in the corridor, Laurie suddenly felt a pang of claustrophobia. Was it being closed in with her friends, or was it being trapped in a lie? Her heart began racing and her hands shook. She wanted to run out of there. But then they would know she was guilty. Guilty of what, though? She hadn't done anything wrong. She just hadn't told her friends about Tobin. It wasn't like she betrayed or hurt anyone. So why was she letting all this get to her? Watching Sharon pass Pam a note, Laurie knocked her English book to the floor.

"Sorry," she mumbled.

The teacher, Mrs. Knox, titled her head toward Laurie. "Everything okay, Miss Matthews?"

All eyes were on her now. Laurie forced a smile. "Everything's fine," she said, bending over to pick up her book.

"Good. Now class," Mrs. Knox continued, "take down this week's vocabulary words." She turned then and began writing them on the blackboard.

Laurie thought her friends should learn the words 'tolerance and humanity.'

Later that evening dinner went by without incident. Conversation was light and not a word was said about Tobin, or even about the guy her mother wanted her to meet at the Selectman's office—if there actually was someone. Eleanor probably knew her husband would side with his daughter anyhow.

"The steak is very tender," her father commented.

"I think marinating helps," her mother responded.

"Did you have a good day at school?" Donald asked, passing the salad bowl to Laurie.

"I did, Daddy," Laurie said, without elaborating, seeing her mother was quiet.

"Eleanor, how was your day?"

Laurie's mother glanced at him. "Fine," she said, pouring Good Seasons dressing over her salad, then handing the bottle to Laurie. "A middle-aged guy applied for a taxi license. We had five dog licenses. It's that time of year."

After clearing the table and stacking the dishes in the dishwasher, Laurie headed straight to her room. No more procrastinating, she thought. Lifting the phone, she dialed Pam's number. Now that Laurie would be seeing Tobin more, it was going to be hard to make excuses for her nightly disappearances. It would relieve tension between her and her mother if her friends backed her up—at least for the time being. Laurie's mother had always liked Pam and Sharon, and she would believe whatever they told her.

"Pam, I need a favor."

"What kind of favor?"

"Just listen, okay?" Laurie said quietly.

"What is it?"

"I need you to tell my mother—if she calls you, that is— to tell her I was with you. And I'm on my way home. Or make up something. I don't care—just tell her something she'll believe. Please."

"You're kidding, right?"

"No, I'm not kidding."

"You want me to lie to your mother? Are you crazy? I can't do that."

"It won't be a lie really. Just think of it as helping out a friend. You really don't know anything. So how can it be a lie?"

"Why? What's going on?"

"I can't tell you right now."

"When then?"

"I don't know."

"I thought we were best friends."

"We are." The line went silent. "Will you do this for me?" Laurie asked her.

"You promise you'll tell me?"

"Yes, I promise."

"Oh, all right. I'll do it."

"Thanks, Pam. It means a lot."

Laurie hoped she could count on her, but she knew Pam could be weak at times. Like the time when she secretly told Pam about the crush she had on their biology teacher, who was only a few years older than them. That information leaked quickly. When Mr. Burns found out, she could have died of embarrassment. But there was no one else Laurie could ask to cover for her, except Sharon, who would squeeze it out of her—hound her to death until Laurie revealed her secret. And Laurie wasn't ready to tell her or Pam about Tobin. She wanted to make sure it worked out first.

Donning her pink bikini, Laurie slipped into jean shorts and a cotton white top. After pulling her sweatshirt over her head, she grabbed a beach towel from the bathroom closet and swung it around her neck. Instead of driving, she would ride her bike. Too many knew her car. As much as she hated sneaking around, she had to—at least for the time being. Her mother was in the garage when she was ready to leave, depositing a bag of trash into one of the barrels.

"Where're you off to?"

"For a swim," Laurie said, releasing the kickstand.

"On your bike?"

"Yeah, well, I need the exercise. I've gained a few pounds since I started driving."

"You don't look any different to me."

"It's right here, Mom," she said, patting her thighs. Leaping onto the seat, Laurie adjusted her gears.

Phew, she didn't ask me who I was going with.

Eleanor called after her. "You meeting Pam and Sharon?"

"Yeah," Laurie shouted, turning onto the street.

She knew the lies would get out of hand. But what choice did she have?

Chapter 33

When Laurie arrived at the pond, Tobin was swimming laps. After leaning her bike against a tree, she laid her towel down. Removing her shorts and sweatshirt, she lifted off her top, dropped it and crept into the water, her arms crossed. Wading, Tobin shot fleeting glances at her.

"You're only making it harder on yourself."

"It's cold," she said with chattering lips.

Tobin made small ripples, pretending to splash her.

"Don't you dare," she said.

"You'll never get in that way."

To keep from being dunked, she dove in. They had this mammoth pool in a serene setting all to themselves. This time when Tobin disappeared under water Laurie didn't panic. He swam by her legs. She yelped when he pulled her down with him. Then he kissed her sweetly and quickly swam away. It was a kiss she had been waiting for.

After swimming a while longer, they went to shore and dried off. Sitting on their towels, Tobin turned to her. "I want to show you something," he said, reaching for his jeans. He pulled out his wallet and leaned next to her.

"Where did you get this?" she asked, looking at the picture of herself.

"I found it at the mall."

"I must've dropped it," she murmured. "You kept it."

He nodded.

She smiled. "I saw you that night. I was so nervous. I had a crush on you back then."

"But you didn't know me."

"Didn't have to. I liked what I saw. And I knew you were a good person."

"How'd you know that? Not by reading the paper, I'm sure."

"I just knew. And I was right."

"I suppose."

"You suppose?"

He laughed. "I guess it depends on who's judging. So, what are your plans after graduation?"

"I'm going to UMass in Boston."

"Yeah? And study what?"

"Anthropology. I want to be a lawyer someday. I want to help people."

"People like us? Like me?"

Laurie looked at him. "Maybe so. That trial was so stupid. It was your people's land for centuries. We had no right. . . ."

"Why?" he asked.

"Why what?"

"Why do you care so much?"

"I don't know—I just do. We're all the same—we should be treated equally."

He changed the subject. "And after college?" he asked.

"Work, of course. Maybe I'll do some travelling first. I definitely want a family someday. Kids. Lots of them. At least an even number of them, so one isn't left out."

Tobin frowned. "Left out?"

"Yeah. That way, they'd each have someone to play with. I was lonely—being an only child. I don't want them to feel that way," she said cupping her hand, sifting sand through it. "I always wished I had a sister.

You know, for a game of Monopoly when it got snowy and twenty below outside."

"Not a brother?"

"That would've been nice, too," she said with a smile. "But you can't shop with brothers or tell them about your boyfriends."

"Boyfriends?"

"You know what I mean."

"Yeah," he said quietly.

"What about you? You'll be out of college before me."

"Pretty much like you. Probably need a decent job—one that pays well, though, before I could think about traveling."

There was silence for a moment then Laurie said, "This may sound strange, but I feel like I've always known you."

Tobin stared at her. "I feel exactly the same way."

"You do?"

"I do," he said with a smile, taking her hand in his, drawing her closer to him. "This feels right;—you feel right." He paused.

"But what?" she asked, staring up at him.

"Your parents. . . ."

"What about them?"

"Will they approve?"

Did Tobin assume with all the fighting that had been going on during the trial that her parents were like the rest? Well, he was half right. At least Laurie's father was impartial. Her mother, however, was another story.

"Doesn't matter. Besides, I'm almost eighteen. I don't think they have much say in it."

"We'll be shot down—everywhere we go."

"Does that bother you?"

"Maybe some, but I worry more about you."

"Me—why me?"

"You're the white girl."

"I don't care what anybody thinks."

He looked at her. "You're different. I like you."

"Oh, thanks. I guess."

"No, I mean—I like who you are."

She smiled. "I like who you are, too."

At that moment, Tobin bent over, wrapped his arms around her and kissed her lightly on the lips. In his arms, she felt warm and safe. She hated to leave, but it was getting late and she knew her mother would be waiting up.

"I really must go."

Tobin held her even tighter. "I don't want to let you go."

"Then don't," she murmured.

"Can I see you tomorrow?"

"Here?" Laurie asked.

He nodded.

She closed her eyes and moved into his good night kiss. She wanted to hang on to the night—and to him. Amazing that someone you hardly knew could also be as comfy to be with as an old friend.

It was close to eleven when she got home. She quietly walked her ten speed into the garage through its side door and tiptoed through the kitchen. Her mother heard her.

"Where have you been? It's late. You should have called."

"I'm sorry—I ran into a friend on the way home. You know how it is—time went by," Laurie murmured.

"A friend?"

"Yeah, someone from school. I really need to get out of these wet clothes," Laurie said, evading, as she headed to the staircase.

"Your dad was getting worried, too. I'll let him know you're home."

"Tell him I'll be down to say good-night."

Laurie wondered what her father had said to her mother to keep her off Laurie's back. For once, it seemed, her mother had listened. Laurie closed her bedroom door and locked it. Then she picked up the phone. After five rings, Laurie assumed Pam was sleeping and hung up. Why else would she avoid answering? *Pam came through for me—otherwise, Mom would've gone berserk.*

In the adjoining bathroom, Laurie abandoned her wet clothes, turned on the shower and stared at her naked body in the large bathroom mirror while the water was warming up. She could smell Tobin all over her. The thought of him touching her made her shiver. She shrunk from the thought of washing him off, losing his scent. She wanted to keep him next to her through the night. In her dreams, she did.

Chapter 34

Pulling into the driveway the next day, Tobin caught a whiff of the lilacs. *What a switch from working with garbage.* Bushes of purple and white thrived in the back yard. He turned off the radio, cutting into a Bob Dylan song, climbed out of the truck, shoved his hands in his pockets and strolled toward the house, whistling.

Laurie had smelled like lavender. And she was warm, tender— open. He was crazy about her. She was everything he could possibly want. But did she really like him? Another of his fantasies? Laurie was sweet and caring. This was the kind of person he was looking for. *Why is it so hard for me to accept this—her? Am I not worthy?*

Hannah was at the kitchen table wolfing down an ice cream sandwich.

"Hey, you up for hitting a few balls?"

"I'd never get a turn. You never strike out," Hannah grumbled.

"You can be up first. What'd ya say?"

"It's so hot. You're not tired after working all day?"

"Nope. It's cooled down a lot. C'mon. Just for an hour."

"I guess."

"While you're getting the bucket and bats, I'll jump in the shower." Tobin turned and hurried down the hallway.

"What about your batting gloves?" Hannah called after him.

"They're in my top drawer."

At the school field where games had ended for the season, a father and his son were finishing up.

"Good job," the father praised, yanking the rim of his son's cap. The small, thin boy smiled. "Thanks, Dad." Tobin imagined the boy dreaming of playing with the Red Sox someday. Tobin had too, once. Not likely now. He had screwed up too much this year.

Hannah struck out right away. "You're up," she said, shuffling toward the mound.

"No. Not yet. You're going to make contact."

"That could take all night."

"I'm going to give you a slower ball. Keep your eye on it."

After a half dozen pitches, Hannah made a base hit. "Did you see that?" she said, excitedly.

"Yeah. Now run to first base before I tag you out."

"You didn't say anything about running. Besides, there's nobody to hit after me."

Tobin focused on the ball and swung. They watched the ball go high and far.

"I'm not going after it."

While she was warming up another pitch, Tobin asked her, "How can a guy tell if a girl really likes him?"

"I don't know. The way she looks at him. She wants to be with him all the time. Why?"

"Do you believe in love at first sight?"

"I suppose. Usually you like someone first. But not necessarily, I guess." She looked up at him. "Oh, I knew you weren't high on drugs. Who is it? Tell me."

"I'll do better than that. I'll bring her over to the house."

Hannah's brow lifted.

Tobin committed himself now. "Sometime this week."

"I'll bug the daylights out of you if you don't."

She will too, he thought. Then he made another homer.

"We're out of balls," Hannah said gratefully.

"The bucket's empty already?"

"You're the one who sent them flying. So you can help me find them."

While looking for the balls, Tobin replayed Hannah's thoughts on love. "The way she looks at you." *That look.* He'd seen it. He was certain. "She wants to be with you all the time." They had made plans to meet again at the pond. She wanted to see him again. That had to mean something.

In the dappled sunlight, Laurie's dear neighbor looked like some nursery queen, tending her already perfect yard. Butterflies flitted from rose to rose. *Charlotte, Charlotte quite contrary or more like Queen of Hearts off with your head.* Laurie backed her car out of the driveway and, halfheartedly, waved. Charlotte's gossipy pearly whites were shimmering. Troublemaker.

Arriving at Pam's, Laurie honked the horn. Usually, Pam would be scrambling out the door before Laurie was in the driveway. After a few minutes had passed and Pam still hadn't come out, Laurie decided to see what was taking her so long. Just as she reached the front step of the farmer's porch, flanked by geraniums, Mrs. Courtney appeared at the screened door.

"Hi, Laurie. I guess Pam forgot to tell you. She stayed at Sharon's last night. Sorry you had to go out of your way."

"Oh, it's okay, Mrs. Courtney. Thanks."

Laurie found it odd that Pam's mother would approve of a sleepover on a school night. She had always been very strict about things like that. She must have figured since it was nearing the end of the school year, not much was going on.

When Laurie pulled into Sharon's driveway, she got a whiff of fresh paint. A man on a ladder in painter's overalls and hat was priming the front of the house in a pale yellow. The Rodneys were particular about getting it painted every two years. Soon Pam came out of the house. Sharon followed behind, wrapping her long hair into a bun, her lips clenching bobby pins.

"We're going to be late," Laurie announced, with her head out the window.

"So, what's new," Sharon retorted, getting into the car. Then she pulled the seat forward so Pam could get into the back. Two minutes later they were on their way to school. At least this late in the year, it was unlikely they would end up with detention again.

"We tried calling you last night," Sharon said, sticking in the last pin.

"You did?" Laurie asked, keeping her eyes on the road. Pam knew better than to call her house.

"Yeah, your phone was busy—for over half an hour."

"Why'd you call? What was up?"

"A bunch of us went to the movies," Pam added.

Laurie knew that meant Pam and Sharon and the guys.

"Where were you?" Sharon asked.

Since when do I have to report in to you?

"Oh, I took a ride—on my bike."

Her friends said nothing for a minute. Then Pam asked, "When's the last time you rode that?"

"I don't know—before I got my license."

They stared at her.

"My ass is getting big," Laurie said. "Probably all the driving...."

"Isn't that something that happens after you have kids?" Pam remarked.

Pam was supposed to be on her side. Had she shot off her mouth? Unless Pam was just going along so Sharon wouldn't get suspicious. If Sharon had known about Laurie's little talk with Pam, she would never have let Laurie off the hook that easily.

Laurie wanted so much to tell her friends about Tobin, but how could she? They would never understand. They simply wouldn't get it.

"Sharon and I were talking it over last night, and we thought we'd wear something wild—the last day of school," Pam said excitedly.

"You game?" Sharon asked, looking at Laurie.

"Depends. What do you have in mind—miniskirts and halter tops?"

Sharon looked devilish. "Not quite."

"I'd like to dress up like a gypsy or a Woodstock hippie," Pam piped in.

"Groovy," Laurie said, making them laugh.

Sharon lifted her brows, widening her eyes. "I think we should dress up like first class whores."

Pam and Laurie gaped at her.

"Well, why not? It'd be fun," Sharon said with a smirk.

"Yeah, well, it would definitely cause commotion," Laurie said.

"So if it did? What are they going to do—throw us out the last day? Sharon grinned. "Unless Laurie, you'd rather we dress up like little Indians."

Laurie ignored the suggestion, hoping her anger wasn't showing. She was tired of her friend's mockery.

The girls ended up ten minutes late getting to school, but nobody seemed concerned. A few of the teachers even held classes outside so their students could enjoy the warm weather.

Yearbooks were handed out, and everybody was milling around comparing photos and quotations, writing farewell messages and wishing each other the best in life. Sharon and Pam had always given the impression they were better than most, so several of the classmates passed by them. Laurie had always been friendly, so she soon had a circle of peers around her wanting her signature, including a shy, lanky boy named Carl.

"I'd be happy to," Laurie said, "if you sign mine."

Carl beamed. Pam and Sharon stood off to the side, snickering. To them he was a nerd, but Laurie bet that one day he would be a rocket scientist or brain surgeon. Who would be pooh-poohing then? When she finished her so-longs with everyone, she looked around for Pam and Sharon. They were nowhere in sight. *Nice. It wouldn't kill them to be friendly once in a while. If they weren't so stuck up, they'd see there are magnificent people in this world.*

Chapter 35

"I hope I didn't forget anything," Eleanor mumbled. "The card, the flowers, the camera. The camera! Donald!"

"I have it right here," he said, holding it up.

Eleanor stopped to fix his crooked tie.

"Laurie, do you have your cap and gown?"

"Yes, Mom."

"Shouldn't you be wearing it?"

"I'll put it on when I get there."

"Where's my purse?" Eleanor asked.

"It's on your shoulder, Mom."

Eleanor shook her head. "Let me get a good look at you." Laurie turned to face her mother. "Doesn't she look stunning, Donald?"

Laurie wore a lilac dress with petite white flowers on the midriff and three quarter length sleeves. She had dabbed pink blush over her high cheekbones and highlighted her lips in pink. Her hair hung shining and straight, the front pulled back in a pearled barrette.

"Yes, my little girl's all grown up."

Laurie had never seen her father so close to tears.

"Well, I guess we're all set," Eleanor said. "We want to get there early to sit up front—so we can take some good pictures."

"Darn. What I'd do with the keys?" her father murmured, fishing in the pockets of his navy blue suit.

"Donald, where did you put them? We can't be late."

"Mom, we've got plenty of time. We still have an hour. Besides, I'm sure the Rodneys will save you a seat."

"If they can, honey. There'll be a lot of people—you have a big class."

Donald grinned. "Just joshing. No need to worry," he said, jingling the keys in front of them.

"Oh, Dad."

"This isn't the time to be playing games, Donald," Eleanor said.

"Just trying to ease the tension, dear."

Eleanor rolled her eyes.

Programs were passed out. The 349 graduating students were listed alphabetically, with honor students like Laurie having asterisks by their names. Hearing her name called, Laurie rose from her chair. On her way to the platform, she saw her parents' smiles and glowing eyes. It was the happiest she had seen them look in a long time. Before returning to her seat, she glanced toward the parking lot. And when she did, there he was, standing there, beside his truck. She lifted her head higher, grinning.

After the last cheers and applause had faded, Laurie found her parents talking to the Rodneys, who had invited them all over to their house for a small party. Eleanor said to Laurie, "Before you go off to take pictures with your friends, let me get one of you and your father."

"Mom, Dad—I'll be right back. I have to see someone," Laurie said, rushing off.

Eleanor looked at Donald. "What did I just say?"

Donald shrugged, his arms lifted, palms upright.

When Laurie reached the parking lot, Tobin was gone. She looked around for his truck, but it was nowhere in sight. She would just have to thank him later. As Laurie headed back to meet her parents, a girl named Rita she had befriended when she first entered Falmouth High raced by her. "Congratulations, Laurie."

"Thanks. You, too."

Laurie knew it would be scary leaving home for the first time, but after everything she had been through with her mother in the past months, she was glad to be going off on her own. Heading back up the cement walkway toward the school, Laurie heard a whistle. Looking to her left, Tobin was leaning against a big elm. She hurried over to him.

"You look great," he said. "Congratulations."

She smiled. "Thanks. I'm really glad you came."

Grabbing hold of both her hands, he said, "I wouldn't have missed it."

Laurie kissed him. "I have to get back. My parents are waiting to take pictures."

"You go. I'll catch you later."

Donald placed his arm around his daughter's waist, and they smiled for the camera. "Now, how about one of you and your mother together?"

"Come on, Mom." Eleanor went and stood beside Laurie.

After her father snapped the shot, Laurie saw Brian headed their way. She turned her head, hoping he would walk on by.

"We made it!" Brian said when she turned back.

"Yeah, we did," Laurie said.

"I can't believe it. It seemed like we waited so long, and now here we are."

Laurie knew Brian would follow in his father's footsteps. He would go to college first then jump right into banking. He had talked about it many times with her, although, she had the impression it really wasn't what he wanted to do. It was the pressure he felt from his parents.

"Hello, Mr. and Mrs. Matthews."

"Hello, Brian. Don't you look nice," Eleanor said, eyeing him in his khaki pants, light blue shirt and navy tie. "Congratulations."

"Yes, congratulations," Donald repeated, shaking Brian's hand. "I bet you're glad you've finally gotten through."

"Yes, sir, I sure am. It's great. Here, Mr. Matthews, hand me the camera," Brian insisted, "let me get the family portrait."

"Oh, I was just wondering who we could ask. Thank you, Brian," Eleanor said with a smile.

Laurie was relieved her mother hadn't suggested that the two of them have their picture taken together. She was sure it was hanging on the edge of her mother's tongue.

"Okay. Everybody together—say cheese." The camera clicked. "One more time to be sure." Brian snapped the camera again and gave it back to Mr. Matthews.

"Thanks, Brian. Congratulations again," Donald said.

Heading away, Brian turned slightly, "See ya later, Laurie."

Laurie wondered if that was a general statement or if he meant at the graduation party. She was hoping there would be enough people there that they could avoid bumping into each other.

Mrs. Rodney had done most of the cooking herself the night before, but still she hired a caterer to help. And as always, the food was superb. For starters: caviar and shrimp cocktail, luscious strawberries, red and green grapes and a variety of cheeses elegantly displayed on Mrs. Rodney's best china and silver. Despite a beautiful three-layered torte that resembled a wedding cake, it was a blonde brownie Laurie carried to the patio. She opted for the wicker chaise lounge next to her mother. Her father had joined the men in a game of croquet.

"She always puts on a nice spread," Karin Courtney commented.

"Doesn't she, though," Eleanor agreed.

"So, what're your plans, Laurie? I know you've had a few options. Still going to Mount Ida?" Mrs. Courtney asked.

"No, I've decided on UMass." Laurie had told her father after the trial but hadn't said anything to her mother until later. As expected, Eleanor didn't take it well, but said little. Probably hoping it was a whim, and Laurie would change her mind.

"Do you still want to be a lawyer? God knows you've got the brains."

"Eventually. I've been thinking about studying anthropology."

"Anthropology? Oh, that's nice," Mrs. Courtney said uncertainly.

Eleanor feigned a smile. "Well, you know how kids are. One day they're going here—the next day they're going somewhere else."

"It seemed like yesterday, Eleanor, they were starting high school. It's hard to believe four years have passed. Where did the time go?"

"Boy, I don't know," Eleanor said, shaking her head. "It does fly, doesn't it?"

"They're getting older—we're getting older," Karin emphasized.

"*Shh.* Don't say that too loudly," Stephanie Rodney said, when she wandered past, carrying a tray of scallops wrapped in bacon.

Graduating from high school was a big step. Seeing how emotional her mother was now, Laurie wondered what she would be like whenever she married. Laurie would be leaving soon, and even though she would be home summers, at least until she finished college, her parents were having a hard time accepting the whole thing, especially her mother. Laurie was beginning to understand it was not only her life that would change.

After the girls had slipped out of their dress clothes into jeans and tank tops, Laurie heard Sharon say to Pam, "Let's get out of here." Then Sharon looked at Laurie. "You ready?"

Laurie nodded. "Yup.*" Why wouldn't I be?* "Mom, we're leaving."

"Where did you say you were going?"

"The beach." Laurie left out which one. The parents had to know there would be drinking, but if Sharon's and Pam's parents approved then her mother and father would consent, too. The girls had always been sensible and their parents knew that and trusted them.

Pam and Sharon nodded.

"You girls have a good time," Donald said, from across the room.

"There are a lot of parties going on. Be careful," Eleanor stated.

"We will, Mrs. Matthews," Sharon responded.

The gang was headed to New Seabury to celebrate with other classmates. Sharon and Pam expected Laurie to go, and she wanted to. In fact, she looked forward to it. Besides, it would probably be the last time she would see many of them. She only wished Tobin could have joined them. He was going to a baseball game, though, with his father and sister. Laurie figured if she became too bored, she would wait until her friends were smashed and slip away to be with him.

The bonfire was huge. Kids were blackening hot dogs and toasting marshmallows on long sticks. Beach chairs and towels were spread across the sand. Laurie chatted with a few people, grabbed a beer from one of the coolers and plopped down next to Sharon and Pam. Soon the night turned chilly enough for the windbreaker she brought along.

One couple who had gone swimming in their clothes had now stripped and wrapped themselves in a blanket. A few walked the flats at low tide, carrying flashlights. Every now and then Laurie caught a whiff of pot, but the majority of them stuck to booze.

"Laurie, why don't you go make out with Brian?" Sharon suggested.

"Why would I do that?"

"I don't know. Maybe you'd warm up, have a little fun."

"I'm having fun."

"Yeah, looks like it. You're not with anyone."

"Why do I have to be with anyone? There are other ways to have a good time."

"Yeah, but you're not even drinking," Sharon noted.

"I'm drinking. See?" Laurie said, holding up her Bud.

"Barely. You've had that same beer for almost an hour."

"So what if I have—is that a problem?" *What—are they keeping track?*

Laurie's friends probably thought if she became drunk, vulnerability would kick in, and she would find Brian attractive. Not a chance.

"No. But ever since you and Brian broke up, I don't know—you've changed somehow."

First of all, there was no break-up because there was never an 'us' to begin with. "Changed?"

"Yeah. You've been acting weird. Like you're hiding something."

"Hiding something? Like what?"

"I don't know. I can't explain it. You make excuses—you don't want to do anything anymore."

"That's not entirely true. I do things with you—went on the buggy ride with you guys. But I'm not going to pretend something's there with Brian when there isn't, just so we can all hang out together. It's not right. Why would you want a fifth wheel hanging around, anyway? Think about it."

They were quiet for a minute. "Yeah, I guess you're right," Pam concluded.

Those who had been partying most of the afternoon and through the evening were now trying to sober up before going home. Surprisingly, the police never patrolled the area, yet they had to know about the graduation party. The cops always seemed to find out about these things before they even happened. But then again there were several gatherings that night, and maybe there were more important complaints.

Laurie gulped down the last swig of beer and walked over to one of the coolers. "What's your name?" a small kid named Tommy asked Laurie when he saw her standing there after grabbing a bottle of beer himself.

Before she could answer him, he began singing. "Is it Mary or Sue?"

"Her name is Laurie. What's it to ya?" Brian asked, stepping in.

"Everything's cool, man," Tommy said, his hands up in a surrendering pose. He probably knew how crazy Brian was; the brawl at school was big talk for a long time.

"Brian, I could have handled it," Laurie said.

"You don't know guys very well, do you? He was putting the moves on you."

"I don't think so. But even if he was—that's my business. I can take care of myself."

"This pig is trying to pick you up. I'm telling you. And I hear he likes to use women. Abuse them. Do bad things to them. Do you know what I mean?"

I think you like to make things up. "He's so drunk I don't think he even knows what he's saying."

"He knows. And he knows a good-looking chick when he sees one."

"Whatever."

Laurie had to be careful what she said to Brian. Evidently her message to him hadn't penetrated and the alcohol only added more confusion. When he bent over and tried to give her a kiss, she turned her head.

"Why'd you do that?" Brian asked.

"You agreed we can be friends. And that's all it can be. It's been a long time now—why can't you accept that?"

She had never given him any hope that they would ever be together, but she wondered if her friends had. Laurie figured they told Brian she would come around sooner or later, especially since they hadn't seen her with anyone else.

"I thought maybe things had changed."

"Well, I'm sorry, but they haven't. Not for me anyway."

"Bitch," he murmured.

"What did you call me?"

"Forget it."

"No. I won't forget it. And don't you ever call me that again. You just want what you want. And if you don't get it, you act like a jerk. I never led you on. Never made you believe we had a chance. So I don't know what your problem is."

"You flirted with me. You were a tease."

"That's so untrue—and you know it."

"I heard you wanted me."

"I never even hinted that. I don't know where you're getting your information, but it's wrong."

Brian walked away and wasted no time finding someone to make out with. When her friends also disappeared behind the dunes, she made her escape.

Chapter 36

It was a beautiful Saturday afternoon. The sun was bright with only a few stationary cumulus clouds. The temperature had reached the high seventies, but there was none of that awful humidity. In the beginning, she had only seen Tobin at night, but now he was filling her afternoons and weekends, too. He worked half-days on Saturdays, but they made a habit of seeing each other afterward. At the pond, when she parked beside him, she knew something was up as soon as she saw his face.

"Get in," Tobin insisted.

"Get in?" Laurie asked. Every day with him was an adventure, and she never knew what to expect next.

He smiled. "You heard me."

Brownie moved over and she hopped in, shutting the door. She patted Brownie, looking him in the eyes. "How you doing today, boy?" Brownie licked her face. She kissed him back. Then she looked at Tobin. "Okay, what's up? Where are we going this time?"

He said not a word until they were down the road a bit. "I don't live far from here."

She looked at him. "You're not thinking. . . ?"

"Exactly. I want you to meet my family."

"For real?"

He nodded. "For real."

"Are you sure this is a good idea? I mean. . . ."

"Yeah, why not?"

Laurie shrugged. *I'm a white girl.* "I don't know."

"You'll like my folks. They're cool."

Laurie felt bad. She had never suggested he meet her family. Her dad would be gracious, but she knew her mom would be reluctant to welcome him. In times like this, she wished she had a sister. Someone she was sure would like Tobin. He was sweet and kind, passionate and exciting. He cared about people, animals—the land. What was not to like about him?

Laurie ran a brush through her hair and clipped it back with a large barrette. Was she presentable? They would be at his house in a matter of minutes. "Do I look all right?"

"You look fantastic."

"You're just saying that."

"I don't say things I don't mean."

Laurie knew that. That's the kind of guy he was—honest, sincere—another great asset that made her like him more. Tobin slowed before a house with a 'For Sale' sign in front of it.

"My Uncle Basil lived there," he said pointing.

"Oh," was all that she could say, seeing the sadness in his eyes. He had told her he spent a lot of time there and how much his uncle had meant to him.

"And this is where I live," he said a minute later, entering a shelled driveway. Laurie saw there was no real landscaping in front of his house, although a beautiful red cedar tree was centered round some azalea bushes. Pine needles carpeted the yard.

"You have a lot of land," Laurie said, noticing no other houses nearby.

"That we do. Nice and private."

His mother opened the door to let them in when she saw them coming. Inside, everything was neat and clean, not showroom perfect like her house, but Laurie immediately felt comfortable there.

"Mom, this is Laurie. The girl I've been telling you about."

"Hello," Myra said nodding, with a big smile.

"Nice to meet you, Mrs. Horvarth."

She nodded. "Something to drink, maybe soda—ice tea?"

"I'm fine. Thank you."

"Isn't she everything I told you she was," Mother?" Tobin blurted.

"Yes," Myra said, nodding again.

Laurie rarely got embarrassed, but her face was heating up. She was glad when Tobin changed the subject to ask where his father and sister were.

"Your father's at a meeting, but Hannah's here. I'll get her," she said, turning to leave.

Laurie waited until his mother disappeared, then she yanked on Tobin's arm. "What did you tell your mother about me?"

"That you were smart—funny—beautiful."

She shook her head.

"Well, you are, you know."

Coming down the small hallway toward the kitchen, Hannah was smiling impishly. Colorful glass beads sparkled around her neck and wrists. Her braided hair circled her head. She was much shorter than her brother and didn't have the high cheekbones he had, but she owned two adorable dimples. The long T-shirt over her cut-off jeans was too large for her; Laurie presumed it belonged to Tobin.

"Hi, Hannah. So, he's your brother, huh?"

Hannah crunched up her nose.

"Oh, really?"

"No. He's okay. I wouldn't trade him."

Tobin stared at them. "Well, that's good to know. You two know each other?"

"Sort of. Everybody knows who Laurie is," Hannah answered.

Laurie looked puzzled. "They do?"

"You're popular. And you're nice, too."

"Gee, thanks. I try." Laurie realized that Tobin was staring at her. *Proud to have her as his*. Laurie only wished Sharon and Pam were nice, too, remembering that awful time at the mall when she had to shove them in a photo booth to keep them from being mean to Hannah and her friends.

"I saw you help Kerry."

Laurie shook her head. "It was nothing."

There was a quiet moment. Then Hannah spoke again. "You're not like them."

Laurie knew who Hannah was referring to. Laurie wished she could defend her friends, but there was nothing to defend.

Tobin intervened. "We've got to go. I'm going to show Laurie around," he said, leading her away.

"Nice to see you again, Hannah," Laurie said, turning.

"Yeah, you too."

Laurie caught his sister giving her brother an approving smile as she stopped to look at a dream catcher hanging on the wall. Tobin gave Laurie a quick peek in each room, showing his quarters last.

"Are you going somewhere?" Laurie asked quietly, noticing the packed bags in his room.

"Yeah, I am. Remember I told you I was saving to go to Wyoming?"

She looked mystified. "I guess I forgot."

"My Uncle Basil and I had this trip planned for a long time. It was his dream to see the Big Medicine Wheel. I didn't want to go without him. Before he died—he made me promise I would."

"I didn't realize you were leaving so soon."

"Yeah. It seemed like ages ago when we planned this. I can't believe it's actually nearing the time to go now."

He led her out the door to the back of the house where they sat in a woven hammock, swinging it back and forth with their feet.

"What were you and my sister talking about? Kerry who?"

"Oh, Kerry Johnson. Rob Killroy tripped him in the cafeteria. He had a tray of food."

"And you came to his rescue?" Tobin asked.

Laurie shrugged, remembering how her friends had stared at her in disbelief—that it was wrong of her to want to do a good thing. "I just helped him clean up the mess. No big deal." She quickly changed the subject. "I like your sister."

"Yeah, she's a good kid."

"Does she rat on her big brother?"

"She wouldn't dare."

Laurie smiled. "You really don't know women, do you?" Then she turned serious. "You have a really nice family, Tobin."

"Thanks. I'm sure you do, too."

"I think you'd like my dad. He's pretty cool. Awesome, actually."

"Are you anything like him?" he asked.

"I think so."

"Then you're probably right. I'm sure I'd get along with him just fine."

She never mentioned her mother, and he didn't ask.

"What's that old building over there?" Laurie asked, pointing.

"That's a chicken coop. At least it was. We don't have any chickens anymore. We used to sell eggs," Tobin said, as they walked toward the dilapidated structure. "I'd take you in, but there's not much to see."

"Take me in anyway; I've never seen one."

"Okay. You asked for it."

"I like the smell," she said looking around, sniffing. "I know it sounds strange, but I do. I don't know why. It's familiar."

"You've smelled it before?"

Laurie nodded. "Yeah. I guess."

Suddenly, an odd looking thing with two legs ran across the slanted planks, between them, making her jump back two feet, falling into hay. Laurie knew what she saw was neither a chicken or a rooster or any animal she knew of. "Oh, my God! What's that?"

He chuckled, extending his hand. She grabbed hold, and he pulled her up.

"Meet Lily. Lily, meet Laurie."

"Lily?" She managed a smile. "What is she?"

"She's a guinea hen. She's the only one we have left. At one time, we had thirty of them."

"Thirty?"

He nodded.

"What happened to them?"

"Fox got several. Some got run over. Others ended up as dinner."

She made a face. "People actually eat them?"

"Why not? If you can handle the gamey taste, it's pretty good."

She shuddered. "You've eaten one?"

"Yeah, once or twice, but I don't particularly care for it."

"What do you feed her?"

"Cracked corn, mainly. She likes birdseed, too. And she loves bugs."

Laurie cringed. "Bugs?"

"Yeah, you know—beetles, spiders. Flies. At least with her being around, we don't have to worry about insects in the summertime."

"She eats bugs, and then you kill her and eat her?"

"Nah, we're not going to kill her, she's like part of the family now—she's been around so long. I think I was thirteen, almost fourteen, when we got Lily."

Laurie calculated quickly. "Wow! That's almost seven years ago. That's a long time."

He gave a quick smile. "Yeah. I guess it is."

After the grand tour, he walked her out into the fresh air and took her hands in his, pulling her close to him. He gently circled her face and lips with his finger. His soft touch made her shiver with desire. He kissed her softy. He was reaching a place deep inside her.

Chapter 37

Driving onto her street, Laurie saw the mailman coming down the sidewalk. Pulling up beside him, she reached her arm out of the car window. "I'll take our mail, Mr. Kingsley."

He handed her a small stack. "You have a nice day, Miss Matthews."

"You, too. Thank you."

When Laurie looked down at the mail on her lap, an odd-shaped parcel stuck out. Extracting it, she saw it was addressed to her. The handwriting was not anyone's she recognized. Glancing to the left hand corner, she saw it came from some place in Czechoslovakia. Who had she met from there and when? The only pen pal she ever had was from Argentina, arranged through the school, but that was years before, when she was ten.

When she opened the bulky envelope, it dawned on her. Excited, she took out the photographs, holding them carefully so she wouldn't smudge them. They were from the lady at the tower. How handsome Tobin looked next to her. The two of them looked like movie stars. She looked in the big envelope again and found a note.

Nice pictures. Hope you like them. You two are beautiful people. Eye-catcher for sure. Enjoy.

Fondly, Mrs. Klaus.

Laurie had jotted down her name and address for the lady that day, but then she forgot about it. It was Tobin she was thinking about. It was their first time together—and in spite of how nervous she was beforehand, not knowing how it would turn out, she had the best time with him. It was the beginning of a beautiful connection. The pictures reflected that.

Inside the house all was quiet. Her mother was still at work. Tuesdays were long days for her. Usually, Eleanor worked half-days, but twice a week, she would put in a full eight hours. Laurie sat at the kitchen table and began laying the pictures across the yellow tablecloth, looking at them over and over again, trying to decide which one she liked best. One in particular caught her eye. Both of them were smiling, and she was leaning against him, his arm around her. He stood erect and solid. His strong face was not only handsome, but he looked heroic. His long, smooth, jet-black hair entwined with her platinum waves. She loved the contrast between them. Eye-catcher. She liked that.

Laurie wanted to show off the photographs, but it would have to be at another time. Seeing some pretty pink stationery her mother had left on the counter, Laurie snatched a couple of sheets, plopped in a chair at the kitchen table and began writing Mrs. Klaus a letter, thanking her. Suddenly, it seemed easier expressing how she felt about Tobin to a stranger than to the people she was supposed to be closest to.

Dear Mrs. Klaus,

I am writing to you to thank you for the pictures of Tobin and me. And yes I do like them very much. They are just beautiful. He is such a wonderful guy. I have never met anyone like him. He's a good person, so kind and gentle. And yes, we do look good together. I wish. . .

Suddenly, the doorbell rang, interrupting her train of thought. Reluctantly, Laurie turned the stationery over and quickly gathered the pictures into a pile. Opening the door, holding it only slightly ajar, she said to her neighbor, "Hello, Mrs. Dunbar. Mother's at work."

"Oh, I know that, dear," Charlotte said, looking past her, her eyes roaming. "I left my planting gloves on the counter. Oh, there they are," she said, trotting past Laurie, practically pushing her out of the way.

Astounded and annoyed at the same time, Laurie followed Charlotte over to the counter, willing her not to notice the unfinished letter.

"You look a little pale, dear. Are you feeling okay?"

That stare of hers sent chills down Laurie. "I'm fine," she said, starting to escort Charlotte out. "I'll tell my mother you stopped by."

At that moment, the phone rang. They stood there looking at each other.

"Aren't you going to get that?"

Laurie looked at the phone, then back. "Yes, of course," she said, grabbing it, keeping one eye on Charlotte. Laurie was afraid she would see the pictures.

"No, this is not Mrs. Matthews—this is her daughter. She's not here right now—I'll have her call you back. Who is this, please?"

The woman on the phone began rattling her name and number. "Just a moment," Laurie interrupted, "let me find something to write with."

Charlotte handed her a pen. Laurie stared at it for a moment, then took it from her. "Go ahead." After Laurie bent down to scribble the caller's name and number, the woman thanked her and hung up.

After putting the phone in its cradle, Laurie turned to Mrs. Dunbar. "Thank you."

Charlotte nodded. "I see you coming and going all the time. You're a busy young lady. I suppose you'll be off to college soon."

"Yes, I will," Laurie said, keeping her responses short as she walked her unwelcome guest to the door. "It was nice seeing you again," Laurie added grudgingly.

"Oh, here comes your mother now," Charlotte said shrilly, spotting Eleanor through the windowpanes, pulling into the driveway.

Thank goodness, Laurie thought.

"I'll see you later, dear."

As soon as Charlotte stepped outside, Laurie ran over to the table to gather up the pictures and her letter, stuffing them into her pocketbook while keeping a watch on the door. There was something about Charlotte that gave Laurie the creeps. She always seemed to be around when she was least wanted.

Taking a couple of deep breaths, Laurie moved back to the counter, lifted the Tupperware cover and cut herself a large piece of chocolate cake. While she was grabbing a glass from the cabinet, her mother writhed through the door carrying a bag of groceries. For once there was no Charlotte trailing behind.

Laurie opened the refrigerator and looked in. "Mom. . . ."

"Yes, I bought some milk," Eleanor said.

"Oh, good. What's chocolate cake or chocolate anything without it?"

"Would you mind cutting me a slice?" Eleanor asked.

"Not at all. How big?"

"Just a sliver. I'm watching my waistline. When you get this age, every pound matters."

"I think you look great."

Laurie thought her mother had a great figure for a woman who had hit forty the year before. And today, she looked especially pretty and slender in her teal green suit, pearls and pageboy haircut, not a single strand out of place.

"Thank you, honey. I'm sorry about the other night. I said things. . . ." she said, shaking her head.

"It's okay."

"No, it's not. I should never have spoken to you like that. I was wrong. I hope you can forgive me?"

"Of course," Laurie said, shoveling cake into her mouth and then gulping down the last of the milk.

"I didn't want to say anything in front of your father this morning. I think I understand why you're doing this." She studied Laurie for a moment. "You have a big heart, Laurie. I know how much you care about people. I think you're feeling sorry for that boy because of what's happened to them. And I understand how you feel."

"Actually, I don't think you do. I like him, Mom. I like him a lot. He's really nice."

Eleanor's mouth tightened. "You know how I feel. You're doing this to spite me."

"No. This has nothing to do with you." "Then maybe it's for attention."

"Well, Mother, you seem to have all the answers. You figure it out," Laurie said flatly, rising.

"I don't appreciate the way you're talking to me."

Laurie walked over to the sink. "And I don't appreciate some of your comments either," she said, scraping the rest of the cake down the disposal. She was tired of her mother continually ruining her appetite—and her life. But Laurie knew it was just the start of what it was going to be like if she stayed with Tobin.

Chapter 38

Halfway down the pathway to John's Pond, Laurie made Tobin stop near an old picnic table. "Let's sit here a minute. I have something I want to show you."

Tobin took a seat on the bench, and she plopped beside him, swinging her pocketbook off her shoulder. Then she unzipped a pouch inside, pulling out the envelope. He looked on curiously.

"Remember when you took me to Scargo Tower?"

He nodded. "Yeah. How can I forget? That was like our first date," he said.

"You remember the couple that pulled up in the Honda?"

"Yeah," he said vaguely.

"The sweet little lady with the fancy camera?"

"Oh, right," he said. "She had a thirty-five millimeter."

"She sent me the pictures she took of us," Laurie said, handing him the envelope. "I think you're going to like them. They came out really nice." She watched him study each photograph. "I'd like to have that one blown up. It's my favorite."

He brushed a few leaves from the table, placing the picture she liked down on it and continued to look at the rest. "I like this one," he said, showing her another.

"But your eyes are closed. See?" she pointed out.

"That's because your hair was blowing in my face."

She flashed him a pouty look. "Sorry. It was windy up there."

"But that's what I love about it. Your hair—you brushing against me. It was great."

"Really?"

He smiled. "Yes. Really."

She watched as he continued studying each one.

"These *are* great. Do we get to share them?"

"Yes, absolutely. There's double prints."

"Oh, maybe you're right," he said, scanning them.

"Wait a minute—some are missing," Laurie stated.

"Are you sure?"

"Yes, I'm sure," she said, grabbing them. "I counted them. And look, there should be two of these, and there's only one. And the same with this one."

Searching frantically, she dumped everything out of her pocketbook. It was never out of her sight. When did her mother get the chance to take them?

Laurie's eyes filled up with tears. "I can't believe her."

"Who?"

"My mother. Who else? Who else could have?" Suddenly, she grew quiet. She had put the pictures in a pile on the table before letting Mrs. Dunbar in.

"You may have just misplaced them."

"No. No," she said, shaking her head. "Mrs. Dunbar stole them. She has no right!"

"Mrs. Dunbar?" Tobin looked confused. "You just said your mother took them."

"That's what I thought, but Mrs. Dunbar—our neighbor—came by when I was looking at them. I had them on the kitchen table. The phone rang. She probably wanted to show my mother."

"They're only pictures. We can take more." Tobin tried comforting her. "Don't get yourself so upset. There's others here. Besides, I'd rather look at you in person."

She managed a small smile. "You don't understand. If my mother sees them, she'll. . . ." He had no idea what she had been through with her mother since the beginning of the trial. And now her mother's disapproval with her new interest in Tobin—and all the lying she was doing to be with him. But she could never tell him that.

"She'll what? Ground you?"

With her hand in his, they walked farther along the green trail, to their own private refuge at the pond. With every step, Laurie drew deep breaths of damp pine. The sun was setting. After a hot, humid afternoon, the light wind and soft lapping of water were refreshing.

Later, they perched high on a bough of an old oak, letting their feet dangle. Bushy-tailed squirrels raced up and down trees, birds chirped in the branches. Peepers sang and a frog jumped off a lily pad. A duck glided across the pond followed by young ones. Laurie imagined she was on a deserted island with him, somewhere far away. They had no boat and no one was coming to rescue them.

"Tobin," she said, with her arm locked into his, "I had this dream."

"What about?"

"These two people. A really pretty woman with very fair skin and a dark man—very handsome, with her."

"Sounds like you and me," he said, smiling.

"Yeah, but see, I had this dream—the same one—before I met you. More than once actually, but not lately—until last night. Sometimes, they have this little girl with them. She has long wavy curls. Her hair's blonde, real blonde. And she's got the cutest smile with these little baby teeth. She's so adorable."

"I wonder if. . . ." Tobin paused.

"If what?" Laurie asked.

"Could the little girl be you?"

"I thought about that. Maybe it is. But then, who are the man and woman? That's what I can't figure out."

"Don't fight your visions. One day it will all come together and make perfect sense."

"Sometimes this family's in a park. It looks like a park anyway. A beautiful place with flower gardens and benches. In the center there's a waterfall with a statue. And the way the sun shines through the overlapping trees—it's heavenly. Once I even saw the three of them in a canoe paddling down a river. And they're always very happy. At least that's how I see them. They're smiling and their eyes sparkle. I don't hear words though. . . ."

He turned and looked at her. "What do you mean—you don't hear words?"

"You know, conversations. Maybe I could get a better feel of who they are if I heard their voices. I don't know, maybe they're from a past life. I've never seen them before. I'd remember if I did. Wouldn't I?"

"Maybe you're a fortune teller and you can see the future. Maybe the little girl is yours."

"But I'm too young for kids," she said.

"Oh, I agree with you there—I'm not ready for kids either. But maybe it's us down the road. When we're older. When we're both through college and working."

Was that a proposal? He would be the perfect guy, but she still had too much to accomplish and so did he. Even so, it was a wonderful dream.

A moment later, he turned and kissed her cheek so gently and tenderly, it stirred every part of her. "You make me dizzy."

He smiled. "That's how I feel when I'm around you—dizzy—all the time. Maybe we should get down, it's late."

"It is," she agreed, glancing at her watch. Time seemed to jet when she was with him.

They climbed down to the lowest branch and jumped, then walked to their vehicles. Opening the door for her, Tobin kissed her goodnight, waited until she got in, then moved toward his truck. She waited until he was behind her before taking off. A half mile up the road Tobin turned left, hitting his horn. She beeped back.

A future with Tobin. Marriage and babies sounded a little scary. But she knew they could be exciting, too, especially with someone you truly cared about. Suddenly, trailing high beams disturbed her daydreams—and her vision. She adjusted the rear view mirror, but the glare was still annoying. She drove a little faster to escape the bright lights. But the car stayed behind her. *If he gets any closer, I'll give him a piggy back ride.* She quickly pulled off the road into a random driveway. Hurling herself around, she watched the car that had been following her crawl past. When an outside light flicked on, she backed out into the road and zoomed home.

Once she was safe inside, she found herself peering out the window every time she heard a motor or saw headlights. Who was following her? She had a right to do what she pleased. It was no one else's business.

Chapter 39

When Sharon called the following day and asked Laurie to meet Pam and her at the beach right away, she figured something was up. What was so urgent? She tried to get Sharon to tell her over the phone, but Sharon quickly hung up.

"I guess I'll see you at the beach," Laurie was left saying to a dial tone.

When Laurie stepped outside to get in her car, she spotted something scrawled across the pollen on the hood. "Indian Lover." She turned off the lawn sprinkler, detached the hose, then blasted water down the windshield and over the hood. There were more words on the trunk. "Watch your back." She cleaned off the rest of the car before Mrs. Dunbar popped over and saw it. She wondered if her parents had noticed it.

Who had done this? The person who followed her the night before?

She knew it could have been anyone, but she was leaning more toward Rob, remembering the names he had called her that horrible day in the cafeteria.

Laurie waited until Sharon shut off the engine of her blue '71 Malibu before getting out of her car and walking over to them. Standing around, Laurie asked, "So what's up? You didn't get me down here to look at the sunset."

After Sharon sucked in a couple drags from her Marlboro, she threw it on the pavement, snuffed it out with her foot and said what was on her mind. "We've covered your ass long enough."

"Yeah, we have. We want to know—what are you up to?" Pam added.

"What am I up to?" Laurie repeated.

"You don't have to play dumb with us. Who is he? Is he married or something?" Sharon asked.

Laurie wondered if *they* had been the ones on her tail last night.

She knew she couldn't hide this relationship forever. "No."

"So you *are* seeing someone," Pam responded, looking satisfied.

"If he's not married—why the secrecy?" Sharon asked.

"Maybe he's famous!"

"In her dreams," Sharon retorted.

Laurie was put on the spot. Even if she said nothing, they would find out eventually. Unless, they already knew and were waiting to hear it from her. Telling them about Tobin was the easy part. Trying to convince them that he was a terrific guy, the best ever, was going to be one of the hardest things she would ever have to do.

"C'mon, who is it? You know we're going to find out. So, you might as well tell us," Sharon demanded, her hands on her hips.

Their expectant faces nearly made Laurie burst. "Oh, all right. If you really must know—I'm seeing Tobin Horvarth," she revealed, letting out a long whistling sigh.

"You're *what?*" Sharon nearly screamed, gaping at her. Her dramatics would ordinarily have made Laurie laugh, but this time she felt sick inside.

"You heard me. I'm dating Tobin."

"Are you nuts? A freaking Indian. Have you lost your mind?"

I'm glad you're happy for me, best friends. "Maybe I have," Laurie shot back, "In thinking you'd understand!"

"You doing it with him?" Pam asked.

Laurie ignored her. Big mistake.

"Oh my God, she is! She's screwing him," Sharon shrieked.

"I think I'm going to puke," Pam said.

"You better pray Brian doesn't find out," Sharon warned.

"Why should Brian give a damn? We never had anything between us really. It's none of his business what I do," Laurie said, remembering her anger at being followed home.

Sharon and Pam looked at each other.

"You're not going to say anything to the guys. Are you? Laurie implored.

They laughed. "Why would we do something like that?" Sharon asked.

"I just don't want any trouble. You know how they can get."

"Let me talk to Pam a minute." They walked a few feet away so that Laurie couldn't hear. Two minutes later they strode back. "Okay," Sharon said.

Laurie frowned. "Okay what?"

"We won't say anything. But we can't guarantee someone else won't."

"Who else knows?" Laurie asked, thinking about the ugly words written on her car.

Sharon nudged Pam. "Let's get out of here."

"See you later, Laurie," Pam said.

Yeah, see ya around.

Laurie watched them get in the Malibu and drive away.

Laurie's anger turned to tears and she cried into her pillow. *How can they say they're my friends? Real friends wouldn't do this.* An hour later, she sat up. Looking around her room, Laurie saw the blue photo album in the open closet. She rolled off the bed and took it off the shelf. Sitting back down, she flipped through the pages, stopping at a snapshot of her with Sharon and Pam, kneeling on a lush green lawn under the big cherry tree in the front of her house, their arms around each other. The beginning of spring: daffodils, lilac and white crocus had all sprung. She remembered the day vividly. They made a pledge they would be friends forever—no matter what. She lay there staring at the three of them, remembering the good times, wishing things were different. If Sharon and Pam couldn't be happy for her, then she didn't want to be around them.

She decided to take a long bath and forget about it. Soaking in the tub, she closed her eyes, freeing her mind of everything. Then she showered, washing her hair. Tobin was always telling her how much he loved her hair. And she loved the way he nuzzled his face into it.

Tobin had tried to discourage her from coming to the pond so often. He was afraid she would get into trouble, but her mind was made up. Summer was short. He would be going back to New Hampshire, and she would be leaving for school in Boston the third week of August. Already, she couldn't stand the thought of not being able to see him every day.

When Laurie left the bathroom, still wrapped in a towel, her phone rang. She couldn't imagine who would be calling so late, unless it was Tobin canceling their evening together. She hoped not. She was looking forward to being with him, especially since the scene with Sharon and Pam. Reluctantly, she picked up the receiver, her heart pounding.

"Yes, this is Laurie. Who's this?"

"This is Rita Sherwood. Do you remember me?"

"Yes, Rita, of course I remember you."

Rita had befriended Laurie when she first moved there. They played tennis together and were both in the drama club at school. Laurie had always liked Rita. She was a sweet girl, attractive and all, but very shy. Laurie had hard time getting Rita to open up, but when she did, she found her to be witty and smart. Rita exhibited a lot of common sense, unlike many kids their age. Pam and Sharon, however, found Rita too much of a "good girl" to include her in their little group. Maybe Rita was just too smart for them. Laurie saw less and less of her. The year before, Rita had been in two of her classes, English and biology, but this year she wasn't in any.

"How've you been?" Laurie asked.

"Fine, thanks. We moved to Connecticut for a while. My father's job didn't work out, so we came back."

"Oh. That's why I haven't seen you around."

There was a pause and Laurie wondered why Rita was calling.

"I probably shouldn't be butting in. . . ." There was a long silence.

"What is it?"

"I don't know if I should be saying anything. I'm not trying to cause trouble for anyone—but I overheard the guys talking. They said they're going after Tobin."

"Guys? What guys? What are you talking about?"

"You know, your friends—Brian, Mike and Rob. I was at the store. The three of them were outside. They said they were going to take care of him. That Tobin would never be with you again."

"This is awful. I can't believe it. I should have known Pam and Sharon couldn't be trusted."

"What?" Rita asked.

Laurie closed her eyes. "Oh, nothing."

"I just thought you should know."

"Thanks for telling me. I appreciate this, Rita. I really do."

"Is there any way I can help?"

"No. I'll take care of it." Laurie wasn't sure how yet, but she would. "Sorry, I've got to go. Bye."

Brian was probably out for some kind of sick revenge, trying to get back at her for leaving him. As for the other two, they never needed any excuse for a brawl. She was meeting Tobin at ten-thirty, and it was only twenty after nine. She had to see him right away, warn him. Who knew what they would start? Immediately she dialed his house, but the line was busy. When she finally got through, a long fifteen minutes later, Hannah answered.

"Hi. Is Tobin there?"

"No. I think he's with my dad. They were going to a baseball game."

Laurie had forgotten. That was why he was meeting her so late. "If he comes home, tell him I need to hear from him A.S.A.P."

"Got it. Is everything okay?"

"Everything's fine. Just have him call me, please."

"I'll give him the message as soon as he gets in."

"Thanks, Hannah."

She picked up the phone again and called Pam. "You said you wouldn't say anything. I trusted you."

"I didn't. Sharon didn't either."

"They're planning to go after Tobin."

"How do you know that?"

"I found out."

"Laurie, you can have anyone you want. Why would you pick him?"

"You just don't get it, do you? I've never been happier. And if you were really my friend, you'd understand."

"I am your friend. We all are. We're just trying to help."

"Help? I don't need your help. I don't need you. Any of you," Laurie cried.

"Laurie, listen to me...."

Before Pam could say any more, Laurie slammed the phone down. Calling Sharon would be a waste of time, too. All that mattered now was Tobin's safety. If anything happened to him, it would be her fault.

Laurie paced the room. When she didn't hear from Tobin, she called his house again. Hannah reassured her that he was still at the game, meaning he was out of harm's way—for the time being. But for how long? She had to do something.

She slipped on a pair of jeans and a short-sleeved shirt, put her long hair up in a bun and slapped on a baseball cap. *Nobody will know it's me.*

When she was certain her parents were settled in for the night, she carefully removed the screen from her window. She climbed as fast as she could down the sturdy white wooden trellis filled with creeping vines, landing in her mother's precious perennial garden. She quickly smoothed away her footprints with a stick and tried to straighten a crumpled flower.

She crept around to the side door of the garage and quietly removed her ten speed. *The game had to be over by now*. She pedaled swiftly across town, shielding her face from car headlights, not knowing who might recognize her and tell her parents. Tobin had wanted to pick her up at the end of her street, but she insisted there was no need. As always, though, he met her halfway, down a dead end road. She knew he was afraid for her at night, but they lived in a safe town. She ditched her bike in the woods and hurried to his truck.

"I've been trying to reach you all night. Did Hannah tell you?" She didn't give him time to answer. "I heard from Rita Sherwood, an old friend. They're coming after you! We have to do something," she said, practically out of breath, after closing the truck's door.

"Calm down," he said softly, wrapping a strand of hair that escaped her bun around her ear. "Who's coming after me?"

"Mike, Rob and Brian. My God, they'll kill you," she cried.

He shifted the gears and drove off.

She looked at him strangely.

Then he grinned. "Let them try."

"They're big. I mean—really big. They're on the football team. There's no telling what they're capable of."

Tobin shrugged.

Laurie wondered if what she was telling him was registering. He didn't have to be cool in front of her. "Tobin, there's only one of you—and three of them!"

"I'll be ready. No matter what. Don't worry."

"I do worry. It's because of me—they want to hurt you."

He pulled off the road and took her hands in his. "It's not your fault. I don't know why you think that. And no one is going to hurt me," he said, wiping away a tear that slid down her cheek.

"But...."

"But nothing. *Shh*," he said, tapping his finger to her lips.

She wanted to believe he would be all right. His confident and valiant response eased her somewhat, but was he putting on this brave front for her benefit?

"Let's forget about it for a moment and go look at the stars," he said. He kissed her and her fears faded.

She took a deep breath. "Okay."

Walking to the pond, he wrapped his arm around her waist. Peepers could be heard nearby and lightning bugs lit their path while small creatures rustled leaves. The only human sound was the distant scream of a far-off siren.

They dropped flat on their backs, their hands cradling their heads as they watched the stars, not thinking of tomorrow, only appreciating this one moment.

"You're like my very own shining star, shimmering in the night, like that one over there," Tobin whispered, pointing to the North Star. "Oh, look," he said. "It just winked at you."

"Am I supposed to make a wish?"

"Yes. Absolutely. I made one."

"What? What'd you wish for?" she implored.

"If one tells, the wish won't come true, Miss Venus," he said with a smile.

"Hmm, Venus? Then you must be my planet—Mars, revolving around me." She shifted her position, to her side, her elbow resting in the sand, her palm supporting her head. "Where did that come from—a woman from Venus—a man from Mars? Are women and men that much different?"

"Well, physically they are. And they are wired a little differently."

"Meaning?" she asked.

"I think women worry too much. Maybe because they have the ability to. Men seem to focus on one thing at a time."

"Oh, okay. Do you know that I wanted to be an astronaut? I wanted to explore outer space. Be another John Glenn."

"A woman on the moon. I like that. So what changed your mind?"

"It was just a childhood fantasy."

"What's your fantasy now?" Tobin asked.

She smiled, moving closer to him. "I think you know."

Later that night, Laurie's worst fear materialized. Rob, Brian and Mike removed Tobin's shirt and pants and tied him to one tree and her to another. They told her if she screamed they would gag her. They whipped his back and legs with a tree limb. The lashes had to be agonizing. The branch whistled through the air and fell again and again. Every muscle in her body grew taut. His body twitched but he never yelled out. Blood dripped from his sores. Still he was silent.

She watched helplessly as Brian placed dried pine needles around the tree. They planned to burn him. She cried, she pleaded, but nothing worked. Finally, she offered herself—her body, anything to free him. But they snickered hatefully.

"You're all used up. Who would want you—after being with that?" Brian said, piercing Tobin with a rod.

"You're so rotten. You'll go to jail for life!"

"Don't think so," Rob said. "They'll be glad to get rid of him. He's been nothing but trouble in this town."

When she saw Brian strike the match to light Tobin on fire, she screamed. She screamed so loud, she thought her tonsils had burst. They shoved a greasy cloth in her mouth.

She gasped for breath, finally waking. Her pillow saturated with sweat. Could they really be that vicious?

An owl hooted. Tobin moved swiftly but quietly through branches and leaves. Then he climbed a huge elm and waited, sitting so still that a small sparrow settled on his shoulder. He listened for footsteps. Voices. Breathing. The woods were silent. Then, there was a rustle of leaves and he knew they were there.

Brian and Rob, each carrying a shovel—Mike, a rake—treaded on each other's heels through a place completely foreign to them. They circled the same area three times. The boys had no idea where they were. *If they're not careful, Tobin thought, they might get caught up in their own little web.*

"Did you hear that?" Mike whispered.

"Hear what?" Rob asked.

A chipmunk darted in front of them into the bushes. Mike jumped back, nearly falling onto Brian.

"Watch where the hell you're going!" Brian gave him a shove. "You're such a pansy."

"Let's stop here," Rob said. "Give me the rake," he said to Mike, handing him the shovel. "Start digging."

"Me?"

"Yeah, you."

"We should've brought gloves," Brian stated, pulling up roots with his bare hands.

"What if he doesn't show up?"

"He'll show up."

"But how are we going to get him?" Mike asked.

"I'll worry about that. You keep shoveling."

"How deep should we go?"

"Until I tell you to stop. He's a big guy."

Once Rob thought the hole was big enough, he crisscrossed sticks across the opening, lightly raking leaves and pine needles on top.

After witnessing their pathetic tactics long enough, Tobin decided it was time to appear. He swung down on a rope, startling them. Once the boys realized Tobin was alone, they quickly surrounded him.

"Come on, Injun boy. Let's see what you got," Rob taunted.

"Doesn't look like the odds are in my favor."

Rob grinned. "What a shame, isn't it guys?"

"See, we never know what an Indian's going to pull," said Mike, the smallest of the three but with the biggest mouth. "You've got to stick to your own kind."

Tobin knew they hated the idea of him being with Laurie, especially Brian, who was still hung up on her. That could make a man go crazy. His silence ticked the guys off all the more.

"Did you hear us, Indian boy? Leave her alone!" Brian said.

"Yeah, I heard you."

"Then you got our message—you're going to stay clear, right?" asked Rob.

"I said I heard you."

"So, what're you telling us—you're going to keep seeing her?" Brian grilled.

"Let's put it this way. I don't accept threats—from anybody."

"Oh, you don't, do you? That's too bad. For you, that is. We have Mr. Tough Guy here. What do you say to that?" Rob asked the others.

"I say he needs to be taught a lesson. One he won't forget," Brian answered.

Watching them march toward him, Tobin thought for sure they had to be the three largest football players he had ever seen, but he was hardly intimidated.

Tobin was pumped, focused, and in a crouched position. Like a cougar with eyes in the back of his head, one by one he sought them out with smooth and quick movements—until Rob pulled a knife on him.

Thanks to Uncle Basil's training, he was able to knock it out of Rob's hand. When Brian quickly picked up a stick, Tobin dislodged it from his fingers before the other boy could blink. His swift swings and kicks tossed and flipped his attackers toward every point of the compass. Rob wouldn't give up and came back for more, while Brian and Mike lay in the bushes groaning. After Tobin aimed for Rob's windpipe, pressing his finger hard between his Adam's apple and the top of his breastbone, it wasn't long before he was down, too. It was over.

Chapter 40

Laurie had been awake since the sun poked through her shades, listening to the birds call to one another. At eight o'clock, she decided to give Rita a ring to see if she was up for a game of tennis. She owed Rita a lot.

"Is nine good for you?" Laurie asked after explaining why she had called.

"I'm free til dinner. I'm going out with my parents."

"So, it's a yes?"

"Definitely."

"Great. See you then. Oh, wait. Can I meet you there?" Laurie didn't mind picking up Rita, but she remembered she was meeting Tobin afterward.

"No problem. Same place, right?"

"Yeah."

The public court, near the school, was in decent shape. At least it was the last time Laurie played there with Sharon and Pam, a couple of months ago now. She wouldn't be meeting them there anymore.

Rita Henley had short, dark blonde hair and green eyes. Though only about five feet four inches and one hundred and two pounds, she was far from delicate. She was strong, agile and had more energy than anyone Laurie knew.

Laurie won the first set but lost the next two to lose the match. Rita was a good opponent. Both of them had been playing since they were young—Laurie since she was eight, Rita a year longer. After a couple of hours of swatting the ball back and forth, they left the court.

They stuffed rackets and balls into their cars and headed to Jeremy's Diner in the center of New Seabury, where they plopped at the counter and ordered ice cream sodas.

"Great game today," Laurie told Rita.

"You're pretty hard to beat."

"You're not so bad yourself."

Rita smiled. "Oh, heck, we're both good."

"I want to thank you, Rita."

"For what?"

"I don't know. The game—and telling me about the guys—what their intentions were."

"Like I said before," Rita said between spoonfuls, "I don't really know Tobin, but he seems like a neat guy. I mean he must be—if you like him."

"You have no idea what that means to me," Laurie gushed in gratitude.

"I don't know why those guys have to be suck jerks. Some take longer to grow up, I guess."

"My mother said even when they're grown up, they're still little boys—they just have bigger toys."

"Good analogy," Rita replied, and the two of them erupted in laughter.

Other than the time Laurie spent with Tobin, she was pretty much alone now. Rita raised her spirits in more ways than she expected. It felt good to be able to really talk to someone again, someone who understood and didn't make judgments. Laurie was sorry she had lost contact with Rita, but now they were friendly again and maybe, just maybe, it was a better time.

"How is Tobin?" Rita suddenly asked.

Laurie smiled. "He's great. Would you like to meet him?"

Rita stared at her for a moment. "Are you serious? When?"

Laurie liked her enthusiasm. This is what she had expected from Sharon and Pam. "What about now? We were planning to see each other after the game anyway. That's the reason I had you meet me."

Rita grinned. "Let's not keep him waiting."

Laurie took a final sip of her soda, left a few dollars on the counter and hopped off the stool. Outside, Laurie waited in her car until Rita pulled up in her brown Corolla; then she stuck her head out the window. "Stay behind me."

Driving to the pond, Laurie realized she had never taken anyone to their "spot," and she wasn't sure how she felt about it. When they got out of their cars, Laurie saw Rita looking around. "What do you think? Pretty cool, huh?"

"How'd you find this place?"

Laurie smiled. "Lots of research. If you want to find something— or someone in this case—bad enough, you will."

Tobin was skimming stones across the water, making Laurie recall their first meeting.

"Tobin, I'd like you to meet my friend, Rita."

Tobin turned around.

"Hi. I've heard a lot about you," Rita said.

"All good, I hope," he said.

"Every bit."

"Tobin, Rita was the one who told me about the guys."

"Thanks. But I took care of that situation," Tobin said. He looked at Laurie. "You don't have to worry anymore."

"What are you saying? What happened?" Laurie asked, forgetting for a minute that Rita was with them.

"They didn't know who they were messing with. I don't think they'll bother us again."

"How can you be so sure?"

"Trust me," he said.

"I trust you, but I don't trust them. They're probably conjuring up something more horrible at this very moment—I know them."

"I don't mean to intervene, but Laurie's right. That bunch is unpredictable," Rita added.

"Why did you keep this from me?" Laurie asked Tobin.

"This is the first I've seen you. Besides, I know how you get. Can we talk about this later?"

"It's beautiful here," Rita said, gazing. "I'm going to get my feet wet. How about it, Laurie?"

Laurie looked at her. "Yeah, sure." Together they sat in the sand, took off their sneakers and socks, and waded into the pond.

"Too bad we don't have our suits with us," Laurie said.

"It's okay. Another time."

There was no doubt Laurie would invite her again. She wondered if Rita had a boyfriend. She had never mentioned anyone, but that didn't mean anything. The focus had been on her and Tobin. Rita was pretty and had such a kind heart. Laurie imagined someone was special to her. "It would be fun to double date sometime."

"Yeah, it would. But I'm not dating anybody right now. I was seeing this one guy—we got along really well. But he moved away."

"Tobin, do you know anybody you could fix her up with?"

"Ah, that's sweet, but I'm really not looking," Rita said.

"But it'd be fun. The four of us could go to a baseball game. Or to a movie or the drive-in."

Laurie loved being alone with Tobin, but once in a while she thought it would be nice if they had another couple to do things with—like it used to be with Sharon, Pam, and the others. She had to admit, though, that it had been a bit too much at times.

"The problem is," Tobin said, "a lot of them around here are burnouts. I don't mean to sound discouraging, but they're either alcoholics or drug addicts. Or both. They're not bad people, they're just screwed up. Seeing their parents lose their jobs, and the way they've been treated. Some of them just don't know who they are. I don't want to fix you up with someone like that."

"It's all right. I can wait."

After sitting a few minutes longer in the sand, talking with the two of them, Rita stood up. "I have to get going. I'll talk to you later, Laurie. Nice meeting you, Tobin."

"Same here. I'm sure we'll be seeing a lot more of you."

"Hope so. Now, if I can find my way out of here...."

"Just stay to your left all the way. When you get to the end of the dirt road, take a right. It'll get you to Main Street," Tobin said.

"Got it," Rita said, flashing Laurie a wink.

After Rita left, Laurie pressed Tobin for more details. "What did they do? They came looking for you here?"

Tobin noddcd.

"How'd they know where to find you?"

"They didn't really. It's more like I found them. They circled around and around like three lost dogs. Actually, it was kind of funny."

Laurie surveyed him carefully. He looked perfectly fine to her, not roughed up, no cuts or bruises. "Come on, there's no way you could've taken on all of them."

"Let's just say we reached an understanding."

"Oh my God, you did! I can't believe it. But how'd you—?"

"I can't tell you all my secrets."

"It must've been something you learned from your Uncle Basil."

He smiled. "Maybe."

She was glad he was all right, but she couldn't imagine the guys just letting it all go. They always had to come out ahead. Especially against an Indian.

Chapter 41

Laurie thought she would surprise Tobin by stopping at his house when he got out of work. She noticed an unfamiliar red Impala parked next to his truck in the driveway. *Was this bad timing?*

Tobin greeted Laurie at the screen door, letting her in and giving her a grand hug.

"Do you have company?" she asked.

"No, my dad's in with someone."

"Oh," she said quietly, figuring the medicine man was doing some healing.

"How was your day?" he asked her.

"Great. Yours?"

"It was good. No complaints."

"You mean nothing out of the ordinary. Like removing dead animals or finding treasures in trash," she said covering her mouth, smirking. Standing in the kitchen, Laurie heard a little girl sniffling and coughing fiercely in another room, sounding almost like whooping cough.

"Is she okay?" Laurie whispered.

"Her mother thinks she has pneumonia. Or close to it."

"Oh, wow. That's serious. Can your dad cure her?"

"He's certainly going to try."

"How about a glass of lemonade? Fresh squeezed lemons?" he asked, taking out two glasses from the cabinet.

She nodded. "Thanks."

When Laurie sat down at the table sipping her drink, she sensed something burning.

"What's that smell?" she asked, sniffing.

"Oh, my dad's burning sage."

"Sage? What's it used for?"

"It clears negative—bad energy," he said quietly.

"That will heal her?"

"Not completely. My dad uses a variety of herbs and plants like goldenseal and burdock root for healing, but he'll probably give her echinacea. It's great for colds. Helps the immune system. And will help build her up."

"Really." She never heard of this before, but she was definitely interested in knowing more.

"Let me grab a few things and we'll get out of here," he said, downing his lemonade.

Tobin went to his room and she suddenly remembered he'd mentioned his fishing pole the day before, so she got up to follow and remind him. She paused in the hallway, in awe, peering into the parlor as she watched the medicine man lift his hands to the ceiling, then hover them over the young patient, mumbling in his language. The room was full of steam and smoke. The little girl was lying very still on a table covered with a white bed sheet, a cloth across her forehead, staring up at Tobin's father like he was her god. She wanted to get closer, see everything the medicine man was doing to help this small child.

"Ready?" he asked, coming out.

"Not yet. Please?" she whispered.

Laurie knew Tobin was ready to leave, but she preferred to stay there, at least for a while. She wanted to get closer, but she knew it was a private session. She maintained her distance as she became increasingly fascinated with the ritual. She noticed the child's mother occupied a chair nearby, not uttering a sound, her head down, eyes closed. Laurie hoped none of them realized she was observing. She was mesmerized by the whole thing.

The girl's coughing stopped. A strong, little voice said, "I feel better, Mommy." Laurie felt the hairs on her arms stand up.

"He'll give her a little token when she leaves," Tobin whispered.

"What kind of token?"

"Probably a unique stone or a charm. I bet he gives her a little animal charm, though."

When they walked outside, Tobin called to Brownie. "Come on, boy," Lying by the front step, Brownie's eyes lifted and he slowly rose, his tail wagging.

The three of them hopped in the truck and headed to John's Pond. The lab immediately started lapping Laurie's face.

"Are you happy to see me? Or are you just happy to go for a ride?" she asked, kissing him on the nose, patting him.

"Probably both."

"What are you thinking about?" Tobin asked her later when they were sitting at the pond.

"Your dad. That was amazing today. It was like your dad performed a miracle. I mean that little girl left there like she was never sick."

He smiled. "Yeah, the medicine man is pretty special. You got to remember, though, not everybody can be cured. It depends on how serious one's illness is. It's hard to keep the body aligned and well, but it can free us from many illnesses. A lot of our sicknesses come from our emotions, even being unbalanced in relationships.

"Relationships?"

"Yeah. Sometimes, certain people are just not healthy for us. And I'm not talking just about lovers. It can be between a parent and a child. Or even a friendship."

She understood that, knowing how sick Sharon and Pam made her feel inside at times. "So, not having any relationships would keep one healthy?"

"Nah, they'd probably get sick or die from loneliness. Humans need each other."

Tobin gave her a lot to mull over. Sitting at the pond, staring out, watching the ducks, she thought about what Tobin said. It all made perfect sense. After witnessing the medicine man's knowledge and skills—the native ways—of helping another, she was so grateful to have been a part of it.

Do you believe in this alternative way of healing?" Tobin asked her as if he read her mind.

"After what I saw today, I do. It just seems more natural—it makes total sense to me. I mean, hearing that little girl so sick and then. . . . It was incredible."

He smiled.

Brownie, who had been napping at his favorite spot near the water, suddenly rose and began to bark in one direction.

"What do you see, boy?" Tobin asked, following his gaze.

"Hey, look," Tobin said to Laurie, pointing to the bird's nest in a maple tree. Laurie and Tobin had observed the mother feeding its young the last few times they were at the pond, but they never saw one take off. A little blue jay spiraled to the ground, flapping its wings rapidly when it landed. It hopped about on its tiny feet, straining for the sky. All at once, it found its wings.

Tobin smiled. "Now that's a miracle."

Chapter 42

Tobin hauled a knapsack out of the closet and started loading it with some of the equipment he would need: compass, sleeping bag, canteen and a flashlight. He had told his boss far enough in advance about his vacation so he could arrange to have some help for Pete while he was gone. Everything was all set. Almost.

Even though he had planned the trip to Wyoming long ago, it hadn't included falling in love. He would miss Laurie. He hated the thought of leaving her even for a day, never mind a week or more. Although he felt secure that nothing would change between them, he still hated the thought of going without her. She had been through hell with family and friends and had given up so much for him. She was strong when he was around her, but how would she hold up while he was gone?

Hannah came and stood by his door. "Laurie's here to see you."

"Tell her to come in," he said.

Laurie appeared in the doorjamb. "Hi. I had to see you before you go," she said, moving into the room.

"I'm not going until tomorrow. You know I wouldn't leave without saying goodbye."

"I know. Can I help in any way?" she asked, looking at the packed bags.

"Thanks, but I just have a few more things here to take care of."

Laurie knelt beside him. "Why don't you let me come with you? I don't start work for a couple of weeks. The timing couldn't be more perfect."

Tobin stared at her for a moment. "Your parents will kill me."

"I'll be eighteen in a few days. There's nothing they can do." She paused. "Unless you don't want me to go." Her voice had turned flat.

"No. It's not that. I just don't want to be starting off on the wrong foot with them. You understand, don't you?"

She nodded.

Then he saw the disappointment on her face. How could he say no to her? Besides, he would like the company. "Ah, why not."

She gave him a crushing hug. "You won't regret this."

I hope not.

Tobin rose at three thirty in the morning, quickly dressed and grabbed a cup of coffee. He had loaded the truck's bed with camping gear and his other belongings before he went to bed, so as not to wake his family in the wee hours. They had said their goodbyes then, and his parents were happy that Laurie was going along. He was happy as well, thinking that it would give them time to really get to know one another.

Flipping on the outside light, Tobin walked out to the truck to do a fast oil change and check the tires. He had just closed the hood one final time when a taxi from Hyannis pulled into the driveway. Laurie, wearing a backpack, stepped out of the rear of the vehicle. She leaned into the taxi and pulled out two medium-sized suitcases. After wiping his hands on an old T-shirt he used for a shop rag, he hustled over to help her. She paid the driver and he lifted both suitcases in to the truck bed.

"We're only going for ten days," he said with a laugh after he loaded her things. "What all do you have in there?"

"Clothes, camera—makeup. You know, girl stuff."

"You don't need makeup. You're good the way you are."

"I really don't wear much. But thank you for that."

After he crammed her belongings under a tarp in the back of the truck next to his, he got back in and looked at her. "I guess we're off." In spite of Laurie's still sleepy eyes, she looked beautiful as ever. He was glad she was coming after all, and he knew his Uncle Basil would've approved, too.

"We could've taken my car, you know," she said.

"I don't think that would've been a good idea. We're fine," he said, peering back at the huge pile that nearly blocked his rear view.

"Yup. We are," she said sighing, as she leaned back against the seat.

While Tobin drove, Laurie pulled out the map and studied the route he had marked on it. He wanted to get there in the shortest amount of time, approximately two days—at least that had been his intention, but he wasn't sure if it was realistic. They planned to share the driving, following Interstate 90 nearly the entire way, covering close to 2300 miles, practically non-stop, except when nature called, or they needed to stretch their legs.

Tobin thought about their destination, Big Medicine Wheel. It was supposed to be traced out in stone on a flat shoulder near the top of a remote 10,000-foot peak. He always had a passion for mountains, beginning in New Hampshire. There was something very powerful about them. *What a rush*, he thought, realizing it was finally happening. He hoped what he was feeling was contagious, that he and Laurie would be looking back at this experience for years to come.

"So, what's it look like? Did they use a certain kind of stone to make it?" Laurie asked.

"Huh?" he asked, awakening from his reverie.

"I was wondering about the wheel—the stones they used. Was there a certain kind?"

"I don't think so, but the rocks are very ancient. Nobody knows for sure, but some think each stone was laid for a famous warrior who died. They say it looks like a big wagon wheel lying on its side."

"A wagon wheel," she murmured. "I can't imagine life back then. I'm sure, though, people were a lot closer. And they didn't worry about things like fitting in and being popular."

"Times change, but people don't. They'll always have the need to compete," he said, thinking about how he felt on the ball field. "Do you worry about those things?"

"No. Not anymore. At least I don't think so. Sometimes it makes it easier though—being liked, that is."

"I know," he said quietly. He himself had hungered for Bill Hogan's respect. But where did it get him? For a moment he imagined walking around campus. Laurie's arm in his—Hogan's envy quite apparent. *Eat your heart out*. But Laurie was not a showpiece and he would never use her in that way.

"Do you miss them?" Tobin asked.

Laurie stared at him. "We got along—dating, playing sports, just hanging out together. I saw a side of them, though, that I could never be a part of. To answer your question—no. We don't have much in common really. It took me a while to figure that out." She took a deep breath. "I do have Rita now."

"She seems nice."

Laurie smiled. "She likes you too."

Suddenly the traffic started to slow. Tobin rolled down his window and popped his head out.

"What's going on? Can you see anything?" Laurie asked.

"It's the toll booths. I forgot," he mumbled, fishing in his pockets.

"I've got plenty of change," Laurie said, pulling her wallet out of her purse.

"I'll give it back to you when we stop somewhere."

"You don't have to. I intend to pay my share. It's only fair," she said, dropping the coins in his palm. Then he handed it over to the attendant and drove through.

After a few miles, Laurie spoke again. "Listen, I don't want you to think I'm just here because I needed to get away."

Tobin turned to look at her. "We all need to get away sometimes. But no, I never thought that."

"Good. Because I know what this trip means to you—and what's important to you is important to me."

"Same here," he said, taking hold of her hand.

There was little to see on the Mass Turnpike, only lines of trees that seemed to go on forever. But talking had passed the time and Tobin felt very connected to her. *Two bodies, one soul*, he thought. When they both said nothing more, Tobin turned up the radio. James Taylor hummed through the speakers, "You've Got a Friend." Listening, Tobin smiled to himself.

After they had finished the coffee in the thermos, they both needed to use the bathroom, so Tobin pulled into the next rest stop. While he was filling the gas tank, Laurie ran into the building to get some snacks from the vending machines. When she came out, she handed him a Dr. Pepper, and he guzzled it at the pump. Laurie gobbled down a package of Twinkies and then climbed behind the wheel.

"It's my turn," she said, her head out the window, watching Tobin screw on the gas cap. "I'll drive from here. Then we can switch again maybe in Ohio or Indiana."

"That's a lot of miles—you sure about that?" he asked, throwing her the keys.

"Piece of cake," she said with a grin, catching them.

After Tobin settled into the passenger's seat, Laurie started the engine. Shifting into gear, she let the clutch out too fast. "Sorry," she said. "Your truck and I were just getting used to each other. It will be a smooth ride from here. I promise."

"Women drivers," he murmured, shaking his head.

"Any other guy would have screamed at me and taken the keys away."

"I'm not any other guy."

"I know that. I mean, we've been cramped in this truck for hours and not once have we gotten into an argument."

"You're not looking for one, are you?"

"No, of course not. I just think it's great that two people can get along so well."

"It's not hard—with you," he said with a slow smile.

Through New York, there was more to look at—the Hudson River, the old Erie Canal locks, fertile flatland. And Syracuse's wildlife preserves had been stocked with blue heron. In Pennsylvania, farmhouses and barns, some kept up well, others run-down, sat on rolling green pastures. How beautiful it looked to Tobin. Suddenly he began imagining a slew of houses spoiling that land. His stomach flopped. What if that happened in Mashpee? He turned to Laurie. At least she would be beautiful forever. He hoped they would be together that long.

In a field, among a family of horses, was one big old cow. "Look!" Laurie leaned out the window.

Tobin smiled to himself. If she got this wild about a cow, he wondered how she would be when she saw a moose or a grizzly. She sure made the trip more interesting.

Turning back to him, she said, "Do you know I don't even know what your favorite food is? Or your favorite color for that matter."

"What? Seeing a cow made you think of that?" he asked, grinning.

She shook her head. "Maybe. But I don't think so."

"Steak—rare. With potatoes. An absolute must. I'm hungry thinking about it. And there's something about the color blue; it reminds me of the sky, the water—your eyes."

She started blushing. "When I have my own house—someday— I'd like to paint each room in a different shade of blue."

"I don't know if you'd want to paint a little girl's room blue."

"Gee, I've never thought about that. You're right. Probably pink instead. Do you want kids someday?"

"Someday. When I have enough money." *To be able to give you the life you're used to.*

"And how much is that?"

"Oh, I don't know. I'm not looking to be the richest man, but I'd like to be able to take my family on trips like this one, one day. I don't want to have to tell them we can't afford it. You know, Laurie, I've always been proud of who I am, where I come from, but so many of my people are broke. And they've come to accept that way of living. That scares the hell out of me."

"It shouldn't. You'll never be in that situation. You have too much ambition, too much drive. And you have dreams. You'd never let that happen."

"I'd like to think so, but sometimes things are out of our control. Trying to make a living—in a white man's world—isn't going to be easy."

"It never is—in any world. I mean, who am I to say? I think, though, the real key to success starts from in here," Laurie said, tapping her heart. "If you're happy with who you are, I think anything's possible."

"Did anyone ever tell you you're a smart woman?"

"Just my dad," she said, flicking a smile.

"You haven't told me yet what *you* like to eat," he said, listening to his own stomach rumble.

"My favorite foods are pizza and Chinese. But right now—anything."

"Then I think it's about time we get some real food," he said, motioning for her to get off the highway.

"I was going to take the next exit anyway."

Within a quarter of a mile, they stopped at a diner in Cleveland. A waitress seated them and handed them each a paper menu. They had already decided when the waitress hustled back to their table.

"What can I get ya to drink?" the middle-aged woman asked, pulling a pencil from behind her ear.

"Two waters, please. And we're ready to order, if it's okay," Tobin added.

"It's fine with me," she said, smacking gum while writing down their request. "I'll be right back with your drinks."

"She reminds me of Laverne on *Laverne and Shirley*," Laurie said. Tobin gave her a questioning look. "The TV sitcom. Those two single women who have those goofy guys who like them. I can't think of their names."

"Sorry. I can't help you out—I don't watch much TV."

"I only watch TV at night. It helps me unwind sometimes," she admitted.

Ten minutes later, the waitress came with their plates. "Here you go, folks," she said, handing Tobin his steak and potato, and Laurie her chicken cacciatore with linguini.

"Looks delicious," she said, delving in.

"Diners always do a great job. My steak is cooked perfectly," he said, after cutting through.

Tobin still found it incredulous he was with the courtroom girl. And here they were having dinner together like a real couple. *How wondrous*, he thought.

"This was great. I'm stuffed," Laurie said, after finishing.

"Yeah, I'm full, too. Guess we're set till breakfast."

When the check came, Laurie dug into her pocketbook for her wallet to pay for her dinner.

"I got this," Tobin said, watching her pull out some bills.

"I thought we agreed on Dutch?"

"We did. Can't I treat a pretty lady—just once?"

She smiled. "Okay. But I got it next time. Then after that. . . ."

He smiled. "If you say so."

Tobin took the wheel, intent on driving through the night. By ten o'clock, though, the white highway line nearly hypnotized him, so he decided it was time to find a spot to sleep. He exited a ramp past Toledo and ended up in the small town of Avery.

Chapter 43

Driving down a desolate road, Tobin slowed in front of a rickety wooden barn with "Rock City" in big white letters painted across the pitched roof.

"You're not thinking about staying . . .?" she asked.

He nodded.

"Okay, I guess."

It looked like the knee-high grass around the barn hadn't been cut in years. He pulled off next to the broken split-rail fence. "Let me take a look around first. I think it's been abandoned for some time, but I want to be sure."

"I'll come with you."

Tobin grabbed the flashlight and they got out of the truck, locking the doors.

"Hello? Anybody around?" Tobin yelled, as they trampled the overgrown field.

There was no answer.

"I guess not." Tobin took hold of her hand. "Let's go in."

They ducked when bats greeted them. Laurie froze, her arm covering her head. Inside, other than a rusty harness, harrow and sickle, there was little else.

Then there was a hooting sound. "What's that?" Laurie whispered, her eyes darting around.

"Just a barn owl. He won't hurt anything. We can always sleep in the car. Although, it won't be very comfortable."

"No," she said. "That's okay."

Laurie didn't have to pretend for him. He knew sleeping in a dusty old barn surely wasn't something she was used to. But he liked that she was a good sport about it. He pulled out his pocketknife and snapped twine from a couple bales of hay, spreading it on the wooden floor. "Not the luxury of a hotel room, but it'll have to do."

"Right now, I don't care. I just want to put my head down somewhere."

Nestled close to each other, they saw several stars break out through a big hole in the roof. And the half-moon lit the shadows. With her head on his open arm, Tobin bent his neck to kiss her. "You near me like this—it's hard to resist you. Even with all your clothes on," he said, grinning.

"Then I guess that's a good thing, because if I was resistible—you probably wouldn't like me. And I wouldn't be here right now."

"That would never happen. Not in a million years. I don't think you could turn me off if you colored your hair green and spit tobacco from those lips," he said, lightly touching them.

She laughed. "I'll remember that." Soon her eyes got heavy and she fell asleep. Tobin quietly sat up and took off his jean jacket, covering her with it. Watching her sleep, he wondered what this fantastic woman, so perfect in every way, saw in him. Whatever it was, she loved him, he thought, smiling to himself as he dozed off.

Morning birds and the clanging of a church bell in the distance roused Tobin at five o'clock. He glanced over at Laurie. She looked so peaceful lying there that he hated to wake her, so he took a walk outside and explored the grassy property, laden with dew. When he came back in, fifteen minutes later, he noticed her stirring. When she opened her eyes, her face was like a daffodil after a gentle rain, moist and vibrant.

"Sleep well?" he asked.

"I guess I did," she said, stretching happily. "I don't remember anything after the stars. How about you?"

"I think I crashed not long after."

"Oh, gosh. What time is it?" she asked, jumping up, brushing herself off.

"No need to rush. After all, this is like a vacation really. And we're not too far off schedule."

"Yeah, right. I'd say by. . . how long have we been here? At least six hours. I thought you wanted to get there as quick as possible."

"I did. That was before—when I thought I was going alone. Why should we have to miss out on everything else?"

She smiled. "You're absolutely right. We should enjoy all of it," she said, handing him his jacket. "Thank you. I wish there was some place to wash up."

"There's an old pump out back. And it actually works."

"Great. Lead me to it," she said, plucking straw from her hair as they headed out.

He pumped while she cupped the water in her hand, splashing it on her face.

"A little cold?" he asked, watching her shudder. "It'll wake you up fast."

"Yeah, if you don't go into shock first," Laurie said, shaking her hands then slipping them into her sweatshirt pockets. "This must've been a really nice place at one time," she said, surveying the grounds. "I can see horses and sheep roaming about. I wonder what happened?"

"It might have been left to their kids and they didn't have the money to take care of it. Unless, they just didn't want to farm. Maybe they wanted to work in the city. That's probably what happened to a lot of the ones we've seen along the way."

"What a shame," she said quietly. "People devote their whole lives to land that meant so much to them, only to have it go to ruin."

"I know. It's hard to think about."

Chapter 44

Before getting back on the highway, they stopped at a country store, grabbing Cokes and a couple of homemade banana muffins that came in fresh daily, according to the clerk. On the way out, Laurie stopped at a swiveling rack filled with postcards and selected half a dozen. They even sold stamps there.

By noon, they had already passed through Indiana and Illinois and were halfway into Wisconsin. If everything went smoothly, no traffic accidents or roadwork, they would be in Wyoming by midnight. Tobin had thought catnaps would be enough, but since Laurie finally admitted she couldn't sleep in motion, at four o'clock he decided to pull into a rest area. However, Laurie was too wired from junk food and caffeine to get any shuteye, so while Tobin slept, she pulled out the postcards. The first one, snow-covered mountains and trees against the ocean blue sky, she addressed to her parents. Now she had to write something on the left side. If she wrote big, there would be less room to get into anything heavy. She didn't want to apologize for leaving. She only wanted to let them know she was thinking about them, tell them not to worry and that she was fine.

Hi Mom and Dad, Temperature's a little cool, but it's sunny. Saw some grand sites. See you soon.

Love, Laurie.

That was short and pleasant, she thought. The way everything should be. Then she picked up a card with beautiful wild horses and wrote to Rita.

Sorry I didn't get to say good-bye—last minute decision. Having a wonderful time. Glad Tobin took me along. We're getting to know each other even better. Will have lots to tell you when I get back. Laurie

She had four more cards to fill out. She thought about her cousins but she wasn't that close to them—hardly knew them really. She figured her grandparents wouldn't appreciate hearing from a granddaughter who had run off with a boy. Even if her mother hadn't told them, a postcard would certainly have them wondering. Maybe she would start a scrapbook with the rest: "Our First Trip Together."

Tobin took the North Folk Highway, a back road west of Pahaska. Still early in their wet season, some roads were closed from heavy rain and snow. "We brought the sun with us," Laurie said to the gas attendant when they stopped to fill up again.

"Glad to hear it. It's always nice to see those rays. Rarely have blue sky in May. Have a good visit, folks."

As they were entering Yellowstone National Park, on the side of the road, a herd of buffalo was grazing. They didn't want to scare the animals, so Tobin turned the engine off, and Laurie quietly took out her camera. Then she got out of the truck, trying to get a closer shot.

"Wow, they're huge mammals. I never realized how big they really were."

"Bison are one of the largest animals in this country. Maybe the largest."

"What are those two doing over there?" she asked, pointing, inching toward them.

"They're fighting. So don't get too close."

Later, holding hands, they stood and watched Old Faithful explode in a tower of superheated steam at Upper Geyser Basin. And they were lucky enough to see the Beehive geyser, which only erupted every few days.

"They're like huge, bubbling mud pots! Reminds me of when I was little—I played in this big dingy puddle after a rainstorm with the kid next door. But really, there's no comparison."

"Did you get in trouble?"

"Yeah. Sure did. My friend and I weren't allowed to see each other for a week after that. But the fun we had was worth it."

Tobin smiled. "I'm really glad you came along."

"Me, too."

Two massive elk sparred in a meadow. Yellowstone River dropped hundreds of feet in two magnificent waterfalls, cutting a canyon deep into the golden-hued rock. Laurie used one roll of film after another. Even though these films would be made into gorgeous pictures, what her eyes actually witnessed on this voyage would be vibrantly imprinted in her memory forever.

Before dark, Laurie helped Tobin build a wigwam from a few bent saplings, loose brush and rugs and mats he'd brought along. Then they added a tarp in case of rain. She was beginning to appreciate the outdoors more than she ever imagined. And she liked the idea of staying in the park; there was so much to do. And Tobin made it even more adventurous.

Once they were snuggled inside, Tobin saw how quiet she had become. "What is it?" What's wrong?"

"It's my mom—she worries a lot."

"Do you want to call her? C'mon," he said, grabbing her hand, "we'll go look for a phone. There's got to be one nearby. It'll make you feel better."

"No," she said, pulling back. "It would just make things worse. I'm sure by now they've read my note. I don't think they'll do anything, though. Plenty of kids my age have taken off—run away—even been drafted and gone to Vietnam. So why would the police waste their time looking for us?"

"I don't know. Maybe because you're Laurie Matthews—a beautiful young white woman—who left with a Wampanoag man?"

"You forgot to put in 'a very handsome one.' My mom and dad must have done something crazy when they were young and in love."

Her parents had planned to take her to the Coonamessett Inn in Falmouth for an elaborate dinner on her birthday. They had already been very generous, buying her the Camaro, an early graduation present. She felt bad about not being there. But she hoped they would eventually understand how much it meant to her to be with Tobin on this trip.

"Hey, I got you something," Tobin said, handing her a small paper bag. "Happy Birthday."

She stared at him.

"My birthday's not until tomorrow."

"I'm a day early. Better than late."

She looked at him and then at the bag.

"Go ahead. Open it."

Peeling away a crown of tissue paper, she discovered an orange glass globe. "Oh, it's a pumpkin. Like Princess Scargo's."

"Do you like it?"

"Yes, I love it! It's perfect," she said, remembering their first date when Tobin told her the two tales of how Scargo Lake came to be, her favorite being the one about the princess. "Thank you."

"As soon as I saw it, I knew I had to get it."

She peered inside.

"Tomorrow, we'll get fish," he said, softly.

She thanked him with a long kiss.

Chapter 45

While browsing in a museum in Sheridan, they saw a collection of Indian arrowheads, hatchets, scrapers, awls and chippings found all over Wyoming. Some were thousands of years old. They listened to a curator tell stories about the people behind them, and the special ways they used these tools.

After hearing a family talking deliriously about their Tongue River cave experience on their way out, Tobin suddenly had a mad desire to explore one. "What do you say? Who knows when we'll get this chance again."

"You're right. Let's do it."

"You don't always have to be agreeable. I mean, if you'd rather do something else."

"No. I think it'd be awesome to go through a dark, cold hole," she said, grinning.

"You're scared?"

"I hate small spaces."

"We can skip this."

"No. I want to."

Tobin watched her shimmy her way through the tiny opening. Probably hoping to exit quickly. Inside, though, she seemed captivated by the little stick figures of people and the sun and stars. Some of the carvings of deer, elk, buffalo and other animals looked prehistoric. They both tried to figure out what the pictures meant, but it was like reading a new language.

"Maybe it was their way of keeping track of special events and ceremonies," Laurie said, running her hand over the images. "Unless, they just wanted others to know how important hunting was."

"It's hard to say. That was a huge part of their lives, though. Without the animals—they wouldn't have survived. There wasn't much else."

Dust-covered and dazzled, Tobin and Laurie eventually exited the mammoth cave and grabbed a sandwich at a little luncheon place close by. There, a young Indian man had left his doggie bag on the table. Tobin flagged him down before he went out the door.

"Thanks. Where you from?" the guy asked him.

"Massachusetts," Tobin replied.

"Both of you?" he asked, looking from Tobin to Laurie.

"Yes. I'm Tobin and this is my girlfriend, Laurie."

"Hi," Laurie said.

"We're from Mashpee. I'm from the Wampanoag Tribe," Tobin added.

"Jonah. Shoshone Tribe. You here on vacation?"

Tobin turned to Laurie. "I guess you can say that. We're here to see the Big Medicine Wheel."

"Why don't you come with me and meet my grandfather? Right about now," Jonah said, looking up at the clock, "he starts telling his stories. Many about Big Medicine Wheel. I've heard them a thousand times. C'mon. Everybody's invited."

"Even the white girl," Laurie whispered to Tobin.

Jonah opened the door to his Jeep—gesturing for them to get in. "What about my truck?" Tobin asked.

"You can leave it here—it'll be all right. It's safe here."

Tobin sensed Laurie was reluctant to leave their belongings, but he felt assured that nothing would be stolen. They hopped into Jonah's jeep, talking with him. Twenty minutes later, in a teepee, they sat listening to the elderly native named Thunderbird recite tales his father had once told him. One in particular grabbed Laurie's attention.

"A great chief—Red Plume—was without food and water for four days."

"How'd he survive?" Laurie asked.

"He found spiritual nourishment. Little people lived along the passage and took him into the earth. They told him red eagle feathers would protect him—be his powerful medicine guide."

"Where did he get the feathers?" Laurie asked.

Tobin wanted to tell Laurie that it was impolite to interrupt, especially a stranger. But her questions hadn't bothered the Shoshone man.

"From a nest. They had fallen. Drifting. He wore one small feather from an eagle's back. That's how the chief got his name. When Red Plume was dying he told his people his spirit would be found at the wheel—and they could talk to him there."

"Did anyone? Did they get any signs from him?" Laurie broke in again.

"One relative, two generations later, had cancer. He went to the mountain and prayed to Red Plume. Through a whistle in the breeze, Red Plume told his cousin where to catch his own feather, 'in the direction the wind blew.' And when his cousin did get his feather, he placed it in his headband where the little people had once told Red Plume to put it."

Laurie didn't give him a chance to finish. "Did his cancer go away?"

"Yup," he nodded. "And he lived twenty more years after that."

"A miracle," Laurie said quietly, absorbing it all.

Thunderbird had, surprisingly, seemed comfortable, even happy, with her inquisitiveness. And her curiosity, so genuine, moved Tobin. She was full of goodness. And seeing her so mindful of things that mattered to him was more than he could have asked for.

On Tuesday morning, they went their separate ways for a while. Tobin wanted to look at guns and bows and arrows. Laurie cared more about the hand-made baskets and quilted blankets she had seen during their travels through the villages, and couldn't resist buying one of each. In one small shop, Laurie was also immediately drawn to a beautiful, beaded white buckskin dress made by an older Shoshone woman. Laurie was very impressed not only with the fine quality of leather but its decorations of horse hair and purple suede.

"Would you like to try it on?" the shopkeeper asked.

Laurie nodded. "Yes. Yes, I would."

She directed Laurie to a small dressing room. Laurie thought the dress fit well. But wanting to see herself in Tobin's eyes, she pulled the curtain aside and asked, "Do you have a mirror somewhere?"

The woman gestured with her dark grey eyes. "Behind that rack over there. It looks very nice on you."

After studying herself in it, Laurie agreed. "I'll take it."

The woman smiled. "Would you like to wear it?"

"Yes. I think I will."

As Laurie fingered the soft fringe trailing over her arm, she was amazed at all the talent and detail that had gone into her new dress. When Laurie was younger she had wanted to try her hand at something nice, something she could take pride in. She tried pottery once, making a small bowl, ringed with deep blues and browns. She thought she had done a good job, considering it was her first time. But her mother told her sharply to give it up, that she didn't have the ability. After that she never tried again.

Laurie looked at her watch. It was close to two. She still had an hour before she was to meet Tobin, so she let a young Indian girl on the sidewalk braid her hair. Now the princess was ready for her prince.

Seeing Tobin coming toward her, Laurie twirled. "So, what do you think?"

Beaming, his eyes wandered over her.

Blushing, she said, "You're not saying anything."

"You take my breath away."

"Thanks," she said, starting to curtsey and then, without knowing why, bowed her head smiling.

Chapter 46

The Big Horn range was rich in game and tumbling crystal clear streams; Tobin couldn't wait to cast his rod in them. He used to fish with his Uncle Basil and his dad, when he was free, practically every weekend growing up. Laurie knew nothing about fishing and refused to try at first, but he finally changed her mind. Tobin uncovered a box of worms and Laurie turned her head away. "What's the matter?"

"I can't touch them! They're slimy."

"They're not bad when they're dipped in chocolate," he said, reaching for one.

Laurie stuck out her tongue and shuddered.

He leaned his head back, pretending to drop it in his mouth.

"Don't! Don't you dare! I'll never kiss you again."

He stopped and looked at her, and then at the worm dangling from his fingers. "Did ya hear that? If I eat you, she won't kiss me again. Sorry, little fella, you're really not worth it."

A few minutes later, perched on a flat boulder with their lines in the water, they sat quietly waiting for the first bite. Tobin thought Laurie was really beginning to enjoy herself and that pleased him.

"I think something's tugging. Yes there is," she said.

"Reel it in. Reel it in!"

"I'm trying. I'm trying," she repeated. "It must be a big one. I think I'm going to need some help."

Tobin flung his rod down and covered her hands with his. "Don't let go."

"I won't. Just tell me when."

"I got it," he said, grasping the pole from her.

"Don't lose him."

"Here he comes. Get the bucket."

"I don't think he'll fit—he's huge!"

"He'll fit."

"I can't believe it. I actually caught a fish!"

"Yeah, you can say that again. This trout must be close to three pounds."

After spending half the afternoon fishing, the sun now sank to its lowest point. Ribbons of crimson stretched along the sky and across Laurie's face, making it glow. Looking at her now, fishing was furthest from Tobin's mind. He gently stroked her face and watched her blue eyes soften as she dissolved into him.

"Come with me," he said, taking her hand and helping her off the rock. They lay down in a thick mat of tall grass and he made love to her. Something deep inside of him emerged; he never felt more connected to anyone. The feeling was inexpressible and as beautiful as she.

Afterward, he lay there, holding her, staring into the vast blueness. Then he turned to her. "Do you know when I saw you in the courtroom that day I thought you were the most beautiful girl—ever."

"What?" she said, her nose crinkling up like a rabbit's. "In those shabby-looking clothes?"

"Yeah. In those clothes, too. But I was thinking more of that black skirt and pink sweater. Those beautiful long legs."

She smiled, shaking her head. "I thought you were pretty hot, too."

"But I truly knew I had fallen in love with you at the pond."

"Me, too," she said, sinking into his arms.

He made love to her again.

An hour later, Laurie was lying on her stomach with her elbows on the ground, her hands cupping her chin. "Look. Over there in the cottonwood tree. See him?" she asked, pointing.

"Oh, it's a meadowlark."

"Look at that beautiful yellow breast."

"Yeah, they're pretty birds," Tobin responded.

"Why are the males the prettiest? Like with the male cardinals. You'd think it'd be the females."

"To distract the predator—so the mothers can protect their young."

"I never knew that. Wow, He thought of everything, didn't He?" she murmured, looking up.

"Yeah, He did a great job."

They stared at the meadowlark until it flew away.

"Do you see those tall, red plumy flowers over there?" Tobin asked, turning to his right.

"I do. I've been admiring them."

"They're Indian Paintbrush. Wyoming's favorite pick. The state's official flower."

"You know about flowers, trees—birds. Is there anything you don't know?"

He smiled. "Plenty. But there is one thing I do know."

"What?"

He moved closer to her, looking into her eyes, "I love you. I'll probably tell you—a million times."

"That's okay. I don't mind. I'll say it back—a million times."

He wanted to be the man she not only desired but deserved. "You should have only the best."

"I thought I already had that. You're not planning to change, are you?"

He shook his head fiercely, rising. "No." Then he asked, "You hungry? You ready to eat your big catch?" He extended his hand.

"I sure am," she said, grabbing hold of it. "I'm famished."

Laurie watched Tobin scale and dress the fish. He started out using a plastic knife, applying raking motions moving from the tail to the head and both sides around the fins up to the gills. When he was through, she rinsed the fish in water. Then she helped him gather wood to build a fire. And while he was cooking her grand catch, she got out the paper plates and plastic silverware.

"So, what do you think?" he asked her after her first bite.

"Pretty tasty," she answered, licking her lips.

"Do you miss the stove or refrigerator?"

"No, not at all. I don't miss any of it," she said with a smile.

Sitting by the flames with her, he couldn't think of any other place he'd rather be.

Chapter 47

The next day they traveled through the early dawn, moving northeast into the mountains. A soft water-color sky in buttery yellow and pale blue dispersed a hint of auburn as the sun rose and the sweet mist in the valleys began to clear. The Medicine Wheel passage was forty-seven miles west of Sheridan, following Route 14A for a twenty-seven mile-stretch. They were getting closer. Even though it was nearing the end of May, it was very cold the farther up they went and beginning to snow. But they had come prepared with woolen gloves, scarves and hats and hiking boots. By sunrise, they had already covered several miles.

Finally, they had to abandon the truck, continuing up some cliffs on foot. Reaching a plateau, they tramped along a rutted road bordered by stone walls. The only sounds were the rustle of their ski jackets, an occasional snapping twig, and their deep breaths as they climbed higher and higher.

Laurie looked like a snow bunny bundled up in her white snowsuit, Tobin thought. The most adorable one ever. "This is going to be all worth it, you'll see," he said. He was speaking of the Big Medicine Wheel, but he was also thinking of her when he said it.

"I never doubted it."

Trekking up the steep scarp wasn't quite as easy as they had anticipated, but they were both young and strong. Tobin realized that Uncle Basil would have had trouble with the climb. He held on to Laurie's hand when he thought she might be getting tired. The snow squalls and the cold wind stung their faces, making their eyes water, but their determination kept them going. The views in the valley below, with the strong and full rivers, were breathtaking.

"How you doing?" he yelled, when he noticed how red her face was getting.

She turned to look at him. "I'm doing fine."

"Just checking."

"Listen, I can make this. Don't worry about me. I think we're insane, though," she yelled into the wind.

"Do you want to turn back?"

"Are you crazy? This is the best time ever!"

That's exactly what he wanted to hear. He loved her passion, her courage and daring. She had made the trip much more fun than if he had gone alone. And it had been her choice.

Finally reaching the very top, at the far end of the narrow ridge, a few hours later, they stood, awed. Looking around, they were both mesmerized not only with the wheel but the benevolence of the white folds in neighboring mountains.

Tobin's eyes fell back to the enormous wheel. He figured the circle of stones was about eighty feet wide with rows extending from a central cairn to a stone rim. Placed around the border of the wheel were five more, but smaller, stone circles. All shimmered in the golden sun.

"It's magnificent," Tobin said, barely breathing.

"Phenomenal," Laurie agreed. "It feels like we're on top of the world."

"We are—sort of."

"I wonder who made this?" she asked, dropping to her knees to get a closer look.

"Nobody knows. Whoever they were—they were extremely gifted, that's for sure."

"How long do you think it's been here?" Laurie asked him.

"They say about three hundred years. Who knows—maybe more?"

"Wow," she said, standing now, counting the lines of stones.

"There should be twenty-eight of them. The days in a lunar month. It was how they established time. I suppose in the same way we use a calendar."

"A calendar," she repeated quietly. "I guess when something's always been there, you don't think about how it got started."

"Everything has a beginning," he said, thinking about theirs.

All alone with this gargantuan stone mystery, a dream had come true. It had always been more Uncle Basil's dream than Tobin's, but now it belonged to all of them.

"If this wheel could only talk, I wonder what it would tell us," Laurie said.

"Archeologists have been trying to figure that out for years. They do know that the early natives made use of the sun and stars in some very refined ways. Each rock is unique and distinct. And each has its own shape, space and time, like the one who placed it there."

"Do you know what I think?"

"No. Tell me."

"I think it was created not only for healing and as a calendar but—to bring people together, like you and me."

"Maybe." Tobin liked the idea, but he wished he knew for sure.

While Laurie grabbed her camera, Tobin fished out his journal and began trying to describe how it all looked to him. There was a lot to absorb, so much of it incomprehensible. People had always sought the high mountain for harmony with the powerful spirits there—that much he knew. He wondered, though, if a stone was laid every time a warrior killed his first living thing or when an animal or bird's name was given to him by his father. Perhaps when an important ceremony like a Pow Wow occurred.

After snapping a last picture, Laurie went over and sat beside him. "What is it?" she asked him. "You look a little glum."

"Oh, nothing. I was just thinking how Uncle Basil would have loved this. How much it would've meant to him."

"I know. But I'm sure he's glad you're here. And I wouldn't be surprised if he was, too."

Suddenly, the wind stirred and the sun seemed brighter. Tobin looked up to the sky. He saw an eagle. Fly high, Eagle. Fly high. In a passing cloud, he thought he saw his uncle's face.

"Let's stay here tonight," Laurie said. She could see how much Tobin missed his uncle. If they spent the night there in the mountains, he could feel closer to him. The mountains were so powerful, and it wasn't just their size that triggered that feeling. The peace, the serenity at that level was amazing. Must have been all the prayers and rituals said there, she thought. Tobin needed such spiritual connection with his late uncle.

"You mean here near the wheel?"

She nodded. "Yeah, why not?"

"It'll be brutally cold. The temperatures could drop well below zero."

"We'll stay warm."

He gave her a slow smile. "Okay, if you really want to do this."

"I do."

They explored the area a little more. Then they both stood in silence, admiring what was before them: the wheel, the mountains and the valleys below. Later Tobin built a fire. They huddled close, sharing a bag of gumdrops and a bottle of white wine he had bought along the way.

"This is a weird combination—wine and gumdrops," she said. "But I like it."

"What's your flavor?" he asked, handing her another handful.

"Green. Spearmint."

"Oh, I think I ate all those," he said.

She nudged him. "No, you didn't. I just ate one. What's yours?"

"Black. Licorice."

"That's my second favorite."

Laurie noticed after a while Tobin got really quiet. The night was winding down and they were both tired, but he was somewhere else.

"You're far away," she finally said.

"I'm sorry," he said, shaking his head. "I never lost anyone close to me before. I didn't know it could be so painful. I guess the way to describe it—like a new sore, open and raw. And you keep waiting to heal. But you know something that deep isn't going to happen that soon. I feel close to him here and comforted that his spirit is near. But. . . ." he trailed off.

"I'm really sorry for your loss. The only persons in my family who died were my grandparents, but I didn't know them. They died when my dad was young. I know I'd feel the same way you do if I lost someone close to me."

They were both quiet, then Laurie said, "I'm glad we decided to stay here tonight."

He searched her eyes. "Yeah. Thank you," he said, pulling her closer to him.

They put up the tent early that evening and soon they burrowed themselves into their sleeping bags. She listened to the ceaseless winds howl until she eventually drifted off. A glimpse of daylight shone through a small opening in the tent. She could hear birds calling to one another. She looked over at Tobin; his sleeping bag was without him. She quickly scrambled out of hers, slipped on her boots and ski jacket and went looking for him.

The air was still very cold; she could see her breath. The sky was slowly opening with snow clouds, sprinkling tiny flakes. She trekked the crunchy ground for at least half an hour, but there was no sign of him. She couldn't imagine where he had wandered off. The wind was picking up again and flakes swirled with it, disturbing her view. She wished she had brought his binoculars. And maybe the compass, too, because she was sure she was lost now.

She knew Tobin was saddened by his uncle's passing and how much he missed him, but she didn't think he'd be so affected that he would leave everything behind, even her. She thought coming here and executing his uncle's aspiration, feeling closer to his spirit, would have made him feel better, at least somewhat. She didn't have to experience a death to know it wasn't easy losing someone you love.

After another half hour of roaming, she saw a figure in the distance coming toward her. "There you are," she cried, running to him.

"I had this dream. Uncle Basil was calling me. I followed his voice."

"Where you sleep-walking?"

"I don't know."

"What happened?"

"I got up and went to the Medicine Wheel, thinking that's where he was. When I got there—it was like I heard him echoing from the mountains. So I started heading that way."

"What was he saying? Just calling your name?"

"Yeah. And he said 'Don't worry.' That he was happy and free of pain."

"Well, that's good. Anything else? Did he say anything else?"

"Yeah. He did. He said he was glad we made it," he said with a slow smile.

We?

Whether Tobin was dreaming or his uncle truly came through didn't matter. This is what he needed. Laurie could tell Tobin was reassured, calmed, knowing his uncle was in a better place now. It made her feel better as well, knowing Tobin's mind was finally at ease.

They walked back to the tent, packed up their gear and began trekking back down the mountain. Leaving was inevitable, but all of a sudden she was getting the blues. They had reached their journey's end, seen and felt the extraordinary along the course, and she was fully satisfied. Still, she wished it could be longer.

"Let's not hurry," she said to him. "Let's keep enjoying—"

"Absolutely," he said.

They were both quiet on the way down, absorbing their surroundings, etching them in their memories. Tobin would stop frequently using both his compass and binoculars, handing them over to Laurie so she could see what he saw.

"Oh my, is that a grizzly!" she shrieked, peering through the glass.

He laughed. "Yeah, but don't worry. He's too far away to have us for dinner."

"Are you sure? I can see his claws. Maybe he can see us. Smell us," she said, backing into him.

"Nope. The benefit of binoculars—they make everything far-off look close. We can watch anything safely," he said, reassuring her.

They trudged across rivers and even stopped to bathe in one, quickly peeling off their clothes and submerging. They smeared a bar of soap on each other, creating suds everywhere.

"I hope we don't get in trouble for this," she said, while he was washing her hair.

"If the Rangers don't catch us," he said with a smile. "They'd arrest us for improper exposure or polluting."

"Maybe both," she said, shivering.

"Your lips are turning purple. Time to get out," he said, dipping one last time.

They were close to where they had abandoned Tobin's truck now. Laurie knew even if her hair formed icicles that the heat inside would melt and dry them.

"Why does it always seem faster coming back?"

"I think getting to your destination always seems longer because of the anticipation. Like the wait to see the Medicine Wheel."

Tobin was right, she thought. When you're looking forward to something, it does seem like forever. The trip had been beyond her expectations. She even felt different.

Chapter 48

Driving back over the Bourne Bridge, Laurie watched the boats glide through the canal. She sat in silence the rest of the way, her stomach churning. She didn't know what to expect, what she was coming home to.

"So, tomorrow's the big day?" Tobin asked.

"Yeah. I hope I can remember everything."

"You will. It's like riding your bike after driving. You think you forgot until you get on. It'll be the same way at the bank."

"I know. You're right," she said quietly.

Laurie was more worried about facing her parents. She knew they had to be angry and disappointed in her. She had never done anything so wild before. She wondered if the consequences of her running off would be just as unimaginable.

"Here we are," Tobin said, when they finally turned onto her street.

Laurie shifted in her seat. During the past two weeks she had felt free from judgment—free from everyone who had tried to hurt and separate them. Now she had returned.

Tobin helped her unload her things, bringing them to the front step. He gave her a kiss. "Good luck."

"Thanks." After watching him leave, she brought her bags into the house. She knew her father was at work and her mother was in the office on Mondays. It would give her time to unpack and do some laundry. Then it dawned on her. Neither one would be working: it was Memorial Day. She wondered if they had gone to a cookout. After starting a wash, she plopped onto her bed, thinking how good it felt. She thought she had closed her eyes for a second, but it was two hours before she opened them again. She caught her mother's shadow out of the corner of her eye.

"Hi, Mom."

"You didn't call or anything. You just took off with that boy."

It's good to see you, too.

Laurie so much wanted to share with her mother the wonderful time she had, remembering how interested her mother had been in the school trip she took to NYC in eighth grade. Back then, though, she was chaperoned. Even if there had been an older adult going along with them, Laurie doubted it would have made much difference. It was more whom she had gone with than anything else.

"Tobin," Laurie murmured.

"What?"

"His name is Tobin, Mother."

"You had us worried sick. I was afraid something had happened to you."

"Well, it didn't, so can we just forget it?"

"I almost called Lieutenant Stein—"

"The police? How could you even think of doing that?"

"I didn't. But I thought about it. I didn't know what else to do."

"I left you and Daddy a note."

Laurie was thankful her mother hadn't reported her missing. The police would have eaten that up. She would die if Tobin went to jail for kidnapping her, or whatever charge they could bring him up on. She would never have forgiven her mother. Or herself. It was her decision to go, and she had assured him it would be all right.

"It wasn't like you were just going down the street with him. You were thousands of miles away."

Her mother had a point. She had never been that far away before, even with them. The furthest she and Tobin had ever gone was twenty miles into Dennis, where they stood at the top of Scargo Tower, touching the sky.

"Mom, I was safe. Tobin took care of me. Look at me, I'm fine. Didn't you get my postcard?"

Eleanor nodded. "You have laundry to finish."

Is that how we finish, Mother?

Laurie would have a talk with her father when he got home. She knew they were both upset, and she did understand. Still, she knew she would do it over again if she had the chance. She hoped her father would be a little more tolerant.

After sticking her clothes in the dryer, she called Rita to let her know she was back. Laurie couldn't wait to tell her about their trip. She knew if anyone would be excited for her, Rita would.

"I want to hear all of it. Don't leave anything out. Do you want to go for a soda?"

"No. I think I better stay around here. My parents aren't too happy with me. Understandably."

"Right. We can always get together another day."

Laurie heard the disappointment in Rita's voice, so she started to fill her in now, just a little bit, on stuff like where they ate and slept. When they got together, Laurie would show her the pictures she had taken and tell her more.

"Rita, imagine me sleeping in a barn."

"No. I can't imagine myself sleeping in one, either. I would've been out of there when I saw those bats."

"It crossed my mind. But I was with Tobin. . . ."

"He's strong and fearless, I'm sure. He certainly knows how to defend himself."

Tobin was fearless, Laurie thought. Brave, yet gentle and warm. And he made her feel completely protected.

"It wasn't just that. I never felt more daring in my life. I would never have climbed a mountain, or explored a cave before—I hate small spaces."

"I get ya—I never liked high places either."

Laurie went on, "When we got to Yellowstone—."

Rita interrupted. "Was the park as great as those pictures I've seen in National Geographic?"

"Better. There's no comparison. You had to be there. It was magnificent! The whole state was beautiful. The mountains—the valleys. We went fishing in one of the rivers. I even learned how to bait a hook," she recounted, remembering how the worms grossed her out. "Then Tobin cleaned the fish and built a fire to cook it."

"It all sounds so romantic."

"It was. Very."

Laurie recalled how she had found his lips as sweet and fresh as new maple syrup. Gingerly running her hands over his smooth bare chest, feeling every ripple of strength along the way. His firm body seemed impenetrable to her, almost inviolable, and his chestnut skin was lustrous as though oil, or some kind of magical potion, seeped from every pore, drawing her into him.

After he had made love to her, she felt something extraordinary—this deep closeness. One she had never felt before with anyone. Now she had truly experienced what others had; it was like rockets and sparklers going off at once.

"Tell me about the Medicine Wheel. Was it everything you expected?"

"Huh?" Laurie was shaken from her reverie.

Laurie had wanted to save the best for when they got together. "More. Much more. It's a very spiritual place. Probably the closest you'll ever get to heaven. You feel so calm and sure of everything there, your mind and body are like—in harmony, at peace. A peace so incredible you want it to live inside of you—always."

"You've made it sound so wonderful. I want to go there."

"You won't be sorry, I can tell you that."

"I'm sure I won't. It would be nice to have someone to go with, though."

Laurie agreed. Rita needed a partner. A boyfriend. It wouldn't have been the same without Tobin. Suddenly, Laurie heard her father's car pull into the driveway. "Rita, my dad just got home. I'll call you later."

Laurie listened for her father to come inside. She gave him a couple of minutes to get settled, then went downstairs. He was in the den, his office, pulling folders from his briefcase. She cleared her throat. He looked up.

"Dad, before you say anything. I know you're mad at me. And you have a right to be. It wasn't right taking off like that." Especially with a boy. "I'm sorry. Sorry I put you through all this. I know you and Mom were worried."

"You seem to know how'd we feel, but still you went ahead and did what you wanted. Your mother hardly slept. She cried every night you were gone. She does care about you."

"I know," Laurie said quietly, remembering the dark circles she saw under her mother's eyes.

"You've never done anything like this before."

I've never been in love like this before.

He went on, "You never gave us any problems. You've always been a good kid."

"And I still am. I feel like I haven't done anything I should be ashamed of. I never want to hurt you or Mom, but I have to be truthful, too. I'm not sorry I went with Tobin. I love this man. Dad, I know you remember what it was like. I had the best time ever. It was a life experience. One I would never have known if I hadn't gone."

He stared at her for a moment, his eyes softening. Unlike her mother, her father was never one to dwell. Once things were said, he didn't want to bring them up again.

"I appreciate your honesty, but that doesn't mean you're off the hook, young lady. You're getting too old to punish. But I want you to promise me you won't do anything like this again." He paused. "Until you're twenty-one."

"Twenty-one?" It seemed like a long way off. Half the kids her age would be married by then, or at least thinking about it, some already with kids of their own. She looked at him. "It's a deal."

"So, what was it like?" he asked, with a smile forming, as they walked together out of his office.

Chapter 49

A pale blue sky broke through occasional showers throughout the warm, late spring morning. Laurie parked her car in the usual employee spot. The private entrance in the back of the building was locked, so she entered through the main lobby. She strolled in cheerfully, ready to go to work. She had even gone out and bought a new lime green, V-neck dress for the first day. She enjoyed the work, but she enjoyed the people, too. The customers had sensed that when she had worked there the previous summer. One afternoon, she had even stayed late to help a woman balance her checkbook, something her late husband had always taken care of. Laurie could still see Mrs. Devon's grateful smile.

In spite of her eagerness, she immediately witnessed a somber setting. She had hoped for a friendly, "Hello, glad to see you again." In fact, everyone seemed more quiet than usual. She noticed a couple of new faces, but the rest had been there for many years. One dark haired woman, named Carol, who was about her mother's age, was opening the vault. Two tellers were counting money from the night deposit bags. Granted, after a long Memorial Day weekend everyone was tired, but the silence was a little too much.

Laurie went straight to the head teller, Sandra Hill, who had trained her the year before. Sandra was thirty-five years old with two young kids in elementary school. It was the perfect job for her because she was able to be home by the time the kids got off the bus. In spite of the age difference between Sandra and her, they hit it off pretty well. Sandra had told Laurie, more than once, that she was a great teller and only wished she was there year round.

"Hey, Sandra, this place is like a morgue. You'd think somebody died or something," Laurie whispered.

"Long weekend, I guess," Sandra said evasively. "Laurie, Mr. Shannon would like to see you in his office."

"Now?"

Sandra buzzed the security door to let her in. "Yeah."

Laurie assumed he wanted to welcome her back and fill her in on any new procedures.

"Brian and I aren't seeing much of each other anymore," Laurie quietly told Sandra.

"I heard," Sandra replied, recounting the money in her drawer.

Since Sandra knew about her and Brian, Laurie wondered if she also knew about Tobin. She figured it had to be getting around— the way gossip raced around Mashpee. Laurie walked down a long hallway, directly to Mr. Shannon's office, third door on the right. She raised a fist to tap on the jamb when she noticed him on the phone. He signaled for her to come in and sit.

She looked around at the wallpaper in eighteenth century country scenes, custom-made curtains and fancy trim work. A handsome brass plaque with his name and rank—President—loomed at the front of his big cherry wood desk. Among the stack of customers' folders were family photos, including Brian's graduation picture. How good-looking he is, Laurie thought. Still, she had never felt with him the constant high Tobin brought her.

Two minutes later, Mr. Shannon was off the phone.

"Mrs. Hill said you wanted to speak to me?"

A tall, distinguished looking gentleman in his early fifties, Mr. Shannon, eyes averted, cleared his throat a couple of times. "Yes. We had to make some adjustments, Laurie," he finally said.

Adjustments? Her eyes narrowed.

"I needed someone before school concluded. It's been very busy here. I'm very sorry, Laurie," he said, extending his hand, out of habit, a courtesy to his appreciative customers, but she had no intention of returning the empty civility. She was no customer, and she was obviously not appreciated.

"What are you saying? You hired someone and now you don't need me?"

"She's older. Mrs. Jones has had a lot of experience. She worked at Capitol for ten years."

"You told me in front of my parents months ago you were going to hire me back. You even made me mark the calendar."

"I'm sorry, I don't remember."

You remember. "Does this have anything to do with me and Brian?"

"No. No, Laurie," he said sincerely, shaking his head. "It's too bad you two weren't able to make a go of it." He paused. "But that has nothing to do with this situation."

"What am I thinking? It's because I'm dating Tobin. That's it, isn't it?"

He fell silent, lowering his head. His body language said it all.

"Oh, God."

He swiveled in his chair and then rose. "I'm sorry. I really am."

"Yeah, me too, Mr. Shannon. Me too." Laurie repeated, glaring at him. "I guess there's lots to be said about a small town." She hurried out of his office, down the hall and through the lobby.

It was a blow to her, but how could she think it would be any different? After all, he was Brian's father. Small town, small minds. She tore out of the parking lot with tears in her eyes. She was more angry than hurt, angry that Mr. Shannon couldn't look her in the eye and tell her the truth.

Without a job, Laurie wasn't sure what she was going to do. Her parents had always given her whatever she needed, but she liked her independence, making her own money. Except now she knew she wouldn't be earning it in Mashpee.

Even though Laurie knew nobody was at home, she was afraid Mrs. Dunbar would trot over and grill her as to why she wasn't at work. She was in no mood for that. Then she remembered she had her suit in the backseat from the last time she took a swim with Tobin. She would change in the bathhouse at the beach. Although, on second thought, she would burn to a crisp if she lay in the sun all day. Since she was already dressed for work, she decided to job hunt instead.

She drove east on Route 28 toward Hyannis, into a town where nobody knew her. Did Mr. Shannon think he was punishing me? If only she knew her legal rights. Still, she wouldn't want the job if he felt that way. She had seen law firms along this road. Since law was something she had always been interested in, the experience would be beneficial. Besides, the thought of working for a lawyer seemed far more intriguing than a teller position. Instead of phoning a firm, though, making an appointment for an interview, she would just show up. Laurie hit the brakes when she saw a big white sign in front of a brick building: "James K. Lake, Attorney."

Wearing an old blue sweatshirt, her jeans rolled up and white thongs on her feet, Laurie walked the beach looking for Tobin. Tall and striking, he was hard to miss, even at night. His tribe was getting ready for a big traditional clambake they called Appanaug. During the full moon, quahogs and mussels were close to the Popponessett shore.

Spotting Tobin, Laurie hurried over to him.

"What're you doing here?"

"If you want, I'll go," she said, turning to leave.

"No, please stay," he said, placing his hand on her shoulder, spinning her around. "I'm just surprised to see you, that's all. I thought you'd be tired, starting work today."

"I don't want to talk about it right now."

"No problem."

"I'd like to help, if it's okay?"

"You bet," he said, wrapping an arm around her waist as they walked.

In pairs, young and old were hunched in the mud, digging for clams, filling their buckets. It was like a contest seeing who could fill their pails first. She could feel the excitement when she and Tobin approached.

Some of the younger children ran over to greet them, grabbing Laurie's hand, showing her where to dig. Laurie knelt down in the cool, wet sand and began scratching. At first she wondered if she had the knack for it. She kept coming up empty-handed from every hole she reached into. Finally, she unearthed her first clam, feeling like she had discovered gold. She held it up for Tobin to see. "Look. I got one!"

He smiled, then kissed her.

"Do that again," said a cute boy, around five, wearing blue swim trunks and a yellow T-shirt.

"Yeah, kiss her. She's pretty," said his little friend, about the same age, with big brown eyes and the longest eyelashes Laurie had ever seen.

"Again, again," the two repeated, excitedly.

Tobin smothered Laurie's face with a half dozen smaller pecks. The children giggled. "You guys want some, too?" Tobin asked them.

They scrunched their noses and ran off.

Later, Laurie and Tobin took a moonlight cruise with some of the others. Six canoes glided across the bay, the air warm and the water waveless.

As Laurie lay against Tobin, his arms around her waist, he asked. "What's wrong?"

She lifted her eyes to meet his. "It's nothing."

"I know when there's something bothering you. I feel the tension in your body. What happened today?"

How could she tell him she believed Mr. Shannon let her go because she was dating him? She couldn't hurt him.

"Did you rob the bank while you were there?" he asked, trying to make her smile.

"No, but maybe I should have. He gave my job away," she finally blurted. "Can you believe it? He said he found someone more qualified. This would have been my second year there. I was never late—I did my job."

"Hey, I know it's rough, but there are plenty of jobs out there. You'll find one."

"I think I already did. Well, it's not definite yet, but I think I have a good chance."

"That's great. Another bank job?"

"I might work for an attorney and be his assistant. Although, I don't know any legal terms, really."

"That's okay, you'll learn them."

She smiled. "I always wanted to be a lawyer." She wished she had been the one representing the tribe.

"There you go. It'll be a perfect start."

Before saying good-night, they cruised the water, alone this time, just the two of them. The stars in the sky shined like diamonds. And she could have stayed in his arms all night, where her troubles seemed to fade.

Chapter 50

All night long Tobin worried about Laurie and wondered if losing her job had anything to do with him. In spite of getting no sleep, he rose promptly at five. It was like he had an internal alarm every year for the big clambake. It took a lot of work, but it was worth it since it was a celebration that made the family ties even tighter, especially between him and his father. Planning and preparing for it was half the fun.

He slipped into his jeans then threw on a blue sleeveless shirt, revealing his muscular arms, and slid his feet into work boots. He knew it was going to be a scorcher of a day and his feet would sweat, but he had heavy work to do. He ran a brush through his hair and tied it back with a rubber band.

His father was already up waiting for him in the kitchen. He also was dressed in jeans and boots, except unlike Tobin's baseball cap, James wore a wide-brim straw hat.

"Ready, son?"

Tobin nodded. "You bet."

Tobin's cousin, Charlie, was waiting for them inside the coffee shop. Instead of ordering the usual, coffee and doughnuts, they added eggs, sausage and home fries. It was going to be a long day. Afterward, Tobin and his father rode with Charlie in his old pickup he used mainly for hauling, leaving the Horvarth station wagon in the parking lot, something they had done for years. The owner, Steve Macklin, gave his permission since he closed up at noon every day.

At the sandpit, they began loading the back of the truck with rocks, some the size of boulders. Tobin and Charlie lifted the heavier ones.

"Damn, these rocks seem to be getting heavier every year," James grunted, as he hefted one up onto the flatbed.

"Yes, Uncle James, I have to agree," Charlie said.

Tobin smirked. "You two are just getting old, that's all."

"You'll be there someday," James said.

"I might get wiser, but I'll never catch up to you two."

Charlie, at thirty-one, though, was amazingly fit. Being a full time cook, or chef, as he preferred to think of himself, in his wife's family restaurant in Falmouth, he put in long hours. Tobin couldn't see how he had time for anything more, much less keeping in shape. Charlie earned a decent salary, enough to get by on, but that was hardly enough for Tobin. He was contemplating a Masters. The more degrees, the higher the pay. Less hassle.

"Hey, I heard you got yourself someone."

Tobin nodded. White girl. "Yeah."

"About time. I'm happy for you, cuz."

"I'm happy for me too," he mumbled, lifting a boulder onto the truck.

"How'd you get so lucky—getting a nice girl like that? Can't be good looks."

That's what I keep asking myself.

Tobin had never thought of himself as being handsome—just an average guy with simple tastes.

Charlie pushed him. "Hey, only joshing with you—I wish you the best, man."

"Thanks," Tobin said, shoving him back, nearly off his feet.

"You want to play rough, let's go," Charlie said.

"Okay, boys," James interrupted. "There's no time for fooling around. We've got work to do."

"Listen to your uncle," Tobin said to Charlie.

Tobin saw his father wiping his forehead. The pit's openness and the air being still made the already warm sun feel hotter. He imagined his father was getting tired. The heat alone was wearisome, never mind the hauling of the rocks.

"Any plans for the future? Marriage? Family?" Charlie asked Tobin.

"I'm too young to think that far ahead."

"Not really. I was twenty-seven, but I wouldn't advise waiting much longer than that."

"Why's that?" Tobin asked, swigging a cold beer.

"You don't want to be old and cranky when you have kids." "Kids! Who's talking about kids?"

"I remember thinking the same way. How old were you, Uncle James, when you had this devilish one?"

"That was a long time ago. I don't know if I can count back that far."

Tobin curled his hands into fists, grinning. "Devilish, huh?"

James intervened by putting himself between them. "That's enough."

Charlie and his wife, Lana, owned a small, three-bedroom ranch and had a new baby on the way. Lana had been in love with Charlie since she was sixteen. They married when she was twenty-one, and they had been happy ever since. Thinking about having that kind of life with Laurie was super. Why did they have to wait? If she wanted to, they could marry as soon as they were both through college. Help each other's dreams come true. Although there hadn't even been a discussion of a life together, Charlie had certainly given him something to mull over. At Charlie's house, he went to the shed with Charlie and lugged out the spruce wood, hammer and common nails. Hammering away, they made three-foot square wooden boxes. Afterward, they rolled out chicken wire, cut it and lined the containers. In the meantime, Lana, Charlie's wife, had come out of the house carrying a tray of lemonade.

"Thank you, honey, but citrus doesn't mix with beer," Charlie said.

"I'll take one," Tobin said, since she had gone to the trouble to bring it to them. "How's it going, Lana? You feeling okay these days—with the heat and all?"

"I'm doing fine. We're doing fine," she corrected herself, rubbing her belly.

"That's good. What're you hoping for, boy or girl?"

"Doesn't matter. We'd be happy with either. Just as long as it's healthy. But a girl would be nice."

"You can always try again."

"Not for a long time. One is plenty—for now. Laurie coming to the clambake?"

Tobin smiled. "Yep."

"I'm looking forward to meeting her. I've heard only nice things."

"She's great," he said, his smile broadening.

Tobin had never taken anyone to the clambake before. Girls had swarmed around him there, flirting, but none of them had appealed to him. Now he had someone he cared about to bring with him.

"See ya later," Lana said, as she turned and walked toward the house.

The sun was still hot at three o'clock when Tobin, his father and Charlie got to the beach. After shoveling a deep enough hole, they laid a bed of rocks then added wood to start a fire. Letting it burn a couple of hours, they raked the coals back and added rockweed.

Soon, some of the women came and placed corn, potatoes and onions, along with sausage and hot dogs, in cheesecloth bags. The wooden boxes, now filled with clams and lobsters, were carefully lowered into the big hot cavity. Charlie and Tobin covered it all with a canvas, sealing it securely with sand. In a few hours after steaming, the feast would be ready for everyone. This year's celebration will be even more special, including Laurie.

Chapter 51

Laurie slid her feet into a pair of moccasins, giving the beautiful white buckskin dress its finishing touch. She liked the way Hannah had braided her hair with deep blue and white beads earlier that morning. The day before, Laurie had helped Hannah pick wild black and red raspberries as a dessert for the big clambake. "It's like the Pow Wow—a homecoming sort of," Hannah had said, excitedly. "You get to see people you don't see every day. There's dancing. Singing. Games. And so much food, you wouldn't believe." Laurie could hardly wait to go.

She held one last glance in the mirror and caught her mother's stunned face.

"You're really taking this too far. I forbid you to leave here dressed like that," Eleanor demanded, crossing her arms. "Putting those clothes on doesn't make you one of them."

"I know that. I'm not trying to be one of them. I like this dress, and I think I have a right to wear what I want."

"Not under my roof, you won't."

"Daddy lives here, too. Doesn't he count for anything?"

"You really think your father would approve?" she snapped.

"As a matter of fact—yes—I think he would. But I really don't need anybody's approval. Not anymore."

"You're still living in this house."

"I'll move out. Is that what you want?"

"You're talking foolishly," Eleanor said quietly.

"Then I'd appreciate it if you'd let me get ready."

"Maybe one of these days, you'll see things my way," Eleanor murmured, leaving the room.

I doubt that. When her mother was gone, Laurie got up and closed the door. She knew her mother wouldn't want her to pack up for good, but at the same time she made it unbearable for Laurie to stay there. The sooner Laurie got out of the house, the better she was going to feel. But college was still weeks away and wishing that away would be like wishing away her time with Tobin. In spite of what her mother thought, she felt just as pretty as Tobin had made her feel the first time she wore it.

From Tobin's house, Laurie rode with his family to the clambake. After the run-in with her mother, she worried about what the Horvarths would think, until Mrs. Horvarth's first words to her.

"You look lovely, dear. That's a gorgeous dress."

"Thank you, Mrs. Horvarth. I bought it in a little shop in Wyoming."

"Yeah, you look pretty cool," Hannah remarked.

Laurie saw Tobin grin. She took a deep breath and laid her head against the car seat, smiling to herself.

As they walked the dusty path, Laurie smelled burning seaweed and as they got nearer, she could see steam billowing from huge pots. Women hovered around the pit, removing the cooked food, chatting happily like morning birds. Older kids played tag while the little ones stuck by their mothers. Dancers were telling stories with their movements, the choreography amazing. Laurie saw one young woman eyeing her dress, or maybe she was eyeing her man. When Laurie looked back at her, she shyly turned her head. Everyone was friendly, though. Each time Tobin received a greeting, they would nod at her, warmly.

After a while, the family went their separate ways. Hannah met up with her friends and Mrs. Horvarth helped put out the food while her husband joined the Peace Pipe ceremony.

"C'mon," Tobin said, grasping Laurie's hand, "I want to introduce you to my cousin Charlie and his wife."

"So nice to finally meet you," Lana said, checking Laurie out from head to toe, with a nod of the head.

"You, too," Laurie said.

"I wanted to do this sooner. But you know how it is. My schedule—Laurie's schedule," Tobin explained. "You two busy with the restaurant. . . ."

Charlie extended his hand to Laurie. "I think he just wanted to keep you all to himself."

Laurie shook Charlie's hand, then turned to meet Tobin's eyes. "Is that right?"

"Not true." Tobin raised a brow. "Well, maybe somewhat."

Laurie couldn't help noticing Lana's enormous stomach. It looked like she could burst at any moment. "When is your baby due?"

"In three weeks. Not soon enough. I wish she'd come now."

"She?" Charlie asked. "Do you know something I don't?"

"No. Not really. For some reason, though, I think it's a girl. Maybe by the way she's been kicking to the music," Lana said, patting her belly. "I think girls are spirited—strong-willed." She looked at Laurie. "Don't you agree?"

"I just think we just know what we want, and we'll go after it. Do whatever it takes. Maybe she's telling you she's ready to come into this world—meet it head-on."

"Lana might be right," Charlie interrupted. "The other night she asked me to get her pistachio and strawberry ice cream. I think if we were having a boy, Lana would want a hot dog and a beer."

"Talk about food, how about getting some?" Tobin suggested.

"Yeah. What are we waiting for?" Charlie asked.

Fish stews and corn chowders, sobaheg (turkey) stew, sausage and onions and all the shellfish the Wampanoag had scooped from the sand the night before topped long tables.

"Everything looks so good," Laurie observed, grabbing a plate for her and Tobin. Just when she thought she couldn't pile anymore on, she would see something too delicious to pass up, like the watermelon— laced with local rum, she had been told.

"Oh, it is. I'm always ready to eat, more so lately," Lana said.

"You can say that again," Charlie teased.

"You've got to remember, she's feeding two," Laurie countered.

The four of them took their food to an old picnic table surrounded by few maple trees. In spite of the slight breeze, Laurie noticed that Lana, dripping from humidity in her sleeveless cotton dress, wiped a strand of wet hair from her face, sticking it behind her ear. "Have you picked out a name for your baby yet?"

"Jasper if it's a boy. Charlie picked out that name. After his grandfather. And Renee if it's a girl. That's why I'm hoping it's a girl," Lana whispered to Laurie.

Laurie was trying to imagine her own stomach being stretched that far, but despite how uncomfortable Lana looked, there was a gleam in her eyes and her cheeks were rosy. Just like she had heard women get when they were pregnant. In the end, she figured it had to be all worth it—having a child with the man you love deeply.

After everyone was done eating, Charlie and Tobin disposed of the empty plates and cups in a nearby trash can. Laurie saw how difficult it was for Lana to get up after sitting for so long.

"Hey, let's go check this out," Tobin suggested, spotting a game of archery in progress.

"We really have to get going. It's tough on Lana. Carrying around that extra weight gets tiring," Charlie said.

"It won't be too much longer. Have Tobin bring you by after this little one's born," Lana said to Laurie.

"I'd be happy to," Tobin said.

"I'd like that. Thanks."

"If you need anything, you know, like a ride to the doctor's office when he's working, just give me a call," Tobin said.

"So far we've been all set, but who's to say? Thanks, Tobin."

"Bye. And good luck with your baby," Laurie said.

She turned to Tobin once they were far enough away. "I like them. They're really nice people."

"I knew you would."

CJ, squatting on a tree stump, shouted at them as they were passing by. "Hey, there. You don't drink what I drink, Tobin. You don't smoke what I smoke, Tobin. You don't think like I think, Tobin. You don't joke like I do, Tobin."

Laurie tugged on Tobin's arm. "Who is that? That sounds like your name stuck into that song I've heard on the radio."

"You don't want to know. Forget him. C'mon," he said, taking her hand and pulling her along.

"It's too bad. He's kind of cute."

Tobin stopped and gave her this stare. It amused her. She had never known him to be jealous before, but there hadn't been a reason yet either.

"I was thinking about Rita. I just thought if you knew him, and he was an okay guy. . . ."

"I'll find her someone, but not him."

"When ya gonna introduce me to your girl, Tobin?" CJ bellowed.

Laurie looked at Tobin. "What harm will it do?"

"You don't know him. He can be a pain in the ass when he's drinking."

"He's not going to let up."

"Okay. But let's make it quick," he said, turning around.

"How's it going, CJ?" Tobin asked flatly, as they walked toward him.

With his eyes half open, he grinned. "I could be doing better."

"You wanted to meet Laurie. Here's your chance."

CJ just stared at her.

"Hello, CJ. Glad to meet you," Laurie said.

"You happy?" he finally asked her.

"Very."

"Tobin's a good man."

She nodded. "Yes he is."

"You take care of her," he said to Tobin.

"I do—always."

CJ kept grinning. Then he gulped down a beer.

"Let's go," Tobin said, steering Laurie in another direction.

"Bye, take care," Laurie said, over her shoulder. "So, what was that all about? I'll bet he's a decent person when he's sober. You weren't very friendly."

"Maybe not," he said abruptly. "Have you ever shot a bow and an arrow?"

"No," she said, staring at the multi-colored target in a field in front of them, wondering why Tobin had changed the subject so quickly. What was it about CJ that Tobin didn't want to talk about?

"Would you like to try?"

Laurie shrugged. "Tell me how it works."

"You see those circles? The innermost one or the bull's eye, if you get it, is worth ten points. And every circle after that goes down a point. You usually stand about thirty meters away. That's about thirty-four yards."

"How do you know if it's thirty-four?"

"You don't have to worry. They've got it figured out. Let me show you."

She watched the way his muscles contracted. Steadying himself, eyes focused, he hit the bull's eye again and again. He wasn't trying to impress her; he was only showing her how. It seemed like everything he did came so effortlessly to him.

"There's your target," he said, pointing. "When you're ready, draw back, aim and then shoot."

She studied it for a few minutes. When she finally released the arrow, it seemed to stop in midair, then fell to the ground. "Yikes," she said, quietly.

"You just need a little more practice."

"A little?"

"Hey, I'd be worried if your aim was a good as mine. You've never done this before. Try again," he insisted. "You'll do better this time."

Concentrating, she never took her eye off the target. Her hand was steady, and she let go with ease. She hit the board. Not a bull's eye, but at least she made contact. One point!

"See, I knew you could do it."

When more people became interested and the competition grew, she dragged him away. It was okay when it was only the two of them, but now there was too much expertise in the game.

The front porch light was on when Laurie arrived home that night. She was glad her mother was in bed. Everything that needed to be said had been, over and over. Her mother could repeat herself a million times; it wouldn't make a difference. She would never give Tobin up.

When she slid under the covers she thought about the wonderful time she had at the clambake. She felt right at home with Tobin's family and his people. And she enjoyed hanging out with Charlie and Lana. Even though they were older, they were easy to talk to. They seemed so much in love, so happy. The way she and Tobin were.

Chapter 52

"Where would you like to go, today?" Tobin asked her the following Saturday when he called.

"I don't care. Anywhere. Let's just get out of here."

"Having a bad day?"

"No. I'm just tired of sitting around. I'll feel better once I start work."

"Have you heard anything?"

"Not yet. I'm sure I will soon." But she was beginning to have doubts. Most summer positions were filled already. She felt she had made a good impression, but Attorney Lake probably considered she would be starting school before she even had a chance to get familiar with the place, never mind legal terms. Laurie kept herself busy reading, riding her bike and swimming, but the days were still long with no one to talk to. Rita worked at a travel agency, so she didn't get to see her much. All she had with Tobin were the weekends basically, since he was working, too. Except for the nights she would sneak out to be with him.

"We're always going to the pond. How about a change? Let's go to Sandy Neck. We can stop at the market, get some sandwiches and have a picnic out on the flats. How about it?"

"You know, I haven't been to the beach that much this summer. Why not? Great idea."

Pushing the grocery cart around with Tobin, Laurie felt married. *That's a scary thought. But not really if Tobin was my husband.*

"Hop on," Tobin said, after Laurie dropped a couple of peaches and plums into the carriage. "I'll give you a ride."

"I'm too heavy. It'll tip over."

"Only if I let go."

As they moved through the aisles, all eyes seemed to be on them. One lady stared so hard she collided with another shopper. "Don't you know it's rude to stare?" Laurie blurted, shocking herself. This was so not her, but the situation made her become someone she wasn't. The woman's mouth gaped, her droopy eyes ballooned as she puffed an aggravated breath and hurried off.

Laurie saw Tobin cover his mouth, trying not to laugh. "She asked for it," Laurie said.

Then an elderly woman dropped an onion. The vegetable rolled on the floor and stopped at Tobin's feet. He stooped, picked it up and handed it to her. She hesitated. Then she grabbed it, never looking at him, stuck it back into the bin and seized another.

Laurie watched her. It doesn't have cooties. In the moment, the incident was funny, but all this disapproval was taking its toll, and Laurie was trying not to let Tobin know it. She didn't know attention could be so contrary, so damaging. Still, there was no reason to hide anymore from anybody. They had nothing to be ashamed of. Laurie had hoped that the more they appeared in public together, the more desensitized people would become. A step toward being accepted. She wanted to believe that anyway, although today didn't look very promising.

Tobin wiped a tear from Laurie's eye.

"Onions," she said, feigning a smile, though she was nowhere near them. She hoped he wouldn't notice.

Once they were alone in the truck, her tears fell. "Why does everything have to be so complicated? Why can't everybody get along?"

"We can't change the way they feel, Laurie," he said softly.

"It's just so stupid," she said, shaking her head.

"I know. Unfortunately, we don't live in a perfect world. But we're not going to let it spoil our day."

"No, we're not," she said, wiping her face.

When they got to the beach, they laid their belongings out on the flats, the tide low. Once they were settled, Tobin fished out the purple and yellow florescent kite he had brought.

"Ready?"

She stood up. "Yup."

There was just enough wind. The kite soared in the sky as they took turns running with it. She lost hold of the string at one point.

"Ahh!" she screeched, reaching for it.

Tobin immediately jumped for it, his long arms and hands outstretched; somehow, he grasped it in time before it was lost to the sky.

Afterward, they strolled along the water's edge. He even stopped and kissed her, the way she remembered seeing that romantic couple together when she had taken Sharon and Pam to see the sunset. How lucky she felt having found him.

They had brought along an umbrella, but Tobin still lathered Laurie with sunscreen. After a couple of hours of lying on the beach, Tobin started packing their stuff. "What are you doing?" Laurie asked him. "I don't want to go home. Not yet."

"Then we won't. I just didn't want you to get burnt—your skin is so fair."

"I'll be okay—I'm well protected with the sunscreen and umbrella."

"Yes, you are. But let's go anyway—I have an idea."

She wondered what he had in mind. With him it was more fun just to wait and find out. She was sort of surprised, though, when he pulled up at his house.

Tobin turned the engine off and looked at her. "Come in for a minute."

Laurie followed him into the house and down the small, narrow hallway, where he stopped midway in front of a closet that resembled a cabinet. He opened the long, slender door and took out a rifle and a handful of bullets.

"Have you ever used one of these?" he asked her.

She shook her head.

"Do you know anything about guns?"

"No," she said, staring at it.

"You will after today."

"I'm afraid of guns. They're dangerous."

"Only if you abuse them. They can't hurt you, if you respect them."

Laurie had a friend back in Newton whose father worked for Brinks. He carried a gun. But Laurie had never actually touched or handled one before. Just the sight of one made her uncomfortable.

"C'mon, follow me," he said.

Whatever she felt about the rifle, she always felt safe with him. He led her outside and into the woods behind his house. About a quarter of a mile in, he veered to the left into a clearing not far from a cranberry bog. He stopped in front of two sawhorses, topped with a large sheet of plywood. He quickly moved them to the side, replaced them with two bricks and two leveled boards. Then, he arranged cans and bottles, taken from a nearby bucket, on top. He proceeded to lay a tarp on the ground, about twenty-five feet away.

"Lesson number one. Never aim a gun at anyone," he said with a wan smile, "unless you plan to use it."

"Are you serious? I wouldn't shoot anybody!"

"I didn't say that. But if it came to your life or someone else's, you might think differently. Now lie flat on your stomach," he said, "and rest on your elbows." He handed her the .22. "Put the butt of the caliber here, firmly against your right shoulder. In your joint," he said, showing her. "Let the stock—this part—balance on your left palm. Put your index finger on the trigger. Your trigger finger," he said.

"Like this?" she asked timidly.

"You're doing great. Take a couple of deep breaths. There's no need to rush."

"What if I don't hit them? Where will the bullets go?"

"Don't concentrate on that. Do you see that pile of sand behind the bottles?"

She nodded.

"That's like a safety net. They'll end up there."

After about half an hour of practice, she started to relax and really enjoy herself. Suddenly, though, a fox appeared, bushy tail erect. She remained motionless. It was the biggest and prettiest fox she had ever seen. Someone was taking care of it, she thought.

"Don't think I'm going to shoot him," she said quietly, laying the rifle down.

Tobin laughed. "You don't have to shoot him or any animal. Besides, he's my friend."

Laurie watched Tobin take a cookie out of his shirt pocket. Evidently expecting to see him, the fox gently took it from Tobin's fingers and ran off into the bush to eat it. She had never seen a wild animal so close to a human before.

"Your friend?"

"Yeah. He came wandering down that path one day," Tobin said, motioning. "He was half the size he is now. He was a little timid at first. But then we hit it off."

"Hit it off?"

"Yeah. Got to know each other. I gave him a chunk of my apple, and we've been buddies ever since."

"What's his name? I mean—did you give him a name?"

He shrugged. "No, I haven't."

She studied him, looking at his glowing reddish fur. "How about calling him Cinnamon?"

"Cinnamon. Hmm. I like it."

The way Cinnamon came to Tobin was like something out of a fairy tale, Laurie thought. But this was real. It was a beautiful sight. It didn't matter if one was an animal or a person; it was easy to be drawn to Tobin. She knew it firsthand.

Chapter 53

Tobin spent half the night pacing, rehearsing what he would say. He had to end it with Laurie. What else could he do?

It was more than just the incident at the market that made him decide. It had been haunting him for weeks. She had lost her job, her friends, and he knew her mother was giving her a hard time, too. She claimed that none of it bothered her, but he knew it did. How could it not? Going out with him didn't seem to be doing her any favors.

When they first met, she was bubbly and happy and nothing got her down. He remembered their first date to Scargo Tower. On the trip to Wyoming, she was carefree and radiant. Lately, though, he hadn't seen that sparkle in her. She seemed uptight; he could feel the tension in her body, and he had seen sadness in her eyes. He knew she was trying to hide it from him, but it was becoming much too obvious.

She was too young. Gorgeous. Smart. She had a bright future ahead of her. What right did he have to take that from her? He had to set her free. But how was he going to do that? He really loved her. How could he pretend he didn't? He remembered how upset she got when she thought he had drowned. And she cried at the courthouse for people she didn't even know. Everything about her was right and good. That's what made it even harder to find the strength to tell her it was over.

They had awoken together to an amber sunrise in Wyoming. She looked so beautiful lying next to him. Was he crazy now to think of throwing her away? No. He knew he was doing what was best for her, even if it felt totally off. He had planned to see her that evening, but he knew if he had to wait until then, he might not tell her at all. It had to be that morning.

He didn't want to meet her at the pond— they had fallen in love there. There was no ideal place, but he had to do it somewhere. He had to be convincing, too. Sure. I can do that.

Finally, he picked up the phone and dialed her number.

"Hi, Tobin."

Already he was having second thoughts just hearing her voice. "I need to see you. At my place."

"Sure. What's up?"

"We'll talk about it when you get here."

"You sound different."

After a few moments of silence, she added, "I'm coming over."

When she got to his house, he ushered her to the backyard where they could have some privacy. His mother was home—not that she would interfere—but the house was small, and he hadn't had time to tell his family about his decision.

"What's going on?" Laurie asked, searching his face.

"Nothing. Well, I mean, yes. There is." Already he felt like he was blowing it.

"You're confusing me."

I'm confusing myself.

"We have to talk," he said, trying not to look at her. It would throw him off. He knew he would say something totally different than he had planned. He might even ask her to marry him. After all, she was everything he ever wanted, and more.

"What about?"

"Us."

"What about 'us'?"

"It's not going to work—you and me."

"You're not making any sense. We're doing just fine."

"No. No, we're not," he said, making his voice as cool as possible.

"I don't understand," she said, tears in the corners of her eyes. "What happened since I saw you last?"

"Nothing. We can't go on like this, Laurie. I can't go on like this."

"Are you telling me you don't want to see me anymore?"

"Exactly. I think this is the way it should be," he said, his voice harsher than he felt.

"What about what I think?"

He didn't answer her.

"Just like that—you want to end it?"

"We're two different people, Laurie. We come from different worlds. It could never work. I don't know what made me think it would." This was harder than he thought. All he really wanted to do was take her in his arms and tell her how much he loved her.

"Really? And when did you figure this all out?"

"I have been thinking about it for a while now."

"I don't believe you. And I don't know why you're doing this. You're being so cruel. This isn't like you." She shook her head, her eyes big with anger and hurt. "You really never want to see me again?"

"Yes," he said firmly. He hoped he sounded like he meant it. His own words were tearing him apart, too. But he couldn't let her know that.

"What about what we have together? How can you just forget that?"

"Please stop asking questions. It doesn't matter."

"It matters to me. And I know it matters to you, too. I don't care what you say."

"I saw the way those people gawked at us in the market. . . .Being with you—I feel like a freak! I'm sorry. I can't help what I feel."

"I gave up everything for you. Everything!" she said, tears streaming down her face.

I know that. That's why I'm doing this.

"All I have is you," she cried as she turned away.

You'll have it all back when I'm out of your life.

Her shoulders trembled, and he could hear her sobbing. Hurting her was the last thing he ever wanted to do. He wanted so badly to run to her, wipe those tears and tell her he didn't mean any of it. He had no other choice, and it was killing him.

Hannah squinted as Tobin looked up at her. Then she shaded the sun with her hand, searching his face. "You look terrible. What's wrong?" she asked, plopping in the hammock next to her brother. "This has something to do with Laurie, doesn't it?"

"It's over," Tobin said.

"What's over? Oh, no. Don't tell me you broke up with her?"

Tobin nodded. "We're not going to see each other anymore."

"She's the best girl you ever had. Are you crazy?"

Tobin couldn't disagree with her there. "Maybe I am," he said quietly.

"You can't let her go. You just can't," she cried.

Tobin had never seen his sister so upset. He knew Hannah liked Laurie; his whole family did, but he didn't realize just how much until now.

"Don't be a fool. Go after her. Don't make the biggest mistake of your life."

"She's not happy, Hannah."

"'Cause you're not with her, that's why. Do you think she's going to feel any better now?"

"It's more than that."

His sister obviously hadn't seen the change in Laurie since they first met. If she had, she would understand why he was doing this.

"You love her. Don't you?"

"With all my heart."

"And she loves you. What else matters?"

What else did matter? He thought he'd been thinking of her, but now he wasn't sure of anything anymore.

Chapter 54

"Are you sure you don't want to come, sweetheart?" Laurie's father asked a second time. "It might make you feel better."

Laurie shook her head. Visiting her Connecticut grandparents was the last thing she wanted to do now, though she usually loved seeing them. "No. Thanks, Daddy, I'll be fine." She had already done her crying, soaking his shirt the night before with her tears.

"Well, you know where to find us."

She really didn't want to hang around the house feeling sorry for herself either, but she didn't know where else to go. Rita had invited her over to hang out with some cousins visiting from Vermont, but she wasn't feeling sociable. Plus, Rita had no idea what had just happened between her and Tobin and would ask too many questions. She wasn't in the mood to talk about it yet. She figured once the word got out about the break-up, Pam and Sharon would probably want to be friends again, but their interpretation of friendship was planets away from hers.

Listening to "Evergreen" on the radio, her heart nearly stopped. Streisand's voice was so beautiful and the lyrics reminded her of Tobin. Songs that were theirs, songs that seemed written just for them, only made her sad now. The last thing in the world Laurie had expected was for Tobin to leave her. After moping awhile, Laurie got up and started hunting for her royal blue silk scarf. It would go nicely with a blouse she bought recently and she wanted to look her best for some crazy reason. Anything to make her feel better. When it wasn't in her drawer, she checked the laundry, then headed to her parents' room. Her mother had probably borrowed it. Laurie didn't mind—her mother paid for most of her clothes anyway.

Rifling through her mother's bureau, Laurie realized she was searching for more than just the scarf but wasn't sure what. Answers, maybe? Was Eleanor going through menopause or something? Laurie knew a girl back in Newton whose mother started at the age of thirty-seven. Her mother was now going on forty-two. At first her friend's mother was stealing candy bars and cigarettes from the supermarket. Then it was Filene's basement. She ripped off price tags in dressing rooms and wore the new stuff out of the store. When they told her she might get jail time, she jumped off a bridge. Luckily, a diver was nearby to save her life. Laurie knew her mother wouldn't do anything that drastic. She was definitely no thief, but she sure had become a stranger.

She didn't find the scarf, but she did find a small silver box far back in the drawer. Curious, she took it out and opened it, to find only a ring of keys. Why did she hide them? After putting it back, Laurie moved to her mother's side of the walk-in closet and started pushing aside dresses and blouses.

Something tickled the top of Laurie's head. She gazed up at the rope dangling from the attic stairs and pulled on it. Climbing them, at the top it was dark and hot. It was ages since she had been up there. All she could see was a ray of outdoor light through two end louvers. Waving her hand above her head, she found the chain to a bright light. Sheets of plywood made paths in several directions.

Labeled cartons filled with tax documents, Christmas ornaments, old dishes and knick-knacks were stacked neatly on the east side of the house. To her far left was an old black trunk she had never been able to open. This time she was determined. Laurie hurried back down the set of stairs and over to her mother's bureau. After snatching the ring of keys inside the silver box, she went back up to the attic. Trying the largest key first, she heard a click. "Yes," she said aloud. Instantly, she was smacked with the pungent whiff of mothballs. Something was being preserved. There on top, safely wrapped in a clear garment bag, was a light blue dress with a white ruffled pinafore, still faintly stained with the chocolate ice cream she had spilled on her fifth birthday. Her mother had worked so hard to make that day perfect.

Digging deeper, she stumbled across an old shoebox. Inside was a mound of faded black and white photographs. She plopped on a small stool directly under the light to get a better look at them. None of the faces or places was familiar to her.

Then she came across a photo of her and her mother when she was six. She remembered that evening clearly. It was just the two of them at home. Her father had gone bowling with some friends. Her mother had taken the ponytail out of her hair. Brushing Laurie's long silky strands, her mother had told her how much she loved her. Eventually, her six-year-old eyes got heavy and her head fell against her mother. Her father had come home and found the two of them cozily wrapped together on the sofa in a "Hallmark pose," as he put it. He quietly set his things down and got out the camera. He said the flashes never even woke them.

Leafing through the pictures, Laurie halted at another. The three people in the photograph were the ones she had seen in her dreams. The man, dark-haired and ruddy-skinned, had a feather near his ear. The woman next to him was fair with long blonde hair. The little girl looked like her. Laurie was definitely no clairvoyant. She must have seen this photo and forgotten about it.

How did my mother know these people?

Laurie's long arms reached further into the trunk under layers of stuff. Her hands touched what felt like a book. Drawing it out, she saw it was a diary. Locked, of course. But she was certain the smaller key on the chain would fit. It did. Thumbing through the pages, she recognized the handwriting. Laurie knew she had no right reading such personal stuff, but she needed to find her way back to her mother. With her legs stretched out, she rested her back against the trunk and began.

August 23, 1963 – It's the beginning of a new work week. Everybody was tired after a long weekend, but I cracked the whip. I try not to be too hard on them but things have to get done. As much as I complain to Donald about what goes on during the day, I love having the upper hand. I like being the boss. Few women have this opportunity. If it wasn't for my father, I wouldn't have this insurance agency. I should be grateful instead of complaining so much.

October 30, 1963 – Ruth Harrison beamed when she announced that her third grandchild, Jessica, took her first step the night before. Then Cynthia, who is two years younger than me, told us that her middle child, Matthew, had lost his first tooth. I really can't relate with them and it bothers me. I never thought it would but it does. I feel more left out than ever.

November 15, 1963 – We were glad Jim and Debbie were able to get a babysitter so they could go out to dinner with us. During the course of the evening they boasted about their kids. I felt a twinge of jealousy. Maybe more than a twinge. Having a child wasn't on my mind before, but lately that's all I've been thinking about.

Laurie found many pages in the diary blank but what truly mattered to her mother was written expressively, keeping her intrigued. She couldn't stop reading.

January 10, 1964 – I'm glad Donald and I talked. He said he'd wanted a child all along but was afraid to tell me because he knew how important my work was to me. I had neglected to tell him that it wasn't as important as it used to be. I thought I'd be content with the agency and I am. Or at least I was. It certainly fills my time but it doesn't fill this emptiness, this void. Now that we know how each of us feels, we're not going to waste any time.

February 19, 1964 – Donald and I have been trying for over a month now and I'm still not pregnant. Maybe we're trying too hard. The doctor told me to relax, take some time off from work if I have to.

March 22, 1964 – I've done everything I'm supposed to and still I can't get pregnant. What if I never can? Maybe this is some kind of punishment for being so selfish for so long. I try not to think like that but nothing's working. The thought of being childless hurts. Please, God, I'm not a bad person. Let me give my husband a child. I don't really think I've done anything so horrible that you should deny me like this.

April 1, 1964 – I saw the doctor today he says I'm healthy and he doesn't see why we would have a problem making a baby. He took more tests. To be safe he checked Donald, too. He said we would know soon. More waiting.

April 8, 1964 – The doctor called and said I wouldn't be able to conceive after all. Donald held me in his arms until I cried myself to sleep.

April 17, 1964 – It's been over a week now since the blow. I'm functioning okay but I feel dead inside. Donald feels bad seeing me like this and he doesn't know what to do. And neither do I.

May 19, 1964 – I've been dreading the weekend. At least work keeps me from thinking about what I'll never have. But Donald came home happy as I've ever seen him. It said he had a surprise for me. I couldn't imagine what it could be. He heard through an acquaintance about an adoption center in Denver. I love him so much. He's going to find out what we have to do next. And the sooner the better.

June 18, 1964 – The adoption agency told us a newborn wouldn't be available for a while. We want a child right away. They want to introduce us to this little Indian girl who came in just the day before. Her parents died in a car accident. I don't recall the tribe. But it doesn't matter. I don't want an Indian. And I really don't want an older child. I want a baby. I want to be able to raise my child my way. For Donald, though, I agreed to meet her. Still, I know I won't change my mind.

June 25, 1964 – Donald and I sat in a waiting room. I don't know who was more nervous, him or me. He always appears calm on the outside. My friend, Diane, gave me a pack of cigarettes before I left. She knows I quit smoking, but told me I still might need them just the same. She was right. In the fifteen minutes we were in the waiting room, I smoked five cigarettes. I'd take a few puffs, snuff it out and light another. I don't know why. I had made up my mind. At least I thought I had.

But then a door finally opened and the most beautiful little girl I had even seen walked into the room. She had almost white blonde hair and big blue eyes. It looked like a halo should be hanging over her head. We just stared at each other for a moment. Somehow, she'd survived the accident. And already I thanked God for that. Donald thought she looked like me. It was hard to believe she was Indian, her skin was so fair.

Laurie's forehead beaded with moisture and she found it hard to take breaths, but not from the stifling attic. Her dreams, her memories were trying to tell her something since so much of her beginning she'd suppressed. But now she had to know everything— even if intruding in someone's privacy was wrong; she couldn't stop reading now.

September 8, 1964 – After all the paper work, legalities, we finally got to take this precious child home with us. Donald says we're alike. I think so, too. I've got great plans for her. We changed her name From Aiyana to Laurie Ann. Nobody has to know anything.

October 15, 1964 – It's been over a month since Laurie's been with us. She is very shy. I wonder if she'll ever come out of it. Some say it's just a phase. The minister spoke to her today in church and she never looked at him. She kept her head down and just nodded at his questions. Donald says I have to give her time. He said a little over four weeks isn't long enough for a child to adjust, especially, with all she's been through. I know he's right. I need to learn to be patient.

June 3, 1965 – Both Donald and I have changed so much since Laurie Ann came into our lives. She brings us so much joy, even after the holidays are long gone. She's a happy child most of the time now. Her parents must have loved her very much. I can't imagine life without her.

Laurie closed the diary, leaped up and immediately dug to the bottom of the trunk, finding a large manila envelope, securely sealed. With trembling fingers, she released the fastener and scratched and peeled away the sticky tape carefully with her fingernails. Inside were sheets of pale, official-looking paper. Quickly scanning them, Laurie slid slowly to the floor. The first record was a birth certificate of a baby girl, born May 24, 1959. The child's father's name was Edward Moon. The mother's full maiden name was Henrietta Sarah Scott. The document said he was a fisherman and she was a homemaker. Beneath that sheet of paper were also two death certificates. The parents were both killed December 26, 1962. What a tragedy, she thought. They were killed the day after Christmas. A little girl was without a mother or father to take care of her. Laurie felt like she had been suddenly smacked on top of her head.

Baby girl born May 24, 1959. My birthday. I am her and these two people were my parents. I made it and they didn't. Not fair. She leaned against the chest. Why couldn't I remember them? I was old enough. I was three. . . .Why was my past kept a secret? Were they so ashamed of where I came from? Ashamed of me, too? Laurie felt like a cement block had been dropped on her chest. It was hard to breathe.

Laurie looked at the photo again. These strangers were her biological parents. Why had those years been blocked from her memory? Maybe there were signs that the people she thought were her parents really weren't, but Laurie never paid attention. Why would she? She had been content with her life—her family. Now she didn't know what to think. She would have to confront them. But what could they say that would make a difference? They hadn't been honest with her.

She sat for a long time, just staring at the picture. Then she glanced at the birth and death certificates again. Numbness fell over her. How could someone's life change so quickly?

Laurie put everything back in the trunk, except for the manila envelope, which she was holding to her chest. She wasn't going to let anything happen to it. If her parents tried to deny it all, she had the proof. Double-checking to see that she left everything the way it should be, Laurie closed the trunk, shut off the light and hurried down the wooden stairs. She had no idea how much time she had spent in the attic and was afraid her parents might come home and catch her. She wasn't ready to deal with them, not yet. There was too much to digest at the moment.

Her first thought was to call Tobin, but she wanted to see his face when she told him. As hurt as she was when he walked away, she had figured out since that he broke up with her to spare her any more heartache. Now they could be together. They were one and the same.

Laurie glanced at the clock on the kitchen wall. It was only a little after three. It would be another hour or so before her parents were home. Her stomach was growling but she was too upset to eat. Still dazed, Laurie went to her bedroom and hid the documents under the mattress. Tomorrow, she would go to the bank and open a deposit box. She wouldn't let anyone take away her past a second time.

Chapter 55

Laurie had hoped to settle down some before approaching her parents, but as soon as she heard their car in the driveway, she ran downstairs. She needed answers.

"Mom, get Dad, I need to talk to you both—right away."

"What is it—what's the urgency?"

"Mom, please."

Eleanor opened the door to the garage and called to her husband. "Donald, could you please come in? Laurie needs to speak with us."

When everyone was in the living room, Laurie demanded, "Why didn't you tell me I was adopted?"

They both stood like deer in front of headlights. "Tell you what?" Eleanor finally asked.

"I know I was adopted. Don't try to deny it."

"Who told you this?" she asked.

"Nobody. I found out on my own."

"If no one told you. . . ." She paused. "You read my diary. Didn't you? That's private. How could you?"

"How could I? You're the one who kept my life your little secret all these years."

Her mother had turned so pale, Laurie thought she was going to pass out.

Donald broke in, "We wanted to tell you. Honestly we did. Didn't we, Eleanor?"

Her mother nodded, her eyes meeting her husband's.

"We thought about telling you when you were small, but then the years just went by. And after a while, it didn't seem that important," he said.

"Maybe not to you!" Her eyes roamed from her father to her mother. "Didn't you ever wonder how I'd feel? I'm not sure I even know who I am anymore."

"You're ours, honey. You'll always be ours," said her father.

"I was never yours. You lied to me. Both of you!"

Seeing her father's face fill with grief made her want to retract her words, but she couldn't now. "Who are my real parents—my birth parents?"

"Well, sweetheart. . . ."

"I don't want Daddy to tell me. I want you to, Mother," Laurie said.

Eleanor's tongue glided over her front teeth, as she twisted her wedding band with her right hand. "Your father surprised me one day. He told me about this adoption agency."

That's a start. Laurie thought Eleanor would be relieved to get it out after all these years, but it was obviously difficult for her.

"Your parents. . . they died in a car accident when you were three."

"Why'd you keep this from me?"

Her mother fell silent.

"Tell me about them. Please."

"We didn't know them, honey," her father said.

"The agency had to tell you something. Where did we live?"

"I don't remember. They may not have told us. Your father was Indian. That I'm sure of. I think your mother, though, was English, maybe Irish."

"What tribe were they from—do you know?"

"It was so long ago. I'm not certain." Donald thought for a moment. "Yes, I remember. It was Southern Ute. I think it's a relation to the Apache."

"So that makes me at least one quarter Indian."

Donald looked at his wife. They both nodded.

"I was afraid of losing you," Eleanor cried.

"Losing me? To who?"

"Them," she said quietly, staring downward.

Them? Then Laurie figured it out. "The Wampanoag?"

Eleanor raised her eyes. "It was selfish of me, I know."

"Selfish? I think that's an understatement. You pretended all these years I was yours. Like you had given birth to me. What gave you that right?"

"We never meant to hurt you, honey. Honestly, we didn't," her father spoke in his wife's defense.

Laurie believed his words. But she wasn't ready to forgive them. At least now she knew why her mother had tried to keep her away from Tobin. She turned away from them, swung her pocketbook over her shoulder and headed to the front door.

"Where are you going?" Eleanor asked.

Laurie said nothing as the screen door swung wide.

"Wait," Eleanor cried.

"Let her go," Donald said, placing a hand on his wife's shoulder. "She has a lot to sort out. Maybe we were wrong, Eleanor. We should've told her long ago."

Laurie banged the brass knocker and waited. When the door finally opened she was relieved to see Rita.

"Are you busy?"

"Not really. Come on in," Rita said.

"I need to talk to you."

"Yeah, sure," Rita replied, studying her as she breezed past.

"Is now okay?" Laurie asked quietly, hoping Rita's parents weren't there. She almost forgot about the cousins.

"Now is fine. I don't expect anybody back for a couple of hours."

"Thanks. I didn't mean to barge in on you like this."

"We can go to my room—just in case. There're some frozen Milky Ways in the fridge. Want one?"

"Maybe later. Thanks."

Rita dropped into a hard chair at the small school desk. "Sit wherever—the bed if you want." Laurie sank onto a window seat piled high with books.

"Just move those aside," Rita said.

All Rita needed was a pen and a pad of paper, and she could be my private shrink, Laurie thought, as she began spilling everything. Divulging her soul was more like it. Laurie first explained her returning dream. Then she told Rita about what she had discovered in the old trunk, handing Rita the picture she found. "These are my parents."

Rita looked at the photo, then at Laurie and said, "You look like your mother."

"I thought so, too. So how could I have forgotten her? Them. My own parents, Rita?" Laurie cried.

"I don't think you did, really. Maybe it was just too painful. I'm sure they've always been in the back of your mind. That's why you've dreamt about them."

Then Rita surprised her. "But it hasn't been so bad, has it? You've had a good life. Haven't you?"

Laurie couldn't dispute that. She had had a great life. A happy one, too. At least until about a year ago, when everything started spiraling downward with her mother. In spite of everything that had happened between them, she knew deep down she still loved both of the people she had known as her parents.

"This bit of knowledge hasn't changed you. You are who you always were."

"They still lied to me. It's like my whole life has been a lie! I always knew I was different."

Rita's green eyes were sympathetic. "Sometimes we say things we don't mean when we're upset."

"Yeah, maybe," Laurie said quietly.

"Finding out you were adopted can be a challenge, but it's not the worst thing to happen. At least you weren't tossed from one foster home to another."

"I guess you're right," Laurie said in a low voice. "It just that. . . ."

"I know, it hurts. And you feel betrayed. But it's not the end of the world. Plenty of people have been adopted, but they haven't been as lucky as you."

"They should have told me."

"Do you think if you had known it would've made a difference? I mean, really, think about it. Maybe they thought at the time it'd be too traumatic to tell you about your parents. You were just a little girl."

"They could have told me when I got stronger. Older."

"Like when?"

"I don't know. Twelve or thirteen."

"Everybody hates their parents then. I'm sure that would've gone over well. Anyway, your parents seem like really nice people."

Rita had her seeing this whole thing from a totally new perspective.

"How do you know so much?" Laurie wondered aloud.

"I was adopted, too."

Laurie looked at her, stunned. "You were? But you're so. . . ."

Rita smiled. "What? Well-adjusted?"

Laurie nodded. "Yeah."

"You are too—so it seems being adopted hasn't hurt either of us. Have you talked to Tobin? What's he think?"

Laurie shook her head, her eyes watering up. "He ended it. He said we're too different."

"That's bull. I don't care what he says. He's mad about you."

"I don't believe it either, or maybe I just don't want to."

"The way you two look at each other. I never saw a couple more in love. You'll be back together." Rita's words made her feel more hopeful. She and Tobin could start fresh.

"I should be going." Laurie gave Rita a long hug. "Thanks. Thanks for everything."

"I'm glad I could help. Hey, before you go, how about that Milky Way?"

"I'd love one. For the road."

Chapter 56

Tobin wondered what Laurie was doing. He remembered the first night he built a small fire for the two of them. They shared a bag of gumdrops and talked until the flames turned to embers. He never thought it was possible to feel that comfortable around someone. She had opened her heart to him. He had thought he was pretty much content on his own, but she had brought a new meaning to his life.

Why had he let her go? How could he have been so stupid? Somehow, it could have worked out. Maybe he hadn't tried hard enough. He wouldn't be able to stand it much longer without her. It had only been thirty-six hours and already he was missing her, far more than he thought possible. He loved her enough to let her go, but selfish or not, now he wanted her back. How was he going to do that?

Would she forgive him for turning her away like that? He should have figured out a solution instead of being so rash. He had said harsh, hurtful words, ones that couldn't be taken back. Why was life so complicated? He wished he had someone he could talk to, to give him advice. Tell him how to win her back. No, he messed things up; he was the only one who could fix this. He started to write her a letter, then crumbled up the paper and threw it to the floor. The right words were hard to find. Would she believe him? After wiping his tears, he began again.

Dear Laurie,

I don't know where to begin. Maybe you won't even read this. But I have to tell you anyway. I don't know what got into me. I said some horrible things that don't deserve to be forgiven. I had the best thing I could ever ask for, and I jeopardized that by saying the things I did to you.

From the first time we met, I knew there was something very special about you, far beyond your exterior beauty, that made me fall in love with you. That love only grew more after getting to know you better. You gave of yourself. And you cared so much about everyone. Even an Indian boy. You had a bright future and I felt I was in the way of that. You were so cheerful and happy; you had so much to offer the world. I just felt being with me I was taking all that from you. Especially when I saw your tears.

You'll probably think I'm crazy. But now I realize there's nothing we can't solve together, no matter how bad something is. Because without you I feel half of me will always be missing.

I hope that your heart will find understanding.

My love for you will never go away.

Tobin

He folded the letter and stuck it in an envelope, writing her name across the front. He sat there for a moment holding his words to her in his hands when he heard his mother nearly choking from a bad cough. He needed to make her some soup.

Chapter 57

Laurie picked up the phone. "Hello?" Hannah sounded breathless. "What's wrong?"

"Tobin's. . . ." Hannah was crying so hard, Laurie couldn't understand her.

"Hannah, what is it? Is Tobin all right?"

"He's been shot! Tobin's been shot, Laurie."

"What?" Please God, he can't be dead.

"He's here at the hospital. . . ."

"Is he going to be okay?" Laurie didn't hear Hannah's answer. "Please tell me Hannah, is he going to be okay?" Laurie repeated.

"They don't know yet."

"I'm on my way," Laurie said, dropping the phone and grabbing her keys from the counter.

Hannah's words pounded in her head. Please. Please. Let him be all right. Who shot him? Why?

On automatic pilot, focusing only on getting there, Laurie zoomed down the street, through red lights and stop signs, praying the whole time. Her tires screeched as she parked close to the ER entrance and ran in. Hannah spotted her right away and hurried over to her.

"Where is he? Can I see him?"

Hannah shook her head. "Nobody can right now. We have to wait. The doctors are working on him"How long has he been in there?"

"Half hour. Forty-five minutes, maybe. I called you as soon as we got here."

"What happened?" Laurie asked quietly.

"Let's sit down." Hannah directed Laurie toward two chairs on the opposite side of the room from the rest of Tobin's family. "It was a cop."

She immediately stood up. "A police officer shot him!"

"Yeah. He thought Tobin had a gun or something."

"What? You're kidding!" Laurie's voice rose. "Tobin would never carry a gun."

"I know. But that's what they said."

"I can't believe this. Where? Where did he get shot?"

"In the chest."

"Oh, God, no," Laurie said, shrinking back down into the chair.

"Tobin's strong. He'll make it, Laurie."

Laurie looked at her. Tobin's baby sister. Comforting her. Their roles should have been reversed.

"Yeah, of course he will," she said, wiping her eyes.

Laurie wanted to talk with Tobin's parents, but she was afraid she would say the wrong thing so she stayed glued to Hannah. The hours ticked by slowly as they waited for news. Laurie and Hannah drank Coke after Coke, others endless cups of coffee. By now most of the Wampanoag community had showed up to pray for the young man who had meant so much to them. One of their own. Reporters crammed the waiting room like vultures. This would be a big story. Gunshot wounds didn't happen on the Cape.

Looking disheveled and tired, Tobin's doctor finally appeared. Hannah hurried back to her family; Laurie stayed where she was. She knew his family liked her, even cared about her, but she didn't feel right joining them. If she were engaged to Tobin it would be a different story, but since she wasn't she gave them their space. She was also afraid of what she might hear.

What is he telling them? Laurie tried to read the doctor's expressions and gestures. Finally, Laurie saw him gently pat James Horvarth's arm.

Seeing Hannah headed toward her, Laurie leapt out of the chair, meeting her halfway. "How is he?"

"They got the bullet."

"Oh," she said, sinking in relief. "Thank God."

"But the next forty-eight hours are crucial," Hannah continued.

"Can we see him?"

"My mother and father are going in first, for a few minutes. Maybe after."

"I *need* to see him, Hannah."

"I know. Me, too. I'm sure we'll get a chance."

"Take this," Hannah said, handing her an envelope. Her name written on it. "It's from Tobin."

Laurie looked down at that sealed letter in her hand.

"He doesn't know I found it. I'm sure he intended for you to have it."

She looked at Hannah. "But shouldn't he be the one giving it to me?"

When Hannah didn't say anything, she knew what she was thinking. She put the letter in her pocketbook; she couldn't read it now.

Laurie watched the doctor usher Mr. and Mrs. Horvarth through the cold white doors. *Tobin, you have to make it. You have to*. Then Laurie wondered if Tobin was responsive. *Will he know me? Or even know I'm here?*

Every time a door opened, she would look up to see if it was Tobin's parents. Then the loudspeaker blared, "Code Blue," and she freaked. It could be anyone, she told herself. It doesn't have to be him.

She flipped through the magazines on the table but they were all a blur. After a while she stood up and began pacing. Realizing the policeman who had been trying to keep bystanders out of the ER was watching her, she stopped and glared at him. *What the hell are you staring at?* Evidently, he read her thoughts. He looked away.

The cold white doors flung open. Mrs. Horvarth stumbled back into the waiting room, crying uncontrollably, her husband holding her up. Laurie saw that his eyes were red, too. She watched Hannah race toward them, a reporter tagging right behind.

Laurie sprang from seat and bolted out of there. She had seen enough. Tobin was gone. How would she live without ever seeing him again?

Eleanor stopped at the mailbox and was looking over the mail in her car when Charlotte rapped on the passenger side window, startling her. Eleanor put the window down to speak with her.

"What is it, Charlotte?"

"You know that Indian boy—the one you disapprove of?"

"You mean Tobin?"

"Yes!"

"What about him?"

Ever since Charlotte had made such a point of showing her the pictures of Laurie and the Horvarth boy, Eleanor had figured out that Charlotte actually enjoyed starting wars. How wretched could anyone be?

"He's been shot."

"Shot? By whom?"

"The police."

"The police?"

"Yeah. I heard it myself. Right here on the radio."

Charlotte carried that small transistor of hers outside whenever she was gardening, even in the rain. Eleanor had shut the music off in the car because of her headache, so she had missed any news. Now she just wished she wasn't hearing it second hand.

"When? When did you hear this?"

"About twenty minutes ago. I'm sure it will come on again."

"You're positive they said Tobin Horvarth?"

"Oh, yes. I'm not mistaken, Eleanor, I know what I heard—it was that Indian boy."

Charlotte's gossip was usually all too accurate. "Charlotte, I have to go. I'll talk to you later."

"Do you think Laurie was with him?"

"I don't know. Let's hope not."

Eleanor tossed her pocketbook and package on a chair and held on to the edge of the kitchen counter. Where was Laurie? Was she with him? Was she all right? If she had been shot, they would have notified her. Someone would have called, wouldn't they? But how? She had been out shopping for a birthday gift for her sister. She had only worked half a day.

She spotted the dangling phone receiver. Laurie must have taken the call and run to him. Her daughter's heart was in one place and one place only. She only hoped Tobin's heart was as true as hers. Eleanor had never wanted anything bad to happen to Tobin. If Tobin didn't pull through, she would never get her daughter back. Never.

"No! No!" Eleanor cried, lowering her head into her hands. *What have I done?*

Eleanor wished Donald was home but she couldn't wait. She picked up the phone and called the hospital to see what she could find out.

"Cape Cod Hospital. How may I direct your call?"

"Yes, my name is Eleanor Matthews. I was wondering how Tobin Horvarth is doing?"

"Are you family?"

"No, but. . . ."

"I'm sorry. I can't give you any information."

She had to relieve her mind. "Wait. Could you at least tell me if my daughter's there? She may have been with him."

"Is she a patient?"

"I don't know—I'm not sure. There was a shooting. . . ."

"What's her name?"

"Laurie Matthews. She's seven—she's eighteen," she said, correcting herself. Hard to believe her little girl was all grown up. A young woman now. "She has long blonde hair, blue eyes." *You can't miss her. She's beautiful. From the day I brought her home.*

Eleanor had felt so blessed. And Laurie had only proved to her through the years how lucky she was to have her in her life. Their lives. Laurie was honest and caring. She remembered the day she brought home a sickly, stray cat and had pleaded with her and Donald to let her keep him and nurse him back to health. Then there was the time when they were in Boston one Christmas Eve when Laurie was six. Donald had bought a bag of pastries, and Laurie held her little hand out holding her favorite doughnut to a homeless woman on the street. Eleanor's eyes welled with tears.

"Let me see."

There was silence. Every second was too long for Eleanor.

"Ma'am?" *Finally.* "No. She's not a patient here."

"Could you check the emergency room? Please."

"I'll have to transfer you."

It took forever until she heard, "Emergency Room. How can I help you?"

For a second, Eleanor couldn't get any sound out.

"Can I help you?" a woman asked again.

"I was checking on my daughter. Her boyfriend, Tobin Horvarth, was shot. Her name is Laurie Matthews. I want to see if she's okay."

"There's no one admitted by that name."

"Oh, thank goodness," she said, breathing deeply. "Wait a minute! Can you tell me anything about Tobin Horvarth? How's he doing?"

"Ma'am, I'm sorry I can't give you that information. Will that be all?"

"Yes. Thank you."

But it wasn't all.

She called a friend at the police station. Mack Stein was from her hometown, Chelsea, and had been a couple grades ahead of her in high school. Her best friend then had dated him. She recently learned he had moved to Mashpee right after he graduated from the Police Academy and joined the force there.

"Mashpee Police Department. Sargent Carter."

"Lieutenant Mack Stein, please."

"And your name?"

"Eleanor Matthews. I'm an old friend."

"He's on another line. Would you care to wait, or would you like him to call you back?"

"It's very important. I'll wait. *I'll try to*. Thank you."

Time required patience and she didn't have much of that right now. Why would a police officer shoot Tobin? She was certain he was a good kid; she knew her daughter wouldn't be with him otherwise. She needed to get to the hospital to be with Laurie. How scared and alone her daughter must be feeling.

"Eleanor?"

"Oh, Mack. Thank heaven. I'm sorry to bother you. I know it's not a good time. I heard about the shooting."

"You and everyone else. The phones haven't stopped."

"I figured as much. I'm not sure if you know, but Tobin is my daughter's boyfriend." Amazingly, she had no trouble mentioning their relationship today.

"Yes. I think I did hear something."

"Is he going to be all right?"

"They don't know yet. The last I heard they were operating on him. Eleanor, hold the line a minute. Something just came in."

She heard a click. *Now what?* She might as well just go to the hospital. She was about to hang up, a minute or so later, when he got back to her. "Eleanor, are you still there?"

"Yes."

"There's been an accident."

Why is he telling me this? "An accident?"

"Does your daughter drive a white '76 Camaro?"

Eleanor felt panic building inside of her. "Yes, she does. Why?"

"Well, I'm afraid she's been in a crash."

"My daughter? Laurie?"

"Yes, Eleanor. The call just came in. She hit a tree."

"No. That can't be. I called the hospital. Laurie's not a patient. She's there with Tobin."

"Well maybe someone else was driving her car?"

Eleanor's voice faded. "No. She would never allow that."

"Are you all right, Eleanor?"

"Mack, I have to go. I have to see my daughter."

"Eleanor, listen to me. You're in no state to drive. I'll have one of my men pick you up and take you to the hospital."

"I have to tell my husband."

"Where is he?"

"I don't know. He's with a client."

"Just leave him a note and tell him where you are. Officer Aiken is on his way."

There was silence. "Eleanor. Eleanor, are you there?"

Chapter 58

Sitting in the sand, her arms wrapped around her knees, Laurie stared out at the water. The sun was bright, drying the ground after yesterday's rain. She smelled the tang of the pines and watched a robin perch on a branch, the way she had so many times with Tobin. Their feet would dangle and they would look up at the stars in the night sky and then at the ripples on John's Pond as the ducks glided across. She wondered what Brownie would do without him. He had already lost his first master. And what about Cinnamon, Tobin's fox friend? She hoped he was around somewhere.

Then she saw him. Peeking from behind a bush. "Don't be afraid." She pulled the peanut butter nib she had gotten at the hospital from her pocketbook and set it on the ground and leaned back. Cinnamon approached cautiously, his dark eyes darting from her to the cracker. She stayed still, not wanting to frighten him away. He was handsome, she thought, his shiny fur full and fluffed as if he had just bathed. He snatched the cracker and dashed off. Then, surprisingly, he came back.

"I'm sorry. It was my last one," she murmured.

His head turning, mouth in motion, it was like he was trying to tell her something. But what? What could he possibly tell her she didn't already know? Tobin was dead. *Dead. Dead.*

"Our friend won't be coming back," she said sadly, trying to make him understand. He tilted his head and looked at her. "I'm going to miss him, too." *Terribly.*

John's Pond was their place. It was where she had fallen in love with him. Tobin had taught her so much, had become her best friend. He was the kind of person people dream about finding their whole lives, but sometimes never do. Why did any of this have to happen?

She read his letter for the third time, as her tears flowed.

All of a sudden, she was sure she felt Tobin's presence, heard him saying, "Don't worry. Everything's going to be all right. Remember, I love you."

Letting his voice nourish her, she whispered, "And I love you," feeling warm and at peace, the way she had felt on top of the sacred mountain. In that instant, she allowed the sadness to leave her. She imagined it floating away into the distant sky.

She opened her eyes and saw Tobin before her. She blinked. He seemed so real—so alive. So touchable. "Am I dreaming?" she asked him softly.

"No, you're not dreaming."

"You're really here?"

Tobin managed a smile, nodding.

Laurie reached out to touch him, noticing his bandages. "I was so scared—I thought. . . ."

He leaned forward in his wheelchair, picked up her hand and kissed it. "*Shh.*"

"You're okay," Laurie said, still not fully believing. The effects of the sedation were wearing off. "What am I doing here?" Laurie asked, looking around.

"You were in an accident."

"*Ouch.* I guess I was," she said, trying to lift her head, noticing her own bruises for the first time. "I left the hospital and I was driving to the pond. That's the last thing I remember."

"You had a concussion. That's probably why your memory's a little foggy. Hey, there're people here to see you," he said quietly, motioning.

Not only were her parents there hovering in the doorway, but Tobin's family as well. It was something Laurie had never dreamed possible—seeing them all together. A nurse who had been standing off to the side walked over and grabbed hold of Tobin's chair. "Sorry, but I've got to get him back to his room. He needs his rest."

"I'll catch you later," Tobin said to Laurie, letting go of her hand.

"Later," she repeated quietly, watching the nurse wheel him away. This time, though, she knew she would be seeing him again.

"Hi, honey," her father said, bending over to kiss her. Then he handed her a bouquet of pink and white roses. "This is from your mom and me."

"Thank you. They're beautiful," she said, smelling them.

Her mother moved in to hug her. "You gave us a big scare."

"I didn't mean to."

"I know. I'm just glad you're all right. We love you," Eleanor said tearfully, her eyes locking with Laurie's.

"I love you both, too," Laurie said softly, feeling the hurt suddenly melt away.

Tobin's family's here," Eleanor said, smiling. "And Rita's on her way."

"Oh, wow."

Laurie saw her mother signal to the Horvarths. Hannah got to her bedside first.

"Oh, Hannah, I'm so sorry. I shouldn't have run out like that. But when I saw your mother crying, I just lost it."

"Hey, forget about it." Hannah moved out of the way so that her parents could get closer to the bed.

"Thank you both for coming," Laurie said.

Mr. Horvarth nodded. "Our pleasure." Then he stood over her for a few minutes, quietly praying.

Afterward, Tobin's mother moved in closer, giving her a warm smile. "When you're feeling better, come by the house. Stay for dinner."

"Thank you. I'd like that."

Laurie's doctor poked his head in. "How's she doing?" he asked. "I don't want to interrupt. I can come back."

"No, that's all right," said Laurie's father.

"Any complaints?" Doctor Sidney asked, moving to her bedside, then shining a pencil-size flashlight into her eyes.

"No. When can I go home?"

"Tomorrow."

"Not until tomorrow?"

"How about the day after then?"

"No. That's okay," Laurie decided, shaking her head. Everyone laughed.

As they were all leaving, Rita poked her head in.

Once Laurie was released from the hospital, she went straight to Tobin's room. She hadn't had a chance to talk to him, only the brief moments when she opened her eyes after the accident.

His breakfast tray was being taken away when she hobbled in. "Anything good?" Laurie asked him, noticing only a half slice of toast left on the plate.

He shrugged. "It's hospital food."

"You did pretty well," she observed, grabbing a chair from against the wall, near a small sink. She was a little unsteady on her feet. The doctor had offered her crutches but she flatly refused, telling him she was a fast healer.

Tobin looked like himself, sitting up in the bed, but she had no idea what kind of pain he was still in. "How are you feeling?"

He grinned. "With my hands?"

"Funny guy. Sounds to me you're well enough to get out of here. Did they give you any idea when?"

"Not yet. I'll probably be here another couple of days. They want to make sure no infection sets in."

There was so much she wanted to say to him, like about her being adopted, but that could wait. Had things changed between them? They had both been through a lot. Did he still love her? She remembered the letter he wrote to her. Yes, things had changed, but not between them.

"My mom's coming to get me. The Camaro's in the shop. I hear it got a decent dent in the front bumper and needs a new windshield. It'll be there for a while."

"That's too bad. That's a beautiful car."

"It's only a car. It'll look like new after Mel's Body Shop fixes it."

"Yeah. They do great work. What about you? Doing okay?" he asked, his eyes examining her from her face down to her sandals.

"A few scratches. A sprained ankle. I'll heal."

"I know your bruises will mend. . . ."

He stopped short. She saw it in his eyes: he wondered if she had healed inside, forgiven him for sending her away. He didn't say anymore until the hospital staff wasn't bothering him for a while.

"Those things I said—I didn't mean any of them. I just thought I was ruining everything for you. You didn't deserve—"

She stopped him, raising her hand, "Don't say any more. None of that matters now."

"But what I did was wrong. I despised myself afterward. If you hated me, I'd understand. I just want you to know one thing—I never stopped loving you. Never. Not for one minute."

"I know that," she said leaning in to kiss him. Closing her eyes, she let her mouth cling to his, her heart pounding the same way it did when she first kissed him. Maybe even harder.

He made a face. "Did you really know?"

"Well, maybe not at first. But if you didn't love me—everything between us would've been a lie. And I know it wasn't." She stopped and looked into his eyes. "I couldn't imagine my life without you."

"Me, too."

"When I saw your mom so upset in the hospital, I thought. . . ."

"Yeah. She'd just heard about CJ. And not knowing if I'd pull through. It was just too much for her."

"What about CJ? How'd he. . . ?"

"Parks had just picked CJ up at his ex-girlfriend's house. He violated another restraining order she had on him. I had no idea he was in the backseat of the cruiser when Parks pulled me over. It was dark and raining hard. CJ saw his chance to make a run for it. But he didn't get very far," he said quietly. "He had just run into the bushes when Park's gun went off. When the investigators went to the crime scene, they found him. Parks was so messed up when he shot me, he forgot about CJ. And when he remembered, he just thought CJ got away. But CJ got the fatal bullet."

"That's awful." She had only met CJ that one time, at the clambake, but still she felt sorry for him. His family. She remembered how she felt when she thought Tobin had died.

"Yeah, if only. . . ."

"If only what?" she asked.

"I hadn't gone to the store. Then he wouldn't have pulled me over. CJ would still be alive."

"You can't think like that. Who's to say it still wouldn't have happened? CJ shouldn't have gone over to that house in the first place. He knew he would be arrested. And he took the risk the minute he decided to get out of that police car."

"Yeah. One that cost him his life."

Chapter 59

Tobin never thought he would see the inside of this cottage again. After he knocked, Mr. Phillips answered right away, opening the door wide like he was expecting him. "Come in, boy."

Tobin glanced left into the kitchen. The dirty dishes were piled high, a cup of coffee, cold, he assumed, left on the table.

"Didn't feel much like cleaning up," Mr. Phillips confessed, directing him into the living room. "Sit down. Would ya like a drink?"

"I really can't stay." Tobin had come to offer his condolences and leave. He looked around. Nothing had changed. Overflowing ashtrays. A leftover TV dinner and two empty whisky bottles cluttered the beat-up coffee table. Tobin figured it had been even worse since CJ's funeral, a week earlier.

"I have Bud. C'mon, have one with me," Mr. Phillips insisted.

Tobin nodded. "Sure."

It had to have been CJ's beer. Mr. Phillips drank only the hard stuff. Pushing aside the newspapers to sit down on the couch, Tobin saw CJ's obituary with his picture. He looked younger. Probably an earlier high school photo because he had dropped out at sixteen. CJ had never paid attention in school, but he loved the attention he got for clowning around. His teachers had tried to get him to settle down and study more, but CJ simply laughed. And then he started getting into trouble. First, when he broke a neighbor's window—accidently, he claimed. Then there was the expensive fishing rod he had stolen across town. "I was just borrowing it," CJ said. Later, there were the speeding tickets and OUI's. Still, he was far too young to die.

CJ had made some wrong choices, but that didn't mean things couldn't have changed. He could've changed. An overwhelming sadness suddenly struck Tobin, and he regretted the stupid little grudge he had held against CJ since fourth grade when CJ called him the "Jolly Green Giant." The thought of never seeing him again made him feel like he had lost something. Maybe part of himself. They were so different, yet they weren't.

Mr. Philips walked back into the room and handed him a beer.

Taking the bottle from him, Tobin said, "I'm sorry about CJ."

Mr. Phillips nodded, sat down and started swilling down Jack Daniels, looking straight ahead. Staring at nothing, really, but the blank TV screen. After guzzling some more, he turned slightly toward Tobin and blurted, "He just wanted to see his baby. She wouldn't let him. CJ loved that kid. It tore him up." The more Mr. Phillips drank—the more freely he talked. And Tobin listened. He wanted to. "CJ's mother ran off. Found herself another man. A rich one, I heard. My boy was only four."

"I didn't know." Tobin hadn't really known CJ, not like he thought. He had never tried to find out differently.

"A boy that age needs a mother. I did the best I could."

"I'm sure you did," Tobin responded automatically. Tobin couldn't imagine what it would have done to him not having his own mother around at that age. And being an only child had to be even tougher for CJ. Lonelier.

They both sat in silence for a moment. Then Tobin was really surprised by Mr. Phillips' next statement.

"He wanted to be like you." Mr. Phillips lowered his eyes. "I told him he didn't know how. Didn't have it in him."

"Me? Why? I don't have anything."

"But you will. You got a strong head. CJ knew that."

CJ had had a lousy beginning. A tragic end. And in between it wasn't much better. *Not fair*, Tobin thought. Maybe it would have been different if CJ had found a girl like Laurie.

"What should I wear? Eleanor asked Laurie, scanning her closet.

"Something cool and comfortable. What about the yellow and green sundress you bought about a month ago? That'll look nice."

"Ah. Good choice. Thank you."

Not in her wildest dreams had Laurie ever imagined her mother going to a Pow Wow. Her mother had accepted the Horvarth's invitation practically on the spot. Accepting Tobin wasn't quite as immediate, but her mother was making a real effort.

"Aren't you going to change? Put on the. . . .? Eleanor asked, looking at her.

Laurie was still in the same halter top, jean shorts and sandals she had worn all morning. "Buckskin? No. Everybody's seen me in it." Laurie loved that dress, but it was the Wampanoags' day, not hers.

Laurie couldn't wait to see Hannah in the one she had made for this special occasion. Hannah had worked hard for months on her beautiful costume. Laurie had even helped her collect berries and other things in the forest to create bright pink dyes to color the porcupine quills that adorned her deerskin dress.

"Are my girls ready?" Donald asked, peeking into the bedroom.

"Almost, Dad."

"I'll be in the car."

Laurie watched her mother run the comb she dipped in water through her airborne hair again. "Mom, you look fine. Let's go."

Tribal nations from across the country were there during the three day event and one of the young women amongst these tribes would be chosen to be Princess of the Year. It was quite an honor. Laurie hoped Hannah would be the lucky one.

Donald immediately wandered off with Mr. Horvarth and Tobin to a pipe ceremony when they got to the Pow Wow. "I've never seen Daddy smoke anything," Laurie whispered to her mother.

Mrs. Horvarth introduced Eleanor to some of her friends and relatives. Laurie had already met many of them at the clambake. Then Mrs. Horvarth and Hannah left to get ready for their performances.

The dancers had made their own outfits with bands of colorful ribbon and beadwork. There were a variety of styles. The men wore turkey and pheasant feathers, some painted, intense and powerful. After watching some of the dancing and applauding with the crowd, Eleanor turned to Laurie, "I'm going to take a look around. Can I get you something on the way back? Hamburger or a hot dog?"

"Just a Coke. Thanks." Then, glancing at her watch, Laurie decided to go with her since according to the program the Horvarths wouldn't be performing for another thirty minutes. "Mom, wait up."

Before grabbing a soda, they stopped at a few of the arts and crafts tables. Coyote, wolf and eagle prints plastered T-shirts and sweatshirts. After handling leather belts with fancy buckles and silver jewelry, Eleanor remarked, "It's amazing—the work they've put in." Laurie nodded with a slight smile. Then Eleanor picked up a dream catcher, studying it.

"Hang it at the head of your bed. All your bad dreams will get caught in the web," said the short dark-skinned vendor. "These prayer beads will trap them and then burn them up."

"What about the good dreams?" Laurie asked. "Where do they go?"

"They'll find their way through this hole in the center," he said pointing to the small open space, "rest on the feathers like dew drops and fade away to the Great Spirit in the morning sun."

"I'll take two," Eleanor said, turning to Laurie. "One for each of us."

"Any particular color?" the man asked.

Laurie shook her head. "You pick," she said to her mom.

Eleanor chose the brown suede for her room and the deep rose for Laurie. "It'll go with your bedspread."

"Yeah, it will go nicely. Thanks."

They got back in time to see some of the men demonstrate fighting and hunting in traditional style. Tobin's feet seemed to hover just above the ground as he told a tracking story with his athletic body. Dazzled by Tobin's dancing, Laurie couldn't take her eyes off him. Neither could her mother.

"Isn't he great, Mom?"

"They're all good. He certainly can dance. And right on beat with the drum, too."

Laurie mentally crossed her fingers, beaming inside.

Then the younger women entered the circle on their toes, kicking high and twirling into the air. Hannah's fringed shawl, like the rest, stretched out like angel wings, highlighting her every movement as she kept graceful pace with the song. Soon, the princess would be picked. Laurie's hands were in prayer position over her mouth, holding her breath when the announcement came.

"Oh my," she said, her eyes wide, turning to her mother. "She won!"

Hannah immediately led the circle dance which consisted of taking the hand of someone in the crowd and in turn that person taking another's. To Laurie's surprise, Hannah took hers, a white person, first and Laurie would never forget the pride she felt as she got to choose the next in line. She grabbed her mother's hand. The circle ended up being very large. Simply beautiful.

Donald eventually caught up with the two of them. "Did you girls have something to eat?"

"We were waiting for you, Dad."

"Shall we get a dog? Or how about if we try one of those buffalo burgers? They looked pretty good."

Laurie glanced at her mom and mouthed "*Buffalo?*"

Just as they were turning away from the arena, Laurie saw Tobin coming their way. He had said he would pop over between shows if he could.

"Wait," Laurie said to her parents.

As he approached Tobin asked, "I hope you're all having a good time."

"We are. I've never seen so many styles of dancing," said Eleanor.

"Yeah. There're quite a few. And we do a lot of practicing."

"I can see that. Very nice."

"Thank you."

Donald broke the short silence that followed. "Eleanor and I haven't danced in years, but seeing all that energy and the beating of that drum made me want to get out there and boogie again."

"Craig Stiles is our drummer. He's great. Without him you don't get that same feel. I have to get back."

When Tobin hurried away, Laurie turned to her father. "Boogie, Dad?"

Donald shrugged. "I thought that was the cool word for dancing today."

Eleanor rolled her eyes. "I don't know what he's been smoking."

Laurie laughed.

The competitions carried on throughout the day. After a few hours, though, Laurie's parents decided to head out. The sun had been really hot and they had done a lot of standing. Her mother had turned down a garden club social, her father a round of golf with a couple of his buddies. Laurie was very grateful they forfeited what they enjoyed to come with her to the Pow Wow. It meant so much to her.

"I'm going to hang around and wait for Tobin," Laurie told them.

"Will you be home for dinner?" Eleanor asked.

"I don't think so." Her parents nodded.

"Thanks for coming."

Laurie watched as they headed back to the car. *And thanks for choosing me.*

Later, Laurie helped Tobin carry what he had worn that day to the truck, except for the small threads of suede he still had on, making him look sexier than ever. "You're a great dancer. My mom even thought so."

"She actually said that?"

"More or less. I even caught her watching you."

"That's a compliment."

"I think she really enjoyed herself today."

"How's that going?" Tobin asked, as he pulled onto the road.

Laurie knew he was asking if they were getting along any better—if she had accepted him. "She's coming around. I mean, she's really trying."

"Well, there's a new beginning."

Yeah. That makes two.

Then Tobin pulled the truck into a small, deserted park. He turned off the engine and shifted his body to look at her. "What? You can't hide things from me."

She started to smile. "Am I that obvious?"

He nodded.

"I've just been waiting for the right time."

"C'mon, let's go talk," he said, motioning to a bench beneath two large maple trees.

They got out of the truck and walked over to the bench and sat down. It overlooked a small koi pond and they relaxed as they gazed at the darting, sun-gold, carroty fish swimming among the fronds. The pool was fed by a small waterfall that trickled joyfully over rocks. Various, graduated flower beds surrounded the pond, their blossoms nodding over its edge and fanning their heady, honey-sweet fragrances. Tobin put his arm around her shoulders. "Remember the dream I told you about that I kept having?" Laurie asked.

"The couple and the little girl?"

"Yeah. Well, you were right—that little girl was me."

"Blonde hair. Cute little smile. Had to be you."

"And that man and that woman I kept seeing with me—they were my parents." She watched his brow crease.

"Were your parents?" he asked, looking puzzled.

"Yeah. I was adopted."

"Adopted? Wait a minute, hold up. Are you telling me that the people you live with now aren't your biological parents?"

"Exactly."

"You've known this?"

"No. Well, maybe I did, sort of. I was very young. . . ."

"What happened?"

"My parents, my real parents, that is, they died when I was three. A train hit our car. I'd forgotten."

"Wow. I don't know what to say. I'm so sorry," he said, wrapping a strand of hair that had come loose from her ponytail around her ear.

"Hey. It's okay. I'm doing okay. At least everything's making sense now."

He stared at her.

"Really. It was a long time ago," she assured him.

"So how did you find out? When?"

"Just before you got shot. I found a picture of the three of us and all the official papers in the attic. I was going to tell you at the hospital, but you'd been through enough."

"Do your parents know that you found out?"

"Yeah. I confronted them. I was really angry with them at first for not telling me. Hurt more than anything, I guess."

"I feel like a real heel."

"Why?"

"I should've been there for you."

"You didn't know. Besides, there was nothing you could've done. I had to sort this out on my own."

"Have you?"

"It's sad I lost my parents so young. But Mom and Dad have been good to me. I have no reason to complain. And someday I can tell my grandkids I had two sets of parents who loved me from the first minute they met me."

"You're amazing. You know that?"

"There's more," she said. "My father, my real father, that is, was Ute. Ute," she repeated, taking the picture she'd found from her pocketbook to show him. "And my birth name was 'Aiyana.'"

He didn't respond.

"Did you hear what I just said?"

He nodded, still staring at the picture. "I heard."

"You don't seem surprised."

"I guess some part of me always knew," he said. He lifted up her chin to kiss her.

Chapter 60

Hand in hand, Laurie and Tobin walked the winding path to John's Pond for the last time that summer. Green leaves hinted at fall with slivers of red. Blades of grass were turning golden. Summer was coming to an end, but "Aiyana," Laurie's given name, meant eternal bloom and that she was "forever flowering." What Tobin had with her was more than just a fling. His love for her would grow and last through every season, year after year.

"I can't believe I'm leaving for college in two days. Where did summer go? It seems like we just met, yet it feels like I've known you all my life."

Tobin looked at her. "That's a good thing. Isn't it?"

She grinned. "I think you know that answer. I'm excited about going to UMass, but I don't want to leave you."

"You're not really. There'll be a phone call or a letter every day. I promise. You'll probably get tired of hearing from me," he said, giving her hand a squeeze.

"That will never happen. At least we'll see each other at Christmas. Maybe we'll even have spring break the same week. I hope."

"Even if we don't, I'll still come and see you."

She stopped him and pointed. They watched one of two lovebirds parked on a branch suddenly take to the sky. The other stayed for a second, then fluttered off in the opposite direction, soon making a complete three sixty, soaring after his mate. "What do you think that was about?"

"They had a little misunderstanding. After she took off, it didn't take him long to realize he'd be a fool to let her get away," he said with a smile.

"And why's that?"

"Because he loved her too much."

She started to smile. "And she felt foolish not recognizing that in the first place."

The water seemed softer than usual on Tobin's feet. Two squirrels raced up a pine and sprang to another. A cluster of sparrows landed only feet away in the sand. Then Cinnamon, the fox they named after his shiny ginger fur, came wandering down the path.

Laurie took out some crackers from her sweatshirt pocket. "I've been waiting for you," she said, smiling at him. Cinnamon approached bravely and snatched them from her fingers.

From the beginning, Tobin had felt Laurie could have been Wampanoag. It wasn't just the way their souls had come together. It was the fascination, the deep respect she had shown for all living things: the Indian Paintbrush flowers in Wyoming, the baby blue jays taking their first flight at John's Pond. Even his wary friend Cinnamon had sensed her gentleness, her warmth, and had let her get up close.

Leaning back on his towel, Tobin unzipped his backpack, taking out the wooden box he had planned to give Laurie before everything happened. After CJ's funeral, he had stopped by his uncle's grave. Now, brushing off the lid, he handed it to her. "Before my uncle died, he said to give this to you."

"We weren't together then. How did he. . . ?"

"He knew."

Tobin watched her take out the wampum bracelet. "It was my Aunt Dot's."

"Oh, that makes it even more special. It's so pretty. Thank you," she said, wrapping it around her wrist. Suddenly her smile turned sober. "I feel terrible. I don't have anything for you."

He cupped her face in his hands and looked into her eyes. "Laurie, I know now what it means to really love someone. And you loving me back—there's no gift greater."

"You're going to make me cry."

"No crying allowed. Let's go for a swim."

Stepping out of her shorts, she said, "I guess this is our last one."

"Maybe for the season. But John's Pond, like us, is going to be around for a long time."

"Our future has just begun." She grinned. "I'll beat you in."

Printed by Libri Plureos GmbH in Germany